PASSION'S PERIL

"Ouch!" Sean yelped, slapping Jessie's hand playfully. "Stop that, wench!" Then he caressed her thigh and she trembled anew.

Jessie's eyes widened and she bolted upright, alarmed not only at his obviously renewed lust but at her own. Then the word he used penetrated her thoughts. "Wench!" Was that what he thought of her? Angry, she struggled to disentangle herself from the sheet and his entwining arms.

Sean's smile was gone, and a puzzled look of concern shadowed his face. "Is aught amiss, Jessie?"

"Nay, but I would not repeat the error I have committed."

"It was not an error, but love we made," he corrected, giving her a cocky smile. "You do tempt a man, Jessie."

"I will try not to tempt you again, Mr. Winthrop."

Other *Leisure Books* by Michele Stegman:

FORTUNE'S MISTRESS

FORTUNE'S SON

MICHELE STEGMAN

LEISURE BOOKS NEW YORK CITY

A LEISURE BOOK®

November 1992

Published by

Dorchester Publishing Co., Inc.
276 Fifth Avenue
New York, NY 10001

Printed in the United States of America.

*To my parents, Gerry and Nelson Holbrook,
and to my sister, Roberta Kess.*

FORTUNE'S SON

Chapter One

1718, Charles Town, South Carolina

"Ooh, there's a handsome one. Maybe he's the one."
Maybelle poked her companion in the ribs and pointed
toward the end of the dock.

"Stop it, Maybelle," the young woman shushed, pushing
down Maybelle's finger. "You're attracting far too much
attention. Besides, you've said that five times in the space
of the last two minutes. Does everything in trousers really
look that good to you?"

Maybelle giggled. "I guess they do, Miss Jessie. But don't
you wonder just a little bit what your husband looks like?
Don't you hope he's handsome and strong and—"

"There's more to a man than good looks!" Jessie snapped
a little more waspishly than she had intended. Of course she
wondered what her husband looked like, what kind of man
he was. She had wondered ever since she had married him by
proxy, sight unseen, six weeks ago in Boston. But after being

cooped up with her maid so long on the ship, the girl's prattle was beginning to wear on her nerves.

"Course there is," Maybelle chatted on. "It's allus grand if they has a shilling or two to spend on a good time."

Jessie sighed. Maybelle was absolutely incorrigible. She turned back toward the *Margaret Anne*. It had been good to stretch her legs a little further than the narrow space aboard the ship. But Charles Town's docks were no place for two women to stray too far, and she had promised Captain Wells she would keep in sight of the ship. He had been too busy to accompany them, and she had been so anxious to debark.

She had expected her new husband to meet her when she arrived and had put on her most attractive gown for him. Not that it would help her looks, she thought. She was too thin by far, and her mouth was too wide and turned down at the corners. She had none of the plump, bosomy fullness of her more attractive younger sisters, nor did she share their fair skin and blond hair. Like her father, her hair was black and straight, her eyes like darkest obsidian. She often wondered if it were indeed his Welsh blood, as her father claimed, or that of some forgotten Indian ancestor that had given her her coloring and high cheekbones.

She shifted her shoulders uncomfortably, beginning to regret wearing her heavy gown. It was fine for Boston, but her day-long wait for her husband in the warm Carolina sun, combined with her anxiety at meeting a man she had wed but knew so little about, had given added weight to the blue velvet making it hang heavy and hot on her.

She had just turned to continue walking when Maybelle clutched her arm, bringing her to a halt. "He's just got to be the one, Miss Jessie." She sighed, staring. "Don't he just turn your innards to water?"

Unable to shake off her distracted maid, Jessie had little choice but to turn and look at the man who had gained Maybelle's latest admiration.

Jessie's breath caught in a quick gasp. He did indeed "turn one's innards into water," she thought, watching a dark-haired, broad-shouldered man halt a wagon near a pile of goods unloaded from some ship. For once she was as caught up in man-watching as her maid. Wondering if some of Maybelle's enthusiasm for men had finally rubbed off on her, she continued to stare as the man secured the reins of the wagon and brushed back a wayward lock of straight, black hair that had fallen across his forehead. It was a wide forehead above dark, arched brows and eyes set too deep for her to tell their color from this distance. He had a fine, straight nose, and full, sensitive lips. Her heart tripped as she thought of how they might feel touching her own.

As her thought made her blush, he glanced her way, and their eyes locked for a moment. Or was it an eternity? She felt suspended in space and time, without breath, but with a heartbeat that had at least tripled. What was wrong with her? Certainly, she had always hoped for a husband and children, a home of her own someday, but she had never before been much impressed by the suitors who had plied eagerly for her hand. She had quickly found faults and flaws with all of them. But it was her own uncertainty as to whether the men were courting her or her father's money which resulted in her rejecting them.

But this wagon driver, totally unknown to her, had, with one glance and in the space of a moment, affected her more deeply than all her former suitors with their anxious looks and straying hands.

Now he let his gaze wonder over her freely and a slow smile spread across his face. She held her breath, mesmerized by his devastating good looks.

Yes, this could well be her husband, she thought, as she gradually exhaled and then breathed deeply. He was driving a wagon that would be needed to transport her trunks and he had stopped at the end of the right dock. Though he was not dressed as well as she thought a prosperous planter should dress, wearing only a simple stained white cotton shirt, dark broadcloth trousers, and heavy shoes, he exuded the air of authority and confidence she would expect in a man who managed a plantation worked by more than a hundred slaves.

With a start, Jessie realized that she was acting like a wanton. If the man was not her husband, she had no right to stare at him. If he was her husband, what must he think of her? Pulling free of Maybelle's grasp and the magnetic pull of the stranger, she turned to hurry back to the ship. But in her haste and flurry, she did not look where she was going and plowed headlong into the thick arms and barrel chest of a sailor.

His arms immediately wrapped themselves around her, and he pulled her close, nearly smothering her in his massive embrace. His unshaven face leered down at her, and even at this early-evening hour, she could smell the rum that fouled his breath.

"Gor!" he said, his eyes alight with liquor and lust. "Yer're a new one, ain't ye? Hardly broke in yet. Well, I can fix that, me girl."

"Let go of me!" Jessie demanded. She pushed against him, struggling in his arms, but it was useless, trying to free herself from his bone-crushing hold.

"Now, now, ye needn't fuss. I know a foin doxie like yerself will cost a sight more'n usual. But I just got paid,

I did, and me pockets is lined with good English coin just waitin' ter be spent on the likes o' ye."

"I said to let me go!" Jessie pounded ineffectually on his chest and regarded in horror the thick, wet lips he was lowering to hers.

Suddenly, a strong, sun-browned arm intervened between her and that reeking mouth, and a smoothly muscled forearm tightened around her assailant's throat. The sailor began to splutter and loosened his grip on her to claw at the tightening band that threatened his life's breath.

Jessie stared in wonder at the corded arms that held the struggling man at bay, marveling at their strength. If she had struggled so helplessly with the sailor, how pitiful would be her plight if these arms ever held her?

"The lady does not want your attention. Do you think you can find one more appreciative of your charms and your coin?" Her rescuer's voice was as pleasant as if he were asking her assailant to join them for tea.

Jessie looked up into the face of the dark-haired stranger grinning at her over the sailor's shoulder. *Blue,* she thought absurdly. *His eyes are blue.*

His grip tightened around the sailor's neck, and his voice took on a more threatening tone. "Or shall I break your neck?"

The sailor's eyes bulged wildly, and he was barely able to shake his head within that stranglehold. As soon as he answered, he was abruptly let go and shoved along the dock. He did not look back, but hurried on his way, not wanting to risk his neck in another bruising encounter. He had had brawls enough with his shipmates. It was not a fight he was seeking this night, but other pleasures.

"My lady," the wagon driver said, giving her an exaggerated bow with an imaginary hat. "May I lend my arm to escort you to your destination?"

Though the bow was done with more than a little humor as the gleam in those arresting blue eyes proclaimed, Jessie noted that it was accomplished with as much grace as any well-practiced gentleman. The man's voice, too, was cultured, though the accent was different from any she had heard. Perhaps its softness was typical of Charles Town. Could this be the man she had wed, coming at last at this late hour to fetch her? She trembled to think it might be so, yet she did not dare to ask him outright.

"Thank you, sir, for your intervention. I would be glad to have your protection," she said, placing her fingers lightly on his arm.

Her hand trembled at the shocking contact with bare, browned skin, hard and muscled, beneath her touch. Her senses reeled again at the added touch of his hand, warm and work-roughened, when he reached to steady hers.

"What is our destination, my lady?"

" 'Tis not far, sir. To the *Margaret Anne* moored at the end of this dock."

"With such a beauty by my side, it would be no strain to escort you to the ends of the earth. Happily, our destinations are the same."

Her heart leapt, nearly certain now that this was her husband. Appraising him sideways from beneath lowered lashes as he guided her through the clutter and bustle of the dock, she was amazed at what fortune had brought her.

Suitor after suitor she had rejected with disdain, preferring to spend her time at her father's shipping office, helping him with the accounts. Papa had often laughed and shaken his head, telling her not to hasten her decision in spite of her mother's protestations that she should have wed long ago. She was pleased that Papa enjoyed her company and help as much as she enjoyed being in the nerve center of as large and prosperous a firm as Ashbrook Shipping.

But Papa was gone now, and he had too long neglected to make the will he had promised. Everything had gone to Mama instead of Jessie, and, too soon, to Jessie's mind, her mother had married Papa's business partner, putting the entire business into Mr. Pierce's grasping hands.

Unlike her father, Mr. Pierce had not enjoyed her company, but had, like her mother, persisted in urging her to marry. With dear Papa dead, her inheritance gone, and her purpose at the company at an end, for her stepfather would not allow her to continue in her job, Boston took on a bleakness she had never before known. She sat for hours by the window with her embroidery on her knee until she knew that the only cure for her melancholia was to leave the town and the home that, for her, had become intolerable. Her two sisters, her mother, her stepfather talked about nothing but her having to marry, marry, marry. And she did want to marry. To marry and have children. To have a home of her own, a man to share a life with. A man whose very touch would melt her heart and who cared not a whit whether she brought him a dowry or only herself.

Those were her dreams, but that was all they were. She had met no man who was as interested in her as in what she brought to the match.

At last she agreed to be wed, not caring anymore who she wed as long as he lived far away from Boston, where memories of her father loomed all too strong. Far away from her mother's seeming betrayal of dear Papa. Far away from the inane chatter of her younger sisters about one man or another and her whole family's constant harping that she marry. If it was only her dowry that her prospective husband wanted, at least she would know where she stood. She would no longer live in limbo, unwanted in her stepfather's home. She would have her own place and would make of it what she could.

As soon as her consent was voiced, her stepfather had arranged her marriage to Jonathan Twill, who managed a plantation in South Carolina for Ashbrook Shipping. After the marriage's consummation, she was to be given deed to the plantation—the only inheritance she would receive from her father's hard-won shipping empire. Or perhaps she should think of it as a bribe, for it was ownership of the plantation that had, more than anything, convinced Mr. Twill to agree to the marriage.

As the days and weeks of the voyage rolled by, taking her farther from Boston and her grief, she began to think more and more about the possible folly of what she had done. She had indeed wondered what kind of man she had wed. She did not have exceedingly high expectations. Not of a man who had taken a bribe to wed her. None of her family, not even her stepfather, had ever met Mr. Twill. But one resolution had grown strong in her mind. When her mother and stepfather came to Charles Town to sign over the plantation, it would be to her alone. Never again would she be dominated. Never again would she let the power of ownership and control slip from her fingers.

Now as she walked beside this sun-bronzed stranger, she marveled at his perfection. Towering over even her slender height, his broad shoulders swung along with an easy, confident grace. The wayward lock of hair had again strayed over his forehead, and with the impish sparkle in his eye and his wide smile, it was impossible not to feel a lifting of her spirits just to look at him. Could this be the man to whom she had plighted her troth? Somehow he did not seem like a man who would agree to marry a woman he had never met just for the control of the plantation she would own.

"Will you be sailing on the *Margaret Anne?*"

His question brought her out of her reverie, and she warmed at the touch of his gaze which seemed to sweep over her like a hot wind, leaving no detail unturned.

"No, sir. I have but newly arrived."

His grin broadened. "Charles Town will be greatly enhanced by so beauteous a lady."

She smiled at him, sure that his words were nothing more than flattery, but appreciating his kindness, nonetheless.

Their conversation ended as he guided her before him up the narrow gangplank. His hand, resting on the small of her back, seemed to burn like a brand even through the layers of velvet, corset, and petticoat. She was not sure if it was relief or disappointment she felt when her feet were safely on the deck and his hand dropped from her.

He turned to help the trailing Maybelle aboard, giving her as much care and attention as he had Jessie. Was he kind or a flirt? she wondered.

Captain Wells hurried toward them, and Jessie's breath caught in her throat. Captain Wells was acquainted with her husband. If the man beside her was Jonathan Twill, she would shortly be apprised of that fact.

But the captain ignored the tall man beside her, giving his attention instead to her. "My apologies, ma'am. I have no idea what has detained your husband, but since we sail early tomorrow, I have made arrangements for you to stay the night with the head of Ashbrook Shipping in the Charles Town office. I believe you are acquainted with Mr. Walker and his wife?"

With sharp disappointment, she glanced toward the handsome stranger where he lounged casually against the ship's rail. His shirt was opened at the throat, and the sea breeze ruffled the loosened ties. It must have been her imagination that

17

made him seem thoroughly at home against the backdrop of the ratlines, rigging, and the scudding white clouds. She had been so eager to believe that he was her husband, to believe that the attraction she had felt for him and which, God help her, she still felt, had been engineered by the same fate that had made them man and wife. But this man was not her husband. Her husband was yet unknown to her and she must not encourage this stranger any more than she already had. He was openly and unabashedly watching her, and the light in those dark blue eyes told her that the attraction she felt for him was reciprocated—an attraction that she must now discourage.

Thrusting her chin a shade higher, she dragged her gaze back to Captain Wells, trying desperately not to let her confusion and disappointment show too much. No one must guess the sense of loss she felt at that moment. "Yes, the Walkers are old friends of mine." She managed to keep her voice from shaking by sheer force of will. "I wondered why they were not here to greet me."

"I have been informed that Mr. Walker is recovering from a recent illness, but you will be welcomed in his home until you can join Mr. Twill."

From the corner of her eye, Jessie saw the smile freeze on the handsome stranger's face and a hardness invade his eyes. Though he continued to lean on the rail propped on one elbow, it was as if a sudden tenseness surged through him, and she wondered why her husband's name should have such an effect on him.

"You there! Are you the driver I sent for?"

The stranger stepped forward at the captain's call, pulling at his forelock as any servant might, nodding in assent.

"Isn't that a Fortune Shipping Company wagon you're driving?"

"Aye, sir, that it is. Since there are three Ashbrook ships in the harbor needing service, your own wagons are a bit busy. But if you'd not be wantin' to use a rival's services . . ." The stranger's voice trailed off.

Though the sparkle still danced in his eyes and his smile had once more become genuine, Jessie noted that his voice did not seem as cultured as it had before. This man was a complete stranger to her. Why then did a sharp pang of disappointment run through her at the knowledge that he was probably no more than a hired driver and not the gentleman she had at first thought? He could never mean anything to her. She was a married woman, her troth plighted to another. It had been no more than wishful thinking on her part that had made him seem more than he was.

"Nay, nay." Captain Wells waved away his objections with his hand. "We sail early tomorrow. The lady's trunks must be taken off now. Foster! Lend a hand here."

The captain made his farewells while the driver and Foster carried her trunks to the waiting wagon. Jessie tried not to watch as the stranger lifted one of her trunks onto his broad shoulders and carried the heavy piece lightly down the gangplank. She tried not to note the magnificent play of his muscles, the sheen of sweat on his sun-darkened skin, the strong grasp of his hands. She tried not to note those things, but she did. And though the day was beginning to fade, it seemed to her to grow warmer, the blue velvet of her dress thicker, heavier, her skin more flushed.

At last the task was done. The captain walked her down the gangplank, and she was once again in the stranger's keeping. She did not take his arm this time as they picked their way through the clutter on the docks. But he walked uncomfortably close, startling her now and then with a guiding hand to her arm or the small of her back. Maybelle walked ahead, and once when she glanced back, Jessie noted that the girl's face displayed an open appreciation of the stranger.

When they reached the wagon, Jessie put out her hand, expecting to be helped to the seat. Instead, the stranger lifted her up, easily hoisting her into the seat, his hands nearly spanning her slender waist. She gasped, feeling the easy strength that lifted her. His hands lingered a moment longer than was necessary and slid caressingly away, straining against the bounds of propriety but not quite enough for her to voice a protest.

He smiled up at her, his one hand resting behind her on the seat, his other on the wagon before her, and though he was no longer touching her, she felt held in his embrace.

"To Mr. Walker's, Mrs. Twill?" His use of her married name irked her. For a moment she imagined his lips forming the soft syllables of her given name. She had no idea what his name was nor was there any reason to ask it. He was but a driver hired to transport her the short distance from the docks to Mr. Walker's. After today, she would probably never see him again. That thought caused her a swift jab of regret which she tried unsuccessfully to squelch. She was a married woman. The way this man affected her, it would be best for all concerned if she never saw him again.

"Yes, please. To Mr. Walker's. He lives on Church Street."

"I know the house."

He turned to lift Maybelle to the back of the wagon, and Jessie gritted her teeth as her maid leaned on those broad shoulders, ran her hands down the length of his arms, and clung briefly to his hands. Her face was an open invitation to him, complete with a winsome smile and batting lashes.

"I'm Maybelle Collins, Mrs. Twill's maid," Maybelle giggled.

"Enchanted to meet you, Miss Collins. I'm Sean Winthrop." In an elegant gesture, Sean tipped an imaginary hat, sending Maybelle into further peals of tittering at his gallantry toward a simple maid.

He climbed up to sit beside Jessie on the narrow seat, their hips touching, their thighs brushing, and took up the reins. Jessie watched in fascination as he maneuvered the team through the traffic, the leather straps entwined through his strong fingers in an expert grip neither too loose nor too tight.

"Will you be going out to Twill's place in the morning?"

"Yes, if Mr. Twill has not come for me by then." Jessie hesitated, not knowing just how to ask Mr. Winthrop her next question. "Do you know Mr. Twill?"

Sean shrugged. "I know who he is and where he lives. We can leave your trunks loaded on the wagon for tonight, and I can pick you up at daylight."

She opened her mouth to protest. She had decided never to see this man again. She had certainly not planned to spend another three or four hours in his company. Judging by how she felt after a few minutes, she hated to think what his close presence on the narrow wagon seat for so long would do to her. It would be no way to greet an unknown husband.

Sean grinned at her discomfiture. "I know Ashbrook and Fortune are rival firms, Mrs. Twill, but I think your husband might forgive your arriving in this wagon."

"Oh, it's not that. It's just that I . . ." What excuse could she give? She sat a little straighter, calling on all her Puritan heritage and training to strengthen her. "That would be fine, Mr. Winthrop."

She was put off by his low chuckle and turned to stare at him. He glanced once in her direction, barely suppressing another smile. Her eyes widened. He knew it was not the matter of the wagons that had caused her discomfort! He knew exactly what was wrong. Reddening, she turned to look primly straight ahead. At least he had had the kindness to pretend that it was the wagons.

They came to a halt before a trim, white-painted house, and Jessie scrambled to get down before Mr. Winthrop could help her. But he had no skirts to hamper him as she did, and he was there with a hand to her arm and one to her waist, guiding her, until she stood beside him. Then he turned to help down a giggling Maybelle who slid along the lean length of him, trying to entice him with every charm she possessed.

Watching her maid, Jessie could almost feel those hardened muscles along her own body and she turned quickly from the sight, giving her attention instead to the woman who was limping down the walk, leaning heavily on her cane.

"Mrs. Walker!" Jessie hurried toward the older woman, happy to at last see a familiar face.

Mrs. Walker held out her free arm to Jessie, a broad smile lighting her face. "Jessie, my dear! I'm so sorry we were not able to meet you. Andrew has been so ill."

"Nothing serious, I hope?" Jessie asked, a worried frown creasing her brow.

"It was. A fever. He's recovering nicely now, but it will be another few days before he's up and about. But come in, child. I'll show you to your room and Maybelle can unpack your things."

"I won't be staying more than just tonight, Mrs. Walker. I'll be going on out to Mr. Twill's plantation tomorrow."

Mrs. Walker glanced at Sean and at the wagon, confusion in her pale blue eyes. "Didn't Mr. Twill come to meet you?"

"No. I was hoping you could tell me why."

The older woman shook her head. "But do come in. Sean can bring your things."

"Just the small case on top," Jessie told Sean.

He bobbed his head and turned to take down the case, again the picture of the perfect servant. Balancing the small trunk on one shoulder, he followed respectfully behind as Mrs. Walker led the way into the house.

"Your room is the first on the left at the top of the stairs," Mrs. Walker instructed. "Pardon me if I don't go up with you." She indicated her cane. "The stairs are so hard for me." She gave Jessie a little push. "Do go up with Sean and open the door for him, will you, my dear?"

Being alone in an upstairs bedroom with Mr. Sean Winthrop, wagoner, was the last thing Jessie wanted, but someone had to open that door for him. Maybelle had already disappeared toward the back of the house in search of the servants' quarters.

Gathering her skirts, Jessie went up the stairs, with Sean trailing behind. She could feel his gaze on her, uncomfortably intimate. Her hips, she realized with a blush, would be right at his eye level. She quickened her steps and hurried to the bedroom door, holding it open with both feet planted firmly in the hall.

Sean shouldered past her into the room. He looked around uncertainly then turned to her. "Where do you want this?"

"Any place," she said irritably, anxious for him to be gone. "There," she said, entering the room and pointing toward the foot of the bed.

In an easy, fluid motion, he set the trunk down. He touched his forelock and bowed. "Will there be anything else, ma 'am?"

Was it her imagination that made it seem as if his manners were but a mockery of a servant's? The way he stood there looking at her, she could easily imagine him stepping forward to sweep her into his arms.

23

"No," she said, her voice a bit shaky as she tried in vain to dispel her imaginings. "That will be all." She wanted to say more, to smile and laugh with him. But what more was to be said? The man was a wagoner, she reminded herself, not a friend of the family.

"Until morning then?"

She shook her head. They stood looking at each other, and he seemed to be waiting for something. Then with a sudden blush, she realized that he was merely waiting for her to precede him from the room. Hurriedly, she turned and went down the stairs, his tread close behind her.

Mrs. Walker was waiting at the foot of the stairs. She smiled warmly at them both. "Will you be taking Mrs. Twill out to the plantation in the morning, Sean?"

"Yes, ma'am," he said.

"Ah," she said approvingly. "Then she'll be in good hands."

"Do you need anything, Mrs. Walker?"

"No, thank you, Sean. You've been too kind to us already." To Jessie's surprise, Mrs. Walker took Sean's hand, patting it as if he were a dear friend. "You run along now."

Again giving Jessie a bow that was totally effaced by the amused gleam in his eyes, Sean left, swinging lightly down the walk and bounding into the wagon.

"You seem to know Mr. Winthrop quite well, Mrs. Walker," Jessie said, wondering at her friend's easy familiarity with the wagoner.

"Sean has been very good to us," Mrs. Walker answered, leading Jessie into the parlor. "I don't know how I would have gotten along without him the last two weeks since Andrew has been so ill. Would you like a little sherry before dinner, my dear?"

"No, thank you."

"Sean stops by nearly every day to see if there's any errand he can run for us. His master must be very kind to give him so much free time, though I've never met the man myself."

Jessie sat down rather harder than she had intended, a tight constriction in her chest. "Master?"

"Yes. Mr. Fortune of Fortune Shipping. Brought Sean with him from Barbados a few weeks ago. Though I don't know of anyone who's met Mr. Fortune. Keeps to himself in that big house of his."

"Mr. Winthrop is a bondslave?"

"Yes, it's a shame, isn't it? Sean's such a nice, young man. Such nice manners."

A bondslave? The knot in in her chest seemed to tighten as her disappointment deepened. Why should it bother her that Sean Winthrop was a bondslave? He was nothing to her, could never be anything to her. Indeed, she assured herself, lifting her chin proudly, even if she was not already wed, she would not want anything to do with a man who could let such a thing happen to him.

Mrs. Walker sat down with a splash of sherry in her glass.

"His manners are very nice," Jessie agreed stiffly. "For a bondslave."

Mrs. Walker gave a very unladylike snort. "For a bondslave? His manners would do justice to a duke."

"He certainly gives himself the airs of one!"

"Why, Jessie, whatever has Sean done to anger you so?"

"Anger me? Nothing. Nothing at all."

Nothing at all, she thought. *Only that Sean Winthrop dredged up all my old dreams of a husband who could send my senses reeling and make me as giddy and glad as a girl again. Dreams and hopes that have to be repressed.*

25

"I'm sorry. I guess I'm just tired and hungry," she said, trying to make amends for her criticism. "The ship's food was not the best." She took a deep breath of the fragrant flavors wafting from the next room as servants bustled about setting out the food. "It will be good to eat decent food again."

"Then go on in to dinner, my dear. I'll go get Andrew. He has insisted on joining us, if you don't mind his being a bit informally dressed?"

"Of course not."

Jessie went into the dining room and seated herself at the table. Within moments she heard a shuffle and looked up to see Mr. Walker in robe and slippers, leaning heavily on a servant and guided by Mrs. Walker. She was shocked to see how ill he looked. Always a rather spare man, he was now nearly nothing but bones. He managed a happy smile when he saw her.

"Jessie, how delighted I am to see you! Just the sight I needed to get me on my feet."

Mrs. Walker helped him into a chair, then sat close beside him. "Just don't overdo it, Andrew. Just long enough to eat, then right back to bed with you."

"Tosh, woman! I'll never get my strength back lying around all day!"

Mrs. Walker said nothing but filled his plate and cut his meat for him as if he were a child. Jessie noticed that he did not object to this attention, and she wondered if he were really strong enough to have joined them.

"I was surprised to hear of your wedding, Jessie. Especially to Jonathan Twill." His wife gave him a warning glare but he ignored her. "Why on earth would you wed a man like that?"

Jessie tried to stiffle the alarm she felt at his choice of words. "Mr. Twill and I have never met. Our wedding was by proxy."

She thought she heard him mutter, "Good God!" but she wasn't sure since his words were muffled in the napkin Mrs. Walker pressed to his lips.

"I'm sure Jessie and Mr. Twill will get along fine, darling. Just give her time. And"—she turned to Jessie, speaking as if there were more to what she said than the surface words, as if she were offering her a safe haven—"if you ever want to come visit with us, no matter how long, you know you will always be welcome here."

Mrs. Walker directed the talk to other matters, her rose garden and the latest styles, but throughout dinner and afterward in her room, Jessie could not shake off the sense of foreboding that the Walkers' words had given her.

Chapter Two

Sean rolled his head back and sighed with exhaustion, easing the strain of the knotted muscles in his back and arms. Shrugging out of his soiled shirt, he tossed it at a nearby chair and pulled off his shoes before stepping onto the thick, Oriental carpet that stretched across his chamber to the downy four-poster bed and ornately carved wardrobe. A movement at the door caught his eye, and he stepped aside for his servant to lug two heavy buckets to the copper tub in the alcove. As the steaming liquid splashed into the tub, Sean stripped off the rest of his clothes and, handing them to the servant, eased his battered frame into the soothing water.

"Will ye be needin' aught else?" the man asked.

"Not tonight, Matt. Thank you," he said in dismissal. Sean relaxed, leaning his head back and closing his eyes.

The sound of footfalls pried open one sagging eyelid, and he glanced up to see not Matt but Mr. Meachum lowering his rotund bulk into a chair beside the tub.

"Matt told me you'd returned, sir."

Sean looked up sharply at the older man, and though not a muscle of his long, lithe frame budged from its relaxed posture, Meachum squirmed beneath the piercing glare of those dark blue eyes. "Do not forget what I am supposed to be, Mr. Meachum. Even within the privacy of these walls, 'twould be best to address me as you would a bondslave. A slip like that within the hearing of the wrong person could cost me my life."

"You're right. Right of course," Meachum said, trying to shift his body into a more comfortable position on the narrow chair. Then he chuckled. "But 'tis hard, seein' ye sprawled there at yer leisure, the same young lordling I've watched grow to manhood."

"It hasn't been easy acting the part of a slave, either, Mr. Meachum." He flexed one thick biceps, wincing as he massaged it. "I thought I was used to hard work."

Meachum chuckled again. "And so you are. But 'tis a different kind of work from the kind done by the son of a wealthy shipowner in Barbados."

Sean's even teeth showed in a wide white slash across the deepness of his tan. "That shipowner's son never knew how good he had it."

Mr. Meachum chuckled. "Your father'll be proud of you, Sean. Saw you at the Walkers' again today. Have you learned aught?"

Sean shook his head. "I've never suspected them. They were transferred to Charles Town but recently and they seem to be good people. But I did hope I could learn something about the workings of Ashbrook Shipping from them by running some of their errands. I think Jonathan Twill is the one we need to watch."

"Twill? What's his connection to Ashbrook? Just an upriver plantation owner, isn't he?"

"It isn't his," Sean said. "I've learned that much. It belongs to Ashbrook Shipping. He just manages it for them, which gives him the connection with Ashbrook. The plantation is conveniently close to our upriver warehouses. And he seems the type to be involved in nefarious undertakings."

"Don't see how you'll learn anything about Twill," Meachum said. "Seems awful closemouthed. Hardly comes to town, keeps people off that plantation."

"I think I know how I can learn about Twill," Sean said, standing up and reaching for a towel. A way that should prove to be a pleasant little diversion, he thought. He had never been one to seduce another man's wife, but if that's what it took to sort this mess out, it might not be too onerous a chore. Mrs. Twill had a mouth that demanded kissing. He wanted to start at those turned-down corners and nibble his way down that slender neck to. . . .

"I hope you're not planning something dangerous, Sean. Your father told me to look out for you and . . ."

Sean laughed mirthlessly. "Not exactly dangerous, Meachum. Twill has taken himself a wife."

"A wife?" Meachum's eyes widened. One did not have to be a longtime resident of Charles Town to hear whispers of the goings-on at Twill's plantation. None of the local ladies of the evening would go there anymore, but his slaves were not so lucky.

"Aye, a wife. But if she married Twill, I doubt that she is half so innocent as she appears." *Not the way she smiled at me when I first met her,* he thought. If that wasn't an open invitation, he had never had one. Why she had cut him off later he had no idea. But he was sure that it would not take much to win that inviting smile from her again.

Meachum scratched his balding pate. "So how will that help you, lad?"

Sean merely cocked a brow at him.

"Ah, yes, well. Harumph."

Sean laughed at Mr. Meachum's discomfiture.

"I know you have a bit of a reputation, Sean. But do you think it's . . . ahem . . . er . . . ethical to use a lady that way, besides being dangerous if Twill finds out?"

"You know I'll be careful, Meachum. As for being ethical, if she's involved with Twill, she deserves whatever she gets."

Sean stepped from the tub, feeling vaguely uneasy about what he had just said so convincingly to his secretary. He hoped he was wrong about the lovely Mrs. Twill. He had to admit that he was unusually attracted to her and he hoped she was as innocent as she looked. But if she was ignorant of what was going on, why would a woman as enticing as Jessie marry Twill? That question led him to conclude that she had to have some ulterior motive. Therefore, she was involved. Besides, he couldn't help remembering the allure of her smile, her look, the easy way she accepted his escort back to her ship—the escort of a stranger. Were those the actions of an innocent?

He rubbed his hair briskly with the towel. Somehow, he would find out what her part in all this was. Even if she wasn't involved, what good would it do him? She was still another man's wife.

The mist had not yet completely risen from the river when Jessie said her farewells to Mrs. Walker. Her hostess pressed a parcel into her hands, explaining that it was sandwiches for lunch.

Thanking Mrs. Walker one last time and giving the woman a parting hug, Jessie turned to the wagon. She glared at Sean and tried to avoid his touch, but he lifted her onto the wagon seat with his hands on her waist just as he had done the day before. He smiled up at her rakishly, and today his hands seemed to linger even longer, sliding onto the roundness of her hip before leaving her.

Maybelle certainly had no qualms about accepting Sean's hands around her waist as he lifted her up. And why should Jessie object if her maid wanted to flirt with another servant? Even if a bondslave were beneath the concupiscent Maybelle?

Jessie watched the broad-shouldered bondslave climb onto the seat beside her. The look in his eye was anything but reassuring. If Mrs. Walker had not spoken so highly of Sean, she would be leery of trusting him to escort her.

It was not just Sean's handsomeness and wandering hands, but her reaction to them. Was the warm Carolina weather already melting her icy Puritan reserve? If so, she must strengthen it. She must never question the gulf between her position and a bondslave's, not if she wanted to keep him at bay and not if she wanted to keep her own desires firmly under control. Pointedly, she squeezed the parcel of sandwiches onto the seat between herself and Sean's lean thighs.

He glared at the parcel, then cocked a brow at her as if he were entirely aware of her need for barriers between them. Then smirking sardonically, he handed the parcel back to Maybelle, leaving Jessie with nothing but several layers of petticoat and gown separating them. It was not enough, she thought as they rattled down the street and headed out of town. It was not enough at all.

The road soon gave way to two ruts with grass and weeds growing in between. Homes were far apart and set amidst wide fields of ripening rice interspersed with untouched stretches of dark forest. Mr. Winthrop was an entertaining guide, pointing out the various homes and telling her what little he knew of their inhabitants.

"I'm sorry I can't tell you more about your new neighbors, Mrs. Twill, but I'm rather new in Charles Town myself," he said, smiling.

"An unwilling immigrant, I'm sure," she answered, as one wheel of the wagon dropped into an unavoidable hole.

Sean grinned as she lurched against him, her soft arm bumping against his hard muscled one. "Unwilling? Why unwilling, madam?"

She gripped the rough edge of the seat, trying to avoid further contact. "Mrs. Walker told me you were brought here from Barbados by your master. A slave has little choice in where he goes."

"True. But I am most glad to be here." Sean clucked softly to the horses, urging them up a slight rise.

"And when you are free? Will you stay in Charles Town?"

He shrugged nonchalantly. "That day is still nearly seven years in the future. Until then, I am content."

"Content?" She stared at him incredulously. How could any man be content to be a slave?

"Aye, content. Why should I not be? I have a lenient master who allows me time to earn extra money to spend as I will."

"And do you apply what you earn against your indenture?"

"There are many pleasures along the road, madam," he said, grinning most suggestively, "and I am not immune to their lure. What little I can earn will not greatly shorten my indenture. Now if I could find a quick way to freedom, I would take it, but I enjoy myself as I can and rest content to let my freedom come when it comes. It might be otherwise if I did not have the best of masters."

"The best of masters? What of yourself, sir? Would you not be your own best master?"

He chuckled, but it seemed as if he laughed at something amusing only to himself. "That was the master who got me sentenced to slavery, madam."

Sentenced? Jessie's eyes widened. It did not seem possible that the handsome, smiling man beside her could be a felon. But what did she know of him, really, besides the fact that she found him far too attractive? She turned her attention to the road ahead, determined to pry no further. She had begun to relent in her opinion of him, thinking that perhaps he had sold his services for a term in exchange for transportation to Barbados to start a new life. That she could perhaps excuse. She had imagined him the son of poor farm folk, anxious to improve his lot, eager for his day of freedom to begin making his fortune in the New World. But a criminal?

Why should she care about him, anyway? What was there that continued to draw her to him in spite of all she had learned? He was certainly handsome, she thought. But so were any number of other men she had known, though perhaps not to Sean's degree of perfection. He had a vitality about him that seemed irrepressible, a *joie de vivre* that was infectious. But now she thought that that quality might be symptomatic of his irresponsibility. A spendthrift criminal who needed to be governed by a master.

Sean urged the horses to the side of the track and brought them to a halt. "The horses need rest and water. We'll stop here for a few minutes and see what Mrs. Walker put in that bag."

He helped them down without pawing her too much and without getting attacked by Maybelle.

Sean handed Jessie the sack of food, and she sat down beneath a tree and pulled out a sandwich. "Sit down, Maybelle. Quit pacing. Why are you suddenly so nervous?"

"Aren't you afraid of snakes, Miss Jessie? How can you sit there in that high grass?" the maid asked, wringing her hands.

Jessie glanced around. "There aren't any snakes here, Maybelle. And if there were, they'd be more afraid of us than we are of them."

"Aren't you afraid of snakes?" asked Sean.

Jessie shook her head. "No. Nor spiders, dead rats, nor frogs. I was teased too much by my cousins when I was little. I decided if they could pick up those things, I could, too. They stopped teasing me."

Sean laughed, and Jessie joined in, feeling pleased somehow that she had met with his approval. He took a leather bucket from the wagon and went to fetch water for the horses from a nearby stream.

Maybelle shuddered, looked around carefully, and kicked a twig or two away before finally sitting gingerly beside Jessie and taking a sandwich.

"He's a handsome one, ain't he?" Maybelle sighed watching Sean water the horses.

He certainly is, Jessie thought, watching the play of his firmly muscled flesh beneath the taut fabric of his shirt. His corded forearms seemed to strain but lightly with the heavy leather bucket as he held it up for each horse to drink its fill. He moved with a grace seldom seen in a man, but it detracted not one whit from his masculinity that seemed to overwhelm Jessie each time he was near.

Forcing her gaze away from Sean, she said, "I think it best if you look elsewhere for a man. Mr. Winthrop is not for you." She wondered if she were not saying it to herself as much as to her maid.

"Why not?" Maybelle challenged with a flounce of her head. "You can't have him. You wouldn't have him even if you could. I don't care if he is a transportee." She bit off a chunk of sandwich and continued watching Sean, trying to catch his eye.

Sean soon joined them, dropping down on the grass and reaching into the bag for a sandwich as if the three of them were old friends on an outing.

"No wonder you are content being a slave," Jessie said, trying not to smile. "You have no idea how to act like one."

Sean cocked an eye at her, and, biting into a sandwich, asked in mock seriousness, "Do I take liberties, my lady?"

Growing warm beneath his bold scrutiny, Jessie remembered the touch of his hands on her waist. "Constantly, Sir Bondslave."

His only answer was a low chuckle as he bit into his sandwich, looking at her as if he wished it were her he was attacking so voraciously.

Maybelle finished her sandwich, then excused herself to look for a private, snake-free place to answer nature's call.

Sean stretched out at Jessie's feet, propped himself on one elbow, and looked up at her. "How long have you known Jonathan Twill?"

Jessie looked down at her sandwich and took another small bite. She did not want to admit that she had never met her husband, that her marriage was an act of desperation which she was already beginning to regret. Especially not to Sean. "Not long," she answered noncommittally.

"Why did you marry him?"

She put down her sandwich and looked indignantly at the man lying so casually at her feet. "That's a rather personal question."

He shrugged, not the least reproved. "You have been asking me some very personal questions. I thought it was my turn."

"That's different."

"Why? Because I'm a slave?"

She started to get up, but his hand on her arm detained her. "You still haven't answered my question. Don't you owe me at least one answer for all those I gave you?"

She shook off his hand. "Very well," she answered stiffly. "It was a business arrangement. A mutually beneficial business arrangement."

"I see," he said shortly. He looked away from her and she could see his jaw clench as if it were not the answer he had hoped for. In one fluid motion he rolled to his feet, casting the remnants of his sandwich into the undergrowth. "If you'll collect Maybelle, we'll be on our way."

When Jessie and Maybelle returned, Sean was again smiling and again helped them aboard with willing and wandering hands, again managing to stay barely within the bounds of propriety. Jessie knew his hands had lingered too long and had strayed slightly off the permitted path, but it was not quite enough for her to give him the reprimand he deserved.

And she needed to reprimand him, for her own peace of mind. She didn't want him to think she welcomed his attentions. She tried to deny even to herself that the feel of his strong hands around her waist was a pleasant one. *I am a married woman*, she reminded herself. *He is but a slave. A sentenced criminal. No matter how his touch arouses you, no matter how closely he resembles the dreams you have cherished of a handsome, loving husband, he is not your husband. Sean is a slave. A man with no prospects, at least not for the next seven years.*

In other circumstances she would have shrugged off the difference in her social status and Sean's as easily as she had braved Bostonian disapproval by working in her father's office. But these were not other circumstances. She was wed and Sean had to be held at arm's length. No. Further. As far away as possible.

And whether her new husband fit her dreams or not, she was wed to him and he awaited her just down the road. If he did not have Sean's overwhelming physical appeal, at least he wasn't a slave nor a felon nor without a future. A future she would bring him, a future they would share. Sean could have no place in that future. It would be wise to remember that. If she felt her breath quicken each time her shoulders brushed Sean's, or his thigh pressed against hers, she would just have to control her feelings.

Sean continued his amiable chatter, and it was hard for Jessie to remain aloof, not to laugh at his jokes, hard not to share in the joy and beauty he pointed out to them. Mrs. Walker was right. He had the manners and easy confidence of a duke. Jouncing along beside him, she found it was all too easy to forget the gulf between their social positions.

When Sean turned the wagon in at a dilapidated gate, and informed her that they were now at her husband's plantation, Jessie felt all the tension return that Sean had banished with his morning banter. As she looked up at the huge overhanging oaks draped in long stands of moss that lined the rutted drive, she wanted to reach over and cling to Sean's arm. Instead, she held her chin higher and clenched her fingers tightly together in her lap as she tried to peer ahead to see the house that was hers.

When Sean halted the team, Jessie gazed in dismay. Her fantasy of an elegant plantation house surrounded by lush flower gardens and a manicured lawn dissolved. Before her was a graying structure that might once have been that elegant house. But it had been left too long at the mercy of the elements to command admiration now. Some of the shutters hung askew, some were missing entirely, and one once grandly towering porch column had fallen away, taking a corner of the porch roof with it. The weed patch near the house was threaded with dirt paths and bare, beaten-down areas where refuse mingled with neglected tools.

A wildly overgrown hedge of crepe myrtle hid the fields from view. There seemed to be no one about. No husband to greet her, no servant to take her things and see to the comfort of the mistress of the manor. She fought the apprehension that clutched at her.

Sean gave her a puzzled look.

"I've never been here before," she said, her voice tight. Her gaze traveled over the disarray and neglect. "It's not exactly what I expected."

Without question, he reached over and gave her stiff fingers a reassuring squeeze. She did not feel the usual tension building at his touch, and she took it for what it was, the comfort offered from one human being to another without regard to wealth or social standing. It gave her the courage she needed at that moment, and for once she welcomed his touch. When she was at last able to give him a wan smile, he let go and got down from the wagon.

He minded his manners helping them down and ushered her up the steps and held her arm as they crossed the loosened porch boards. The door protested being opened, scraping an arced trail in the dirt in the entry. The interior of the house reflected the exterior. The once grand furnishings were sadly neglected and badly used.

They could hear muted voices from upstairs, and Sean guided her steps upward and down a hall. The door of one room was open and it was from there the voices came.

Stepping to the doorway, a stench of illness and filth assailed her nostrils, almost making her retreat.

The room was shut up, with closed windows and drawn drapes. Dust motes danced in the few shafts of light that penetrated the dimness. Two people stood by a bed, looking down on the lone occupant, a man whose shallow breathing and jaundiced skin proclaimed him a victim of a severe fever.

The man, so tall he towered over the woman, turned at Jessie's entrance, drawing the attention of the quadroon to her. The tall white man looked at Jessie so contemptuously it made her skin crawl.

She felt Sean's hand tighten at the small of her back and it gave her strength. "This is Mrs. Jonathan Twill," he said. "You should have been expecting her."

Jessie swallowed and looked at the tall man. He was completely bald and his face scarred, perhaps from a bad bout of smallpox, and it added to the feeling of evil she had when she looked at him. Her apprehension grew when she thought that this man might be her husband. He let his gaze travel over her as if appraising her for sale, and wherever it touched her, she felt defiled.

"Twill's 'bout dead," he said, jerking his thumb in the direction of the man on the bed. "Fever's got 'im. I'm Jackson, the overseer."

Jessie tried not to let her relief show too visibly that Jackson was not the husband she had traveled so far to join. But now her vision was drawn to the sick man, the man who was her husband. He was a large heavyset, man, but his flesh was sadly wasted, his skin a sallow shade not entirely due to his illness. His hair was matted, several days' growth of beard stubbled his cheeks, and the bedclothes, rumpled and frayed, had not been washed in some time. An overflowing chamber pot sat in a corner, nearly hidden by mounds of clothing and debris but making itself evident by its smell.

As she surveyed the room, her anger began to mount. She had little knowledge of Jonathan Twill's character, but no one deserved to be so neglected and poorly cared for in sickness. She had given her vow to love and to cherish this man in sickness and in health until death parted them. She had not expected to have to answer to the more difficult part of that vow so soon, but he was her husband and he was sick. Perhaps Mr. Jackson had given up on Jonathan Twill, but that didn't mean he could not yet be saved. And she was determined to do all she could to nurse him through this illness.

"You," she said to the young quadroon woman who leaned indolently against the bedpost, "what is your name?"

"Josie," the woman answered impudently, tossing her head, making the gold hoops in her ears dance.

"Josie, ma'am," Jessie corrected in a tone that made the woman straighten from her slouch and glare at her. "Open the windows and take out that chamber pot."

Jackson stepped forward, and the woman relaxed against the post, as if waiting to see if she really had to obey.

"I'll take care of things here, Miz Twill. You just go on back to town." His words were drawled almost in a challenge.

Jessie could feel Sean edge forward, his hand on her waist telling her that he was there to protect her if necessary, but not interfering as yet. She appreciated his presence, but he seemed to know, as she did, that this was something she had to handle herself or she would never be mistress here. She stepped away from Sean's touch.

She felt like pointing out to Jackson just how poorly he had evidently taken care of things so far. But she controlled her tongue. "Mr. Twill is my husband. I am mistress here now, and I will take charge. I appreciate the offer of your services. There is one thing you can do and that is to fetch a doctor."

She stepped aside obviously dismissing him and giving Jackson room to leave. He glared at her, but there was little he could do but obey her. He stomped out, giving her a look that said that he was not finished with her yet. Maybelle barely had time to scurry out of his way.

Josie still lounged against the bedpost, snickering.

"When you have finished the chore I gave you, there are other things that need doing," Jessie said, and this time there was no denying the snap in her voice.

Josie looked at her a moment longer, her eyes narrowed and calculating, as if considering whether to obey. Then suddenly she moved away from the bed and began opening windows.

"We'll need some water heated for washing and cleaning," she said to Josie, who looked at her as if she were asking the impossible.

"I'll see to it, Mrs. Twill," Sean said. He gave her a reassuring nod as he left, and somehow, the burden she had to face seemed lighter just knowing that he was there to help.

Jessie stepped closer to the bed and looked down on the man to whom her troth was plighted. He moaned suddenly and thrashed around, startling her. His eyes opened, and he looked around but did not seem to really see her. He licked fever-dried lips.

A bedside table was littered with cups and bowls containing a variety of stale and questionable contents, but there was no water or anything liquid she felt was safe to offer Mr. Twill to ease his thirst.

"Maybelle," she began.

Maybelle nodded and hurried over to gather up several of the cups. "I'll get some water."

With her nose wrinkled in distaste, Josie picked up the chamber pot and left, holding the offensive thing as far from her as possible. *She acts as if she has never done such menial work in her life*, Jessie thought. She watched her go, her hips swaying, her bright skirts aswirl, her gold bangles jingling. Maybe Josie's role in this household had not included cleaning. If not, she would soon learn. From the condition of this room, it seemed that until now no one had taken much interest in cleaning.

Jessie turned to look down at Mr. Twill. His eyes were closed again, but he moved restlessly, further rumpling the covers and grayed linens.

He sported a thick crop of dark brown hair. That seemed to be his one good feature, Jessie thought, but even that was lank with oil and dirt. His beard, several days from a barbering, was sprinkled white. His eyes, sunken from the dehydrating fever, were ringed by dark shadows, but it was clear that his present illness was not entirely responsible for the ravages she saw on his face. A pile of empty liquor bottles tossed into one corner gave mute evidence to her conclusion.

His nightshirt gaped open at his neck and Jessie could see part of a massive chest, covered by thick, curly hair. But even as massive as that chest was, the belly was larger, though slack now from his illness. His outflung arm was large-boned and at one time probably well-muscled. Now the flesh was loose and wasted by disuse, dissipation, and disease. This man could have stood tall and commanding, exuding an air of authority. Though he was by no means handsome, he could have been impressive. But he was not. What had happened to him to bring him to this pass? she wondered.

Jessie dumped the contents from a straight-backed chair and pulled it beside the bed. A coiled whip fell to the floor. It was too long for a riding crop. She shuddered. What did that say about the character of the man she was married to? There were over a hundred slaves on this plantation. Did he use it on them?

She sat down slowly, her legs beginning to shake in reaction to what she had encountered so far. Though the chamber pot was gone and the breeze from the now-open windows was bringing fresh air into the room, the staleness, the smell, the closeness were nauseating. Or was it the picture of Jonathan Twill's character emerging from the evidence around her that was causing this knot to grow in her stomach?

She had imagined arriving at a well-run plantation, greeted by her new husband bending over her hand to place a welcoming kiss on her fingers that would run like fire into her heart, sparking a searing romance between them. He would be tall and handsome, strong of character, and elegantly dressed.

Jessie looked around at the clothing strewn on the floor, on chairs, on the bed, and hanging out of the open cupboard. They were of cheap material, cheaply made, and none of it very clean or in good repair. Jonathan Twill was hardly an elegant dresser.

He moaned, thrashing again, licking his dry lips. Jessie stood and straightened the covers, then pushed back the hair from his face. His skin was burning, and she did not have a cool cloth to soothe his brow. What was taking Maybelle so long?

She heard a rattle of dishes before she saw her maid enter. Jessie moved the rest of the dishes on the bedside table to clear a place for the tray Maybelle carried.

"Sorry I took so long, Miss Jessie," Maybelle said. "I had to wash some dishes to use. There weren't any clean ones." She put down the tray on which she had placed a pitcher of water, a glass, a small basin of warm water, and a ragged cloth. Then she gathered the remaining dirty dishes onto the tray.

Removing her bonnet, Jessie handed it to Maybelle. "Unpack our clothes in one of the other bedrooms and find my gray work dress. Then we'll see about bringing some order to this room and cleaning up Mr. Twill."

"Yes'm," Maybelle said. Tray in hand, she turned to go.

"And find that Josie. She should have been back by now."

Jessie lifted Mr. Twill's head and placed the glass of water to his lips. He took a swallow before turning away.

Dipping the cloth into the basin, she bathed Twill's forehead, his neck, hoping this would bring down the fever. She washed his hands, noting the uneven nails thick with ground-in grime. Wrinkling her nose at the smell of his body, unwashed and sick, she fought down her nausea. This is the man who would hold her in his arms, with whom she would share this bed. She shuddered. But not until both were clean and he was well! She closed her eyes for a moment. Would she be able to bear it even then? She would have to, wouldn't she? But it was hardly what she had hoped to find at the end of her journey.

Unbidden, the image of Sean Winthrop came to her, sunshine-scented and smiling, a spark of joy in his eyes, firm, muscled flesh and strong hands touching her, searing, kindling a warm response within her. That was what she had hoped to find. He was what she had pictured. Perhaps he dressed no better than Jonathan Twill, but his clothes were clean, well cared for, his hair shining clean, his nails pared.

She forced her eyes open, ordering her mind to shut out that image. What proof did she have that Sean's character was any better than that of the man who lay sick in this bed? Had not Sean been sentenced to bondage for some crime? At least her husband was no criminal.

"You wanted me, Miz Twill?" Josie lounged impudently in the doorway, her arms crossed beneath her shapely bosom.

45

Jessie straightened. "Yes, stay with Mr. Twill while I change."

Josie shrugged. "Why? He ain't goin' nowhere."

Jessie bit down her anger at the woman's uncaring attitude. "Bathe his face and hands. It will help bring down the fever. And try to get some water into him. He will need a lot of care if he is to recover." On her way out the door, Jessie handed the wet cloth to the slave.

Jessie went down the hall to the next room. Maybelle was there, stripping the bed and mumbling something about filth. The sheets were nearly as gray and rumpled as the ones on Mr. Twill's bed.

"I thought you'd like this room, Miss Jessie," Maybelle said. "It's in the best condition, even though it's none too clean, either. I laid out the dress you wanted." She nodded to where the gray dress was draped over Jessie's traveling trunk, as if Maybelle had not wanted it soiled by contact with anything in the room.

"Thank you, Maybelle," Jessie said, shutting the door and beginning to unbutton her blue velvet with shaky hands. "It's hardly what we expected, is it?"

Maybelle turned with the wadded sheets in her hands and grinned, a determined look in her eye. "Not yet!"

Chapter Three

Jonathan Twill had been washed and shaved, his nails cleaned as best as possible, his hair washed, his nightshirt changed. Jessie could tell that they had caused him some discomfort with their ministrations, but he seemed to be resting more comfortably now, though still feverish. His skin seemed even yellower now than it had earlier this afternoon when she had first arrived. Or was that caused by the glow of the setting sun?

With Maybelle's and Josie's help, Jessie had brought order to Mr. Twill's room. She could not yet think of it as hers as well. Sean had also helped, moving the heavy cupboard so they could clean behind it, keeping a supply of hot water available for the washing, and even helping hang the heavy wet sheets to dry.

Mr. Twill now rested on clean linen, and Maybelle was putting freshly laundered sheets on Jessie's bed and cleaning her room. Josie was supposed to be making supper.

Jessie's stomach rumbled. Lunch seemed a long time ago. Wringing out a cloth, she continued to bathe Mr. Twill's face, neck, and hands with the tepid water, but the fever continued. He drank whenever she offered him water.

Hearing the sound of footsteps, Jessie looked up, expecting to see Maybelle. But Sean Winthrop stood in the doorway, nearly filling it. Her breath quickened, and she straightened slowly from her task, the ache in her back forgotten. The same glow from the setting sun that turned Jonathan Twill's skin an unhealthier shade of yellow was far kinder to Sean. His skin seemed golden in that glow, radiant and full of life, warm and sensual. His hair, recently washed and still wet, shone. His whole body seemed to cry out for her touch, and she wanted nothing more than to run her hands over that bronzed skin, over the muscled chest straining against the fabric of his shirt.

Fiercely, she forced her eyes away from that awful temptation. Unfortunately, it came to rest on the face of her husband, slack-jowled and sallow. *It is only because of his illness,* she told herself. *But whatever his physical condition this man is your husband, not the one standing in that doorway.* It would be best for her to remember that, and to stay on completely formal terms with Mr. Sean Winthrop.

"Mr. Winthrop," she said stiffly.

He walked toward her, graceful as a cat, yet exuding a masculine prowess that threatened to overwhelm her. He reached out to take the cloth from her and she flinched when his fingers touched hers.

"Let me do that," he said. "You go on down and have some supper. I'll take care of Mr. Twill."

"No, really, you've done too much already, Sean," she said, hanging on to the cloth.

Smiling crookedly, he gently pried the cloth from her fingers. "I don't mind, as long as you continue to call me Sean."

Shaken, she stepped back. So much for her resolve to remain on formal terms with him. Where Sean was concerned she seemed to have very little strength.

He took her by the shoulders and turned her, pushing her toward the door.

"Thank you, Sean," she said, turning to give him a smile before leaving.

Hungry as she was, Jessie took the time to wander through the house before going down to the kitchen. Since she had spent the bulk of the afternoon cleaning and caring for her husband, there had been little chance for her to explore. There were five rooms on the second floor. The master bedroom, the one she was going to use, Maybelle's, and two others. Her maid had managed to bring some semblance of order to Jessie's room and to her own, but the last two rooms were the worst. Broken furniture was scattered in piles of refuse. Old leaves had sifted into one room through a broken window. She shut the door. She would deal with that later.

The wallpaper in the hallway was loose and torn in places, she noted. The wall sconces held no candles, and one was broken. As she descended the stairs, the balustrade wobbled beneath her hand. Downstairs there was a parlor with tall French windows and a dining room with a long table and buffet. The pieces were fine but in desperate need of cleaning and refinishing. There was a library with empty shelves and dark paneling, and a small sitting room.

A tiny office held a desk piled high with papers, ledgers, plumes, and inkwells. Other papers cluttered the floor, some in stacks along the wall, others in untidy heaps. She felt the anger rise inside her at the filth and disarray of the plantation. Jonathan Twill was supposed to be the manager here for

Ashbrook Shipping and it seemed he had taken that responsibility lightly. She could only hope he had run the farming of the plantation with more efficiency and care.

Holding a tight rein on her rage, she left the office, and followed the narrow hall to the kitchen located at the back of the house instead of in a separate building as she had heard was customary in the South.

Josie was sitting at the kitchen table, hunched over a plate. The woman looked up when Jessie entered, but did not stand or even stop eating. Jessie's brow arched, but she was too tired to begin training a servant to show proper respect. She dropped into the chair at the head of the table and began filling her plate. There was not much, only potatoes and some kind of meat cooked together as a stew and cornbread. The cornbread was not bad and the stew, though simple, was hearty.

"This is very good, Josie," Jessie complimented.

Josie shrugged. "I didn't make it."

"Then who did?" Jessie knew Maybelle had no talent in the kitchen.

"Massa Sean. He make de cornbread and stew. I jes put out de plates."

Sean, a cook? The bondslave continued to surprise her. Jessie glanced up to where she had left Sean tending her husband. She had much to thank Sean for.

When she finished her meal, Jessie spooned some of the broth into a bowl for her husband. He might not be able to eat any solid food in his present condition, but as long as he was drinking, he could partake of a nourishing broth as well as water.

When she went back upstairs, Sean was lifting Mr. Twill's head to give him a drink.

"Here," Jessie said, "give him this instead. We need to get some nourishment into him."

Sean nodded and spooned some of the liquid into the man's mouth. Mr. Twill was awake and looking around, but seemed entirely unaware of what he was seeing. He took only a few spoonful before turning away. Then with a hacking convulsion, he vomited. Sean caught most of it in the basin, then gently used the cloth to clean Twill's face. Then the sick man turned over and went back to sleep.

Jessie looked at Sean in amazement. Not many men would have performed that service for another with such calm. But she was dismayed that her husband could not keep the broth down.

Sean smiled encouragingly at her. "He'll eat when he's better," he said.

She only nodded, but the thought that maybe Mr. Twill wouldn't get better clung to her. "I'll take over now," she said.

"There's not much you can do for him right now," he told her. "Sleep is the best healer." Then giving her hands a reassuring squeeze, he said, "I'll be back later."

"Thank you for everything, Sean." She smiled and added as he was going out the door, "Supper was delicious."

It was sometime in the middle of the night when Sean returned, carrying a blanket. "I thought you'd still be here," he said, pulling her up from her chair. "Off to bed with you."

"He might wake and need something," she protested over a yawn.

"I'll stay with him. I'll sleep there on the floor. I doubt that he'll wake tonight, but if he does, I'll hear him. Get some rest, Mrs. Twill."

After the day she had had, her trip out to the plantation, the emotional strain of finding a house in near ruin and a dangerously ill husband, the cleaning, and the tending, Jessie could hardly stumble from the room, let alone protest any further. She was asleep before her head hit her pillow.

The next morning she barely took time to fix her hair and straighten the rumples from the dress she had fallen asleep in before she went back to Jonathan Twill's room.

Sean was at the window, looking out, but turned when he heard her and nearly gasped. How lovely she looked in the morning light, even with rest-robbed eyes and wearing her dull gray work dress. But it was the look in her eyes that stirred him, the way she looked at him as if she were hungry for him. If her husband had not been lying on the bed between them, Sean would have been sorely tempted to pull her down upon it. Judging from her lips, softly parted, her quickening breath, the hardening nipples faintly evident beneath her dress, it would not be difficult to seduce the very lovely Mrs. Twill. But the moment was not right, and she must have realized that as well as he, for she turned her eyes away.

"How is he?" she asked, peering down at her husband.

"Sleeping now. He woke earlier, ate some." She glanced up hopefully. He could almost feel the heat from her body, hear the rapid beating of her heart. He shook his head. "It came right back up."

"He any better?"

Jessie turned at the sound of Jackson's gruff voice jarring them both from their thoughts. The overseer loomed in the doorway, seeming to sneer at Mr. Twill.

Jessie straightened, her lips set in a grim line at the man's cockiness. "Well, Mr. Jackson, have you returned with the doctor?"

"Nah. He said there weren't nothin' more he could do for Mr. Twill. I could have told you that 'cause the doctor been here before and done all he could. But you wanted me to go and I went. Now, is he any better 'cause there's stuff I need to ask 'im about."

Incensed by his arrogance, Jessie stiffened, determined to put the insolent overseer in his place. "While my husband is ill, Mr. Jackson, I am in charge here. If there's anything you need, ask me."

The look he gave her was that of a person who had just found a spider in his soup. "I guess I'll be makin' the decisions around here fer a while." He glanced again at the still form on the bed then back to Jessie, letting his gaze travel over her in the most lewd manner she had ever experienced. "Maybe from now on."

He started to turn away, but Jessie stopped him. "I will make the decisions here, Mr. Jackson," she said firmly.

He turned back to her. Hefting his trousers, he gave her a derisive grin. "Jes what could you tell me about the north field, Miz Twill?" he asked, curling his lip.

"The north field?" Jessie asked uncertainly.

"Yeah," he said scornfully. "Is the rice mature enough? Should I drain the field or not?"

"I . . . I . . ." Jessie's voice trailed off. She had wanted to be firm with this oaf, establish her authority. But he was right. What did she know about the maturity of a rice field?

"I know a bit about rice, Mrs. Twill," Sean offered. "We grow some on Barbados. Perhaps I could help."

She looked at Sean with a great deal of relief and gratitude. "Thank you, Mr. Winthrop. You have been a great help to me. I would appreciate your opinion on that field. Perhaps you and Mr. Jackson could come to some decision about it."

Jackson snorted and stomped out.

Sean stood a moment, looking at her. "As soon as I survey that field, I'll have to get back to Charles Town, Jessie."

She experienced a moment of panic at his announcement, her hand reaching out as if to stop him, but she drew it back, tucking it shakily beneath the other. She wanted to throw herself into Sean's arms, to beg him to stay, but she merely nodded. Sean had been a big help to her, but she couldn't depend on him forever.

He stepped toward her, drawn by her aborted gesture. "I'll come back in a day or two. Is there anything I can bring when I come back?"

"No." She hesitated a moment, awkward. But in spite of social dictates, she extended her hand to him, offering not just her hand in that simple gesture, but her thanks, her whole-hearted appreciation, and, perhaps, even her longing. "Thank you again for all your help."

He could not resist taking her hand and was heartened when her fingers curled around his enticingly. Was she offering him more than a parting handshake? he wondered, for she seemed to be pulling him closer with her smoky look, her downturned mouth, the sway of her body toward his. Was he misinterpreting these signals? Yet she did not resist when, instead of simply shaking her hand, he lifted it to his lips, turned it up and gave her a kiss on her wrist that promised more than he could say in words. The throbbing pulse at her throat seemed to answer that promise with one of her own, sending a silent message to him with each pounding beat. Could any invitation have been more blatant? If he had had qualms about his plan to seduce Jonathan Twill's wife, they were more than soothed now. This woman must know what she was doing to him, what she was suggesting with every nuance of her body. When the time came, it would not be seduction, but a mutual pleasuring. Of that he was certain.

It was with difficulty that he pried his fingers loose from hers, tore his gaze away, and turned to go.

The echo of his steps was gone long before Jessie recovered from the sensual trance he seemed to weave around her.

Jessie stayed at Jonathan Twill's bedside most of the day. She gave him water to drink when he roused enough to take it, and tried once or twice to get some more broth into him, but he couldn't keep it down.

That night, she, Maybelle, and Josie took turns sitting with him. He slept most of the time, leaving them little to do. It was during the long hours as she sat by his side in the darkness that Jessie at last had time to think about what the future might hold for her.

If Jonathan Twill recovered, what would her life with him be like? She shuddered to think of him touching her. She knew so little about him, but that little did not sit well with her. That whip had not been the only instrument of torture they had found when they cleaned out the room. And there had been even more empty liquor bottles beneath the filthy clothes. And what kind of man would keep Jackson on? She had had no chance to look further into the office downstairs, but its total disorderliness spoke volumes to her when added to the filth, clutter, and decay in the rest of the house. Then there was Josie. Had she been Twill's paramour? Was it a willing relationship on her part, or had he forced himself on his slave?

Jessie buried her head in her hands. Was she letting her imagination run rampant in the night? Almost, because of those things, she hoped Jonathan Twill would die. But that thought had barely surfaced before her guilt shoved it away again. Besides, what would she do if her husband died? Could she run this plantation without him? Would Jackson take orders from her? Would the slaves accept her authority? What orders could she give anyway? She had come here expecting to run a household, not a rice plantation. Mr. Jackson had made it plain to her just how little she knew about planting.

But surely she could learn. She laughed derisively at herself. Back home in Boston, she hadn't even been able to make the houseplants flourish. Her sister, Abby, was the one with the green thumb. Any plant under Jessie's care was under a slow death sentence. Did she really think she could grow more than two hundred acres of rice?

Probably not. Certainly not without help. And she certainly couldn't look to Mr. Jackson for that help.

Toward morning, Mr. Twill began moaning and thrashing, scratching at his arms, his chest. Jessie pushed up his sleeves, could see no reason for his itching, but worried that he would hurt himself.

It was full light when Maybelle came in with a breakfast tray.

"Why don't you get some rest, Miss Jessie?" she suggested, setting down the tray.

Jessie merely shook her head, pushed back her hair, and began eating her breakfast of eggs and ham. The eggs were greasy with hard brown edges and broken yolks, the ham barely warm. With difficulty, she forced some of it down.

Twill began scratching again, and Jessie again looked at his arms and chest.

"Why is he scratching?" she asked her maid. "Do you see any rash?"

Maybelle shook her head. "He just looks yellow and puffy."

"Get that jar of skin cream my sister gave me. Maybe that will soothe him."

But the cream did not help at all. Periodically during the day, Twill would rouse, drink, and then scratch as if tormented.

Mr. Jackson came that afternoon to check on him and to ask Jessie questions she could not answer. She had no choice but to leave things to Mr. Jackson's judgment for now.

"As I said," he sneered as he turned triumphantly to leave, "I guess I'll be makin' the decisions around here from now on."

That night Jonathan Twill seemed weaker and when Jessie returned from her all too brief rest the next morning, Josie greeted her with a doleful shake of her head.

"Dat man gonna die."

Jessie looked at her husband with alarm. "Die? What makes you say that?"

" 'Cause he ain't peein'."

Alarmed, Jessie checked the padding of folded towels under her husband. It was dry. Josie was right. He had not passed water for the two and a half days she had been here. She looked at his face. It had filled out, his eyes were no longer sunken. But it was an unhealthy puffiness.

"But he's drinking plenty of water," Jessie protested.

"Plenty goin' in but nothin' comin' out. Dat man's gonna die." With that pronouncement, Josie sauntered out of the room, unconcerned.

Jessie sat down in the chair that was now so familiar and looked at her husband. There was still no sign of a rash, though there were long scratches on his arms where he had clawed himself. His face and hands were even puffier, his color an alarming shade of yellow. His skin was still hot. As she bent over to bathe his chest with tepid water, she stopped in alarm. She could clearly hear a rale in his chest as he labored to breathe.

"No!" she gasped, tears beginning to roll unnoticed down her face as she struggled to prop him up with extra pillows. Mr. Walker had recovered from a serious fever, surely this man, younger, stronger, heftier, could recover, too.

In the semi-upright position, he seemed to breathe a little easier, and she dried her tears with the back of her hand. He was going to be all right, she told herself. Her dream was not dead yet. He would run this plantation, and she would take charge of the house. They would invest in shipping. There would be friends and parties. Life would be gracious.

Twill moaned, licked his dry lips, his gaze seeking the cup of water. Quickly, she grabbed it, then paused. Should she give him more water? If he was passing no water and it was collecting in his tissues, wouldn't giving him more make him worse? She didn't know. He seemed now to be reaching toward the cup, his hand wavering weakly. She put the cup to his lips but allowed him only a sip or two before taking it away.

His hand dropped and his eyes closed, though she was not sure he slept. Shakily, she put the cup down. What if she was doing the wrong thing by limiting his water? How could she know? Tiredly, she sank back into the chair. She could only follow her instincts and hope she was right.

But as the day passed the rale got worse, his breathing more labored. She propped him higher, but it helped only for a while. She could hear a gurgle in his throat with each difficult breath he drew. He struggled harder, wheezing more, gurgling, coughing, choking, until she thought she could not stand to listen to him any longer.

Maybelle offered several times to relieve her, but she refused, continuing to bathe his face and chest to bring down the fever, smoothing on the skin cream to try to relieve the itching, keeping him propped up, and giving him only tiny sips of water to ease the dryness in his mouth.

It was just after noon when she looked up to find Sean beside her. Just his presence seemed to lend her strength. When he put his arm around her waist in a purely comforting gesture, she leaned against him, gathering courage, comfort, strength. It all seemed to flow into her from him, and she wanted nothing more than to remain in his arms forever.

"How is he?" he asked.

Mutely, she shook her head. The horrible raling in Twill's chest and throat was answer enough. That was when it stopped so suddenly that at first she wasn't sure what had happened. Then with a start she straightened, then gasped.

Sean bent over Twill's chest, listening for a heartbeat, feeling at his throat and wrist. He turned to her about to speak. She was on the verge of throwing herself into his comforting arms when a voice intruded.

"He dead?" Josie asked, standing at the end of the bed, her hand on her hip.

"Yes, he's dead," Sean affirmed.

Josie merely shrugged and left, seemingly unaffected.

Sean gathered Jessie into his arms, and she went gladly, enfolding herself in his strength, the enveloping warmth of his arms. How good it was to lean on a strength other than her own for a moment, to smell a healthy cleanliness instead of the sour smell of fever, to feel firm, masculine flesh. How long she stood there, she did not know; she only knew that she never wanted to leave. She had no tears, only a tired numbness. But suddenly she was aware that someone had come into the room.

Pushing away from Sean, she turned to see Josie and Jackson standing there. Jackson had a grim smirk of satisfaction on his face, his fists on his hips. Two field hands were with the overseer, and Jessie was shocked at her first sight of two of the slaves who now belonged to her. They were thin and cowed, their clothes little better than rags. Josie, on the other hand, seemed as impudently disrespectful as ever.

"Josie said he was dead. 'Bout time," he grunted. "Mose, Bill, wrap 'im in that blanket and take 'im on down."

Jessie straightened, lifting her chin. "Leave him. My husband will neither be buried hastily nor without a minister."

Jackson gave her a mocking grin. "In this heat, we got to get 'im in the ground quick. There ain't no time for no minister."

Josie snickered.

Realizing Jackson was right, Jessie gave a brief nod.

"Though we may have to do without a minister, Mr. Twill will be buried properly—and tonight, Mr. Jackson," she said firmly. "Since you are so anxious to see him buried, you can see to digging the grave."

She indicated he was dismissed, and he stomped out, jerking a thumb at the two field hands, who followed mutely.

"We'll need to get him cleaned up, to press one of his suits, and to get some kind of a coffin," Jessie said, one hand at the arch of her aching back, the other absently running through her hair.

"I'll see to a coffin," Sean said. "And a marker." With a reassuring smile, he left and again she felt his aura of competence which seemed to lighten her burden.

With Josie and Maybelle to help, they washed Mr. Twill one last time, shaved, and dressed him.

When, at Jessie's request, Mr. Jackson brought the two men back to carry her husband out to his coffin, the overseer looked at the dead man with a sneer. "A waste of time if ye ask me. He ain't goin' to smell any sweeter or rot any slower with a shave and clean clothes."

"I didn't ask you, but I'll remember that when we bury you, Mr. Jackson," Jessie said, smiling sweetly.

Jackson snorted and turned his back to her, ordering the two slaves to take up their burden.

When they at last stood at the graveside, Jessie was satisfied with the way her husband had been laid to rest, except for not having a minister. As she watched the two slaves fill in the grave she had time to think for the first time that day. But she was too tired to think, too tired and too disheartened.

Her husband was dead and her dream of living a comfortable life with him at her side was being shoveled into a grave. There was no partner to help her, to lean on, to share with, to love. How would she ever manage to run the plantation alone? She knew nothing about growing rice, or managing slaves, or surviving in this climate.

She looked at the faces gathered around the grave. Josie seemed willing enough to help, though somewhat inept, and would be a help to her only with constant supervision and prodding. Jessie wondered why she had been tolerated as a housemaid. She wondered again if it was some other service she had provided for Jonathan Twill. Josie was certainly shapely enough, and the gold bangles that jingled constantly at her wrist and the hoops in her ears gave evidence that she had been favored.

Maybelle was a lady's maid. She could help with cleaning and laundry, but Jessie knew from past experience that the girl was hopeless in the kitchen.

And what of Mr. Jackson? He made her skin crawl just to look at him with his leering looks and sneers, but did that mean he wasn't a good overseer? Could he be depended on to bring in a good crop and to supervise the slaves? His eyes met hers and, suppressing a shudder, she turned away with a proud toss of her head.

The two slaves were nearly done filling in the grave, and she wondered about them. Were they adequately fed, clothed, housed? There were over one hundred slaves on this plantation who were now her responsibility, and she could not leave their welfare entirely to Mr. Jackson. Mentally, she added them to her list of things to do. Tomorrow she would inspect the slave quarters.

Then her eyes were drawn to the tall, broad-shouldered bondslave standing with wide-spread feet across from her, strong, virile, tugging at her heart at the mere sight of him. His simple cotton shirt was open at his throat, and he held a battered hat in his hands. Fine, strong hands, she thought, looking at them. The wind touseled his hair and played with the loosened ties of his shirt. He was dressed little better than the blacks who wielded the shovels. His status as bondslave was clear, yet he somehow exuded an air of authority. It was to him the slaves looked when they finished their task, and it was he who dismissed them. Except for the way he was dressed, this was how she had pictured her husband. With little effort, she could imagine that he was her husband. It was he who had given her comfort and support this day and since her arrival. It was he who set her blood to racing.

When they started back to the house, Sean took her arm, and she found his touch welcome, comforting. She had asked little of him today, but whenever a task needed doing, he had seen to it, from directing the making of the coffin to being certain that food was on the table. No job was beneath his dignity, yet his dignity never seemed to suffer.

But she could not lean forever on Sean, she thought, as tempting as that was. He would have to return to Charles Town tonight. He had been here to help when she most needed him, but from now on she was on her own.

She walked a little taller, holding her chin up. After all, wasn't this what she had wanted? Independence. Now she had a little more of it than she had bargained for, but she was determined that nothing was going to change it. She would never go back to her stepfather's home in Boston, never be financially dependent on him again. This plantation was hers or would be as soon as her parents arrived and signed the papers next week. And she was determined that it would remain hers and that someday, it would be something to be proud of.

It was a long time later that Jessie was at last alone in her room. Unable to sleep, she stood at the window, looking out across a lawn tamed by moonlight. The weeds and bare patches were not so glaringly evident in that gentle light. A faint breeze stirred the curtains against her cheek in a caress. It was a soft and calm night, the warmth almost tangible around her. The night she should have been sharing with a new husband. A vision of Sean rose unbidden to her thoughts. Sean, as she had first seen him, pulling his wagon to a halt at the dock, thinking then that he could well be her husband. Sean, leaning against the railing of the ship, his hair whipped by the salt-tanged breeze. Sean, helpful, supportive.

Moonlight pooled at her feet and splashed onto the long, white cambric gown she wore. A whisper of cloth, it had been intended for her wedding night.

She thought of the gross form they had buried that afternoon and shuddered. His was not the face and figure she had imagined when she pictured herself as the mistress of a Southern plantation.

Again, irrepressibly, Sean's body came to mind. A tall, lean body with dark hair and eyes of such a deep blue that they sometimes appeared black. How easily he had fit her dreams with his ready smile and blood-warming gaze. How easily she had been ready to accept him as her husband. Even now, it was not difficult to remember the feel of his hands on her as he lifted her into the wagon seat and let his caress stray onto her hip.

She had been quickly disabused of that dream as well. Sean Winthrop was not at all what he had at first seemed. He was no wealthy planter. He was not even free. He was also no concern of hers, she thought, shaking her head as if that would free her thoughts of him. Her hair, long, black, and straight, tumbled about her shoulders. Absently, she pushed it back where it lay in sharp contrast against her moonlight-whitened gown.

She wished there was at least someone to talk to.

Maybe a glass of wine will make me sleep, she thought. Hadn't she seen a liquor cabinet in the parlor? She picked up her robe, but it was warm tonight and no one would be about at this hour. She let the garment fall back onto the bed and slipped into the hall.

The house was quiet and dark except where the moonlight crept in, softening the rundown, shabby house. It was enough to light her way but not enough to show the threadbare patches in the carpet. The walls did not seem in such dire need of painting, and the grime did not show on the chandeliers. The soft radiance showed what the house once was, and what it could be again. Here in the pale light, it was as if her dream had materialized. If only her dream of a husband who would share her life and a night of love could be conjured up as easily.

Ever since her first kiss, stolen beneath a twig of mistletoe when she was sixteen, she had wondered what it would be like to be possessed by a man, to know the full onslaught of passion. A passion that had occasionally been stirred by other beaux, but never to an uncontrollable depth. Never to the depth Sean had stirred it with one touch. She had looked forward to her wedding night, to overturn finally the caldron of passion that smoldered within her. A caldron that had been brought to a kinetic simmer by a certain blue-eyed bondsman. A caldron whose boiling she would have to tamp once again.

She sighed and started down the stairs. It had all been too much—the loss of her father and her work in the shipping office, her comfortable life in Boston. And what had replaced it? Not the husband and life she had expected. That was gone, too.

The door to the parlor was open, and she hurried across the room, her bare feet making only a whisper of sound. The liquor cabinet was next to the French doors and was not locked. She took out a bottle and a glass, their clinking sounding loud in the quiet room.

She heard a soft rustle of cloth, then a deep, masculine voice said, "Pour me a glass and I'll join you."

Chapter Four

Jessie gasped and whirled, backing into the French door, the wine and glass clasped to her chest. The room seemed obscured by shadows, and the moonlight, spilling through the leafy branches of a tree, played tricks with the furniture, catching her eye with movements of light and shadow.

"Who—" It was all she could manage to ask.

" 'Tis I, Jessie."

The soothing accents of the now-familiar, low-timbred voice stirred through her, and her tightened nerves relaxed. Sean! It was not some ogre of the night, or worse, the fearsome Jackson. She trembled with relief. She saw him now, rising from the sofa, his hair tousled, his shirt loose about him. He came toward her, and she was glad to see that he had not removed his trousers, for the wide cotton shirt hung only to his thighs. But it made her acutely aware of her own apparel, and she wished she had worn her robe. She was glad that only moonlight lit the room. She did not realize, as Sean realized all too well, just how much the sheerness of her gown was emphasized by that wan light.

"Sean! What are you doing here?"

With a smile that warmed her as much as any wine could, he took the decanter and the glass from her nerveless fingers. Setting the glass on the liquor cabinet, he filled it with red wine, then found another glass and filled it as well.

"Sleeping."

He handed her a brimming glass, pressing it into her fear-chilled fingers. The warmth of his fingers brushing hers shocked her, and she spilled a drop of wine. But his hand quickly steadied hers and pushed the glass upward to her lips.

Jessie did not have to be urged to take a long draught of the wine.

His eyes passed over her in warmth and admiration, glowing softly in the half light, leaving little doubt as to his thoughts.

Her hand fluttered to her chest, drawing his gaze to the slim whiteness of her hand and its futile effort to conceal what the lacy gown accentuated. Her dishabille, being here alone with the very man who had claimed her thoughts earlier, the lateness of the hour, all combined to shatter her composure. "I must go," she said, turning to set down her glass.

"You have not finished your wine."

He stayed her with a caress to her hand that shredded her poise completely. She could almost feel it wafting to the floor in a thousand pieces.

"I can finish it in my room." She tried desperately to keep her voice steady, nonchalant, but her hand gripped the goblet so tightly she thought that the cut design of it must forever be branded on her hand.

"And leave me to drink alone?"

Even in the pale light, she could see the flash of his smile inviting her to stay. An invitation that was becoming increasingly difficult to decline.

"I think it would be wise."

"And when have wine and wisdom ever gone together?"

She laughed, knowing within her the truth of those words, knowing that to remain with him was very unwise indeed, but reluctant to take her leave.

"I want to thank you for all your help today, Sean." She twirled the glass in her hand, still feeling the tingle where he had touched her.

"Is that why you came down?"

He stepped closer to her and she was assaulted by his nearness. He must have bathed and laundered his clothes sometime that afternoon, for he smelled freshly washed.

"I couldn't sleep. I thought some wine . . ." She shrugged and waved her nearly empty glass.

He refilled it and she drank again as if to prove that it was the reason she had come downstairs in the middle of a dangerous riot of moonlight.

Was it that enchanting light that made him seem even handsomer than the dream she had held so dear for so long? Or was it the wine?

She took another long, calming drink to cool the flush she felt blossoming within her, then noted where his eyes strayed. The decolletage of the gown was planned to lead a man's eyes downward. Designed for her wedding night, the gown did little to conceal what lay beneath it, and the little that was hidden would have encouraged even the dullest imagination to new heights.

Sean's imagination was far from dull. Yet even his lusty mind had conjured nothing to compare to the enticing woman who stood before him clothed in a wispy web of lace and moonlight. His hand trembled as he groped for his own glass of wine, but he dared not take his eyes from this midnight apparition lest it vanish.

Sean took a large gulp and reached to place his glass back on the cabinet. His shirt gaped, letting a ray of light fall upon the mat of dark hair covering his strongly muscled chest.

Jessie's gaze followed that moonbeam, noting that his body was perfect, his shoulders wide. *Wide enough to help bear a world of troubles,* she thought. *Wide enough and strong enough.* The shirt gaped further, exposing more of the dark hair that trailed downward to where it disappeared inside his trousers. It was but a brief glance, but her heart skipped to a more rapid tempo. The clink of his glass on the hardwood of the liquor cabinet startled her, drawing her attention to his hands. Fine, strong hands. The fingers were work roughened, yet their touch could be gentle, comforting as when he had held her hand this afternoon. That touch could also excite, she thought, remembering the feel of it on her. It was just such a touch that she had dreamed, had hoped, she would feel from her husband this night. A touch she had yearned for. A touch that would lure her ever closer, excite her to unquenchable desire, and urge her to a blissful passion. Here before her was the body and face she had longed for, never really believing it was a hope that could truly materialize as it had in the man she saw before her.

That he was not her husband mattered less to her at this moment than the fact that she had dreamed him and he was here. And, if she judged aright from the warm glow in his eyes, as impassioned as she was.

His eyes were large and luminous in the mystical light, and Jessie could feel their warmth as they slowly moved over her. A warmth that was answered by a growing warmth within her.

She looked away from his impassioned gaze, unable to bear it. She knew she should flee to her room as quickly as her feet could carry her. But she could not flee him any more than she could deny her own desire. Yet because she knew she should, she spoke once more to try to turn them from the course she now knew they were set upon, to try once more to deny the magic that was being spun about them with tender filaments of moonlight.

Though her words were guileless, her voice was husky with desire. "Your master must have expected your return by now. Will he not take it amiss that you stay away?"

Shadows played over his face as he stepped closer to her. She could feel the heat from his body, and her own seemed to tingle in anticipation of the touch of his skin on hers.

"He knows who I'm with. It will not surprise him that I stay overlong," he answered, his voice as soft as the night that half-shielded him.

Hesitantly, he touched the line of her jaw with one finger, drawing it toward the point of her chin. She closed her eyes at the contact. Though light, it was as if that one simple touch of his finger to her face was more than just a touch. She felt that contact from the depths of his being to hers, melding them, fusing them into one, making of them one being more completely than any ceremony in a church or any signing of proxy documents could ever do. This was the kind of wedding night she had dreamed of. Though she had been denied the rest of her dream—the life of sharing, the gracious plantation life, a caring, loving husband—she would not be denied this one night of love. Not be denied this man whom she had envisioned in her dreams. On her arrival, she had mistaken Sean for the husband she would share her life with. For this one night, he would be that husband.

When he spoke, his voice was full of wonder. "What vision have my dreams brought forth from the darkness?" he whispered. "For surely no woman of flesh and blood could be half so lovely."

Jessie gasped at his words and pressed back against the door, watching hypnotically as the tree-filtered light danced across his face. "It must be a night for dreams. Surely this must be one." She leaned toward him. Invitingly, she lifted her face to his.

"A night such as this is indeed one for fantasies, but I assure you I am no dream. You, however, are too lovely to be real."

Jessie's lips glistened, and Sean bent to taste her wine-wet mouth. He found there a brew far headier than any dream-conjured wine, and he was wont to linger, gently tasting, nibbling one delectable lip and then the other, exploring her mouth with a thoroughness that would engrave its shape forever in his mind. No dream could have this much substance, yet what else could have brought her to him?

He had watched her that morning he brought her here in the wagon, the gentle movement of her hands, the precise little way she tilted her head when she spoke, the grace with which she sat on the grass to eat. He had been unnerved each time her thigh brushed his or when his hands touched her, lifting her from the wagon.

There were times when there seemed to be a spontaneous warmth between them. He had dreamed of her, but never dreamed that she would come to him this night. He had planned her seduction, planned to use her, then, uncertain of her involvement in this whole affair, had changed his mind. Yet here she was, leaning toward him, inviting his caress, his ardent advances. He could not deny that he wanted the lovely Mrs. Twill.

Any qualms he felt about taking her, he pushed aside. Was she not inviting his attentions? Surely she could not be the innocent she looked. Had she not wed Twill because of their past business associations? A business that Sean was convinced included theft and piracy. He had but to prove it. To press his advantage with the desirable widow would further his cause in a most enjoyable way. He tried to tell himself that his mission was the reason he pressed her, but his body did not accept that answer. Jessie Twill was a woman to set any man's lust ablaze—and his admiration. She had faced enormous difficulties in the past few days and had handled them with grace and firmness.

But it was not her managerial talents that interested him now. It was her mouth, warm and willing, soft beneath his probing possessiveness. It was her breasts, high and round, their dark centers teasing him from behind a nearly transparent shield of lace. It was the lush curve of her hips and the dark triangle that nestled between her thighs awaiting his awakening touch.

Jessie sighed as the fire of Sean's kiss flowed into her like brandy on a winter-chilled night. Here was the soporific she sought. But unlike wine that dulled everything, this heady draught aroused her senses with new awareness, and her mouth came alive beneath his.

She leaned toward him, but was stopped by the harsh rim of the glass she held. Vaguely, she felt him pluck it from her fingers, heard the ringing sound of it being set down. His hand returned to pull her more firmly against him, caressing her waist, her hip, the base of her breast, while his kiss, his drugging, awakening kiss, continued to hold her enthralled.

His kiss deepened, and she drank it in as if it were a fiery liquid. The fingers of one hand tangled in her hair, then trailed over her cheek, caught drops of that liquid, ignited it, and drew it down her throat, spilling fire down the slender column of her neck, along her soft collarbone. Wherever his flesh touched hers, a conflagration followed, fueled by his burning kiss. Downward, downward his fingers drew a smoldering trail. The gossamer barrier of her gown, barely protecting the pink peaks of her breasts, was brushed aside as easily as a cobweb, and his fingers continued along their searing path, at last conquering one rounded mound.

She gasped as new ecstasies burst inside her, and the trail of fire raged out of control. She wanted only his touch, his lips, his hands, his rock-hard frame pressing against her. Her desire was ablaze, fueled by his kisses and his touch and she succumbed to the fiery storm willingly, wantonly.

He pushed her gown from her shoulders, and it floated to her feet. He stood back a moment to survey her, and his gaze warmed her further.

"My God, Jessie," he said in awe, his voice husky, throbbing with passion, "you are more beautiful than any woman has a right to be."

He scooped her up and, holding her so close he could feel her wildly beating heart, he carried her quickly to the sofa, laying her down on the cool sheet he had discarded. He paused a moment to pull off his shirt, his trousers, then he was beside her, flesh touching flesh in searing contact.

Jessie was as aware of his desire as she was her own, each heightening the other.

Her hair had fallen across her breast, and he sifted it through his fingers, savoring its silken texture so like the softness of the breast beneath it. Almost impatiently, he brushed aside her hair to capture her breast gently. Caressing it, he pulled its pink crest into his mouth to taste, tease, torment.

A moaning Jessie wrapped her arms about him, running her hands over the smooth, rippling muscles of his back, feeling their strength as he pulled her closer to him.

His hand slid over her rounded hip, traveled to the flat plain of her belly, and down into the triangle of dense, black hair. Stroking, probing, his fingers found the sweet, warm moistness they sought.

Jessie lifted her hips, opening her thighs, wanting more. But still he continued his play, arousing, fueling the fire of her passion to uncontrollable heights until she thought she would die, consumed in the flame. Yet still her desire grew until it had to be fulfilled. She clutched him to her, wanting him closer, closer, wanting him to be part of her. She felt a moment's trepidation when he lifted himself above her and slid between her thighs, his manhood pressing against her.

She trembled and he paused.

Looking down at her, he could see her momentary fear. "Jessie?" he asked.

She knew without question that if she asked him to stop, he would. That alone shredded the last wisp of her fear and banished it forever. She smiled at him, winding her arms firmly around his neck. He thrust inside her and she felt a sharp pang. She saw his look of surprise, then closed her eyes as the flame they had kindled together became a bonfire, drawing them into a swirling, sweet inferno that swept them beyond anything they had ever known. The inferno blazed, burned, flamed, then subsided to a warm glow—the warm, gentle glow of contentment.

As they lay side by side, his arm around her, her head on his shoulder, her fingers absently twisted a bit of hair on his chest. Wonderingly, she thought of what had just happened to her. There had been that one brief pain, but otherwise, her "wedding night" was all she could have asked for. Sean's touch could not have been gentler or surer. Even now he continued to caress her, pressing her close to his side. Willingly, she snuggled against him, her curves fitting perfectly into his, enjoying the lean, hard feel of him. She wished she could stay there forever. She wished that he was really her husband, that they could awaken together in the morning, come down to dine in an elegant setting, and begin their life together.

But this had been no wedding night. She was a widow in charge of a large rice plantation and Sean was a bondslave. He was not her husband. There was no husband at all anymore. The house was not elegant and would not be for some time. She sighed and pressed closer to him, resting her head on his chest, trying to hold on to her dream for a few moments more. But it was fading with each passing beat of the heart she could hear thudding so strongly within him.

He still held her, but she knew she must leave before she fell asleep in his arms and was discovered by a servant in the morning.

She could wish, she could dream, but reality came creeping back. She knew what this night had meant to her, why she had succumbed to, even sought, Sean's embrace. But now she wondered what it had meant to Sean. Was she no more than another in a string of conquests? Would he boast tomorrow in the tavern how he, a mere bondslave, had coupled with Mrs. Jonathan Twill? Her face burned at the thought, and she pulled at the strand of hair twined around her fingers.

"Ouch!" Sean yelped, slapping her hand playfully. "Stop that, wench!" Then he caressed her thigh and she trembled anew.

Her eyes widened and she bolted upright, alarmed not only at his obviously renewed lust but at her own. Was one forever haunted by a need for more once one had tasted the forbidden fruit?

Then the word he had used penetrated her thoughts. "Wench!" Was that what he thought of her? A willing wench, no better than the dockside harlot the drunken sailor had mistaken her for?

Angry, embarrassed that her dream-clouded perception of him had caused her to give herself willingly to this bondslave, who saw this night as no more than another lustful romp, she struggled to disentangle herself from the sheet and his entwining arms.

He smiled and tried to pull her back into the comforting curve of his arm.

She pushed him away with a snarled, "Wench, is it?"

"Aye. Wench," he agreed with a lusty grin. "Come back here. I have a growing desire that only you can allay."

That desire was only too evident, and she scrambled off the sofa, gritting her teeth at being called a wench a second time.

He followed her from the sofa, reaching for her, but she backed away, snatching the sheet to cover herself. "Nay! Do not touch me!" Even in her anger, she could admire his lithe, naked body, the grace of the hands he lifted to her as if in supplication. A tremor passed through her and she thought, *If he touches me, I am lost. The magic in those hands is enough to fog my reason, overcome my indignation, shred my pride*. The only hope that she would not again succumb to her passion was the knowledge that on the morrow he would be gone. Soon, his master would return to Barbados and take his bondslave with him. She would never have to see Sean again. At that thought, she felt a pang sharper than the one she had felt during their lovemaking.

He dropped his hands, and she trembled from relief, she told herself, not disappointment.

His smile was gone, and a puzzled look of concern shadowed his face. "Is aught amiss, Jessie?"

"Nay, but I would not repeat the error I have committed." And it was an error, she told herself. For she would ever want him, would ever measure all other men by his gentleness and passion.

"It was not an error, but love we made," he corrected, giving her a cocky smile.

"I doubt there was much love in it but overmuch lust."

"Aye, there was that, too," he agreed. "And as you can see I have more. You do tempt a man, Jessie."

She gazed at his unabashed nakedness and the evidence of his desire, and pulled the sheet more tightly about her. "I will try not to tempt you again, Mr. Winthrop," she said archly, turning away.

She heard a low chuckle rumble from his chest. "I do not think you can avoid it. I am tempted already."

Raising her chin, she said, "You will just have to control your lust. There can be no repeat of . . . of this."

"This? And what was 'this'?"

"It was but an uncontrolled moment. I . . . It will never happen again."

With that, she fled up the stairs. He heard the soft closing of her door, and thought he heard a quickly muffled sob. Then all was still.

He stood bemused, thinking of her, his first impressions thrown akilter, wondering anew why she had given herself to him so freely. With his suspicions of her already high, he had thought her an experienced woman of the world, that the looks, the touches she had given him were clear invitations in spite of the fact that she had a husband. He had been proven completely wrong. She had been a virgin, and now he saw her actions in an entirely new light—those of an innocent, unaware of their effect. A sudden hope sprang up within him. Was she also innocent of other things? Or was that merely hope with no substance in reality?

He bent to pick up his trousers and jabbed his legs into them. Just because a woman was innocent of men did not mean she was innocent of theft and piracy. He hoped she was innocent, for there was now no denying his attraction to the lovely Widow Twill. He shook his head. There was still evidence against her. Her own words indicated that her association with Twill had been a mutually beneficial business arrangement. As far as he had found out, there was little legitimate business between Twill and Ashford shipping. The plantation was more a liability than an asset to the company.

Looking around for his shirt, he spotted her gown where it had fallen by the French doors. He picked it up and crushed it to his chest, intoxicated again by her fragrance which still clung to the cloth. It felt so soft and light, almost insubstantial, almost as if it could have been a bit of witch-spun moonlight. Had she bewitched him or had it been the moonlight?

Shaking his head he returned to the sofa to toss in sleeplessness.

Except for the persistent hammering coming from somewhere outside, Jessie awoke with a feeling of well-being and contentment. She stretched, every nerve ending in her body atingle, delighting in the sensuous feel of the sheets against her naked skin. She opened her eyes and gasped, suddenly very aware of why she was naked, why her body was experiencing such hedonistic sensations.

There, crumpled on the floor, was the sheet she had fled in last night. On its surface, glaring up at her accusingly, were a few dried drops of blood, the evidence of her lost virginity.

Her gown! She had left it downstairs. Jessie jumped up, and began yanking on her clothes, heedless of exactly what she wore, or how. Her hair received a hasty brushing, a quick twist into a low knot at her nape and she was flying down the stairs. She had to find that gown before anyone else did!

At the doorway to the parlor, she paused. What if Sean were still here? Could she face him without blushing? She doubted it. And how would she then retrieve her gown? Could she prance into the room, smile at him, pick up her gown and leave? More likely he would smile at *her*. A provocative, knowing smile that would infuriate her if it did not shame her to death first.

Hesitantly, she peeked into the room. No one was there, and she breathed a sigh of relief, at the same time angry at herself for having to sneak around in her own house. She scanned the room. Then, in panic, she looked again. There was no sign of her discarded gown, as if it had been a wisp of moonlight put to rout by the morning sun, she thought.

Who had taken it? Sean? Doubtful. What would he do with it? He had had his way with her, used her for his own ends. Why would he want her gown?

Could one of the servants have found it? She thought she had heard Maybelle beginning to stir in her room but the girl could have come down earlier. Could Josie have found it? How could she find out? Surely she couldn't casually ask if someone had happened to find her crumpled and discarded gown in the very room where a very handsome bondslave had spent the night.

Jessie sighed. She would just have to wait and hope it turned up. She rubbed her temple, to soothe away the beginnings of a headache. That hammering. It sounded almost cheery. Too cheery. Who could be hammering so happily this morning?

Jessie went out to the back of the house to see, and the sight of bare broad shoulders and lean, well-muscled arms greeted her. Sean looked up with a board in one hand and a hammer in the other and smiled at her.

"Good morning, Jessie," he said, seeming far too pleased with himself and far too familiar. A familiarity that reminded her all too embarrassingly of last night.

Jessie flushed but lifted her head proudly. "Mrs. Twill, to you, Mr. Winthrop!" she said, trying to regain some small shred of her pride.

She could tell he was trying to hold back another smile but doing very poorly. Was he laughing at her? "Mrs. Twill? Mr. Winthrop? So formal this morning. 'Twas not so last night."

She raised her chin another notch and tried desperately not to blush again. "A gentleman would not have mentioned that."

He seemed to mull over her words. "A gentleman, is it? I thought I was but a poor slave and no gentleman at all."

"You are a slave. It would do you well not to forget it. A slave who should be getting back to his master, not . . . not . . ." She stammered to a halt, looking about her. "What are you doing out here, hammering?"

"Are you so anxious to be rid of me?"

"I am concerned for you. I would not like to see you flogged by your master because you dallied too long on your errand."

Sean chuckled. "There is little chance of that, my lady," he said, stressing, it seemed to Jessie, the "my lady."

Annoyed, she said, "Then 'tis certain that your master is too lenient with you. Mayhap a good flogging is just what you need!"

"First you don't want to see me flogged, then you do." He shook his head and gave a deep mock sigh. "They say lovers can be fickle."

"Mr. Winthrop! We are not . . ." she trailed off, realizing just how much she had raised her voice, then with difficulty, calmed herself and finished softly, "We are not lovers."

He only grinned at her as if to deny her words and picked up his board and hammer again.

"Mr. Winthrop, what are you doing?" she asked in exasperation.

"Right now," he said, his face a picture of seriousness, "I'm mending a privy. I couldn't bear the thought of it collapsing on you some moonless night. You do seem wont to wander about at night."

Jessie decided to ignore his innuendo. "It does seem to be in need of repair," she said. The little building tilted to the side, and several boards were broken, leaving wide gaps in its walls.

Sean looked around. "Along with everything else around here." He took another nail and began to hammer the board into place.

"Don't you need to get back to Charles Town?" she asked yet again.

He finished nailing the board and stood up. He towered over her, and she looked up at the mouth she had kissed last night, the face she had caressed, and could feel again the rush of emotion that threatened to sweep her out of control again. She tried not to let her eyes stray to the black hair on his chest, tried not to follow the curling wisps that trailed downward. Desperately, she tried not to think of those arms around her, the hardness of his chest pressed against her softness.

He was standing much too close and she could almost feel the warmth from his hard-muscled body. Or was it the morning sun? But it was not the sun. It was his gaze that warmed her as it traveled over her features.

"You look very kissable this morning, Mrs. Twill," he said as casually as if commenting on the brightness of the day, and it was a moment before the meaning of his words filled her mind.

No matter how handsome his face, how appealing his smile, how his lightest touch could affect her, Sean Winthrop was still a bondslave, though he seemed as wont to forget it as she. He had no right to address her so. "You forget yourself, Mr. Winthrop," she said coldly.

His brow arched. He was still standing much too close to her. "Mr. Winthrop? I prefer it when you call me Sean."

"I do not wish to encourage any . . . further familiarity, I assure you."

"Because I am a slave?"

"Yes," she agreed, grasping for any reason to have nothing more to do with this man. "Because you are a slave."

He ran a finger lightly along the soft ridge of her jaw sending a ripple of warmth through her. "Aye, a slave. But still a man, Jessie."

She turned her head away from his hand. "You must remember that I am but newly a widow."

His teeth flashed in a grin. "But not a mourning one, I think," he said, turning her face back to his.

"My feelings have nothing to do with the proprieties!"

He grasped her about the waist and, pulling her hard against his lean frame, looked down into her face with a gleam in his eyes. "Then I will deal with your feelings and leave the proprieties to someone else," he whispered huskily, and his lips descended on hers.

His mouth claimed hers as if he were the master and she the bondslave, bending her will completely to his. She could not think, could not move, could not breathe. She could only submit to the warm pressure of his lips as they explored hers, pulling from her a yearning excitement that rushed to give to him all he demanded.

And then that warmth was gone, the warmth of his lips a memory, the warmth of his arms slid from her, the warmth of his body moved away. She opened eyes she had not realized she had closed and regained her senses.

Why had she let him kiss her? Could she have stopped him even if she had wanted to? Good Lord! What had she become in the short time since her arrival in Carolina? She had been prepared to submit herself to a husband, had even looked forward to it. But Sean Winthrop was not her husband nor could he be. She wanted a husband to share her life on this plantation. What did Sean know about running a plantation? About investments in shipping? About the intricate steps of a minuet? An elegant ball or lavish dinner? He was a slave. A petty criminal sentenced for—for what? She did not even know. Yet last night she had . . . And today she had stood here and let him kiss her like a common trollop. And she had enjoyed it! It must not happen again. It would not happen again. She was the mistress of a great plantation. He was but a slave. Someone else's slave. He would be gone this day, and she would never see or speak to him again. She must keep her distance now and protect what was left of her heart.

She held her head up proudly and looked him in the face. She felt a decided warmth but she tried to put all the iciness of a Boston winter into her eyes and prayed that the shakiness she felt did not betray her as she spoke.

"My feelings are of no concern to you, Bondslave Winthrop! From now on confine yourself to the proprieties and behave as befits our respective positions! I suggest that you leave as soon as you can for Charles Town."

She thought her reprimand was more than adequate to quell the most adamant pursuit, but his frustrating attempt not to smile told her that Sean Winthrop was bolder than any man, slave or free, had a right to be.

"Do you think I might have a bite of breakfast first? 'Tis a long way to Charles Town. My services may not be needed now, but I think you have not been displeased with them so far."

Angrily, she gritted her teeth. Would the oaf never stop referring to last night? Had she not made it plain enough that last night was but a chance encounter, not the beginnings of an affair?

Turning to leave, she said stiffly over her shoulder, "I will call you when your breakfast is ready, Mister Winthrop." Then, with all the dignity she could muster, she headed for the kitchen.

The kitchen was a large, spacious room with a fireplace across one end. The morning light revealed the dirt and cobwebs that clung in corners and beneath the long table in the center of the room. Various dried herbs hung along one wall. Jessie fingered them, noting that most of them were old, their leaves dusty and no longer as aromatic as they should be. Opening a large cupboard, she found a haphazard collection of flour, sugar, tea, and grains. Eggs and clabbered milk sat on a work table.

There was no sign of Josie, and Jessie's anger began to rise. The girl should have had the fire going by now and breakfast well underway.

There was a door next to the fireplace and, opening it, Jessie found a cozy room tucked behind the fireplace and in it, Josie was sleeping in a rumpled bed.

Jessie shook the woman's shoulder and, with a stretch as sensuous as a cat's, Josie opened her eyes. She looked Jessie up and down, and Jessie thought there was a brief sneer on her face before she lowered her eyes and sat up, saying, "I'm sorry, Miss Jessie. I purely must have overslept."

Josie reached for her blouse, and Jessie noted the silk chemise, wondering how a slave could have come by such a fine garment. But she said nothing as she led the way back to the kitchen.

"Get the fire going, Josie," Jessie said, pulling out a bowl to stir up pancake batter. "Then find a bucket and mop and clean this kitchen. I want a sparkle on this floor. And the windows, too," she added, noting the accumulation of grime that made it almost impossible to see outside.

"The windows upstairs could use a good cleaning, too," Maybelle said, coming into the kitchen. She carried a load of dirty curtains she had stripped from the bedroom windows.

"I'll sure try, Miz Jessie, but I doan' know when I'm gonna get all that done," grumbled Josie, bending over the fireplace to set a small blaze going.

"Today," Jessie answered her. "This morning, in fact."

Jessie began making the pancakes and scrambling eggs while Maybelle set the table.

"How many places should I set, Miss Jessie?" she asked. "Will Mr. Jackson be joining us?"

"Marse Jackson eats in his own cabin," Josie answered.

"Four places, Maybelle," Jessie said, relieved that she would not have to face the odious Mr. Jackson at breakfast. "Mr. Winthrop will be coming in."

Jessie noted a lightening of Maybelle's step, more of a swing to her hips, at that announcement, and saw the girl stop to smooth back her hair and to straighten her collar.

Let her have him, Jessie thought, turning the pancakes so hard drops of grease sizzled into the fire. If Maybelle wanted a bondslave with seven years still on his indenture, then she was welcome to him. With Maybelle to entice him, maybe Sean would find fresh game for his wandering hands and kisses. But somehow that picture did not give her the satisfaction she thought it would.

Sean entered in just as Jessie was setting the platter of pancakes on the table. She looked up as his body filled the doorway. His freshly washed hair glistened wetly in the light. He had donned his shirt, and in places it clung damply to his muscled torso. His eyes were deep in shadow, but she knew he followed her movements, and had trouble keeping her hand from shaking as she poured cups of tea from the steaming kettle.

"I thought you'd left," Maybelle said to Sean, swaying up to him. "I'm glad to see you're still here."

Jessie set the kettle down with a clatter, startling Maybelle and raising Sean's brows in a questioning arc. "Breakfast is ready," she said.

She went to the head of the table but found Sean already there, holding her chair for her.

"My lady," he said, helping her as elegantly as any lord.

An amused smile flitted over his lips, and she forced the memory of his kiss to the back of her mind. His hand slid along her arm in a brief caress, but her indignant glare was lost on him as he moved away to sit at the other end of the table. He took his place as if he were master here instead of slave, and Jessie began to wonder at the wisdom of eating with the servants rather than sitting alone in the as yet unfit dining room.

He grinned at her making her feel warmer than when she had bent over the fire turning pancakes. Obviously, he had taken no note of her reprimand. Before she could snub him as he deserved, Maybelle distracted him with the platter of ham, engaging him in banal conversation.

Between bites, Jessie watched her maid and the bondslave. Sean's good humor and wide smiles were infectious, sending both Maybelle and Josie into peals of laughter. He was certainly handsome, she thought. A feathery lock of his shining clean black hair fell over his forehead and looked so soft and fine she longed to feel its texture. Instead, her fingers brushed the rough pottery cup beside her plate and she took a sip of her tea to distract her mind from the too-handsome features of one Sean Winthrop, too-bold bondslave.

She couldn't shut out their chatter, however, and became annoyed at their laughter. Although Sean tried to include her with his smiles, she avoided their banter, turning away from the look of warmth in his eyes as they raked over her. Finishing the last of her tea, she stood up. "Josie, will you find Mr. Jackson? I'd like a horse saddled for me, and I want him to show me around the plantation."

Sean rose to his feet, his chair scraping back over the flagstone floor. Jessie could not help noticing the smooth, fluid grace of his motion as his tall form unfolded, up and up until he towered over all of them.

"Mr. Jackson is out in the fields, Mrs. Twill. I'll saddle the horses and take you out to him."

Sean started for the door without waiting for her to accept or to reject his help. Taking charge seemed to come as naturally to him as taking liberties. Surprising qualities in a slave, she mused.

Watching the play of muscle over his shoulders as he turned slightly sideways to go through the door, Jessie was not at all sure she should ride out with him. Yet she could not deny that she was glad she would not have to meet with Mr. Jackson alone.

Giving Maybelle and Josie a list of instructions, Jessie fetched a hat and went out to the stables, following an overgrown path through a garden that was more weed than flower.

Chapter Five

The stable door hung askew, and even before she entered, Jessie's nose told her that it had been some time since the stable had been cleaned. The normal fresh smell of hay and horse was overpowered by the muck that was piled deep in each stall. The shafts of light that penetrated the dimness were alive with dust motes—the dust that lay thick on jumbled piles of broken harness and on a once fine carriage.

Sean turned at her entrance, and a beam of light fell across his face, lighting his eyes to a bright sapphire-blue. Eyes that seemed to brighten as they swept appreciatively over her before he turned to continue his work. He was grooming one of the horses, running his hands over its back and belly to assure himself that there were no burrs to irritate the horse once it was saddled. Jessie noticed how gently he touched the horse, how its ears twitched as Sean clucked softly to it. Shaking out a musty blanket, he put it over the horse's back and saddled it, then put a sidesaddle on the second horse for her.

He led the horses into the sunlight, and she got her first good look at them. They were not the fine riding animals her father had kept, but they seemed adequate.

Sean bent and, with a smile, folded his hands together to help her mount. She stepped onto his waiting hands, trying not to notice his fresh-washed scent, now mingled with horse and leather as she brushed his shoulder. His hands were warm and gentle as he guided her foot into a stirrup; then he handed her the reins and mounted his own horse.

He led the way past the crepe myrtle bushes and down a path. She noted that he rode easily, guiding the horse casually, obviously very much at ease in a saddle. He turned to check on her, and a leafy shadow fell across his eyes, making him look, for a moment, very much like a mounted bandit. Had that been the crime for which he had been sentenced to slavery? Had he been a highwayman? She snorted at her overactive imagination. More likely he was a cutpurse, saved from the gallows by the need for cheap labor in the colonies.

They rode between rice fields until the path widened and he dropped back to ride beside her. She felt his gaze on her warmer than the Carolina sun. Was there no way to discourage this overbold bondslave? Worse, was there no way to discourage the warmth that grew within her when he looked at her like that? She shrugged and tried to relax. He would be gone within the hour, and she would have so much to worry about that she would have no time to think of one very handsome, blue-eyed bondslave.

"The plantation boundary is there at that line of trees," Sean said, pointing ahead. "To the right, it runs down to the river. To the left, it runs up through that stand of timber."

"For a recent arrival to Charles Town, you seem to know a lot about the Twill plantation," she said.

Sean drew his horse to a halt, and Jessie stopped beside him, their thighs nearly brushing. He leaned forward in his saddle, and his eyes seemed to glow as he looked across at the lush, ripening grain on the next plantation.

"That's because it happens to border on Fortune property," he said. With a broad wave of his hand, he indicated the sweep of the land. "Five hundred acres of timber, rice, and rich upland bordering on the river."

She looked at him in surprise, seeing a pride there as if the land were his own. Strange that a slave would feel that way about his master's land, she thought.

"It isn't much now," he continued. "There's just a few acres of rice planted. Not even a house yet. But one day, this will be the pride of the Fortune family. Yes," he mused more to himself than to her, "the pride of the Fortunes. Fortune's Pride."

Fortune's Pride. She could almost see what he was describing. It was not so different from what she had imagined her own plantation to be.

They sat silently, and for a moment Jessie was content to share this particular dream. She had wanted so much to believe it, to share it with a husband. That hope had been put to rest only the day before. Now there was no one to share her dream. No one but a bondslave whose dream was of a grand plantation that was not even his own, but his master's.

"Fortune's Pride," she said. "Is that what Mr. Fortune calls his plantation?"

He turned to look at her, and she could see the dream still warm and alive in his eyes. Then he smiled.

"Yes." He gave his head one, quick, definitive shake. "That's what Mr. Fortune is going to call it. Fortune's Pride."

Sean urged his horse onward, and Jessie followed, noting that the bondslave before her continued to gaze at the neighboring land with a quiet satisfaction.

They entered a dense wood, and Jessie heard the sounds of sawing and cutting. She soon saw the cause of the noise. A wide swath was cut through the wood, with large trees on the ground, indiscriminately crushing the smaller ones, while slaves worked at cutting away the limbs and tops of the trees. She glanced at Sean and noted a look of disgust on his face that echoed her own at this wanton destruction to obtain good timber.

Jessie heard a loud crack that was not the crack of splintering wood and an answering yelp of pain. Then Mr. Jackson's voice boomed out, "Get back to work, you lazy, burr-headed oaf!"

Jackson again raised his whip, bringing it down smartly on the back of a cowering slave. Before he could strike a third time, however, Jessie set spurs to her horse and, without thought to her own safety, drove it between the slave and the overseer.

Jackson looked up in surprise, then a sneer took shape on his thick lips. "You are interfering in something that does not concern you, Miz Twill."

"The prevention of cruelty always concerns me, Mr. Jackson."

Jackson again raised the whip as if to strike her or her horse, but Sean drove his horse toward the man, nearly knocking him from his feet.

"You bumbling bondslave!" Jackson yelped, and raised his whip yet again, this time choosing Sean as his target.

"I doubt that Mr. Fortune would care to see his property abused," Sean said, resting his hands casually on the pommel of his saddle.

Jackson lowered the whip, for the moment forestalled. He knew it could gain him little to harm the property of the powerful Mr. Fortune. "You may rest assured, slave," he spat, "that I will inform Mr. Fortune of your interference when next I see him. Perhaps between us we can yet strip the hide from your carcass."

Sean laughed. "Mr. Fortune is far too fond of me to allow that."

"Fond of you, is he?" the overseer mocked. "You sound as if you are privy to his very thoughts."

"To many of them," Sean admitted.

Jackson's eyes narrowed. "And I suppose there is little you don't know about his business."

"His business?" Sean shrugged. "I suppose I know as much about it as he does."

Jackson seemed to mull that over for a moment, was on the verge of saying something more, but changed his mind. Jessie caught his attention once more, and he turned toward her. He coiled the whip slowly, letting his fingers slide slowly along its length, as if relishing the feel of it while his gaze never left Jessie. Her skin began to crawl. It was as if the thoughts that lurked behind that gaze concerned her and the whip he was fingering.

"I thought you would have returned to Charles Town by now, Miz Twill," he drawled, ignoring her reference to his cruelty.

"I have no intention of returning to Charles Town, Mr. Jackson. Mr. Winthrop was kind enough to help me find you so you could show me around my plantation."

Jackson eyed Sean and dismissed him, knowing that the bondslave would soon be out of the way.

"Your plantation?" he sneered. "This plantation belongs to Ashbrook Shipping."

"That's true. My hus . . . Mr. Twill only managed it for them."

Jackson grinned. "Now that Twill's dead when do you plan to return to Charles Town?"

"Why, I will stay here and run this plantation. I admit I know next to nothing about rice and plantation life, but I can learn."

Jackson snorted, clearly enjoying her discomfort. "Do you think Ashbrook Shipping will let a woman newly from Boston who knows very little about running a plantation remain in charge of their holding?"

"It will not belong to Ashbrook Shipping. It was to be a wedding present after my arrival here."

"Do you really think they will sign this plantation over to you?" Jackson almost laughed.

"Why shouldn't they?"

"A woman alone?"

"I don't see that it makes any difference. They were to sign it over to my husband and me. Since I am now his widow . . ."

"But are you?" The overseer's eyes pierced hers.

"Of course I am! My marriage may have been by proxy, but it was perfectly legal."

"And when was it consummated?"

"Consu . . ." Jessie blushed at the man's crudity.

"It wasn't, was it? Twill was near dead when you got here. I understand he never fully regained consciousness. I don't think a marriage can be consummated with a man as far gone as Twill was." Jackson was nearly chuckling outright now.

"My marriage is none of your business, Mr. Jackson!" Jessie leaned toward him from her high perch, indignant at his prying.

"I think what Mr. Jackson is getting at, Mrs. Twill," Sean put in calmly, "is that without that consummation, your marriage can, in the eyes of the law, be considered void."

"Void?"

"Aye, *Mrs.* Twill," Jackson sneered. "I think you own as little here as one of them blacks there." Jackson waved his whip toward the laboring slaves. "And got less right to be here. You might just as well save yourself a lot of trouble and go back where you came from. Whatever Twill promised you, I doubt you'll get anything now."

Jessie sat up straighter on her horse, angry at this man's insolence, his sneers, the crude way he had referred to her lack of a legal marriage. "There is one thing you are discounting, Mr. Jackson. Or perhaps you didn't know that I am an Ashbrook by birth. I doubt that my family will throw me off a plantation they have promised me. I fully intend to take over from Mr. Twill and do every job he was doing for Ashbrook Shipping. You may find that I have abilities that will surprise you."

Jackson looked up at her, genuine shock on his face.

Sean also seemed surprised at this information but did no more than raise his brows.

Jessie smiled triumphantly. "Now, Mr. Jackson, if you will be so good as to show me around so that I might get acquainted with my plantation?"

The overseer glared at her, his eyes twin pools of black hatred. He stood a moment, slapping his leg with the coiled whip, and then turned to mount his horse. He gestured to another white man to take over and started to lead Jessie from the clearing, but she stopped him.

"Let's start here, shall we?" She indicated the timber and the slaves who had not stopped their labors.

"We're cutting timber," he said, his voice a surly growl. "That's clear enough." Even to a fool, his tone implied.

"Do you plan to plant crops here?" she asked.

"This hillside?" He shook his head as if she were indeed a fool.

"Then, Mr. Jackson, I would suggest that you leave the undergrowth and the smaller trees intact. In fact, that is more than a suggestion. That is an order. Take only the larger trees, make only one small road in and out of this stand, and be very careful not to damage any more than you must. Something must be left for the future besides barren, eroded hillside."

Jackson's mouth gaped, but there was nothing he could do or say. He snapped it shut and nodded his angry acquiescence.

Sean was smiling broadly, and when he caught her eye, he nodded his approval, letting his own gaze rove over her in a way that caused her to blush. She wondered why he had not excused himself and returned to Charles Town now that there was nothing to keep him here. Did he think that after last night there might be a reason to linger in spite of her reproof this morning? Whatever the reason he stayed, she was glad. He had protected her again from Jackson's attack. She had already decided that as soon as she held the reins to this plantation firmly and legally in her hands, Jackson would be given notice and sent packing.

Sean might not be adverse to taking advantage of any encouragement she gave him, but she felt sure that he would not force his unwanted attention on her. It was her own desires she needed to hold in check when she was around this man. The result of that, she had experienced last night. She turned away from Sean's admiring glances. Was he thinking of those moonlit moments as often as she?

She turned her attention back to Jackson. It was much easier to arm herself against his resentment and his leers than the least of Sean's warm glances.

"Why are so many of these men chained?" she asked.

"They are slaves," Jackson snapped, as if explaining to a

rather stupid child. "Slaves have a tendency to run. These won't."

"Where would they go in this wilderness? Only a desperate man would try to escape into that," she said, waving her hand vaguely westward at the vast, seemingly endless forest.

"These men are desperate," he answered.

"Even those?" She nodded toward several white men toiling beside the blacks.

"Bondslaves are the worst!" Jackson spat contemptuously and glanced meaningfully at Sean. "They'll turn on you quicker 'n a black and take to their heels the first chance they get."

"I have little acquaintance with slaves, but I think they must not be too different from bondslaves. We have bondslaves even in Boston, and they seldom flee their masters if they are fairly treated. I want the chains off these men today. And get rid of the whip, too, Mr. Jackson. Slaves they may be, but they are men, not animals." Pulling at the reins of her horse, she set it into a canter, cutting off any argument Mr. Jackson may have voiced.

The two men caught up with her at the edge of the wood, and she slowed her horse to a walk.

"That path there, Mr. Jackson," Jessie said, turning her horse toward a narrow trail that led toward the river, "where does it lead?"

The overseer cut in front of Jessie. " 'Tis naught but an old shed. No longer used." He urged his horse around hers, trying to turn them back toward the fields.

"I would like to see it, Mr. Jackson," Jessie persisted.

Jackson laughed uneasily, it seemed to Sean. He glanced at Sean, then back to Jessie. "It really is dangerous, Miz Twill. Near to collapse. Nothing there but spiders and rats."

Sean glanced toward the river. The top of a shed could

barely be seen through the trees. To him, Mr. Jackson had seemed far too anxious not to show them the shed. What was there that the overseer did not want them to see? Perhaps he would have a look on his own later on. But for now Sean followed in the overseer's wake, interested in every facet of rice growing.

For the next hour Mr. Jackson seemed much more affable, talking volubly, and showing them the best parts of the plantation, the rich stands of timber, the flooded fields of ripening grain, the small dock where the produce of the plantation was loaded for shipment downstream.

While approving much that was being done, Jessie was quick to note any neglect, a fence that needed repair, a worn harness, broken tools that should have been mended rather than cast aside.

Jackson urged his horse onward, pointing ahead to a field where slaves were building a dike. "This field is being prepared for planting next year," he said, and Jessie and Sean followed him toward a group of workers.

Several slaves, watched carefully by a slave overseer with a whip, dug in the earth, carrying baskets full of dirt to build a long dike around the field. One slave, stopped, bending over his shovel to cough. For his moment of respite, he was paid a stinging lash that sent him back to work, although his hacking cough did not abate.

"You! Come here," Jessie called to the slave.

The black only paused long enough to look up but continued working, glancing fearfully at the overseer.

She gestured to the slave and called again, and this time, hesitantly, the man approached. He tottered weakly as he stood beside her horse, and she could hear the rale and wheeze of his breathing.

"Mr. Jackson, this man is not well."

Jackson looked down at the man and shrugged. "He's well enough to stand. He's well enough to work."

Sean saw the fire leap into Jessie's eyes. "Is that how you judge the fitness of a slave to work? This man needs rest and care."

"If we coddle every slave who sneezes, they'd all be sneezing."

"Nevertheless, this man is ill. I want him relieved of duty right now."

Seeing the implacable set to her jaw, Jackson gave in but could not help adding, "Very well, *Mrs.* Twill, but if you want to see this place turn a profit this year, we can't be pamperin' every slave who gets a little sick."

"This man is more than just a little sick, Mr. Jackson. If we are to turn a profit, it seems logical to see to the health of our slaves."

Jackson gave an uncaring shrug. "It's cheaper and a far sight easier to replace 'em than to cure 'em."

"Healthy people are better workers, Mr. Jackson. I want their ills tended to." She started to urge her horse on down the path, then pulled it to a quick halt. "My God," she said, jumping from her horse. She approached a laboring slave, reaching out to turn his back to her. She had caught a quick glimpse of it as she rode by him, but now at close range, she could see it was crisscrossed with blood-encrusted welts. "Mr. Jackson, what happened to this man?"

"A troublemaker. He was whipped."

Staring in horror at the man's back, his manacled wrists, his shackled feet, Jessie was speechless for a long moment as her rage built. She rounded on Jackson, spots of angry color in her cheeks, but he did not give her a chance to vent her vehemence.

"This ain't Boston, Miz Twill! You'll find things a bit different on a rice plantation than in a tea parlor. If you can't stomach what has to be done to keep the blacks in line, then go back to Boston!" With a mocking bow, he said, "I think that's about it, Miz Twill. You've seen all you need to. If you'll excuse me, I'll get back to the timbering."

Jessie fought for calmness. Until Mr. Pierce signed the deed when he and her mother arrived next week, and her ownership of this plantation was assured, it could do the slaves more harm than good to antagonize Mr. Jackson. But once everything was settled, firing the overseer was the first thing she would do. She glanced at Sean and was glad to see a look on his face as angry as her own.

"You have not yet shown me the slave quarters, Mr. Jackson," Jessie said, halting the overseer in the act of turning his horse.

"There's no need to go troubling yourself over that, ma'am," Jackson said in such a patronizing tone that it made Jessie's hair bristle.

Too often she had faced men who thought she was no more than an ornament or merely a visitor in her father's office. It had never taken her long to impress upon a prospective client that she knew as much about running a shipping company as her father. And knew more about keeping the books. She was not about to let Mr. Jackson, a mere employee, continue to condescend to her as if she were a bothersome child.

"There is nothing on this plantation that is too much trouble to inform myself about, Mr. Jackson," she said sharply. "I'm sure I can find the quarters myself, but I would like you to be present when I inspect them. I'm sure there will be some things that you will need to be apprised of so that you can correct them."

Jackson glared at her, and his smile of acquiescence was more like a gritting of his teeth. But he waited while Sean helped Jessie to remount, then led the way to the quarters, jerking his horse's head around so hard that Sean winced at his cruelty.

When they reached the slave compound, Jessie was so appalled that she dismounted and leaned against her horse as she looked around. The cabins were in worse shape than the outhouse Sean had repaired that morning. Shutters were askew or dangled from one rusty hinge. If the cabins had ever been whitewashed, there was little evidence of it left. Scattered piles of refuse were covered with swarms of flies. A few ragged women glared at her covertly as they stirred pots hung above smoky fires. There were few children, and they were nearly naked and clung to the women fearfully. The whole plantation was so far from the picture she had carried in her imagination of happy workers, decently clothed, decently fed, who would smile happily at their mistress, that she did not know where to unleash her fury first.

Then she saw the post in the center of the compound. Thick and solidly set, a pair of manacles dangled from its top.

"What is that?" Jessie pointed to the post, so enraged she could barely get the words out.

"A whipping post," Jackson said arrogantly and without apology.

Once or twice, Jessie opened her mouth to speak without success. Finally, through gritted teeth she said, "Get me an axe."

"What?" Jackson asked.

"An axe, Mr. Jackson," Jessie said confronting the overseer with such authority and rage that he dared not disobey.

In moments she held an axe in her hands. She marched up to the post and without another word, began to hack at its base, angrily, furiously, as if all the cruelty and injustice she had seen that day were centered in that

101

one object. It was an excellent outlet for her fury, though she made little progress in destroying the post. Her anger was dissipating and tears were beginning to well in her eyes when a strong, sun-browned hand took the axe.

She looked up at Sean. The concern and anger she felt were mirrored in his eyes. If she felt as she did about the treatment of the slaves, what must a man feel who was one of them? He only nodded and she moved out of his way. With strokes as angry as hers had been but more efficient, he attacked the post. Soon it was wobbling, and together they pushed it over.

The women and children had gathered in a crowd. When the post fell, Jessie could see grim satisfaction in their eyes. "Burn it," was all she said to them.

They looked at each other a moment, wondering what it could mean, then, in sudden understanding, they joyously assaulted the post, lugging it toward one of the fires.

"Mr. Jackson," Jessie said, glaring at the overseer, "you may return to work now. I will have a list of work orders for you tomorrow."

With that, she turned on her heel and marched toward the house. It was a short distance, but a tree-shaded path effectively screened the unpleasant sight of the quarters from the house.

Jackson threw himself onto his horse, viciously kicking the poor beast into a gallop. A smiling blue-eyed bondslave gathered the reins to Jessie's horse to return it to the stable to rub it down.

Traitorous moonlight again streamed through the window when Jessie came into her room that night. So beautiful, she thought, yet so dangerous. As she approached the window to close the curtain against that beguiling light, a shadow

102

moved in the corner, rose from a chair, and became the form of a man.

"Sean! What are you doing here?" Jessie demanded, frightened, then slowly letting out her breath.

A low chuckle emanated from the shadows. "It seems you are forever asking me that same question."

"With good reason!"

He moved between her and the window, and his arm reached out to brace against the window frame. "The moonlight is even more beautiful tonight," he said.

Jessie swallowed hard. The dim light revealed the outline of his muscled frame through his loosened shirt and highlighted his profile as he turned half to her, half to the scene outside. The blackness of his hair seemed to fade away into the night. It was not hard to remember the silky feel of it or the strength of those corded arms when they had circled her.

It was not easy to keep her voice steady. "I do not have time to discuss the moonlight, Mr. Winthrop. I am tired and would seek my rest."

Again she heard that low chuckle, felt it vibrate within her own chest, and felt a warmth where it touched her. He turned toward her, dropping his hand. His face was completely shadowed, but she could feel his gaze on her as surely as if he stood in the sunlight. She stood in the full rays of that knave of a moon.

"Aye," he said softly. " 'Twas little rest you had last night."

She writhed beneath his reminder and was glad that the light was not plentiful enough for him to see the blush she felt rise to her cheeks. Then she felt him touching her, the light caress of his fingers on her neck. She could not blame him for coming to her room, not after the wanton way she had behaved the night before. But she could not let that happen again.

"Nay!" She jerked away, moved to the door, and flung it open, shaking her head. "You overstep your bounds, Mr. Winthrop. You have no further business here. I must ask you to leave first thing in the morning."

Sean stepped away from the window and came toward her with an easy grace. Why did she think of a master swordsman when he moved like that?

He stopped close in front of her. Too close. "I came to return something you lost," he said, sweeping a hand toward the bed.

Her glance followed the gesture. Sprawled in a ray of moonlight was her lost nightgown. "Oh! You found it!" She snatched up the gown in relief, crushing it to her chest. Then, realizing what a strong reminder it was of last night, she quickly put it behind her, as if its absence could erase the memory of what lay so heavily between them. "I . . . Thank you for returning it."

"I thought it was best to return it in private."

"Yes," she said, but she wished it had not been in moonlit privacy.

"I would like to see you in it again," he said, his voice so husky with desire that she started, her eyes widening as she looked up at him.

It was as if breathing had suddenly become the most diffi-cult thing in the world. "We both know that is impossible," she said, using what little breath she had left.

"Is it?" Again his hand reached out to caress her throat, his fingers weaving a spell with the moonlight.

For a moment she reveled in that gentle touch. Then she moved away. The love of a bondslave was not for her. Love? It was not love. Merely lust. She shook her head. A whisper was all she could manage. "Please go."

"You have not yet paid me for returning your gown," he said.

She looked up at him, wondering what he meant. But he gave her no time to ask. His lips accosted hers, besieged them, attacked them unmercifully but with all the gentleness of the treacherous moonlight that swirled about them. Her will surrendered to that onslaught and crumbled defenseless at his feet. Then he was gone, leaving her alone with moonlight and shadows. Only the soft sound of his feet going down the stairs gave any evidence at all that he had ever been there.

Sean leaned against the bole of a live oak and looked up at the window. Jessie's window. He let the cool night breeze waft over him, cooling him. It had not been easy walking out of that room just now. But he had had to leave before he got so emotionally involved with Jessie that he wouldn't be able to see her guilt even if it were laid before him. Or innocence, he couldn't help thinking. There was still a chance that she was completely innocent in this business.

But he was finding the Widow Twill much more interesting than he had imagined he would. It was not just that her mouth had tasted every bit as delectable as he had thought it would, but so had her smooth skin.

She had been an innocent last night, as far as knowing a man was concerned. She had come to him perhaps from loneliness and seeking comfort after what had been a trying time for her. And he had not been able to resist her and had seen no reason to. He had thought her a woman of the world, knowledgeable. Instead he had found a virgin. He had thought only to use her as a possible co-conspirator in piracy for his own ends. Yet today she had shone him another side of her. Her compassion, strength, courage. There was much to admire in Jessie Ashbrook Twill besides a body that sent him wild even thinking about it.

Even if she was far too proud. His mouth twisted with discontent. Did she really think a bondslave beneath her, or was she just using that Boston pride of hers to shield herself from emotional entanglements? Would she spurn his attentions if she knew he was not the slave he pretended to be? Would she welcome the son of a wealthy shipowner? He shook his head. He did not yet dare trust her with that information. He still had no proof that she was not involved in the nefarious business he had suspected Twill of.

But how could he use her, gain information from her, when just being around her made him nearly lose all reason? So he had walked out when, with but a little further urging on his part, he could have again shared a delicious hour with her. No, he must keep his reason when dealing with Jessie. There were indications of her innocence, but there were just as many indications of her guilt.

He remembered how quickly she had acquiesced when Jackson did not want to show her that shed. What was in it? Was there something there that they did not want a bondslave belonging to Mr. Fortune to see? Had she followed Jackson's lead to keep a mutually beneficial secret? She had informed Jackson in no uncertain terms that she intended to take over every aspect of Twill's work. Did that include leadership of a ring of pirates? Her dislike of Jackson did not seemed feigned. But dislike of a partner had never stopped mutually profitable business dealings. She had married Twill for financial reasons. She had admitted as much, and Twill had been no more likeable than Jackson.

"Won't do ye no good moonin' around out here under her window like a hound."

Sean turned at the sound of the voice. Jackson stood slightly to Sean's left and behind him. The overseer had not washed or changed from his day's labors but had been drinking. He held a slim-necked bottle as he stood looking up at Jessie's window.

"That one ain't goin' to have nothin' to do with no bondslave," he said, taking a long pull at the bottle. As an afterthought, he held out the bottle to Sean.

Sean took it and swallowed a small swig, nearly choking on the vile concoction.

Jackson laughed as he reached to reclaim his bottle. "Used to fancier stuff, eh?" He nodded toward the window. "Them's fancy goods there, but don't get your hopes—nor nothin' else up!" He snickered at his own crude remark.

"That one ain't goin' to even spit at a bondslave. She looks at me as if I was dirt. And I'm a free man. I ain't never been a slave neither." He hitched up his drooping trousers as if being a free man was the only requirement for respect.

"You may as well get on back to Charles Town and your high-and-mighty Mr. Fortune afore he sends out searchers for you." Jackson looked sideways at Sean. "Or does he really trust you as much as you say?"

Sean's brows rose in sudden understanding. He had wondered what had made the irascible Mr. Jackson suddenly so friendly to a mere slave. It seemed Mr. Jackson was after information, too. Sean found a chuckle hard to contain. Judging from Jackson's ineptitude, Twill must have been the brains in the operation. But if Sean could play Jackson out, pretend to give him what he wanted. . . .

"Sure he trusts me," Sean said, putting more than a little braggadocio into his voice. "The fool doesn't know what a lock is. A good thing for me, too. A man in my position, without wages, that is, always has a need for a bit of cash for clothes and doxies and such."

Jackson chuckled evilly. "So you steal a bit now and then."

"I never said that!" Sean said as if suddenly alarmed at

what he had revealed. "It's just that I can usually manage to find a loose coin or two about the place. It's never enough, but I make do. Not that I couldn't use more."

"Couldn't we all?" Jackson asked, taking another long pull from the bottle, then offering it again to Sean.

"That we could," Sean agreed, forcing himself to accept another drink. "Fortune's easy enough and generous. Let's me earn extra money on my own. But earning money is hard work. I deserve an easy coin or two."

"Mayhap I can help you there, Winthrop," Jackson said with a nonchalance that was laughably feigned.

"Oh?"

"Aye. That is if you're not above selling a little somethin' of Fortune's that he'll never miss." The look Jackson gave him was supposed to be sly and knowing.

"And what would that be, Mr. Jackson?"

"Information, Winthrop. Information."

Sean merely raised his brows to encourage the overseer to continue.

"The man's been devilish clever of late. Shippin' things out before anybody even knew he had 'em on hand." He shook his head as if being clever was not very kind of Mr. Fortune. "If you was to apprise me of shippin' times and cargo lists and such like, I know somebody who'd be willin' to pay for the knowledge."

Sean cocked his brow at that tidbit. He had thought that Twill was the man in charge of the land end of the piracy ring. But he was dead. Had he been wrong about Twill? He glanced again at Jessie's window. Or had he merely been replaced?

"And who is this person, Mr. Jackson?" Sean asked casually, as if it really was of little importance to him.

But Jackson was not quite as thickheaded as he appeared.

He merely laughed. "Now that's my secret, ain't it? If I was to tell you, how would I get my cut?"

"You're a clever man, Jackson. I can see that. And I'm a greedy one. I'll see what I can come up with for you and your boss." Unconsciously, he glanced again at Jessie's window as if hoping that Jackson would confirm or deny his suspicions. Then he muttered, "But the pay better be worth it!"

"Ah, it will, Winthrop," Jackson said, turning away. Then over his shoulder he added, "But what you get here will be from me—not her!" His laughter rang out, fading as he left.

But his last comment had done nothing to ease Sean's suspicions concerning the very desirable Widow Twill.

Chapter Six

"Thank you again, Mr. Winthrop, for all your help," Jessie said. She stood beside the wagon that had brought her to this plantation, and Sean stood beside her, seemingly reluctant to leave. Jessie pressed a parcel into his hands and at his uplifted brow, she explained, "Sandwiches. For your lunch."

"Jessie, I . . ."

She stepped back, avoiding his slim, sun-browned fingers that reached out to touch her. It would hardly be appropriate to throw herself into a bondslave's arms and cling to him, especially in front of her home in broad daylight. It was only with the tightest control that she kept herself from doing just that. If he touched her, she was sure that her control would crumble. She ignored his intimate use of her name, trying desperately not to let him see how she felt inside, how she would miss him. She forced a smile to her lips, trying, however, not to put too much warmth in it. Not only must he be encouraged to leave, she must try to forget him as well.

"If you don't get going, Mr. Winthrop, I shall have to pack

you a dinner as well," she said lightly.

Sean put the package on the wagon seat and leaned against the wagon, his elbow propped on the seat with his hand dangling. His shirt sleeves were rolled back, exposing his corded forearm, and Jessie pulled her gaze from the play of muscle there. Sean tilted his head to look at her, his blue eyes even now glinting with desire as they swept over her.

"I can stay if you need me, Jessie," he said.

She shook her head.

He straightened to reach for her again but was stopped by a clatter of hooves. They watched the horse and rider come toward them. A large spirited chestnut stallion tossed its head, but the rider seemed to have little difficulty controlling the beast. The man was well-dressed in smooth-fitting doeskin breeches tucked into high-topped riding boots and a bottle-green coat with fashionably wide cuffs. He pulled the steed to a halt and swept off his oversized tricorn and bowed from atop the prancing animal. He wore a wig that hung past his shoulders and curled into the ruffles at his throat. But his large brown eyes were alive and his smile infectious.

"Mrs. Twill?"

At Jessie's nod, the man leaped from his mount, flung the reins to Sean, and in a flamboyant gesture, took Jessie's hand, and bent low to kiss her fingers.

"Jason Soames, my lady. At your service."

"Delighted to meet you, Mr. Soames," Jessie said, a bit overwhelmed. Noting the man's questioning glance at Sean, Jessie introduced him. "Sean Winthrop, Mr. Soames."

"Ah," the man began effusively, extending his hand, "a fellow planter?"

"No, sir, a bondslave," Sean replied in the same effusive tone, not in the least nonplussed when the other's expression changed from one of warm greeting to cool aloofness.

"Oh," Mr. Soames uttered, letting his hand drop, completely dismissing Sean from consideration. Mr. Soames turned back to Jessie, the warm smile again in place, his eyes glittering as they assessed her. "I heard Twill was taking a wife and thought I would stop by and offer you a welcome to Carolina. I never dreamed he'd find such a lovely gem."

"Why thank you, Mr. Soames," Jessie said, cheered by a hearty welcome at last.

Soames again bowed elegantly, unhampered by his horse this time. His gaze took in the drooping porch roof, the weed-choked lawn, the peeling paint. "It is regrettable that such a jewel should be put into such a rough setting, but I'm sure that things will soon shape up."

Jessie didn't know whether to blush at the man's reference to the shoddily kept home or to warm at his compliment to her. But Mr. Soames gave her little time for either, sweeping on into his next speech.

"Just where is Twill? Must congratulate him on finding a beauty. He'll be the envy of every man in Carolina, and Carolina will be the envy of every other colony when word gets out of your beauty and charm."

Jessie glance uneasily at Sean, wondering how she should break the news of her husband's death to this neighbor. Sean saved her the trouble.

"Mr. Twill died the day before yesterday, Mr. Soames," he said quietly.

Jason Soames's eyes did not leave Jessie's face, but his back stiffened and his brows arched haughtily. "I was not addressing you, Mr. Winthrop! A bondslave must learn not to intrude in the conversation of his betters."

Jessie opened her mouth to defend Sean, then glanced at him. He was unsuccessfully hiding a smirk, as if Jason Soames were an ass. Sean was not the least rebuffed by

Mr. Soames's reprimand. She shut her mouth. Perhaps Jason Soames was right. Sean Winthrop seemed to have a talent for forgetting his proper role as a bondslave. Indeed, for a condemned felon, he seemed remarkably at ease in the presence of his "betters." She wondered if he were as at home with his fellow slaves.

Her reverie was interrupted by Mr. Soames again taking her hand in his. "My dear lady," he effused, this time eyeing her with real delight, as if he would devour her. "May I be the first to offer my condolences?"

"Thank you, Mr. Soames," she said solemnly.

"Jason, please! We are neighbors. May I hope that we may be something more?"

Her hand was beginning to sweat, held as it was in the enfolding warmth of his. She was going to pull her hand free and suggest that they did not know each other well enough yet for the familiarity of first names, but she happened to catch Sean rolling his eyes. Why, the rogue was laughing at Soames! Did he dare to think a mere bondslave was better than the owner of a Carolina plantation? It could certainly not be because of his status. Was it because he had bedded her? Did he think that he now had a claim to her on which none other dared trespass? She lifted her chin, determined to show him just how wrong he was. It was time, as Mr. Soames . . . as Jason had said, to put this bondslave in his place. And that place must be far from her heart.

With a winning smile she laid her free hand on Soames' clutching one. "How kind of you, Jason. Do call me Jessie. I'm sure we'll be the best of friends."

She was encouraged by the disappearance of Sean's smugness and the almost audible grinding of his teeth.

"Mr. Winthrop was just leaving," she said pointedly, dismissing Sean, but hoping he did not turn away before he saw her beam at Soames again. "Do come in. I'll have my maid bring us something cool to drink and we can talk. It will be good to have someone to talk to besides servants."

Why didn't she feel the satisfaction she thought she would when Sean clapped his hat on his head, leaped into the wagon, and slapped the reins just a shade too hard over the horses' rumps? She heard the wagon clatter away down the drive, but did not let herself turn to watch it go. Instead, she forced a bright smile to her lips and led her guest inside.

Calling for Maybelle to bring them a cool drink, Jessie ushered Jason into the parlor. It seemed far shabbier by daylight than it had in the moon's softening glow. Jason took a seat on the sofa, exactly where she and Sean had . . . Jessie could not help blushing, remembering what she had done there. Was it possible that the heat of their lovemaking had not seared a brand into that piece of furniture?

She tried to smile as she sat on the chair next to the sofa, and saw Jason's hand touch the cushion. Surely there was nothing there, no dregs of passion, no remaining heat, no telltale stains. Surely it was only the stirring of her memory that brought the burning flush to her cheeks.

Then she saw the wineglasses. The glasses were still where she and Sean had left them, the night before last, and she wondered why they hadn't been removed. Sitting on the liquor cabinet in full sight, the red remnants of wine glistened accusingly in the sunlight now streaming through the window. Could her neighbor fail to notice them? What would he think, seeing two half-emptied glasses of wine sitting there in mid-morning?

Maybelle appeared with a pitcher of lemonade and two tall glasses on a tray. Sprigs of fresh mint floated in the pitcher and sat on the edge of each glass. She had included a plate of biscuits left from this morning's breakfast. The maid spied the wine glasses and lifted them with a questioning arc of her brows. But, thankfully, she said nothing as she took them away to the kitchen, and Jessie breathed a small sigh at the disappearance of this one bit of incriminating evidence.

Yet it did little to lessen the feeling of Sean's presence in the room. Was it guilt that made her see him, feel him, hear him everywhere?

She forced her attention back to her guest. She had missed what he had said, but since he was laughing, she smiled as if she, too, had enjoyed his story. It was enough to encourage him to launch into another tale. He was a gifted storyteller, and Jessie was soon clutching her sides over the escapades of the young daughter of Jason's neighbor. For the first time since she had arrived in Carolina, she laughed out loud even, at times, giggling like a schoolgirl at Jason's gossipy tidbits. "No, no, it's true," he said, finishing a story about another neighbor. "Albert Baines lost the same horse three times. He's paid more in rewards for its return than he paid for it in the first place."

"Jason, do you know everyone in Carolina?" Jessie asked, gasping for breath.

"Not everyone." He leaned close to her as if to share a confidence, placing his hand familiarly on hers. "But I do know at least one story about everyone." He cocked his head and looked at her. "Except you. What brings a lovely lady like yourself to this?" He nodded his head toward the worst of the decay in the parlor.

Jessie suddenly realized how intimately they were sitting. They had both leaned forward in their laughter, and Jason was now quite openly holding her hand on her knee. Disconcerted, she pulled her hand away and sat back. She was relieved that Jason did not pursue her further, but also sat back as if expecting to hear her story.

When she remained silent, he said, "Come, come, my dear. I may know a lot of good stories. That doesn't mean that I tell them all. I do know how to keep a confidence."

She could understand why Jason knew stories about everyone. He would be eminently easy to confide in. In spite of his gossipiness, she felt she could trust Jason Soames. But she was not sure she wanted to tell her story to anyone. "I came because this is where my husband lived," she finally said.

"And now you are alone." Jason's eyes twinkled then softened. He again leaned forward and took up her hand, patting it in a friendly way.

"Not really," she said, giving his hand a squeeze. "I seem to have one very good neighbor."

He laughed and rose without letting her hand go. "That you do, my dear. I must go now, but if you need me for anything, you have but to send me word. I'll stop by often to check on you."

He tucked her arm in his and continued his good-natured chatter out to the porch where he said good-bye, bending low over her hand and kissing it. Then with a grand sweep of his tricorn, he leaped onto the back of his stallion, setting the steed to prancing. When the horse reared, he waved his hat to Jessie once more. Clapping his hat on, he gave the horse its head and was soon lost to sight.

Late in the morning four days later in the cramped, cluttered little office, Jessie pushed back her chair and rubbed her eyes. There was so much to do, so much to take care of. Like the work in her father's shipping office, it was challenging, but the details were different. Instead of what cargo should be taken on which ship and where to send it, it was how many yards of cloth would be needed to clothe nearly two hundred people, what foodstuffs could be grown on the plantation, and what had to be ordered, and what other supplies would be needed.

She had spent yesterday morning going through the slave cabins one by one, talking to the women, writing down their needs and wants, deciding which things would be needed right away, which could wait. She had directed some of the women to remake Mr. Twill's clothes for the men, but was dismayed to find so few of them skilled in needlework. There was an old loom in the attic, but none of the women knew how to use it, and her own skills were very limited.

There was no whitewash available, but the cabins could at least be cleaned and repaired. Much to Mr. Jackson's annoyance, she had taken some of the men from his crews and kept them at the compound to begin the repair work. Already she could see a new pride in the women. They stood straighter and looked her in the eye when she passed. By the end of the day, some of them were even smiling at her.

This morning, after getting the repairs underway and setting Josie and Maybelle to some cleaning chores in the house, she had entered Mr. Twill's dark, cluttered little office. She had thought of writing to her mother and Mr. Pierce about Twill's death, but realized they would already be on their way by now. She would just have to wait until their arrival to inform them of it. What if Jackson was right and Mr. Pierce wouldn't give her the plantation? But she pushed that thought away. There were piles of papers to sort through, and she needed to find the account book to see what money was available. She had spent a long time just straightening and cleaning up enough of the mess so that she could work. Her dress was dirt-smeared, and she felt gritty and tired.

Now she stood up and stretched, glaring at the piles of papers that seemed to taunt her. She had not found an account book, but she felt she had made some progress in deciding priorities and making lists of the things she needed from town.

The air in the small room was stifling, and Jessie wanted nothing more than to go for a good gallop and let the fresh air clear the cobwebs from her head. And from her hair, too, she thought, pulling one of the clingy webs from a loose strand. She smoothed her hair back and decided that she would go for a ride. Neither a plantation nor a shipping business could be run entirely from an office. While riding, she would check up on Mr. Jackson and take a look around on her own.

At the stable Jessie pushed back the heavy gate, lifting it slightly since it hung askew and dragged badly. Everyone was busy in the fields or working in the slave quarters. She had put the stable far down on the list of necessary repairs. She lifted her skirt. At least the worst of the muck had been cleared out and fresh straw laid down.

Not wanting to call anyone away from his work, she saddled her own horse. It was not a task unknown to her. In Boston, she had often gone riding before her family or the servants were astir. Choosing the same horse she had ridden with Sean, she realized that she actually missed the bondslave. But she shoved the thought aside. He would not be riding with her this day or any other. He was gone, and if she ever saw him again, it would be in Charles Town. She would see him at his work, loading barrels or chests into a wagon. His skin would be glistening with sweat, his muscles standing out in bold relief against the strain of his load. She would nod regally as she passed. He would nod his head in grateful acknowledgment that she remembered him.

Jessie grimaced as the fanciful image shattered. More likely he would give her a lusty smile, leave his work to greet her as if he expected her to throw herself into his arms, and completely destroy her composure. His boldness knew no bounds.

She tightened the cinch with an angry jerk and led the horse to the mounting block and climbed on. She gave the mare a little kick and headed it down the same path she and Sean had taken. The cool shadows soon gave way to the brightly lit path between the fields, and she urged her mount into an easy canter. The slaves working on the dike looked up to see her pass, and one or two actually waved.

As she neared the end of her plantation, she could see the Fortune plantation ahead, its one rice field shining green in the sun. She pulled to a halt and looked around, deciding which way to go. Again she noted the path that led down to the river and the top of the shed she had asked Jackson about. Perhaps she should inspect it. If the shed were as bad as the overseer claimed, perhaps it should be pulled down. She remembered his description of it as infested with snakes and rats, but since those things had never bothered her, she turned the mare's head in that direction.

The overgrown path to the shed showed signs of recent usage, and she wondered what else might be located in this part of the plantation. Jessie leaned down to pass under low-hanging branches and pushed aside brambles that caught at her skirt.

Then she was at the shed. Her brows wrinkled into a puzzled frown. This was no tumble-down shack full of vermin but a relatively new building built up on supports to keep it dry. She dismounted to the soft, sandy soil and, holding her skirts up, went around to the front of the shed and up the four steps to its door. There was a sturdy lock in place and no windows. She pushed against the door, but it was solid and did not give at all under her weight.

Turning, she looked toward the river. There was a narrow, twisting trail through the underbrush, but she could not see the river at all. From the river, the shed would be invisible, and she knew that it was only by chance that she had spotted its roof through the trees the other day. Jackson had deliberately lied about its condition and now that she thought about it, she realized that he had distracted her attention and avoided showing it to her. What purpose would a hidden, nearly inaccessible shed like this serve on a rice plantation?

If this were a storage shed for goods that would be shipped, why was it hidden from the river? Why wasn't there a dock built here to facilitate loading? For that matter, why couldn't the goods be brought to the river dock near the house? There were plenty of sheds there and most of them were empty. What was Jackson trying to hide behind that sturdy portal? Or was she being unnecessarily suspicious?

She would ask Jackson about the shed when she saw him, but for now she had more important things to worry about than a locked shed.

Jessie used the step to remount her horse, turned it in the narrow space in front of the shed, and headed back to the house.

Though the breeze was scarcely sufficient to fill even the small sail of the little skiff that plied its way upriver, there was no doubt that there was great skill in the hand at the tiller. For even though the slight breeze blew in the wrong direction, the skiff made steady, if languid, headway, zigzagging in a tightly controlled tacking pattern. The lone occupant of the craft did not seem preoccupied with sailing the boat, but lounged at the stern, making the necessary adjustments to sail and tiller with the easy nonchalance of one long acquainted with ships.

The sun, sifting through the overhanging trees, made a dappled pattern on Sean's strong, broad shoulders, now bared to that errant breeze. His black hair glistened in the stray sunbeams, and his blue eyes reflected the color of the sky. A relaxed smile played across his sensuous lips that parted to reveal strong, white teeth as he gazed about him, his eye caught now and then by a chattering squirrel or a bright flash of a bird's wing.

When the skiff came abreast of the Twill plantation, Sean kept it close to the other side of the river, barely visible in the shadow of overhanging branches. Then at the edge of the Fortune plantation the skiff crossed the river and came about, edging slowly along the shore back toward the Twill holdings. Crossing the boundary between the plantations, the skiff slowed, and the sail sagged at the deliberate depletion of its wind.

His blue eyes narrowed, scanning the shore closely. After a short distance the skiff came about, again luffing into the wind, and sailed back to the border of the Fortune plantation. There it turned and sailed again close to the shore while Sean scanned the shore even more closely. It was on the third repetition of this pattern that Sean gave a soft expletive and turned the craft into the low branches and nosed into the sand. Jumping out, he secured the craft and followed the narrow twisting trail he had found. It ended just where he had expected—at a shed well hidden from the river.

But the condition of the shed surprised him. Jackson had claimed that the shed was deserted, dilapidated, vermin-infested. The shed was new and solid—and locked. Sean looked around then knelt, his hand reaching out to examine the prints he had found in the sandy soil. Mingled with the hoofprints was another trail. But it was not the large print of a masculine boot but the small, heeled print of a woman.

A frown clouded Sean's brow, and his jaw clenched as his fingers traced that delicate print. Who else could it belong to but Jessie? The slaves were barefoot for the most part or wore simple clogs and did not ride horses. And what other lady held no fear of the rats and snakes Jackson had claimed held sway here? Or did she come here knowing there was no reason to fear? Was this one more piece of evidence implicating the lovely Mrs. Twill in the illegal deeds centered in this area? Or had she merely come investigating as he had?

He stood, shaking his head, a grim smile playing about his lips. Mrs. Twill might just hold the key to the unsolved thefts and piracies. But whether she did or not, he would enjoy finding out.

Sean tossed down the clump of soil and dusted his hands. He had planned to ask the lovely widow to go for a sail on the river this afternoon. He had thought of little else than Jessie for the last two days—her lips soft and yielding beneath his questing ones; her smooth, satiny skin, quivering in anticipation at his touch; and the silkiness of her hair entwined in his fingers, trailing across his naked chest, glimmering in the moonlight. Her softness—and her strength. How undaunted she had been when faced with a rundown plantation, a belligerent overseer, and sullen slaves. But that very strength could also give her the courage necessary to engage in piracy to recoup her fortunes. But could a woman engaged in piracy, no matter how distant her connection with the actual thefts, be as compassionate as he had seen Jessie be with her slaves?

She was a paradox. A very pretty paradox. A mystery he would relish investigating. Turning, he made his way to the river along the twisting, nearly nonexistent trail. He shoved the skiff into the water and jumped in, then pulled on his shirt before setting the sail.

With the wind at his back, it was an easy, quick sail to the Twill plantation. Slackening the sail, he edged the little craft up to the rickety dock and tossed a line around a timber.

The house stood back from the river across what should have been a large gracious lawn bordered by flower gardens. It was now so overgrown it was hard to follow the brick walkway that led up from the river.

Sean found his way to the back of the house and entered by the kitchen. If he wanted to talk Jessie into an afternoon's sail, he had better not go in the front door and give her a reason to complain that he again did not know his place as a mere bondslave. He grimaced. He would be glad when this masquerade was over and he could again walk in the front door of any home—especially Jessie's. He wondered what she would say if she knew that the bondslave who didn't know his place was no bondslave at all. He gave a mirthless laugh. Perhaps in time he would be able to tell her. But until he knew for sure whether she was involved in piracy, perhaps even the instigator of the thefts, she was the last person he could confide in.

Sean had no sooner stepped inside than the smell of something burning assailed him. A haze of smoke enveloped him. Through the pall, he could just make out Josie bent over a pot, mumbling.

"She 'spects me to cook, then Miss High and Mighty goin' to eat burned beans and soggy cornbread. What I know 'bout cookin' could fit into one of dem beans. Even one of dem little black charred ones."

The bondsman left the door open and began waving a hastily grabbed towel at the smoke. "Josie, what on earth happened?"

The slave jumped and turned toward him, brandishing a large wooden spoon. "Don't ever 'spect me to cook again!"

"I won't, I promise." Sean couldn't help laughing at the mixture of helplessness and anger on Josie's face. Folding the towel to use as a hot pad, he took the smoking pot out into the yard and doused it with water from a bucket.

Josie stood looking down at the ruined beans in the blackened pot. Shaking her head, she said, "We goin' to have a late supper tonight. That's for sure."

Sean patted her consolingly on the shoulder. "Maybe I can help."

She glared up at him, waiting.

"I have a basket full of food out in my skiff. If I can convince Miss Jessie to go for a sail with me, I'll feed her before we come back and you won't have to."

"That be jes fine. Dat woman been gettin' into ever'ting around here. Doan give a body no rest at all. 'Josie clean this, Josie wash that, Josie mend this.' She busy, too, but never too busy to make sure ever'body else jes as busy." Josie shook her head again. "It sure be good to see her go off for a spell. She's back in that office again. You take her out o' there, Marse Sean. And if you doan bring her back till late, nobody here goin' to worry."

Chuckling, Sean made his way through the still-smoky kitchen and down the hall toward the small office. Jessie was just coming out, a concerned look on her face. When she saw him, a smile briefly lit her face, and she unconsciously held out her hand in greeting. Sean took her slender fingers in his own, his heart leaping at the contact. He longed to kiss those fingertips, those red lips, to sweep her into his arms and bury his face in the softness of her hair, to. . . .

Mentally, he gave himself a shake. One moment in her presence and he was ready to forget his suspicions in the wake of his desires. Besides, he thought, he doubted if that kind of attention would be well received by the lovely widow. Not from him. Not from a bondslave.

"Sean! What has happened?"

"Only Josie disposing of the most of your supper."

Jessie groaned. "Not again?"

Sean chuckled as he took her arm and, turning her, guided her away from the smoky kitchen. "Some soggy-looking cornbread and some burned bits of beans is all that's left. And those are soaking in the cold water I doused them with."

"That girl is impossible!" Jessie complained. She went back into the office and sat down by the desk. Since it was the only chair, Sean leaned against the doorjamb and folded his arms across his chest. Content to lean there, he smiled at Jessie and listened to the sweet tones of her voice, velvet soft even in exasperation.

"She does try, but she can't sew a straight seam. Her cooking is a disaster, and she makes as much of a mess when she cleans up. In Boston, a servant like that would be turned out. Here"—she shrugged and shook her head—"what can I do? You don't just tell slaves they're fired. They're yours and you're stuck with them."

"You could always sell her," Sean suggested, chortling at Jessie's description, "but if she's as bad as you say, you might have to pay someone to take her!"

Jessie's mouth twitched, and she could not stop a giggle.

Sean was glad to see her laugh again. He had been struck by the tiredness in Jessie's face, the darkness shadowing her eyes.

"Since your supper is ruined, Mrs. Twill, would you consider dining with me?"

"With you?"

"I have a basket full of fried chicken, baked potatoes, fresh rolls, turnovers, cheese, wine . . ." He ticked the items off on his fingers. "Much better than burned beans and soggy cornbread. We could take a sail, find a nice place, and dine *al fresco*." He cocked his brows, waiting for her answer.

"A sail?" she asked.

"I came upriver in a skiff."

"And just what brings you upriver?"

"I had faint hopes that I could persuade you to go for a sail and share my dinner. Thanks to Josie, there shouldn't be much persuading to do. If you don't, you might not get any supper at all."

She hesitated, wanting to go, afraid to trust herself with him for a whole, free afternoon.

"I don't know, Sean. I have so much to do." She gestured toward the pile of papers still needing her attention. "I . . ."

He saw her hesitation and reached for her, pulling her up by her arm. "It will keep. You need to eat anyway, and a little time away from all this clutter will do you good."

He gave her little time to protest but led her to the front door, taking her shawl from a peg and pushing her ahead of him.

She turned but he barred her way. "Really, Sean, I shouldn't."

He held her firmly by the arms, facing him. "You need an outing, Mrs. Twill. I can see in your face how hard you've been working." He smiled and ran a finger along her jaw, so tempted to pull her to him and kiss every inch of it that his hand shook. Or was it Jessie trembling beneath his touch?

Her chest heaved and a flush invaded her cheeks. "I don't think it would be very proper," she said.

"Because I'm a mere bondslave?" His finger continued its tormenting course along her throat.

Her pulse quickened and she avoided his eyes. *No,* she thought, *because you are the most virile, handsome man I've ever met. Because your slightest touch sets me afire and I don't trust myself with you.* But out loud she only said, "Yes."

"Can you not forget that for one afternoon? I will call you by your given name like an equal and make you laugh. We'll sail upriver to a secluded spot and—"

"And could I trust you to behave?" she interrupted, pushing his hand away from its dangerous downward course. "I would trust a gentleman. But a bondslave?"

"My word is my bond. I will give it as freely as a free man and be as bound by it as I am by my indenture. For this afternoon, I vow to play the gentleman." He dropped his hands from her and stepped back as if to prove his promise.

Momentarily Jessie composed herself, and almost wished she had not extracted that promise from him. But she knew she could not go with him without it, and the proposed outing greatly appealed to her. It had been a long time since she had gone off for an afternoon's sail. She used to do it all the time when she was a girl.

"I must look a mess," she said, reaching up to smooth her hair.

Sean chuckled and nodded his agreement. "Have you been cleaning fireplaces?"

She tossed her head coyly. "A gentleman would not have agreed with me."

"I thought a gentleman always agreed with a lady, especially when she's right."

"You're impossible!"

"Just like Josie?"

"Never that bad!" She laughed.

"I'm new at this gentleman business. You'll have to help me. What would a gentleman have said?"

"Oh, something flattering," she said vaguely.

"Flattering?" He shook his head and stared deep into her eyes, and a warmth seemed to leap from him into her very being. "I could never flatter you, Jessie. Flattery is but a pretty lie. There is no compliment I could give you that would come close to flattery. It would all be true."

Jessie could scarcely breathe, but she forced a lightness into her voice. "Being a gentleman may be new to you, 'my lord,' but you learn very quickly."

"Then shall we go, my lady? Your royal barge awaits."

Grinning, she nodded happily and set off down the over-grown walk to the river. Sean followed a pace behind, carefully not touching her. Not touching at all. Yet she felt his presence, his magnetism, as if his body reached to envelop hers and hers welcomed that enfolding touch.

Chapter Seven

When Jessie stepped onto the dock, she felt Sean's hand on her arm, steadying her. The waiting skiff looked trim enough, clean and well kept. Jessie could see the promised basket tucked under the stern seat.

She lifted her hand, testing the wind. There was but a whiff of a breeze and that an errant one. She was well versed in sailing a ship, but how much could a felonious bondslave know? Would Sean be able to sail in this whimsical wind? Had the wind been steadier when he came upriver?

"Can you sail this thing?" she asked dubiously.

Mockingly, Sean drew himself up as if insulted. "Can you doubt me, my lady? Remember, for the afternoon, I am a gentleman."

Jessie laughed at his foolery. "Being a gentleman does not necessarily make one a good sailor. In this situation I'd rather trust myself to a good sailor than to a gentleman who has never hoisted a sail."

Sean gave her a leering grin. "If my lady prefers a lusty

sailor to a gentleman, she has but to release me from my vow and I will comply and happily."

He leaned suggestively forward, and she pushed him back with one pointed finger. "I'll trust that this *gentleman* knows how to sail. But if you don't, I have some small skill as a sailor myself."

"You, my lady?"

"Do you forget that I am an Ashbrook by birth? I was practically raised on ships."

"You are in competent hands," he assured her. He helped her into the craft and, casting loose the binding rope, jumped aboard himself. "I am no stranger to ships myself."

Jessie settled herself near the bow, out of the way of tiller and sail. She looked doubtfully at the limp sail but decided to let Sean prove his boast. If he found himself in difficulties, she would come to his aid.

Sean's boast did not prove an empty one. With the capability of an accomplished seaman, he set the small sail to catch each puff of wind, and the craft made its way upstream in a tacking pattern. Though their progress was languid, it was steady, and Sean's handling of the skiff was smooth and seemingly effortless.

To her knowledgeable eye, it was plain Sean was well acquainted with sailing. She thought of that first day they had met, when he had stood aboard the ship that had brought her to the Carolinas. So it had not been entirely her imagination that had made him seem at home, leaning casually on the ship's railing, his hand laid upon the rigging, his shirt open to the wind that tossed the white scudding clouds about.

"Where did you learn to sail, Sean?"

He drew his gaze downward from adjusting the sail and smiled at her as if his memories of the past were pleasant ones. "My father taught me."

She leaned back against a soft cushion, imagining Sean as a boy being taught to sail by his father, a crusty but tender old salt. What trouble had Sean gotten into that had sent him into bondage? Had it broken the old man's heart?

"Your father was a sailor?"

She heard the soft rumble of Sean's chuckle. "He was a pirate."

She looked up sharply. There was a broad grin on her companion's face, almost, she thought, as if he were proud that his father had been a pirate.

Her carefully constructed fantasy crumbled. "So. Misdeeds run in the family, Bondslave Winthrop."

"Tsk, tsk," he said, holding up a warning finger. "Remember our pledge. For the afternoon I am a gentleman."

She relaxed against the cushion, feeling the skiff's gentle sway. Leaning back, looking at him through half-closed eyes, she could imagine him being a gentleman as easily as a pirate. One role seemed to fit upon those broad shoulders as well as the other. Unfortunately, she knew which of them was the true picture.

The skiff rocked gently and she closed her eyes. Her exhaustion soon put her to sleep. She dreamed of Sean first as a gentleman, dancing with her in swaying rhythm, then as a pirate, carrying her off in his swaying ship. When the swaying stopped, she woke to see Sean bending over her, the back of his hand stroking her cheek. In the aftermath of her dream, she almost put her arms around his neck to draw him down to her, but the remnants of sleep fell from her in time and she stretched her arms instead.

Sitting up, she looked around. They were at another dock further up the river. This dock was newly built and sturdy, the boards not yet grayed by the weather.

Sean set the basket on the dock, then helped her ashore.

"Where are we?" she asked.

"The Fortune plantation," he answered. "And for this afternoon, since I am a gentleman, I will show it to you as if it were mine."

She laughed as she took the arm he so elegantly offered and looked up at him. He was looking out over the clearing to the fields beyond, and again she was struck by the odd incongruity of a slave taking such pride in his master's possessions.

They walked to the top of a grassy knoll and Sean set the basket down. "This will one day be my dining room," he said. His hand swept out. "There will be a row of windows there to afford a view of the river while I dine. There will be a terrace just outside the window and a garden. Glass doors will open out to it and let in the breeze."

She looked where he indicated and could see what he described. It was a beautiful view. "It's a perfect spot for a house," she said. "Is this where Mr. Fortune really plans to build?"

He touched a finger to her nose chidingly. "Yes, this is where I will really build my house."

She laughed, remembering their afternoon's game. "Where will the parlor be, Sir Gentleman?"

He led her a few steps to the right. "Here beside the dining room and also opening onto the terrace."

"What else does your dream house contain?" she asked.

He shrugged. "The usual rooms. Kitchen, bedrooms, library . . ." He paused to look down at her suggestively, "A nursery."

She ignored his leer and turned away, breaking off a stem of grass to twirl in her hands. "Just how many children do you plan to have, Sir Gentleman?"

"At least a dozen." He stepped behind her, and she felt his

fingers trace along her shoulder. "If I have the right woman to wife, it will be a pleasure to make them."

Her breath caught. Surely he was not suggesting that she could be that woman. No, not even Sean would be so bold. She stepped away from his touch. His conversation struck too close to her own thoughts when she had mistaken Sean for her husband. She pointed to some buildings some distance from the house. "What are those?"

"Would you like to see?"

She nodded and he took her hand. They walked along the river to the buildings. At their approach, a man stepped out of one of the buildings with a flintlock in his hands. Jessie gasped, but Sean squeezed her hand reassuringly and waved to the man.

The man returned Sean's wave and shouldered the weapon. Obviously, they knew each other. The two men shook hands then Sean introduced her.

"This is Bill Flinders, Mrs. Twill. He guards Mr. Fortune's upriver warehouse."

Jessie smiled and nodded to the man who turned a deep red and, tugging a quick salute to her, mumbled a hasty comment and left.

Jessie wondered what she had done to scare the man off like that until Sean explained. "Bill's very shy, Mrs. Twill, especially around women. That's why he's glad to have a lonely job like this. The only people he has to talk to are a few trappers when they bring in furs."

"Furs?" she asked.

"Mr. Fortune buys furs, stores them here, then ships them out when there's enough."

She looked around at the numerous sheds. "These are all full of furs?"

"Some of them are for the rice crop, some for tools, timber.

Only this one is for furs." He chose a key from a ring, set it into the lock, and swung open the door.

The interior was dim, and dust motes danced merrily in the sunbeams that pierced the gloom. Sean led Jessie to the back of the shed where bundled furs were stacked.

"There aren't many here right now, but the trappers will be bringing in the last of this year's trappings soon. When this shed is full, Mr. Fortune will send a ship upriver to load the furs for shipment to England."

Jessie nodded, reaching out to feel the soft pelts. "They're beautiful."

There was not much else to see and they left the shed, Sean carefully locked the door behind them.

To her surprise, he did not lead her back to the site of the house and their waiting lunch but took her up the slope away from the river. There, a large field of ripening rice spread out before her. Sean knelt and examined the rice, checked the water level, and walked a ways along the edge of the dike, kneeling once or twice to check its strength before returning to her.

"I wanted to check on the rice before I went back to Charles Town," he said, and she wondered again at how solicitous Sean was of his master's possessions.

Jessie looked at the crop, neatly transplanted into even rows, and a sudden question struck her.

Someone had to have planted this crop, made the dikes, irrigated the field, but she saw no sign of slave cabins. "Sean, where are Mr. Fortune's slaves?"

The bondsman stood, running some loose soil from one hand to another. "Slaves?"

"The ones who planted this crop. Where are they? I see no cabins or . . ." She shrugged, looking for some evidence of habitation.

"There are no slaves," Sean said brusquely and his fist tightened, squeezing the soil he held into a misshapened lump.

"No slaves?" She saw the grim set of Sean's jaw and could well understand his aversion to slavery. In spite of his lenient master and easy manner, she wondered if his bondage did not sometimes chafe him dearly.

"Men are hired to do the work as they are needed." Sean tossed the clump from his hand and dusted it on his pants. "Mr. Fortune does not hold with slavery," he said curtly.

"Yet he owns a bondslave," she said softly.

"A bondsman is not a slave. Mr. Fortune holds the bond of many men. They work out their indebtedness to him and then are free to go where they will."

"As you will?"

"As I will," he agreed.

"Someday, perhaps," she said. "But seven years is not very soon."

He reached up to smooth back a strand of her hair that the wind had blown free. He smiled down at her. "But even so, I am no man's slave. And perhaps I will yet find a way to shorten my bondage."

"I thought you were content to be Mr. Fortune's bondslave," she reminded him.

The hand that had smoothed her hair trailed down along her throat, and his eyes raked over her with a hard yearning evident in them. "Circumstances change," he said.

Though the sun was waning, it suddenly seemed warm. She stood as firmly rooted as the sod she stood upon. Was he telling her that she was the circumstance that had changed his contented life? Surely that could not be the case. He looked down at her, a deep intensity in his eyes, and she thought for a moment that he was going to kiss her.

135

Before she was able to decide whether to let him as she wanted to or deny him as she knew she should, he had stepped away from her, the light teasing twinkle back in his eyes.

"What circumstances have changed for you in two days?" she asked.

He shrugged. "A man, as well as a woman, may change his mind. There are things I would do that my bondage hampers."

"I have not seen any evidence of your bondage hampering your activities in any way. You seem free enough to come and go as you will. You speak when you will, and your bondage seems not to constrain you in any way from saying what you would to a slave or to a free man alike."

"Nay, madam, I am far from free to speak as I would." His eyes held her and his fingers softly caressed her cheek. "I have held my tongue when I longed to tell you how beautiful you are, how my heart leaps at the sight of you, how full of joy I feel when you are near. I want to tell you how I long to touch you and yearn for the closeness of your silken skin yet I am silenced by my station for I know you would but scorn my words. My loins ache for wanting you and yet I dare not speak of it to you for I am not free. If I thought my words would fall on approving ears, you would know the fullness of my craving, for I would tell it all to you and then I would . . ."

Her eyes widened at the fervor of his speech. Could he really feel so deeply for her so soon? Then, hearing the drift of his words, she hastened to halt them. "Not even a free man would dare express so much, much less a gentleman," she chided, although her words were gently spoken.

"You are right. And I am not just a free man this afternoon. I am a gentleman." He smiled at her. "Therefore I will not say those things to you."

She turned away, warmed by his ardor more than she

wanted to admit. "I think, my lord, you have already said them."

He laughed. Then, holding out his hand to her, he asked, "Hungry?"

She nodded, and he took her arm to help her down the slope as decorously as any gentleman born and bred.

When they reached the storage sheds, she caught a glimpse of Bill peeking out at them but he disappeared as soon as she nodded in his direction.

Sean pulled her arm through his, and they walked side by side down the tree-lined lane back to their dinner.

In the "dining room" Jessie sat on the grass and Sean served her. There was crisp fried chicken, still slightly warm, rolls with a yeasty fragrance, and turnovers so light and flaky she couldn't remember when she had had finer. The wine was smooth and satisfying. If this meal was any indication, Mr. Fortune was more than generous with his bondslave.

Licking the last of a turnover from her sticky fingers, Jessie looked over at Sean with a mischievous gleam in her eye. "I think Mr. Fortune's cook is almost as good as mine," she said.

Sean looked up in surprise then chuckled. "Almost. Do you think Josie would be willing to give lessons? Especially on cooking beans?"

Jessie shook her head. "That recipe is an old family secret. Charred beans *à la* Josie."

Sean let out an exaggerated sigh. "Why do you think I took you out this afternoon?" he asked. "I was hoping to pry the secret out of you."

Now she chuckled. "My lips are sealed. Especially when Josie cooks!"

"That," he said, "sounds like a bit of good advice."

Satisfied to repletion, Jessie leaned back, letting the

freshening breeze flow over her. Sean began putting away the remnants of their meal, and she handed him her plate and napkin. Their fingers touched and with one hand Sean took the things. With the other he grasped her hand.

"You should always be this carefree, Jessie," he said, seeing how much she had relaxed in the last hours. "It becomes you."

"It's hard to be carefree. I've taken on a lot of worries."

Her hand trembled slightly in his, and he wondered if those worries included theft. He caressed her slender fingers feeling the delicate bones, the now work-roughened skin. Could such hands direct a band of thieving miscreants? But he had also seen her snap at Jackson, take charge of an entire plantation with authority and confidence.

"I want to thank you for this afternoon, Sean. You've been a big help to me since I came to Charles Town."

She squeezed his hand in a simple gesture of thanks and began to pull away, but he held her fast. "You speak as if you are ready to leave."

She laughed, and pulling her hand free, stood up. "I'm not. But I must." Nodding her head toward the lowering sun, she continued, "You took me away from duties that can only be delayed, not forgotten. I'll be up half the night to pay for this afternoon."

Sean leered up at her with a teasing grin, "I had no idea you intended to pay me that way."

"Sean! You're supposed to be a gentleman!"

He shrugged in mock innocence. "I thought the afternoon was over."

"Not until you deliver me to my door, Sir Bondslave."

Sean finished gathering the dishes into the basket, continuing his banter. "Does a gentleman never make such suggestions to a lady?"

"Never!" Jessie answered, taking up the game. Primly, as if she were the grandest lady in the world, she straightened her sleeves, and smoothed her skirt. "With his lady, he is always chaste and pure."

Shaking his head in puzzled wonder Sean asked, "Then where do all those newborn ladies and gentlemen come from, I wonder?"

She tried hard to suppress a giggle, but it was impossible, and soon the delight and freedom of the afternoon came bubbling out, and they laughed long and hard together.

On the way back down the river, Jessie sat in the stern with Sean, and this time, it was she who directed the set of the sails, her hand at the tiller. It was with a nod of appreciative approval that Sean helped her nose the craft to the rickety Twill dock.

All too soon Sean was delivering her to her door, standing close to her on that crumbling porch, saying good-bye.

"Did this mock gentleman comport himself well, my lady?" he asked, offering her a gallant bow.

She leaned back against the wall, studying him as if trying to decide if there wasn't more to him than a mere bondslave. "As well as any gentleman of my acquaintance. If I didn't know better, I would say you were a gentleman born and bred."

He propped a hand against the wall behind her, an impish grin lighting his face. "And then you remember that pirate father of mine."

Her lips twisted when he mentioned that souring memory. It was almost as if he really never wanted her to forget what he was—a bondslave, a felon, the son of a pirate. Certainly never a gentleman. "Yes," she said dispiritedly, "then I remember that pirate father of yours."

He leaned closer. She could feel the warmth from his body,

his breath on her hair. She started to move away but he lifted her face to his and his eyes held her. She could feel her breath quicken, feel the furor of her pounding heart as if it called out to his.

His arm came around her, pulling her into his embrace, an embrace which seemed to her the most natural place in the world for her to be. Then his mouth was boldly plundering hers, and she surrendered to that piracy, becoming a willing partner in that punishment.

For an eternity that passed but in a moment they stood, lips clinging to lips, body pressed to body, yearning answering yearning. Then he drew away, taking some part of her soul with him.

She lowered her gaze, ashamed that once again he could so easily make her forget herself so completely. In spite of the hammering blood coursing through her and the shakiness of her knees, she was determined to pass this off lightly. Forcing a smile to her lips, she looked up at him. "That was certainly no gentleman who just kissed me."

He cocked a black brow at her. "Quite right, my lady. By your own terms the afternoon is over. You are at your door, and I have shed the veneer of a gentleman."

"And returned to the ways your father taught you."

He smiled lightheartedly. "A pirate is never loath to steal a kiss from a winsome lass."

"Is that what you are, Sean?" she asked, turning serious eyes up to him. "Is that what you were sent into bondage for? Are you a pirate?"

"Now?" He laughed. "Now I am merely a humble bondslave who must return to his duties." He stood away from her and turned to eye the setting of the sun. "And I must be on my way or I'll not make it back to Charles Town before full dark." He drew out a folded paper and handed it to her.

"The Walkers asked me to give this to you. If you want to send an answer, I'll be upriver again tomorrow."

With that, he was off, waving back over his shoulder as he made his way around the house and out of sight.

Jessie took the letter into her office and sat at the desk to read it. It was in Mrs. Walker's generous, loopy scrawl.

"Dear Jessie," it said, "Sean has informed us of the death of Mr. Twill. May we express our condolences on your being made a widow so soon after your arrival.

"We have had a letter from your stepfather, Mr. Pierce, stating that he and your mother will arrive via the *Harper* on Tuesday. I'm sure that circumstances being what they are they will insist that you return to Boston with them. We will be sorry to lose you so soon after your arrival, but we understand that you will be anxious to accompany them back home. Being alone on that plantation must be difficult for any woman but especially for one so young and unused to plantation life. Please feel free to come to Charles Town and stay with us until their arrival. Sincerely, Lucy Walker."

Jessie let the letter slip from her fingers. Go back to Boston? She clenched her fists and stood up. Never! What did she have back there? An empty, mundane existence. Here, she could make her own life, build this plantation into what it should be, perhaps later invest in shipping. In time, now that Twill was dead, she would marry someone of her own choosing, the someone she had dreamed of, the someone she could share her life with fully.

Maybe she should have written her mother and stepfather of Twill's death, and told them not to come. She shook her head. No, by the time her husband had died, they were well on their way. Besides, she wanted her stepfather to come and sign over the plantation to her. But would he now? Would he insist she return to Boston?

Jessie chewed on a knuckle. No, there was no going back for her. She had had a little independence and she liked it. It wasn't easy by any means, but she was determined not to return to Boston and live under Mr. Pierce's thumb again.

Legally, however, she might have no recourse. As a widow, she would be free to live anywhere. But as Mr. Jackson had so crudely pointed out, her marriage had never been consummated, and that would be easy to prove. Jonathan Twill had been too ill when she arrived and there were too many people who knew that. Legally, her marriage was null and void, and in the eyes of the law, she was still Pierce's ward. If he knew that Twill was dead, and that her marriage was unconsummated, he might insist that she return to Boston. She knew that Pierce had married her off to Twill because he wanted something from him. But Twill was dead. What reason could her stepfather have for letting her have the plantation now? It would be more likely that he would force her to return to Boston and use her again in some other "deal."

If she refused to return to Boston, how could she live if she didn't have the plantation? Her stepfather had never done more than promise to give her this plantation once her marriage to Twill was consummated. How could she make him give it to her now if he decided it would suit his purpose more to have her in Boston?

And her mother! Mother had been nearly hysterical hearing that her daughter wanted to live in such an uncivilized place as Charles Town. And then not even to live in town but out in the wilderness! She didn't understand why Jessie couldn't just marry some nice boy from Boston. To her way of thinking, Boston was the only decent place to live. Mother would certainly not hear of Jessie remaining here on her own without a husband. She would insist that her daughter return to Boston.

Jessie began to pace. Surely there had to be a way to convince them to give her the plantation and let her stay. For an hour she came up with one plea after another, discarding each as she thought of her mother and stepfather's reaction.

Sighing, she slumped into her chair. The only thing Mr. Pierce and her mother would accept would be a living, breathing Jonathan Twill beside her. But he was dead. If only Sean Winthrop who had met her at the dock upon her arrival had been her husband as she had first thought.

Jessie sat bolt upright, with a sudden inspirational glint in her eyes. She had mistaken Sean for her husband because she had never met Jonathan Twill. But her mother and Mr. Pierce had never met him, either.

Was what she was thinking too wild a scheme to work? She rose and began to pace again, excitedly this time.

What if she could convince her mother and stepfather that Jonathan Twill was very much alive and well? Then, once Mr. Pierce had signed over the plantation and returned to Boston, she could write to them of her husband's untimely death.

But they would want to meet this husband of hers. She couldn't just tell them he was off on a trip somewhere. She would have to present them with a flesh-and-blood mate, a man who could fool anyone with his manners and charm. And it had to be someone willing to help her. Of the men she knew here in Charles Town, only one had all the necessary qualifications—Sean Winthrop.

Could she really hope to fool Mr. Pierce and her mother with a substitute husband? Mrs. Walker thought he had the manners of a duke. Jessie herself had seen just this afternoon just how convincing the felonious ex-pirate bondslave could be when he played the part of a gentleman.

Jessie shrugged aside the guilt at such a deception. It would only be for a short time. But would Sean be willing to help her? Maybe if she offered to pay off a year of his indenture, he would. She had found some cash, enough to pay off the full year's indenture and for a few short-term expenses.

She took out her small hoard of cash and began to plan. She would have to buy a decent outfit or two for Sean. She shoved a few coins to one side, then more to pay his year's indenture. He would have to move in. The master bedroom had been cleaned and Twill's things removed. Sean could have that room. She would have to get rid of Jackson and Josie for a few days. Perhaps send them to Williamsburg for supplies. She shoved more coins to the side. Maybelle might be a cat in heat, especially when it came to Sean, but she was loyal enough to trust.

The Walkers would help once she explained the situation to them, she was sure. They had never approved of Mr. Pierce and his business methods in the first place, which was why they had been sent to Charles Town.

Thankfully, Twill had been a recluse and recently arrived in the colony himself. There wouldn't be a problem with running into old friends. She would see that her visitors stayed close to the Walkers and to the plantation during their short sojourn. It was unlikely that many would yet know of her husband's death. Any question could be temporarily turned aside by simply pointing to the living man beside her. If that man was a bondslave in disguise, how many people in the upper circles of society would recognize him?

Having made that decision, she went to work on the accounts. There were precious few coins left, and she had to move some of them to the growing pile for paying bills. What little was left would not stretch until the harvest if there were any more expenses. She might have to take out a loan against her future crop, she thought. Her worry was interrupted by Josie's insolent step.

"Dat man here again," Josie informed her.

"Mr. Winthrop?" Jessie asked, wondering what could have brought Sean back tonight.

"No. The other one. Dat fancy man," Josie said indolently.

"Mr. Soames?"

"Dat's de one," she said, and disappeared back into the kitchen.

Hastily, Jessie gathered up her papers, returning them to her desk drawer. Jason Soames had been a daily visitor since she had first met him four days ago. His visits were usually brief, but always lively and entertaining, leaving Jessie feeling as if a whirlwind had come and gone. But she enjoyed the brief visits and was beginning to look forward to them.

Jason was waiting on the porch. Josie had not even shown the man into the parlor or offered him a cool drink. He turned when he heard Jessie, his large brown eyes becoming alive and warm when he saw her. Dropping his feather-trimmed tricorn to the porch, he reached out for her with both hands, taking hers, squeezing them as he kissed her cheek in greeting. For most men, it would have been an outrageous liberty, but for Jason, it was simply the outpouring of his effusive nature, and Jessie accepted it in the spirit it was offered.

"Jason!" she greeted. "You are late in your visit today."

His whole face lit up when he smiled broadly and completely. "Did you despair that I would not come?" he asked hopefully.

"Completely!" she said, laughing, taking up his playful mood. "I was inconsolable!"

"Ah," he sympathized. "Tomorrow I will be sure to come early!"

"No," she said with a little moue, "not tomorrow."

He looked devastated. "You are punishing me!"

Jessie laughed. "I would never be so cruel. Besides, I

145

wouldn't rob myself to punish you. Your visits are delightful." He looked as hopeful as a pup at her words. Surely he did not take this flirtation seriously? She laughed at herself. Certainly not such a worldly man as Jason Soames! "I am going to Charles Town tomorrow," she explained.

"Then I must stay longer today," he said. "If that is all right with you?"

His big eyes looked at her so pleadingly she could not refuse him in spite of the work waiting for her. "Of course!" She put her hand on his arm, and he grasped it immediately as if she had offered him some incredible gift. "Will you come in?" she asked.

"Let us walk," he suggested.

They strolled down the drive, arm in arm, and he launched into one of his stories. For an hour he entertained her and drew her out as well. Then he left on his prancing stallion, letting the beast have just enough slack to dance and release some of its energy but not enough to lose control of it.

As she watched him canter down the drive, she suddenly realized that it had never occurred to her to ask him to play the role of her husband. She chuckled to herself when she thought of it. He might be willing, but, somehow, she could not imagine him pulling it off. No, it would have to be Sean. And she stood for a moment in bemusement when she realized she was glad. Briefly, she wondered how she would keep Jason away while her parents were here. Perhaps she could tell him she was going to be away. She shrugged. She would think of something.

The next morning Jessie watched anxiously for Sean's arrival while she oversaw the repair of some of the slave cabins. There were fourteen cabins, most of them needing new roofs, whitewash, a new board here and there. The area had been cleaned, the hinges and shutters repaired, but the work was going slowly. The slaves were needed in the fields so close to harvest time. When she at last spotted the small white sail of Sean's skiff, she didn't know whether to run down to meet him or to await his arrival at the house. So much depended on his agreeing to help her. But what if he laughed in her face?

She shook her head. She couldn't imagine Sean doing that. However, she could easily imagine him refusing to take part in her charade. Yet he was a convicted felon. Why should a little deception bother him? She didn't know, but she felt that whatever he had been, deceit was not part of Sean's character and that thought troubled her. No, not troubled her. Confused her. It was almost as if there were two Seans. A decent, upright, honest one, and the ex-pirate, felonious bondslave. And it was the second Sean who never seemed quite believable.

Jessie shaded her eyes and watched the skiff bump gently into the dock, and then the sail drop. She sighed. Well, it would have to be the second Sean she appealed to. Somehow her feet had begun to move of their own accord, and she tripped down the walk toward the dock. She told herself that it was anxiety that twisted her heart and propelled her forward, and not because she was glad to see Sean again. She forced herself to slow down, and not appear quite so anxious. But Sean had already seen her. His infectious smile spread joy through her as he half ran toward her.

As he turned the tiller, heading the little skiff toward the battered dock at Jessie's plantation, a troubled frown creased Sean's brow. He had been quite troubled by his meeting with Governor Johnson and Colonel William Rhett this morning. Sean had agreed to help Rhett bring an end to the raids and piracy in the area as the Fortune ships had too often been targets of piracy. Several more plantation houses along the James and Cooper Rivers had also been broken into, silver plate and cash, furs and valuable carpets stolen. There had been no deaths so far, but one or two men had been knocked unconscious when they had inadvertently stumbled into the path of the miscreants. But Mr. Campbell's report was unsettling.

The Campbell plantation had been plundered the night before, and it was harder than ever not to have some suspicions about Jessie. The raiders had come from the river, broken into the house, and taken several pieces of valuable silver. Mr. Campbell had been awakened by a noise, but by the time he came downstairs, the thieves were running toward their boat. He fired a shot that went wide of its mark. Much chagrined, the stout Mr. Campbell had blamed his poor marksmanship on being surprised to see a woman with the band. A tall, slender woman. A woman who knew well how to handle a sailboat.

Sean tied his skiff to the rickety dock and looked up in time to see Jessie running down the walk toward him. He couldn't help but be thrilled at the sight of her, her face alight, her skirts flying about her willowy form. She was a sight to make any man's pulse race. It was hard to look at her and believe that she could be anything but the innocent she appeared to be. If only the evidence didn't keep pointing toward her. Hadn't she said yesterday that she would be up half the night working? The same night that the Campbell's had been raided? Was he reading more into her words than she had meant?

But right now she looked so delicious, hurrying toward him as if she desired him as much as he wanted her. He couldn't help running toward her, his arms stretching out of their own accord to enfold her. But she suddenly slowed, then stopped, folding her arms primly.

He stopped before her, forcing his own arms down. They trembled in their effort to touch her, but he firmly put them behind him, clasping one hand with the other. He searched her face for signs of sleeplessness. Had she been raiding? But all he could see was the sparkle and snap in her black eyes, the flush coloring her cheeks, her lips trembling. Lips he could remember tasting just yesterday.

"Good morning, my lady. You look none the worse for having spent half the night at work." His words were lightly spoken yet there was a challenge in them, a hope that she would disprove his suspicions, and claim to have slept the night through.

"Perhaps because the night's work turned more profitable than I had anticipated," she answered.

He frowned. Her words did not contain the assurance he was looking for. Could the profit she mentioned be Campbell silver? Quickly, he erased his frown, which was easily done when he looked at her lovely face.

"Gold and silver or only silver?" he asked, hoping to confirm or to allay his suspicions.

She laughed, a bit uneasily, it seemed to him. "Nothing so valuable as gold, I'm afraid."

He looked up at her standing on the step above him and wanted to shake her. Shake her into telling him everything, shake her into telling him there was nothing to his fears. Then, when he was done shaking her, he wanted to taste that honey-sweet mouth again and watch those down-turned corners of her mouth turn up, transforming her face from sultry to beguiling.

She twisted her hands, and it seemed as if her smile was forced. "Sean, there's something I have to ask you."

"Whatever my lady wills," he said nonchalantly, though his heart wrenched.

Jessie looked around. There were slaves watching from the quarters. "Not here," she said. "Come inside." She turned, and Sean followed her gently swaying hips up the walk and into the house.

Chapter Eight

Leading the way into the house, Jessie could feel Sean's eyes on her, and she forced down the feeling of warmth that tried to steal over her. It was going to be hard enough to ask Sean to play the part of her husband for a week without making him think she wanted more than pretense. In the kitchen, Maybelle was arguing with Josie over the proper way to prepare a pot of stew. Her maid managed to take time out to smile enticingly at Sean, but the bondsman merely nodded to her and passed on, much to Maybelle's annoyance.

Entering her office, Jessie paced up and down a moment. She had rehearsed her speech a hundred times, but Sean's presence seemed to take on an extra dimension in the tiny room. She could almost feel the heat from his sun-drenched hair, smell the scent of the sea that he carried. She had no doubt that the whirlpool she felt inside was stirred by the light in Sean's eyes, the smile that twitched at his lips. Yet she sensed a reticence in him, too, as if he wanted to take her in his arms but was deliberately holding back for some reason. Whatever the reason, she was glad for it because she was not sure she could have resisted him. She had to put some distance between them or she would never be able to make this proposal—this arrangement—she hastily corrected herself, in businesslike terms.

Sitting down at her desk, she folded her hands in front of her and looked across at him from her position of authority. A position he immediately destroyed by perching casually on the edge of her desk, crossing his arms across his chest, and cocking a questioning brow at her. She shifted, unnerved by his closeness.

Taking a deep breath, she began, "As you know, I was sent here by my stepfather as Jonathan Twill's wife. I was to . . . to help him with this end of the business." She saw a frown momentarily cross Sean's face, but it was gone so quickly she was not sure she had really seen it. She continued, "The wedding was by proxy and"—she blushed and clenched her hands tightly—"obviously unconsummated."

She looked up at him, then back down at her hands in an unspoken plea that he refrain from mentioning that he was quite aware that she had been innocent of any man until that moonlit night in the parlor. Sean merely nodded encouragingly and she went on.

"My mother and Mr. Pierce are coming to Charles Town. This plantation was to be mine and my husband's wedding present. If I have no husband, they won't sign it over to me, and will expect me to return to Boston with them. If they find out my marriage was not consummated, I might have no choice but to go with them."

She lifted her gaze to his, and though her voice remained steady, there was a silent plea in her eyes. "I have tasted freedom, Sean. I want to keep my independence. But I have to prove to them that I can handle things here on my own. I can't do that unless they give me a chance. They don't think I can run things here without Twill, but I can. And for that chance I need this plantation. By rights, it should have been mine and I want it."

She paused and Sean knew that she was about to ask for his help. He gave her a small smile.

Encouraged, she continued, "Sean, I know Mr. Pierce. He will never sign this plantation over to me unless Jonathan Twill is standing beside me, alive and well." Her hands clenched tightly, she asked, "For one week, will you be Jonathan Twill?"

Sean stared at Jessie, for once completely taken aback. He had been prepared for a number of pleas from asking his help with a recalcitrant slave to advice on handling Jackson. He had even been half prepared for her to ask him to join her band of pirates. But to ask him to impersonate Jonathan Twill to fool her mother and stepfather was the last thing he would have thought of. He couldn't help admire her thinking—and her plan. He frowned. It was just this kind of bold, unconventional thinking that had made the pirates' preying on the plantations and ships in Charles Town so successful—especially on the Fortune ships and holdings.

Looking at her sitting there with her wide, anxious eyes, her chin held high, needing his help but too proud to beg, he wanted nothing more than to cradle her in his arms and do everything he could to protect and help her. Maybe the best thing to do was to refuse her, making sure that she returned to Boston and away from this whole tangle.

He rejected that idea as soon as it came to him. If she were innocent, she would not only resent him for not helping, he would destroy her chance of building the independent life she wanted. If she were guilty, he would be throwing away a very good chance to get inside the ring and bring it to its knees that much sooner.

She was waiting for his answer, and he knew much depended upon it for her. But she must never suspect his real reasons for helping her, especially not his determination to use her to work his way closer to the pirates. Whether she was the leader or not, the raiders had come from this area, and the closer he was to their center, the better. He must convince her that lust was his main reason for agreeing to her scheme and that would not be difficult to do.

Again letting his gaze rove over her, he allowed a lecherous grin to play over his face. "Aye," he breathed, "I will be your husband for as long as you wish. Though it surprises me that you would consider a mere bondslave for the position. Or is it the mock gentleman you wish for your mock husband?"

He reached out to draw her close. With a haughty lift to her chin, she moved away.

"I am confused, my lady. Just exactly what did you have in mind?"

"Not what your lusty mind is imagining, I am sure."

He shrugged. "Then the game has lost much of its appeal."

"I'm willing to pay you, Mr. Winthrop, if your master is willing to lend me your services. I will pay off a year of your indenture for your help."

"Though I would like to see its end, my bondage does not sit too heavily upon me. Other inducements would be more to my liking."

"I can offer few other 'inducements,' Mr. Winthrop."

"You could call me Sean."

"Jon would be more appropriate if you are going to play the part of Jonathan Twill."

He shrugged. "Sean, Jon. 'Tis the same name in two tongues." Sean sat back down on the desk, leaning close

154

to her and smiling suggestively. "What are those few other inducements you can offer, Jessie?"

She leaned back in her chair, templing her fingers and looking at him over them. "We will have to do something about getting you some clothes. After all, a plantation owner can hardly go around dressed as you do."

There was also the added inducement of being close to Jessie, he thought. To see her supple grace each day, perhaps to hold her in his arms once more, to smell the fragrance of her hair, to hear her soft moan of pleasure as he caressed her, to taste her sweet mouth. He raked her hungrily with his eyes, letting his gaze travel slowly over her slender waist, her full breasts, the throbbing in the hollow of her throat.

Sean's lips twitched in amusement as if she had offered an apple to the owner of an orchard. "I have clothes of my own which I think will be adequate." He paused, waiting for her to offer a further inducement.

Ignoring his innuendo, she continued briskly, "You will stay here, of course. Since my visitors are due to arrive the day after tomorrow, it would be best if you moved in tomorrow. If you don't mind, I will accompany you back to Charles Town to make arrangements with the Walkers and see Mr. Fortune." She tapped a pen nervously on the desk. "Do you think he will mind lending me your services for a time? We don't have to tell him why."

She looked uncertainly to Sean and was annoyed to see a flicker of amusement on his face.

"I'll speak with Mr. Fortune myself," Sean said, unable to restrain a chuckle. "I don't think he will have any objections."

Nodding gratefully, Jessie gave a little sigh of relief. "I'll have to figure out what to do with Jackson and Josie," she mused. "They both know you aren't Twill, and I don't trust either of them not to give us away. I thought I might send them to Williamsburg for some supplies."

"I'll see what I can come up with," Sean said thoughtfully.

She stood up. "I'll just have to pack a few things for overnight and I'll be ready to go." She went briskly to the door, then paused. Without turning to face him, she said, "And, Sean. Thank you."

Sean watched the sway of her shapely hips as she left. There were other aspects to this plan of hers. She must realize how such a charade would throw them into a physical closeness he could well take advantage of. Maybe she was not as adverse to Sean Winthrop, bondslave, as she tried to act, or maybe he was the only man she could think of to help her. Thinking of the men she knew in Charles Town, he could see that her options were certainly limited. Did she trust him so much? If she were guilty of preying on the local planters, with particular attention on all Fortune shipping, it seemed strange that she would invite Mr. Fortune's bondslave into her home and confidence. Had he been wrong about her? Was she innocent?

Yet nothing Jessie had said supported her innocence. Indeed, every word she uttered seemed to confirm her guilt. She wanted to "handle things on this end." If Ashbrook Shipping were behind the pirate raids, what else could she mean but that she had taken up the standard from Twill's lifeless fingers?

Now she was asking him to help her. The raids had started shortly after Pierce had taken over Ashbrook Shipping. Jessie was an Ashbrook by birth. Was she trying to make herself indispensable to Pierce? Or did she merely need the means to remain independent of him as she claimed? Would the added income from piracy insure the independence she prized so highly? She must know that it would be some time before the plantation would be profitable enough to be stable and give her a decent income. Had she turned to piracy to subsidize the plantation, or was the plantation merely a front to be used and then discarded?

He got up from the desk to do some pacing of his own with his head down and his hands clasped behind him. From what she had said, he was convinced that if she were part of the pirate ring at all, she was new to the business. Perhaps he could keep her from getting too deeply involved, perhaps even protect her from the scoundrels she would have to deal with, even from Pierce's influence, and from the law, when the ring was rounded up. But he couldn't help her if she went back to Boston.

What better means could he use to meet all those goals than by taking part in the deception she offered? Perhaps even Pierce would confide in him. Sean lifted his head, grinning. He had hated the necessity of his role as bondslave. Now he would be a gentleman pretending to be a bondslave pretending to be a gentleman. It was enough to make his head swim. But by taking on this double role, he felt sure that this whole business would be over even sooner than he had hoped.

It was much quicker to Charles Town by river than it had been by wagon over rutted roads. In the nearly two weeks since Jessie had last seen the town, the docks seemed even busier. Sean escorted her through the busy streets and left her in the care of the Walkers, promising to return for her the next afternoon.

The Walkers were understandably reluctant to partake of such deceit as Jessie proposed, but after listening to her reasons, they at last agreed. They spent the evening and the next morning making plans for Jessie's guests' upcoming visit. By the time Sean came for her that afternoon, she was beginning to wonder if her ruse would work, but she was determined to at least try.

Sean and Jessie walked the short distance to the dock, Sean carrying Jessie's overnight bag, his other hand resting possessively on the small of her back. It felt comforting to have it there, Jessie thought, but hastened to remind herself that she must not begin to lean too heavily on Sean. If she wanted to be independent, she must learn to lean only on herself.

She glanced at Sean. He was wearing the same cotton shirt, rough breeches, and brogans he had worn when she had first met him. As usual, they were clean, but they were not the dress clothes she thought a gentleman planter should wear. She wondered if these were the clothes he would wear when impersonating Jonathan Twill, but she hated to embarrass him by pointing out their inadequacy.

"Are you sure you have no need of new clothes for this venture, Sean?" she asked him tentatively.

The bondslave's lips twitched in amusement as he answered, "I think you'll find my wardrobe satisfactory."

Jessie said no more. She could only hope his appearance would not embarrass him. Then she laughed to herself. She couldn't imagine Sean being embarrassed in any situation. And thinking of how effortlessly he played the role of gentleman, she doubted that anyone would ever mistake him for anything else even in the shabbiest clothing. Still, she hoped that his clothes were at least decent.

To Jessie's surprise, Sean led her, not to his usual skiff, but to a small sloop, the *Fortune*. Seeing her surprised hesitation, he shrugged apologetically. "My trunks wouldn't fit into the skiff. The *Fortune* happened to be in the harbor ready to sail today. It isn't much out of the crew's way to take us upriver first. We'll be more comfortable in the sloop than in the wagon."

It seemed that the sloop had merely been waiting for the two of them before getting underway. The gangplank was hauled up, and the captain called orders to the hands. Jessie looked at Sean with wide eyes.

"Does Mr. Fortune know how his bondslave appropriates his ships and rearranges their schedules to suit his comfort?"

Sean chuckled and leaned against the rail, one browned hand clutching the rigging. Again Jessie was struck by how at home he looked on the deck of a ship with his hair wind-tossed and his shirt open at the throat. "He knows and approves, my lady. You need not fear for the hide on my back. 'Tis safe enough from the lash."

" 'He knows and approves'?" she quoted. "Just how much of this scheme did you reveal to your master?"

Sean shrugged innocently. "Why, all of it."

"All?" Jessie asked in dismay.

Sean smiled. "Mr. Fortune has more of a sense of humor than most, Jessie. Especially when the joke, a mild deception that may cost them a valuable plantation, is on Ashbrook Shipping. When I explained the situation, he saw the justice in it. In fact"—he motioned to two people who were sitting on a coil of rope—"he has made a sizeable contribution to seeing that the scheme does not go awry."

The couple, a man about Sean's age and a heavyset woman with tinges of gray in her hair, came forward.

"Matt Webb is to be my personal servant," he said, clapping the man on the shoulder in a familiar manner that made Jessie wonder if they were bondslaves together. "Letitia Mullins is"—he leaned closer to Jessie, with a gleam in his eye and licking his lips—"the cook."

Jessie's mouth gaped. "Not Mr. Fortune's own cook?"

Sean gave a slow satisfied nod. "The very same."

Jessie smiled warmly at the woman. "Madam, I am most glad to have you. I have tasted the wonders you perform and can only wonder at the generosity of Mr. Fortune to let you go even for a week."

Letitia gave a pleased, deep-throated laugh. "He's heard about Josie's cooking. Seems he's mighty fond of this bondslave of his and wants to protect him from it."

"Josie won't be there, Letty. Mrs. Twill would have had to cook," Sean said. "I might have ended up eating worse."

Letty patted Jessie's arm. "No wonder you're so thin. Don't you worry none. I'll make sure you get something decent on the table for you and your folks."

"I also thought it might make your mother and Mr. Pierce more content to stay put if they had an inviting table to look forward to for every meal," Sean said.

Letty and Matt excused themselves and sat down again, looking up the river.

"It seems you've thought a lot about this. Now all I have to do is get rid of Josie and Jackson."

Sean leaned his forearms on the rail. "That's another reason for bringing the *Fortune* upriver. The two of them can sail on her to Williamsburg."

"On the *Fortune?*"

"You said there are things there that you need to send someone to buy. Yard goods for slave clothing newly shipped from England, tools." He shrugged. "Whatever might be needed on a plantation. Things that need a

160

woman's eye as well as a man's. The *Fortune* can take them to Williamsburg and return them at the end of a week."

Jessie nodded, thinking of the list she had made. Most of the things could be obtained in Charles Town, but there were a few things she thought they might have trouble finding. She had had to set aside more money than she had anticipated to send Josie and Jackson to Williamsburg, and now her cash supply was sorely lessened. The necessity for taking out a loan loomed closer, but what choice did she have but to give up and return to Boston?

After the ship was well under sail, the captain, Thomas Reading, introduced himself and entertained them with sea stories during their trip. It was not long before they sighted the rickety dock at the plantation, and Captain Reading's attention was taken up with docking maneuvers.

Matt helped Sean carry some trunks ashore, then the *Fortune* began hoisting sail to leave.

"She has some cargo to load upriver," Sean explained. "She'll be back in the morning to pick up Josie and Jackson, and we can sail back to Charles Town to meet your mother and Mr. Pierce."

Jessie wondered just how much Sean had changed the *Fortune*'s plans and how much they had just happened to fit her needs so conveniently.

She was amazed at the size of Sean's trunk. Along with Matt and Letty's smaller ones and the two servants, the skiff would have indeed been swamped.

"I take it the trunk is another loan from Mr. Fortune?" Jessie asked, noting the Fortune name tooled on the leather straps.

Noting where her gaze fell, Sean fingered one strap. "Ah, uh, yes," he agreed.

"I do hope the clothes inside are yours." She could just see herself trying to explain to her relatives why her husband wore ill-fitting clothes.

"Assuredly, my love," he answered, and she noticed that his eyes had an odd twinkle to them. "Though Mr. Fortune and I are of a similar size."

"I look forward to meeting the legendary and so generous Mr. Fortune."

"You shall, Jessie, you shall. Now, to which room do I take this?"

"The master bedroom, of course. The one where Mr. Twill . . ."

She had no need to go on. Sean nodded, and he and Matt each took up a strap and carried the trunk up the walk and into the house.

Jessie followed them, pausing to tell Josie to find Jackson and for the two of them to see her in her office. Then she went upstairs. The master bedroom had been thoroughly cleaned, the piles of garbage thrown out, the old clothing given to the slaves, the bed linens boiled and aired, and potpourri freshened every corner. It presented a stark contrast to the way she had first seen it. Still, she had not been able to bring herself to move into it but had kept her smaller room down the hall. Now, Sean's presence, and Matt's quiet efficiency, as he opened drawers and doors deciding where to place Sean's things, seemed to banish the last shadow of the former occupant.

"Where are your things, Jessie?" Sean asked, scanning the empty cupboards and drawers.

"Down the hall, in my own room," she answered. Certainly, he didn't think they would actually share a room, did he?

162

Sean winced as if he had been wounded. "Separate bedrooms, my love?" he asked, reaching out to finger the bow at her neckline in a most familiar way.

"I need you to *pretend* to be my husband," she said, pushing his hand away. "I don't think it is necessary to actually . . ."

"It is not the way a man and wife would live who have *consummated* their marriage," he said, reiterating her reason for his role as Jonathan Twill.

He leaned so close to her she felt that there was barely room to breathe; indeed, the room had grown considerably warmer. "But it would seem to everyone that you and I were . . ." She struggled for a word, blushing.

"Intimate?" he supplied.

Her blush deepened.

"Isn't that the whole purpose of this charade?" he asked, his fingers trailing down her throat, pouring molten lava into the center of her being. "To appear as if you and your husband are intimate?"

She gritted her teeth, trying desperately to ignore the smoldering embers just beneath the surface of her reserve. She moved away from him, pulling her cool, New England aloofness about her like a shield. "It's to prove he's *alive*."

"Any man who is alive and your husband would never tolerate separate bedrooms, madam," he told her with conviction, as his gaze traveled over her body piercing her icy reserve and setting the embers within her ablaze. How could she share a room with him for a week and not be seared by that fire?

She turned away from him, bemused, trying to control herself. He moved closer to her, took her gently by the shoulders, and sighing as if fighting a battle within himself, turned her to face him. The fire in his eyes was banked and he spoke reassuringly. "I will sleep on a pallet on the floor, Jessie. We need not share a bed simply because we share a room."

Biting her lip, subduing her own fire, she nodded her head. "I'll have Maybelle move my things." Seeing the quick renewal of the hope in Sean's eye, she hastened to add firmly, "You *will* sleep on your pallet."

After asking Maybelle to move her things to the master bedroom, Jessie headed down the stairs. Maybelle had not approved of her mistress's decision and let her know what she thought in terms only a familiar, longtime acquaintance allowed. That Maybelle still had hopes of catching Sean's eye herself did not escape Jessie. She sighed and headed for her office. Josie and Jackson would be waiting for her by now.

When she entered the room, Mr. Jackson was sprawled in a chair and did not bother to get up, though he eyed her in a way that made her most uncomfortable. She thought she caught a calculating look from Josie, who leaned casually against the desk, but the quadroon dropped her eyes and made a quick curtsey.

Jessie sat down behind her desk, drew out a sheet of paper, and unlocked her cash box, carefully removing the coins she had allotted for their trip.

Briskly writing a list of instructions, referring to the list she had made of the things she needed, she spoke to the two of them.

"I'm sending the two of you to Williamsburg to purchase supplies. You will sail in the morning aboard the *Fortune*," she said.

Jackson sat up, and Jessie saw him glance at Josie. She could have understood a wicked leer at the slave, but his look seemed to be asking her for instructions.

She looked at Josie but the woman had again lowered her eyes.

Jackson stood up, clearing his throat. "This is a bad time to be leaving, Miz Twill," he said, and Jessie felt that he had soiled her name, the way he seemed to smirk as he said it. "The harvest'll be comin' in soon and if I don't break that new gang in, they ain't goin' to be worth dirt."

"I got lots to do, too, Miz Twill," Josie twanged in agreement with the overseer. "Cain't rightly go off and leave you now. Ain't there nobody else can go?"

Jessie sat back in her chair. She had thought they would be thrilled to travel a bit, to have some freedom, to see another town, shop. Any other slave on the place would have jumped at the chance, but Josie seemed even more reluctant to leave than Jackson.

"You two are the best choice. The *Fortune* will dock here tomorrow."

Josie glanced again at Jackson, then launched into another objection. "But what about them pirates?" she wailed. "That's a Fortune ship you be sendin' us on. Ain't many of them as gets out safe nowdays. You want me killed an' . . . an'—" Josie sniffled to a stop.

Jessie was amazed at the extent of the quadroon's knowledge about the shipping in the area. And it was true that more Fortune ships were attacked than any others. But the *Fortune* was small and unimportant, just a coastal trader, and she had to be rid of these two for the next week. "You'll be back here within the week," she assured Josie.

Jessie saw Josie eye Jackson and shrug, and Jackson acquiesced, though growling something about the slaves getting totally out of hand by the time he got back.

Jessie sat forward, stuffed the instructions and the money into an oilskin pouch, and held it out to Jackson. "Mr.

Winthrop will be here to handle things while you're gone."

"A slave takin' care of slaves," Jackson sneered, hefting the pouch and grimacing at its lightness. "I doubt if any work gets done around here in the next week. I can see I'll have to kick a few backsides to get them niggers back in line when I get back."

Without so much as a respectful nod to her, Jackson left and Josie trailed behind him.

"You'll kick no backsides when you get back, Mr. Jackson," Jessie muttered to herself. "If all goes well, you'll be fired as soon as you come back."

"The nerve of that man!"

Jessie looked up to see Maybelle stamping into the room, red-faced with anger, her arms akimbo, her skirts aswirl.

"What man, Maybelle?"

"He actually thinks he knows more about starching a lady's petticoat than I do! Says he'll be glad to share his recipe for starch with me. Says he'll be glad to show me how to organize your wardrobe better. Then he has the audacity to ask me if I'll tell him how I get the shine on your shoes! As if I'd tell him anything!" She crossed her arms and flopped down in the chair Jackson had vacated, and Jessie thought she could actually hear her growl.

"What man, Maybelle?" she repeated, but it was as if her maid had not heard her. She continued to rant on, and Jessie thought she had never heard any sailor run through a man's ancestry quite as thoroughly as Maybelle did. Astounded at her maid's vocabulary, Jessie sat back and chuckled. She had never heard the lustful Maybelle ever speak this way about a man before. Her thoughts had always seemed to run in favor of the masculine half of humanity.

Jessie waited until Maybelle's tirade had run its lengthy course, then calmly asked again, "What man, Maybelle?"

Maybelle sat up in surprise almost as if she hadn't been aware Jessie was there. "Why that insufferable Matthew Webb, of course. Thank goodness we only have to put up with him for a week!" And with that, she flounced out.

So Maybelle had finally met her match, Jessie thought, chuckling. Well, it was about time.

Chapter Nine

With company coming, a decent cook in the place, and a "husband," getting the dining room in order was essential. After her meeting with Jackson and Josie, Jessie spent the rest of the afternoon working on it. With Maybelle and Josie to help, she took down the curtains. One look at their frayed threads and she knew they would never stand a good washing, so they aired them and shook out as much dust as they could. Hopefully, there would be enough money to buy new ones after the harvest.

Jessie instructed Josie to scrub the walls and though the slave worked with a will, she seemed to slop water everywhere, making streaks and splattering the furniture. It was as if she had never cleaned anything in her life, so Jessie told Maybelle to help her. Matt hauled water in and out for them, but all he got for his help from Maybelle was a haughty sniff and an uplifted chin. After conferring with Jackson on what needed to be done in the next week, Sean helped move some of the heavier pieces so they could clean behind them and dragged out the rugs for a good beating, while Jessie rubbed beeswax into the table and buffet until it shone.

At last the room was as ready as they could make it. Josie went to help in the kitchen, and Maybelle left to heat water for Jessie's bath. Jessie silently took inventory. There was no silver, no fine china, not even a decent tablecloth to be found. The rugs were handmade of braided rags and considerably worn. It was as if the house had been ransacked of all its valuables. But it was clean, Jessie thought, and, hopefully, would soon be hers. She ran her fingers over the lustrous tabletop. The furniture was good, though, and took a shine well.

Sean had left an hour before to get some work done outside. He came back in now, sweaty and dirty, strands of his fine black hair sticking to his forehead. He carried a hat and riding crop which he slapped absently against his leg as he strode down the hall, whistling softly to himself.

He looks like the lord of the manor, Jessie thought when she saw him, *totally at home here as if he really does own the place.*

He stopped in the doorway, and nodded his head in approval at their afternoon's work. "Finished right on time," he said. "I came through the kitchen, and Letty is just about ready to serve dinner."

Jessie suddenly realized how late it was and how hungry she was. Thoughts of the sumptuous delicacies that Letty was capable of made her head swim.

Sean put an arm around her waist, drawing her close. "Is that dreamy look of anticipation for me?" he asked.

She pushed against his chest, hard and strong beneath her touch, resisting the impulse to let him hold her. "'Tis for the food Letty is preparing," she corrected him.

In mock thespian tones, he misquoted, "Ah, that I were a bean upon that plate that I might touch those lips!"

Jessie giggled, moving out of his embrace with the lightness of a dancer. "I hope your acting improves or we'll fool no one this next week."

Sean looked completely crestfallen. "Spurned! Both as a man and an actor!"

"Surely not!" Jessie answered. "I am in sore need of a husband this week."

"I am most willing to play the part in full, my lady," Sean said, his eyes alight, as he reached for her again.

Laughing, Jessie eluded him. "You are too willing by far, sir. A little less will and a little better acting is what I desire!"

Brushing by him, skipping out of range of his reaching hands, she ran up the stairs.

For a moment Sean stood looking up after her. "'Tis not all I desire!"

Jessie had not dressed formally for dinner, but she had donned one of her better dresses. When she came into the dining room, Sean was already there. He turned at her entrance, and his eyes raked her appreciatively. Darkness had fallen and only candle glow lighted his face, bronzing his skin with lush life, pulsing, flickering, a reflection of the strong pulse within her that throbbed faster and faster with each moment that she gazed at him.

His shirt was open at the throat, a simple, cotton workshirt as he always wore, clean and smelling of sunshine. It did not cling damply to his muscled form as his shirt had that afternoon, but she knew every curve of flesh and sinew and bone that hid beneath that cloth was as hard as steel, as smooth as satin. And with great difficulty, she tore her eyes away.

Sean came toward her, graceful as a fencing master, and held out his arm for her as elegantly as any gentleman of her acquaintance. As usual, his sleeves were rolled up, and she tried to still the trembling in her fingers when they touched his bare forearm, feeling his strength, his hardness.

"You are lovely tonight, Mrs. Twill," he murmured near her ear.

She winced at the sound of her married name. For some reason she hated the sound of it from his lips. "Jessie," she corrected.

His brow cocked askance, and his mouth twisted in amusement. "Is the bondslave at last permitted the use of your Christian name?"

"Not a bondslave," she said, reminding him of their roles for the coming week. "You are my husband."

As he held her chair for her and seated her, he bent down, closer than was necessary, his lips brushing her hair, his fingers lightly caressing her arm. "Am I?"

I thought you were once. The thought flitted unbidden and unwelcome through her mind, pulling another behind, one she thought well buried—*I wish it had been you.*

She pulled her napkin from its ring and clutched it tightly in her lap. It had been cut from an old sheet, she noticed, and not yet hemmed. But it matched the tablecloth which was a clean sheet. Two places had been set at the table with the crockery from the kitchen, and candles were positioned in the center in pewter holders.

Sean sat at the head of the table, his gaze tangled in hers, when Josie entered carrying a tray. She kicked the door out of her way and set the tray on the buffet with a clatter. Taking up two steaming bowls, she nearly succeeded in dumping the soup she was serving into Jessie's lap. Jessie steadied the bowl, then watched as the slave merely turned to serve Sean instead of serving from the proper side.

Taking the edge of her apron, Josie mopped up a few drops of spilled soup, then turned to bring a basket of hot rolls which she plopped down on the corner of the table. She shoved them into the center of the table, wrinkling the cloth. Dusting her hands, she picked up the tray, and banging it absently against her leg, she left the room without a dismissal, a curtsey, or a "Will there be anything else?" And she had forgotten to pour the wine. Thank goodness it would be Maybelle and not Josie who would be serving at the table next week, Jessie thought.

Sean seemed amused rather than annoyed at Josie's inadequacies, and Jessie couldn't help seeing the humor in the slave's behavior.

"She doesn't know how to clean," Sean said, referring to that afternoon, with a wry twist to his features, "she doesn't know how to serve, and she certainly can't cook. What did she do around here?"

Jessie remembered Josie's fine silk chemise, the gold hoop earrings, and the gold bangles. It was not hard to guess what her work had been. "I'll have to give her some training when she comes back," was all she said.

Sean got up to pour the wine himself. As the rose liquid splashed into her glass, she was reminded of the first time she and Sean had shared a glass of wine. There had been no candlelight that night, only the radiance of the moon streaming in from the French windows. From where she was sitting, she could see into the parlor, see the sofa where . . . She tore her eyes away, forcing a smile to her lips.

"The candlelight becomes you, Jessie," Sean said, and she thought she caught a slight emphasis on the word "candlelight." Was he also remembering that night? Was he hoping for a repeat of it? Of course he would be, she thought, biting hard into a roll. Why else had he agreed to this charade? Hadn't he told her that paying off a year of his indenture weighed less with him than "other inducements?" Perhaps there was more scoundrel to him than met the eye.

She watched as he ate a spoonful of soup, buttered his roll, and bit into it with strong teeth. If she didn't know better, if he were dressed better, it would be easy to think Sean was the gentleman he mocked so well. As Mrs. Walker had said, Sean had the manners of a duke when he chose to use them.

She had to admit there were gentlemen aplenty with few enough coins in their purses who could afford to dress no better than Sean. And she would rather have a poorly dressed gentleman than a well-clad scoundrel at her table. But what was Sean? Anyone could learn fine manners, she thought. But Sean's manners seemed a part of him, as natural to him as breathing. He was not merely a poorly dressed gentleman, yet it was hard to believe he was really a convicted felon. He didn't seem to fit either role. Nothing about him seemed to fit just right. There had to be more to Sean. She could only hope that he would fit his role this next week well enough to fool Samuel Pierce.

Sean took up his wineglass and sipped from it, studying her over its rim. The flame from the candle flickered on his face, highlighting the fine cast of his nose, the deepness of his eyes, the strength of his jaw. It glistened on his wine-wet mouth, and reflected in his eyes, joining the flame that already leaped there when he looked at her.

She could not help but be warmed by the flame in his eyes. The soup that a moment before had delighted her tongue was now tasteless in her mouth. *There are other delights to taste,* her senses shouted at her as she watched Sean lick a last drop of wine from his lips.

Jessie was wrenched from her thoughts by a returning Josie clattering through the door with her tray. She again thumped the tray down on the buffet and carried two plates to the table.

"Y'all done?" she asked. Without waiting for an answer, she set down one plate, using it to shove Jessie's still half-full bowl out of the way and placing the plate before her. She plopped down Sean's plate the same way. Eyeing the soup bowls doubtfully, she said, "I guess I'll just leave 'em in case y'all want to finish." Then she picked up her tray and, humming in a self-satisfied way, sashayed out of the room.

Jessie was caught between a laugh and a groan.

"You do have your work cut out for you," Sean commented, chuckling.

Jessie nodded in agreement, then her attention was caught by the food on her plate. There were succulent pieces of tender chicken in a white sauce over rice, peas, and slices of spiced peach. "Josie has met her match," Jessie said, savoring a mouthful. "How could Mr. Fortune give up Letty for a whole week?"

Sean smiled. "I suppose he didn't want his favorite bondslave dying of food poisoning."

Jessie looked askance at the cocksure man beside her. "He must be awfully fond of you to give up such fine dining for a week."

A look of wry amusement, barely hidden, passed over Sean's fine features. "I assure you, my lady, Mr. Fortune dines as well tonight as I do."

"Nevertheless," she said, "I shall have to thank him for his generosity when I meet him."

"Actually, he had an ulterior motive in sending Letty along," Sean said seriously.

Jessie looked up questioningly as she picked up her wineglass.

Sean leaned over conspiratorily. "He was hoping to discover Josie's secret recipe for beans."

Nearly choking on her last sip of wine, Jessie quickly set her glass down and pressed her napkin to her lips as she laughed.

Sean took her glass, filled it, and held it out to her. He was still smiling at his joke, but the look in his eyes shook the laughter from her, filling her with a warmth that made her fingers tremble as she reached out to take her glass. His fingers brushed hers, and the shock of his touch nearly caused her to drop the glass. But she steadied herself and looked down into the wine, refusing to become entangled in his spellbinding gaze again. She drank and began to chatter, while she ate, about the weather, the crops, the cleaning yet to be done, the excellence of Mr. Fortune's cook. Anything to fill the space between them, to enlarge that space, using it as a buffer to keep the kindling flames within them apart.

Sean ate slowly, contributing an occasional comment, continuing to look at her as if it were she he hungered for.

How will I ever make it through the next week, she wondered to herself, *sleeping in the same room with him, when his mere gaze can melt me into a shameless puddle of desire?*

Maybelle put the finishing touches to Jessie's hair which glistened in the bright morning sunlight streaming through the window.

"I still think this is all a mistake," Maybelle grumbled. "Sleeping in the same room with Mr. Winthrop and not even married to him."

Jessie sighed. For a woman who twitched her skirts at every man who crossed her path, Maybelle could be paradoxically moral when it came to Jessie's welfare.

"I didn't sleep in the same room with him," she said.

"But you will tonight. And every night for a week. What will people think?" She shoved the last pin into place with a little too much vigor.

"They will think we are married," Jessie said, wincing. "Which is exactly what we want them to think."

"Having that no-good man around here for a week!" Maybelle muttered.

Jessie looked at her maid in surprise. Was it jealousy causing Maybelle's angry mood? She had certainly flirted enough with Sean that first day. "I thought you liked Sean?"

"Sean?" Maybelle seemed confused for a moment. "Oh, Mr. Winthrop! I don't mean Mr. Winthrop. He's fine. It's that man of his. That Matthew Webb!"

To hide her smile, Jessie bent to close her valise. Unconsciously, Maybelle spoke of Sean as if he were indeed the master here and was now far removed from her consideration. If Sean fit into his role so well that he could even convince someone who knew better, maybe their scheme would work after all.

"What has Matt done, Maybelle?" Jessie asked.

"What has he done?" Maybelle drew herself up indignantly, her brown curls jiggling about her narrow face. "Why, he tried to kiss me!"

Jessie could barely restrain her laughter. Maybelle insulted by a kiss? She shook her head. It was beyond her why her maid would take exception to Matt Webb. The man seemed quiet and efficient and was young and pleasant-looking. Maybe it was because the man tried to kiss her and Maybelle preferred to do the chasing!

"Try to put up with him, Maybelle," Jessie told her. "The week will be gone before you know it and they will both be gone."

"Hmph!" Maybelle snorted as if that day could not come soon enough, but Jessie felt a pang when she thought of never seeing Sean again.

Maybelle grabbed Jessie's shawl and put it around her shoulders. "You better get going, Miss Jessie. I saw the *Fortune* coming in just when I came up."

Jessie nodded, knotting her shawl and picking up her valise. "You'll take care of things here?" she asked, indicating the room. Maybelle had already moved most of her things into the master bedroom, and only a few of her personal things remained.

Maybelle nodded, a disapproving pucker souring her face. "If that insufferable man has left any room for your things!"

Jessie was sure that Maybelle had to be exaggerating. Sean could not possibly have that many clothes. She was simply finding fault with the other servant. Hastily, she gave Maybelle a quick hug and hurried down the stairs and outside.

At the top of the walk, Jessie paused to look down at the *Fortune* riding in jaunty contrast to the rickety dock. She could see a sullen Josie already aboard, sitting on a coil of rope. Jackson lounged nearby against a mast. Captain Reading stood on the dock, talking to a tall well-dressed man. Sean was nowhere in sight, but she was sure he would not be long and Jessie started down the walk, wondering who was talking with the captain. He had his back to her and had on a large tricorn so she could see little of him, but he seemed vaguely familiar. Even from this distance, she could tell that the man's clothes were of superb cut, fitting smoothly over his broad shoulders. His hands were clasped behind his back, and as Jessie came closer, she could see that the spotless ruffles at his cuffs were edged with a fine, narrow lace. Fine attire indeed for an early Tuesday morning. Was this some successful upriver plantation owner whom the *Fortune* had picked up to take into Charles Town?

Captain Reading smiled at her as she stepped onto the dock. As the captain tipped his hat, the strange man turned. In one quick glance, she noted that the man wore his own

177

unpowdered hair cropped short. Black straight hair. And blue eyes that gleamed in an unmistakable, unforgettable way when they saw her.

"Sean!"

"Good morning, my lady," he said, sweeping his tricorn off his head and into an elegant, well-accomplished bow.

Excusing himself, Captain Reading went aboard his ship and started giving orders to get ready to sail.

Jessie could only stare at the bondsman before her. From the gathered lace at his throat to the silver buckles on his shoes, Sean was the perfect picture of a well-to-do gentleman. No one would ever guess now that he was a indentured felon. Yet she could not believe that a bondslave could possibly afford such finery. Not sure she could believe her eyes, Jessie reached out to finger the fine fabric of his coat, noting the vest richly embroidered with silver threads.

Remembering Sean had said that he and his master were the same size, she asked incredulously, "These clothes, Sean, surely your master wouldn't loan you his clothes. You didn't—"

"Nay, madam, the clothes are mine," he assured her with amusement. "Honestly bought. I take it you find them adequate for our charade?"

The clothes he wore were by no means cheap. Surely he must have the equivalent of a year's indenture on his back. Why the fool had bought such expensive clothes instead of paying off his indenture was more than she could understand. He had told her that his bondage did not weigh heavily upon him, but surely a man would prefer his freedom to clothes, wouldn't he? Had she misjudged Sean? Was he so frivolous that he gave no thought to using his money more wisely than this?

"More than adequate, I should think!" she snapped, her disappointment in his character voicing itself as annoyance.

Her hand was still on his chest, and she jerked it away as if to prevent any further feeling between them. But he caught her hand in his, brought her fingers to his lips and, in a light assault to her senses, briefly kissed them. "Then, madam, shall we go aboard? The captain is ready to sail."

All the way down river, Jessie alternated between annoyance at what she saw as a serious flaw in Sean's character and trying to fit it to what she knew of him. Until now, she had not seen him in anything but his simple work clothes. He had not seemed to give a care to what he wore, except that he was always scrupulously clean. Whether fixing a privy or talking to her neighbor, Jason Soames, it was his air of self-worth rather than what he put on his back that had seemed more important to him. Even now, watching him, he did not seem overly concerned about his clothes. He did not seem awkward in his splendid outfit, but wore it with the same casual indifference with which he wore his work clothes, as if he were as used to one kind as he was to the other. She shook her head. It was another piece of the puzzle that just did not fit.

The *Fortune* was much faster than Sean's little skiff, and it was not long before they were docking in Charles Town. The little sloop stopped only long enough to set Jessie and Sean ashore, then cast off again, carrying Josie and Jackson away for the next week.

Sean guided her through the bustle of the dock, and they walked the short distance to the Walkers' where they would await the arrival of the *Harper* which was bringing her mother and Mr. Pierce.

Mrs. Walker was waiting for them, leaning on her cane, one arm outstretched in greeting.

"Jessie! Sean!" She hugged them each in turn and urged them inside where Mr. Walker awaited them. Sean took the older man's hand and shook it.

"Don't you look fine, Sean!" Mrs. Walker said, sitting down by the tea service. She poured a cupful and held it out to Jessie. "Doesn't he look wonderful, Jessie?"

Jessie took the cup, turning her eyes toward the tall bondsman. He stood by the fireplace, his tricorn held beneath one arm, smiling down at her. Mrs. Walker had always welcomed Sean in her home, but with his fine apparel, he no longer looked out of place. His coat hung open, and the form-fitting vest emphasized the breadth of his chest, the slimness of his hips. Close-fitting breeches met smooth, silk stockings, both of which showed off the trimness of his well-muscled legs. Jessie swallowed some of the scalding tea. *Yes, he looks wonderful,* she thought. *Natural and as at ease as any lord.*

Sean sat down across from her, accepting a cup from Mrs. Walker, and the talk turned to plans for entertaining their expected guests. Not least in all of their thoughts and their conversation was how to keep the Pierces from finding out that Jonathan Twill was dead, replaced for the week by an impostor.

Not more than an hour had gone by before a boy rapped on the door bringing the message that the *Harper* had been sighted and would be docking soon.

Since Sean had often worked at the docks and was well known there, they thought it best that he stay with Mrs. Walker. Mr. Walker would accompany Jessie to the dock to meet her mother and the head of Ashbrook Shipping.

"Are you sure you're up to the walk?" Jessie asked the older man as they stepped into the hot sunlight.

Mr. Walker chuckled. "I need the exercise. If it were up to Lucy, I would still be tucked into bed with her spooning thin gruel into me."

By the time they reached the dock, the *Harper* was just putting out her gangplank. Jessie could see the stern visage of Mr. Pierce, his gaze running over the cargo piled on the dock as if already calculating its worth. Then she saw her mother, clinging with white knuckles onto the railing with a stoic smile on her pale features. Spotting Jessie, she bravely let go of the railing with one hand to wave a kerchief at her daughter.

Jessie returned the wave, glad to see a member of her family again. As her mother came to the head of the gangplank, Jessie could see that her chalk-white face was tinged with green, evidence that her mother was still the poorest of sailors. She had to appreciate the strength of will it had taken for her mother to make this voyage as much as she hated sailing. It gave her more than a twinge of guilt to think how she would be deceiving her mother this week.

Shakily, Mrs. Pierce made her way to the dock, her arm held by her husband, though he seemed to have little patience with his wife's frailties.

Jessie embraced her mother, bending to her shorter stature, and kissing her cheek.

"Oh, my dear!" Mrs. Pierce fluttered. "I thought I'd never have solid ground beneath me again!"

Bobbing a curtsey to her stepfather, Jessie inquired politely, "How was your voyage, sir?"

"Fine," he replied curtly, nodding to Mr. Walker.

"Fine! My darling Jessie, it was terrible!" Mrs. Pierce wailed. "Nothing but high wind and rocking the whole trip!"

"You are safe at last, my dear lady," Mr. Walker assured her, bending over her hand with a gallant bow.

181

Jessie hid a smile. She knew that if there was any kick at all to the sea, her mother would consider it a veritable gale.

"Shall we go?" Mr. Walker asked, indicating the way with a wave of his hand. "You'll stay with Lucy and me tonight, of course, and go on to Jessie's plantation tomorrow. Knowing how you hate to sail, I've arranged for wagons to take you. They'll load your things from the ship and be ready to leave early in the morning."

"I had hoped to visit the office before going out to the plantation," Mr. Pierce said. "I would like to take a look at things while I'm here."

They began to walk, Mr. Pierce and Mr. Walker in front, with Jessie and her mother arm in arm behind. "I was sure you would," Mr. Walker said. "But most of the account books and records are at my house. I've been ill and have been doing most of my work at home, you see."

"Nothing serious, I hope!" Jessie's mother exclaimed.

"Just a bit of fever, ma'am. I'm well over it now."

Jessie started to protest that his illness was more serious than that, but decided that it would be best not to alert her mother to the dangers of disease here in Charles Town. She wanted to give her no excuse for demanding that Jessie return to a safer clime.

"I thought your husband would be meeting us, Jessie." Her mother wore a polite, inquiring smile, but Jessie could see the real concern behind it. She knew her mother was worried about the kind of husband he was, and Jessie appreciated her concern.

"He stayed to keep Mrs. Walker company." She smiled reassuringly and patted her mother's hand. "We're almost there." She pointed to the white-painted house just ahead.

Her mother nodded, but Jessie noted that the worried creases did not lessen. Guilt again pricked Jessie at this sign of her mother's deep care. But even though Jessie knew what Sean really was, she was counting on the fact that his manners and dress were fine enough to reassure the most worried of mothers.

Mrs. Walker was at the front door to greet them, ushering them into the parlor where Sean stood awaiting them. Jessie's mother voiced her approval at her first sight of "Jonathan Twill" by a sharply indrawn breath and a quickly exhaled, "Oh my!"

Jessie had to admit that Sean made a wonderful impression. Dressed as he was, she could find no flaw to mar the perfection of his form. The deep blue of his coat emphasized the color of his eyes, and the white ruffles at his throat and wrists contrasted with his deep tan. It was plain that there was no padding necessary to his coat. The excellent cut of the garment lay smoothly over his naturally broad shoulders and tapered to his slim hips. The muscles of his legs were barely concealed beneath the trim fit of his breeches.

When Sean bent over Mrs. Pierce's hand, she actually giggled like a schoolgirl. At Sean's polite greeting, Jessie could see the tension ebb from her mother, and Mrs. Pierce looked at her daughter with relief and a nod of approval.

Mr. Pierce greeted Sean coolly, not offering his hand and eyeing him suspiciously. And though Sean smiled and gave a little bow, Jessie knew him well enough to recognize his restrained greeting. Not understanding the tension between the two men but wishing to ease it, Jessie stepped between them, smiling.

Remembering to call Sean "Jonathan," she said, "Jonathan has had some experience sailing."

"Yes," Sean said, taking up her cue and sliding his arm around her waist. "Jessie and I have had some nice outings in a skiff on the river."

Jessie tried to ignore the way his hand continued to caress her waist. She forced a smile to her lips and tread warningly on Sean's toe.

"Jessie always did love to sail," Mrs. Pierce said, "though I prefer other modes of travel myself."

"I would say that is an understatement, Mother." Jessie laughed. "Not only have you always detested sailing, it seems not to like you, either. I seem to recall a definite tinge of green on your face when you landed today, which is entirely gone now."

Ignoring her warning tread, Sean pulled Jessie closer as any loving husband might. "I'm glad Jessie likes to sail. It has always been one of the delights of my life."

There was warm sincerity in his words making Jessie wonder just what he was remembering. Was it those sailing lessons with his father? Or had he gone aroving with his pirate father and longed for the buccaneering freedom of the high seas?

His hand had made its way up to caress the slope of her bare shoulder, sending chills through her. She glared at him and would have pushed his hand away but dared not in front of Mr. Pierce and her mother. They must appear in every way to be contentedly married, but did this bold bondslave have to take advantage of the situation? She could only smile and occasionally get in a sharp prod to his ribs which he blithely ignored, but she would be sure to take him to task for his behavior later.

They all exchanged pleasantries for a few minutes longer, then were called in to dinner.

The first course was served, and the talk naturally turned to shipping.

"So I think the Charles Town office will show a profit this year," Mr. Walker said, concluding a rather long speech.

"Fortune Shipping has not been quite so fortunate of late," Sean put in. "Pirates have taken their toll."

"Pirates!" Mrs. Pierce exclaimed, letting her soup spoon clatter into her bowl, her light blue eyes becoming round and fearful. "You mean there is actual danger?"

"Now, Mama," Jessie soothed, giving Sean a scolding glare for bringing up the subject. "There's no reason for you to worry."

"But if there are *pirates*!" Mrs. Pierce quavered.

"Jessie is right, Mrs. Pierce," Sean assured her. "Ashbrook Shipping seems to suffer the least from these brigands." He looked at Mr. Pierce. "Perhaps you could tell us why."

His voice was pleasant, inquiring, but Jessie caught a thread of tension beneath his words, as if he were throwing out a challenge to her stepfather.

"Perhaps our captains are more skilled and can more easily elude the cutthroats." Mr. Pierce smiled at Sean, but the smile did not reach his eyes. "What other reason could there possibly be?"

Jessie didn't understand why, but her stepfather's words seemed to carry even more of a challenge in them.

Mr. Walker laughed to ease the tension, and jokingly said, "Perhaps the pirates mistake the black-and-white banner of Ashbrook Shipping for one of their own."

Sean smiled, but his look at Mr. Pierce was more suggestive than pleasant. "You may not be far off the mark, Mr. Walker."

Mr. Pierce merely laughed. "Then perhaps Mr. Fortune would be wise to fly the Ashbrook flag on his masts. If he keeps losing ships, he will soon be forced to sell out to us, anyway."

"I doubt that Mr. Fortune will give in so easily as that, Mr. Pierce," Sean said amiably. "I doubt it very much."

Mr. Pierce merely arched a haughty brow and sipped his wine.

No more was said of pirates, and Jessie managed to distract her mother by suggesting an outing to see the shops in town. There was nothing Mrs. Pierce liked more than to browse, and she and Jessie were soon on their way with Sean as their escort. Her stepfather and Mr. Walker planned to spend the rest of the afternoon talking business and going over the books.

Mrs. Pierce bought several lengths of material for dresses for herself and Jessie's two younger sisters, and talked of Sarah's possible betrothal to her long-standing sweetheart. Abby, Jessie's youngest sister, could still not choose between several beaux, though Mrs. Pierce was hoping she would soon settle on one of them. Mrs. Pierce filled Jessie in on the rest of the gossip, and Jessie listened politely, surprising even herself at how little she had missed Boston.

Jessie fingered a few of the fabrics but made no purchases, though she eyed a set of china longingly. There just wasn't enough money to waste right now.

Jessie was aware that Sean watched her and her mother and that he did very little shopping himself. But between shops, he would pull her arm through his and handle her with an easy familiarity that made Jessie definitely uneasy because she enjoyed his touch too much. She would definitely have to speak with Sean tonight when they were alone.

That evening after supper Mrs. Pierce suggested another walk to see what sights Charles Town held besides shops. Mrs. Walker stayed at home, but the rest of them took a long stroll. Mr. Walker pointed out the bastions that protected the town along with the various meeting houses, the Presbyterian, the Quaker, and the Anabaptist.

When they returned, Mrs. Pierce said she would retire, and everyone agreed that it had been a long day.

Mrs. Walker directed her guests to their rooms, stopping Jessie at the bottom of the stairs with a look that asked if she were sure she wanted to go through with her plan. "Your room is the one you had before, Jessie," she said, watching Mr. and Mrs. Pierce go up the stairs.

Jessie bent to kiss Mrs. Walker on the cheek, and whispered softly so that her mother could not hear but making sure Sean, standing beside her, could. "I'm sure Sean will be a perfect gentleman, Mrs. Walker."

Mrs. Walker gave Sean a warning glance. "Yes, I'm sure he will be."

Sean could not keep the amusement from his eyes as he looked down at the two women. "I shall be the model of gentlemanly comportment," he said, bending over Mrs. Walker's hand. Then he turned to follow Jessie up the stairs to their room, his hand riding familiarly on the small of her back.

Chapter Ten

At the top of the steps, Jessie paused with her hand on the latch of her door to nod a last good night to her mother who was further down the hall. Her mother's gaze shifted from Jessie to Sean and back to Jessie. It was a happy gaze, assured. Jessie was acutely aware of Sean's hand where it touched her in a possessive, husbandly manner, and knew that this sign of affection assured her mother that her daughter's marriage was a good one. For that reason, she did not throw off his hand but stood casually for a moment as if accustomed to his touch.

But she was not accustomed to Sean's touch. No matter how slight, how fleeting, she knew she would never become accustomed to the searing warmth that his touch sent through her. Never take for granted the havoc one brief contact with this man made of her senses, her nerves, her coherent thoughts.

She entered the room, the same she had used on her arrival in Charles Town, the same room she had stood in so awkwardly before, directing a handsome bondslave where to put her trunk. His presence had been disturbing then. Now, feeling him enter behind her, hearing him close the door, she felt an even deeper awkwardness. This time he would not be leaving.

She looked about the room. The bedcovers were turned back invitingly, but an extra pillow and comforter had been placed pointedly, it seemed to her, on a long narrow settee beneath the window.

Sean also noticed them, and she heard the low rumble of his chuckle. "Mrs. Walker has provided for my comfort, I see."

She half expected him to add that he would be far more comfortable sharing the bed, but to her relief he didn't. The last time she was in this room alone with Sean, she had imagined him sweeping her into a husbandly embrace. It was something she could imagine even easier now.

He shrugged out of his coat and folded it over a chair back. Panicking, she cast her eyes around the room. Her nightdress, the most modest one she owned, lay across the foot of the bed, but there was nowhere to change. There was no adjoining changing room, no shielding screen, not even a high piece of furniture to duck behind.

Sean turned to her, loosening his cravat. The full, loose sleeves of his fine cambric shirt contrasted to the trim fit of the waistcoat which superbly molded itself to his lean torso. The lace gathered at his wrists did not detract from the strength of his sun-browned hands as his fingers worked at the silver buttons of his waistcoat.

Daily she had seen Sean in less than he wore now; indeed, she had once seen him in far less. But the intimacy of watching him undress shattered her reserve, and she turned away to finger a book on a table by the bed. It was a well-thumbed

Bible. Had it so been put there purposely to remind them that they were not wed?

"The hour is late, Jessie. 'Tis time to be abed."

Her nerves already atwitter, Sean's voice startled her, causing her to send the Bible tumbling to the floor. Gasping, she reached for it and her fingers met his. She jerked her hand away as if burned.

Glancing at the open pages he held, Sean's lips spread into a slow smile as he handed the open book to her. She could not help but notice the passage. "By night on my bed I sought him whom my soul loveth: I sought him, but I found him not."

Reddening, she slammed the Bible shut, jerking her hand away from his. Had he seen that passage? Was that why he was smiling at her? Silently, she gritted her teeth. It was probably a coincidence. Probably the lout couldn't even read.

"You can keep your hands to yourself, Mr. Winthrop!" she said rather more sharply than she had intended.

He cocked a brow at her. "I merely returned the book, Mrs. Twill," he said as formally as if they had just met in a fashionable salon. But somehow his coolness only served to fluster her more.

It was not that casual, though devastating, brushing of fingers just now that she meant but the evening full of caresses. The touch of his hand at her waist, his hand clasping hers, the familiar brushing of her cheek, shoulder, and arm. Shattering touches scattered over the hours of the afternoon and evening but accumulating along her heightened nerves until she feared that even one more such nonchalant touch would shatter forever her Puritan-based wall of defensive reserve. She had meant to speak to him about his familiarity with her that evening, and there was no better time than now. Now when she needed so desperately to rebuild her protective shield.

"I did not mean here and now in this room. I mean when we are in company!"

A smile flirted briefly with his lips, "Meaning that it is all right for me to touch you when we are alone?" His smile was then unleashed and spread into a happy leer as he reached for her.

"Certainly not!" she snapped, backing away.

But she was trapped with the bed and the table forming a corner holding her in. She lifted her chin proudly. His mere closeness set her trembling, her breasts tingling with anticipation. She had to keep him from her or she would be in his arms, a willing accomplice to her own seduction.

"Didn't you promise Mrs. Walker that you would behave like a gentleman?"

He made a mockery of being deflated. "So I did." He grinned wryly at her, though his gaze still raked her hungrily. "Though how so many little ladies and gentlemen, as I said before, get born is a marvel to me if gentlemen are put off this easily!"

Chortling, he moved away from her. Her weakened knees forced her to sink onto the edge of the bed. She heard him moving about, removing the rest of his clothing. By the time she had gathered her scattered defenses and turned around, he had rolled himself in the coverlet Mrs. Walker had provided and lay with his back to the room. Thankfully, she quickly undressed, put on her nightgown, and slipped into bed, putting out the last candle on her way.

The sweetly acrid scent of the extinguished flame wafted about her in the darkness. There was no moonlight tonight. She stiffened when she heard a rustle from the settee, but Sean was only shifting position. She tried to relax her body, tense with longing, and frustration. How would she survive a whole week of this?

*   *   *

Her mother's shocked face mirrored the dismay Jessie had felt the first time she had seen the plantation house. When Sean handed Mrs. Pierce down from the wagon seat, she came to Jessie and put an arm around her, comforting and supporting without saying a word. Jessie accepted her support and hugged her mother reassuringly, returning comfort of her own. But her mother's dismay gave Jessie hope. If the plantation seemed so bad, so unprofitable, perhaps her stepfather would be all too glad to sign it over and be rid of it.

They had gotten a late start that morning, and it was already late afternoon. Letty was setting out tea and refreshments on the veranda overlooking the river, so Jessie led them out there. The four of them sat beneath the trees and had their tea; then Jessie took her mother on a tour of the house while Sean showed her stepfather around.

At last she showed her mother to her room. Mrs. Pierce sat on a rocker and removed her shoes, rubbing her feet in relief, her face creased in thought. Jessie bustled around, opening her mother's trunks which had not yet been unpacked, taking out a robe, a brush.

"Jessie, are you sure you're happy here?" Mrs. Pierce asked.

Jessie stopped what she was doing to kneel at her mother's feet and to lean into her lap.

"Of course, Mother. Why shouldn't I be?"

Mrs. Pierce looked around at the shabbiness, the peeling, faded wallpaper, the threadbare rug, poorly made to begin with, the sparseness of the furnishings. "It's just that . . ." She faltered as her hands fluttered in a gesture of bewilderment at her surroundings.

"That there is so much to do?" Jessie asked. "But that will be the fun part. Building this into what *I* want. Making it wholly mine."

"But to start with so little, to have to build so much!"

"Others have started with far less, Mother."

Mrs. Pierce smiled a little sad smile and caressed Jessie's hair. "At least you have your husband to help you," she said. "Jonathan seems like a wonderful man." The tears of relief that had been threatening ever since she had first seen Sean leaning so tall and magnificent against Mrs. Walker's mantle glistened in her eyes. "You are happy with him, aren't you?"

Jessie laid her head on her mother's lap wishing she could confide in her, longing to cry, to feel the comfort of her mother's arms. But she had to smile, to reassure her mother that all was as it seemed. "I'm happy, Mother."

That evening Jessie had dallied in her bath in the little cubicle that adjoined the master bedroom. She had heard Sean dressing in there, his deep voice interspersed with the quiet voice of Matt Webb, his "servant." Sean had left, and then she had heard a sharp altercation between Matt and Maybelle. The exact nature of the quarrel was unclear, muffled as it was by the heavy door, but that Maybelle had emerged second best was clear from the expression on her face as she came into the tiny room to help Jessie dress.

As Maybelle assisted her, an unceasing string of muttered threats and dire warnings directed at the hapless and thankfully absent valet fell from her lips. Jessie shook her head, again astounded that Sean's valet could upset her maid so much. *So,* Jessie thought, *the indomitable Maybelle has at last met a man strong enough to stand up to her*. She smiled at the thought.

Ready at last, Jessie went down to the parlor. Her mother and stepfather were seated, sipping an aperitif. Sean was standing by the French doors and looked up when he saw her enter. She caught her breath. She had almost expected Sean to be dressed in his simple garb, saving his one good outfit. Yet the clothes he wore were anything but simple. A deep burgundy coat, expertly tailored, fit smoothly over a snug-fitting waistcoat intricately embroidered with gold thread. Breeches of dark cream to match the waistcoat fit to perfection over the smooth muscles of his thighs. Gold buckles on shoes dyed burgundy to match his coat shone softly. Elegant lace frothed at his wrists and throat, in itself an expense beyond most journeymen. Altogether, Sean's outfit was within the means of only a wealthy few. But this bondslave wore it with a casual nonchalance.

While she wondered again why he did not spend his money to purchase his freedom, she could not but admire the lean length of him. Splendid even in his work clothes, tonight there was no flaw to be found in him. She doubted that he would have been refused admittance to court.

He came toward her, stepping with that easy grace she had often admired, the deep blue of his eyes growing warm as they traveled the length of her.

"How like a pair we look tonight, my love," he murmured as he lifted her hand to his lips.

Blushing, she realized how planned their outfits looked, how husbandly and wifely contrived, for unknowingly she had chosen a gown of burgundy silk trimmed with cream lace. The brush of his lips on her fingers entwined with the whispered endearment and the warm desire shining in his eyes caught at her heart. She had to remind herself that they were but playacting for the benefit of her mother and Mr. Pierce.

"You look very elegant, my dear," Jessie said, tossing him an endearment of her own but in a tone that clearly told him it was not for his ears she said it.

He led her to a place on the sofa, earning a hard glare for his caress to her waist which strayed a bit too far and lingered a bit too long. But he ignored her reproving eyes, for he was drunk with her mere presence. Her low-cut gown framed her rounded breasts in a lace as creamy white as her skin. They rose, seeming to invite his touch and his fingers tingled with anticipation. They were as tempting as food to a starving man and his mouth hungered to taste their sweetness again.

He dragged his gaze away, trying to harden himself against the onslaught of her beauty, her sweetness, all the fascinating facets of her that entrapped him. He smiled wryly to himself as he sat down next to her. There was only one thing about him that was hardening—and that was not his resolve.

Jessie and her mother were chatting about redecorating the parlor. Mrs. Pierce was going on about how delightful a mauve print wallpaper would look with darker drapes while Jessie was holding out for painted white walls and more formal blue drapes. Sean looked askance at the parlor, shuddering to think of it decked out in mauve, but it was an argument he planned to stay well out of.

He leaned back, listening, unconsciously letting his fingers stray along the soft curve of Jessie's neck. It was a husbandly gesture that was not lost on Mrs. Pierce but which sent waves of distracting pleasure coursing through Jessie. She told herself that it was only because of her mother that she did not throw off his hand and give Sean a severe scolding.

Finally Maybelle announced that dinner was ready and Sean rose, taking Jessie by the hand and drawing her arm through his so closely that she could feel the warmth of his body next to hers and smell the freshness of his sun-dried shirt. She looked at him and could almost taste his lips on hers. Why did her mind continue to wander along such paths? Swallowing hard, she tried to ignore the assault to her senses and gave him a hard jab in the ribs.

He only smiled at her and led her into the dining room. He held her chair for her, and took the opportunity to enjoy a most luscious view of her bosom. A light lilac fragrance, mingling with the clean-washed scent of her, swirled up to him, and it was with a slight headiness that he took his seat at the head of the table.

A clean white sheet again served as a tablecloth and the best of the kitchen crockery was arranged at each place. Four pieces of cut stemware had been added from the liquor cabinet, and Sean noticed that the rim of his was chipped. But the center of the table was so overflowing with flowers, so artfully arranged, that one tended not to notice the inadequacies of the place settings.

But Mrs. Pierce noticed. "My darling!" she said to Jessie. "If I had known you needed china, I would have brought some as a wedding gift!"

"I should think the plantation is wedding gift enough," Mr. Pierce said tersely, looking meaningfully at Sean.

"Of course, Samuel," Jessie's mother said hesitantly. "I just thought something personal, something just from me . . ." Her voice trailed off uncertainly, and she gave her husband a silent, pleading look.

Mr. Pierce grimaced, his lips thinning into a hard line of disgust. "Very well, Amanda, if you feel you must."

Amanda's eyes sparkled happily with her husband's grudging consent, and she turned back to her daughter. "I know just the pattern you'll want. I saw it in a shop in Boston a few days ago. I thought of you then but never dreamed you didn't have anything at all decent." She babbled on gaily as the meal continued, the perfection of Letty's offerings exclaimed upon as course followed course.

Jessie was glad to see her mother's interest in helping set up her household. Dishes, drapes, linens, and looms were all brought up and discussed.

Her stepfather asked about the slaves, the soil, the crops. Jessie couldn't help admiring the way Sean handled himself and the situation. He answered Mr. Pierce's questions knowledgeably, as if he really were the master. His manners were beyond reproach, and he spoke with the ease of one among equals. She marveled at the bondslave's acting ability.

She watched as Sean explained some facet of plantation life to her stepfather and again that unbidden thought arose to plague her: If only this wasn't all a sham. If only this man were really her husband. Perhaps she could overlook the fact that Sean was a bondslave, even excuse the crimes that had led to his sentence. But could she overlook the extravagant thoughtlessness of a man who spent coin on clothing beyond his means and needs instead of freedom? If he were free, would he be less of a spendthrift? Was he a man with whom to build the life she dreamed of? Or would he be more likely to waste every coin she hoped to hoard? If they were married, he would have legal control of all that was hers and as his wife she would have little to say about how their money was spent. Perhaps he did need a master to curb a reckless nature! She wanted freedom. She did not want to put herself into marital bondage to a wastrel bondslave.

"Is there no overseer to help with the running of the plantation?" Mr. Pierce's question shook Jessie from her reverie, and she exchanged a quick glance with Sean.

"He is away on business, just now," Sean answered smoothly, and Jessie breathed a sigh of relief at her co-conspirator's quick reply. She noted a brief moue of annoyance on her stepfather's face and wondered why the overseer's absence should concern him.

Dinner was soon over, and the four of them went to the parlor for the rest of the evening. Sean was pleasantly entertaining, keeping their wineglasses or teacups filled, while he told several stories that were nearly as amusing as Jason Soames's. But as good as Jason was at putting people at ease, Jessie doubted that he could have pulled off this charade with the verve and confidence that Sean showed. No, she was certain of it.

Amanda was still chuckling when she rose to say good night. "It has been a long day," she said, beaming happily at Jessie and Sean. "But a good one knowing my daughter is settled so happily." She squeezed Sean's hand and left, followed by her husband.

Since Jessie had dismissed Maybelle and the other servants for the night, Sean put out the candles, except for one to light their way before following Jessie to their room.

It was quite dark in the room, and Jessie stopped inside the door, waiting for Sean to bring the light. Sean entered and closed the door, setting the candle on a table. He stood behind her, and she felt his breath fall softly on her hair and the caress of his fingers along her neck.

"Shall we be abed, my love?"

She looked up at him, arching her brows. Though she was aflame at his nearness, she knew she must be cool to him or his bed would not be a pallet on the floor this night.

"There is no need to continue the charade now, Mr. Winthrop."

"Charade?"

He leaned closer and she could feel the warmth of his body drawing her. Or was it the heat of her own growing desire?

" 'Tis no charade I play when I say I desire you." His fingers continued their course across the slope of her shoulder and returned to stroke her nape. " 'Tis no charade that I long for the touch of your skin on mine." He bent to nuzzle his face in her hair. "That the soft splendor of your tresses would put to shame the finest silk. That your lips entice me to near madness."

Though her heart thudded with the onslaught of his seductive words, she knew how easily their passion could flare and she danced away from him as he sought her mouth.

Picking up the candle and keeping just out of his reach, she said, "Then, sir, it is well that your pallet is thin and the floor is hard. Perhaps the feel of it against your bones will give you something else to think on this night!"

With that, she slipped into the bathing cubicle and shut the door, leaving him in darkness. She heard him groping, muttering curses when he banged a shin, then stubbed a toe, and she giggled at his trials.

"You're a black-hearted wench to laugh at a man in his distress!" he growled, and she heard yet another thump and a yelp.

She only laughed harder. "At least it is a different kind of distress than that which you were complaining of a moment ago. A bump on the shin is not likely to drive you mad."

"As you surely will!"

All grew quiet in the other room, and Jessie put the candle down to undress. That was when her own distress began. She had forgotten that her dress fastened down the back and without Maybelle's help, she could not remove it. Yet her maid was long abed. She could not very well stumble through the house and wake Maybelle just to undo a few buttons. She had no recourse but to ask Sean to help. She gritted her teeth and opened the door.

Sean stood just outside, leaning against the wall as if he had been waiting for her. His oversized grin did naught to lessen her distress. "I wondered how long it would take you to remember that your dress fastened down the back."

Setting her hands on her hips, she glared at him. "How observant of you to have noticed just where a lady's dress is fastened! Did you also take note of Maybelle's and my mother's?"

"Jealous, my love?"

"Certainly not!"

"You have no reason to be. I assure you, I had eyes only for you. Any other woman could appear with no dress on at all and I doubt I would even notice."

Jessie merely arched her brows in disbelief.

"You, however—" he began.

"I, however, do not have to appear without clothes. You manage to undress me with your every glance."

"I would rather do it with my hands," he said, trying unsuccessfully not to smile. "If you'll just turn around, my love."

"I am not your love!" she said, presenting her back to him. "And do try to keep your hands to yourself."

"You set me a near impossible task!" he moaned at her injunction. He finished loosening her dress with what to her seemed like practiced skill.

"It must be, for your hands were ever touching me this evening. My parents are convinced you are my husband. It is not necessary for you to touch me constantly and so intimately." *And therefore confound my reason*, she added to herself.

" 'Tis how I would treat you were you truly my wife, Jessie," he said, and she closed her eyes at the tenderness of his words. "Do you think that any man, wed to such as you, could keep his hands from the softness of your cheek, your slender neck, the sweet curve of your bare shoulder?"

His fingers touched where his words led them, sending a calming warmth through her cheek, throat, and shoulder as his hand slid downward.

"And where fingers touch, lips are wont to taste." He bent to brush his lips along her shoulder, nibbling upward, testing one corner of her mouth, then the other before finding the center to savor fully the softness of her lips.

Her breath seemed lost in some forgotten eternity, her reason shattered, and she knew only his mouth on hers, the warm embrace of his arms. At last, from somewhere, she found the strength to pull away, out of his embrace, and into an unbearable void.

"But I am not truly your wife," she said, crossing her arms in a gesture to forestall any further intimacy. "I am not your wife at all."

"No," he said tonelessly, dropping his arms, "you are not my wife." He forced a smile to his lips. "My pallet will be hard indeed, my love."

It was the next afternoon on her way out to the veranda with tea that Jessie happened to look out the window. "Good Lord!" Jessie exclaimed, and Sean turned to follow her gaze.

An elegantly dressed man on a prancing black stallion was riding toward the house.

"Good Lord!" Sean echoed. "It's Soames."

Fortunately, Jessie's mother and Mr. Pierce were not in the house. They were on the veranda, awaiting afternoon tea which Sean was helping Jessie bring.

Jessie turned to Sean, a stricken look on her face. "He knows Twill is dead. If he comes in here—"

She didn't have to finish. Sean set down the tray he was carrying. "I'll get rid of him."

"No." Jessie stopped him with a hand to his arm. "He also knows you're a bondslave. I doubt he'll take orders from you. I'd better go."

Sean's lips compressed, and he squeezed her hand resting on his arm. "If you have any trouble . . ."

She laughed. "I won't have any trouble. Just keep my parents busy."

She lifted her skirts and hurried out the door to meet her visitor on the porch, wishing she had dealt with warning Soames off when she had thought of him days ago.

Sean waited to see how Jessie fared. The friendly greeting Jessie gave her neighbor told him that Soames was not an infrequent nor an unwelcome visitor. How could she allow Soames such liberties yet fend off Sean's every touch, every caress? Damn this role of bondslave! Gritting his teeth in angry frustration, he picked up his tray and went out to the veranda.

"Jason! How good to see you!" Jessie exclaimed, accepting his usual kiss to her cheek, the embrace of his hands in hers.

"You look lovely, as usual, Jessie," Jason said, his large brown eyes shining softly as he gazed down at her. "I have missed you."

She laughed a light little trill. "It has only been three days!"

"Four, counting today," Jason corrected. "An eternity. Tell me you have missed me," he insisted playfully. "Even if you have to lie just a bit."

"I did miss you," she told him, and was surprised to realize that it was the truth. Jason had been a great comfort to her in her first two weeks in the colony and good company. "And I don't have to lie to say it." But she was a bit disconcerted to see how much joy sprang up in his eyes at her words.

"Will you walk with me?" he asked.

"Not today, Jason. I really have too much to do." She shrugged helplessly when she saw his disappointment. "It is just that you have come at a bad time." There was more truth to that than she wanted him to know.

"Then I suppose I must leave." His smile did not waver, but the happy gleam in his eyes was gone as if snatched away by her denial.

She didn't want to send him away like this. She did enjoy his company. She thought quickly. "Can you come tomorrow? Early? We can go riding together."

"My dear! Can you ride?" The spark had returned to his eyes.

"Of course. I love horses. Though I doubt if I can keep up with that spirited creature," she said, nodding toward the impatient stallion.

"Jessie! What a delight! My horses are my treasure. I never thought to ask if you could ride. It gives me great joy to think that you could share my interest in horses. Shall I bring a mare for you?"

"I have my own mount," she said quickly. She didn't want him riding up to the house again while her parents were here. They might see him next time and have to be introduced. If he came early enough, her parents would still be abed. She would be ready and meet him in the road. "I'll be ready early in the morning. Very early."

"I do love an early-morning ride," he said with enthusiasm. "A half hour past dawn?"

She agreed, submitted her cheek for his good-bye kiss, and watched with relief as he rode away. Then she hurried out to the veranda, trying to think of some reason to give for her delay.

* * *

As Sean closed the door to their room that night, Jessie let out a deep sigh. Another difficult day done! Two more days here, then one at the Walkers' and her mother and stepfather would be gone, her deception over. If it weren't for the strain of maintaining her charade at all times, she could have enjoyed her mother's visit so much more. As it was, she had to guard her every word.

"Tired, my love?"

She felt Sean behind her, felt his fingers move over her neck, her shoulders, soothing, massaging, prying out the knots of tension that had built up over the day.

"Mmm," she moaned, relaxing beneath his ministrations, knowing that with Sean she need not pretend. With Sean, she could relax and be herself.

"Would you like a little wine to unwind?"

Thinking of the last time she had shared a glass of wine alone with Sean late at night and where it had led, she smiled. Well, perhaps she couldn't let down her guard completely with him. She shook her head. "It's just so trying, having to be so careful all the time. Today when Mother and I walked through the slave quarters, I was so afraid one of the slaves would say something, ask some question about you and arouse her suspicion. And then on top of everything, Jason showed up!"

She felt his hands move to the top fastening of her dress.

"Shall I?" he asked.

She nodded and he began undoing the back of her dress.

"How did you get rid of our foppish friend anyway?" he asked with a twinge of disdain in his voice.

Jessie opened her mouth to defend Jason. How dare a cloddish bondslave criticize a gentleman planter? But Sean was hardly cloddish. She thought of the quiet elegance of his clothing, the smooth polish of his manners. In comparison, Jason was certainly more than a bit flamboyant, but it was his style. It was . . . it was Jason.

"I told him to come back early tomorrow morning and I would go riding with him," she said airily, tossing her head as she moved away from him to her dresser.

"You what?" He stood, his arms akimbo, glaring at her.

She turned to face him. "You take your role as my husband too seriously, Bondslave Winthrop! We are not truly wed. I can go riding with whomever I choose."

"With that pompous peacock?" Sean shrugged out of his coat, tossing it toward a chair and missing.

Removing her earrings and necklace, Jessie threw them in her jewel box and slapped the lid shut. "I'm going and that's the end of it."

"Alone?" Sean jerked off his cravat and began unbuttoning his waistcoat.

Jessie spun toward him, her hands on her hips. Her loosened dress gaped wide, and irritably, she shoved it down and off, kicking free of it. "You didn't find any objection to me sailing off alone with you the other day! And Jason is not a pompous peacock!"

"Would you prefer prancing popinjay?" He tore off his shirt and waistcoat together, wadding them into a ball before aiming them angrily at the rest of his things that had landed haphazardly near the chair. "How do you know you can trust him?"

Her black eyes snapping, Jessie kicked off her shoes and stripped off her stockings, matching Sean shoe for shoe and stocking for stocking. "He's behaved very well whenever I've been alone with him. Unlike you, he does not try to ravish me every chance he gets." Angrily, she began to rip the pins from her hair, throwing them onto the dresser so hard most of them bounced off.

"Then I question his manhood."

"He's a gentleman!"

"Ah, there's that word again. Like magic, it protects a maiden from even being desired. How often has he come sniffing around here, anyway?"

"You're jealous!" she snapped, glaring at him, daring him to deny it.

"Jealous? Aye," he growled. "When a man such as Jason Soames can court you openly and I have not the right to so much as touch your hand, I am jealous."

She faced him, her hair tumbling wildly about her shoulders, her breasts straining against the gentle confines of her chemise. "For someone with so little right, you have tresspassed oft enough. Lacking the right has not kept your hands from straying! If my virtue, what's left of it, is in any danger, it is not from Jason but from you."

"Then why didn't you ask Jason to play the role of your husband this week?" Roughly, he pulled her into his arms. "Were you afraid he would try this? Or were you afraid he wouldn't?" His mouth came crashing down on hers, hard, demanding, hungry.

Surprised, Jessie put her hands up to push him away. But they came into contact with bare, warm flesh, hard and muscled beneath her touch. Moving up, they roved through the thick hair on his chest, felt the deep curve of his collarbone, the corded muscles at his neck, the soft fan of hair at his nape. Her touch generated a hunger within her to match his, and she turned from trying to escape his embrace to cling closer. Her mouth sought his as desperately as his searched out the hidden depths of hers.

His hands began a thorough exploration of her, one rambling through the wildly tumbled thicket of her midnight hair, the other descending along her spine to curve around her shapely buttock. He pulled her closer, and she came willingly, pressing avidly against him.

His hand trailed down her throat, across her shoulder, pushed aside her chemise, and continued its exploration around the slope of her breast. Leaving her mouth wanting, his mouth tore away to follow where his hand led. Down the column of her throat, along the ridge of her collarbone and across to the base of her breast, his mouth left in the wake of its passage a searing hunger that grew enormously within her at his gentle assault on her breast. Her hunger for him deepened as his lips at last conquered the rosebud peak, drawing from her a submissive sigh.

His hands were quick to loosen the final ties of her protective chemise and to send it to ignominious defeat upon the floor. The rest of their clothes followed and were heedlessly trod upon as he swept her to him and lay her down on his pallet.

As his tongue teased, his hand found its way through the dark triangle between her thighs. He found her open and hungry for him, and he lifted himself above her to feed that hunger, tantalizingly slow, until she lifted herself to take him completely in, wrapping her arms around him to keep him securely where her body desired him.

Tormentingly, he moved within her, now feeding her raging desire, now withdrawing until her anguish drove her to lift her hips for more. When it seemed as if she would die with wanting him, she found fulfillment and hers entreated his own to follow quickly so that they reached completion together, fully sated.

They lay together, savoring each other until Jessie slipped into sleep.

Propped on an elbow, Sean looked down at Jessie. There was not much to see in the darkness, but he could feel her. Like a kitten, she snuggled against him and he heard the rhythmic breathing of peaceful sleep. Softly, his hand trailed over her, wanting to learn every line of her body. There was no longer any doubt in his mind that he wanted her, now and forever, and would ask her to marry him when both their charades were played out. He would tell her his true identity, lay his wealth at her feet, and tell her that, by birth and breeding, he was as much a gentleman as any. Then she would come eagerly into his arms and consent to wed him. He frowned at that picture and shook his head. If he had wanted to wed a woman impressed with his wealth and position, he could have had any number of women ere now. But he wanted Jessie and he wanted her to accept him for himself, to want him, not what he could give her. How could he ever be sure of that unless he asked her to marry him while she still thought him a bondslave? Would she accept him as she knew him now?

"I think you will, eventually," he whispered softly to her. "There's more to you than a shallow woman seeking wealth and security. Even if you don't realize it yourself yet. You just need time."

He smiled in wonder. When had he changed from chiding himself for wanting a woman who might be involved in piracy and theft to wanting her whether she was or not? And how could he protect her if she was?

Jessie, my love, he thought, *how you confound my very senses! How can I love a woman who can be so callous as to steal from her neighbors for her own enrichment?"*

Yet where was that callousness? His hand touched only softness. In her dealings with her slaves, he had detected no callousness. Surely her involvement with the pirates, if there was any, was that of an innocent entangled. Yet, the thought came unbidden to remind him, she could plan and execute such a charade as they were now involved in. Was she then incapable of other charades, other less savory roles? Only by working harder to bring an end to the piracy could he find out. Then, if necessary, he would find some way to protect her and to make her his.

Chapter Eleven

Dawn had barely touched her eyes when Jessie woke warm and contented, pressed so close to Sean that she was soothed by the steady beat of his heart. She was tired. Sometime in the middle of the night she had been aroused again by Sean's touch intruding into her sleep. She smiled at the pleasure he had given her and wondered if other men were as gentle, as strong, as generous in their lovemaking. She sighed. There was no place she would rather be than right here, right now. But dawn was breaking and Jason would soon be here. She had to be on the road, awaiting him. She slipped from under the coverlet, groaning as her aching body let her know that a thin pallet on a hard floor was no place for prolonged love-making.

As she got up Sean stirred. He did not say anything, but she could feel his eyes on her as she groped in the near darkness for her riding clothes and boots. She smiled, knowing he watched as she dressed. She pushed her feet determined-ly into her boots, brushed her hair into a tight coil, and was reaching for her crop when she felt his arms around her.

His hand stole up to entrap her breast as he bent to nuzzle her neck. "I know you must go, Jessie," he said. "Just remember that it is to me that you return."

She leaned back against him, enjoying one last embrace. *Yes,* she thought, *yes.* Then a guilty thought stole into her mind. *This is wrong,* it said, but she pushed the thought away. How could something wrong feel so right?

Then his hands slid from her, and she fled, knowing that if she looked back, she might not be able to go at all.

A heavy mist obscured the road, and long streamers of moss hung eerily from the overhanging oaks. Jessie peered down the road as far as she could see, holding her horse steady.

She heard Jason before she saw him, materializing through the lifting fog. He started when he saw her; then his face lit up with a wide smile.

"Jessie! You are early. I thought I would have at least a half-hour's wait ahead of me. I should have known you are not the typical woman to keep a man waiting." By this time he had reached her side and leaned from his saddle to give her a kiss on the cheek.

"I have never been one to dawdle, Jason," she said. "Where shall we ride?"

"I would like to show you my place," he said hesitantly. "I know you would not be properly chaperoned, my dear, but I promise you—"

Jessie cut him off with a trilling laugh and a hand laid softly on his arm. "Jason, if I did not trust you, I would not be out here alone with you now. I would love to visit your home."

"My dear!" he exclaimed happily, lifting her hand to kiss. "I assure you, your trust will not be misplaced."

He turned his horse, and they rode side by side down the rutted track. As Jason had told her, it was not far to his home and soon they were turning off the road onto a tree-lined drive that hid the house from view.

They approached the house from the back because it was built to face the river as that was how most visitors arrived at Jason's home. He then led her around to the front before they dismounted. He tossed his reins to a waiting slave boy, then helped Jessie down. A butler opened the door, bowing, a broad smile of welcome on his face.

The grounds had been carefully tended, the walks of crushed oystershell edged neatly and lined by flower beds. The house was brick with neat white shutters and trim. There was no peeling paint here, no neglect nor decay.

Jessie looked out over the wide expanse of river. "It's a lovely setting, Jason!"

His eyes roved over her appreciatively. "Yes," he agreed, squeezing her hand meaningfully. "A lovely setting. It but needs a jewel for a centerpiece."

She looked up at him in surprise. Was she the jewel he referred to? She wasn't sure what to say.

Jason must have sensed her discomfort, for he laughed grandly and pulled her arm through his. "Shall we walk or would you rather go inside first?"

Jessie smiled at him, grateful that he did not press her. "I would like to walk a little first."

He showed her the gardens around the house, extensive ones that included a patch of herbs near the kitchen door. Some of them were unfamiliar to her, and he promised to send her some cuttings along with directions for their use. Then he took her to the stables. They were nearly as large as the house, a true horseman's delight. Large, roomy stalls were being cleaned and fresh bedding laid in. Most of the horses were out in a large pasture, some of them kicking up their heels. Her own horse was there, enjoying a portion of oats, and nickered in recognition when she passed by.

She leaned against a fence, watching the horses. "They're magnificent, Jason!" She pointed to a foal nuzzling his mother for food. "He looks like the stallion you ride."

"You've a fine eye, Jessie. 'Tis his son, that one. And I think he may outshine his father when he grows up."

They were heading back to the house when Jessie saw a path through a stand of trees.

"Where does that path lead?" she asked

"To the slave quarters."

She looked at him with interest. "May I see? I am in the process of repairing my own slaves' quarters and could use some ideas and suggestions."

"Of course," he replied, and they headed down the path.

Set in a circle, the rough log cabins with dirt floors were crude, but better homes than many free farmers could boast of. Several vegetable patches were surrounded by circular woven fences, and chickens pecked underfoot and there were a few pigs. Several children played within the circle of cabins, their faces dirty from their games, but they looked healthy and were well dressed. They jumped up and down when they saw Jason approaching and ran to him, shouting out greetings, white grins flashing in stark contrast to their black faces.

"No, no," Jason said, laughing. "I've nothing for you today. Run along now."

Several women smiled and nodded but hung back shyly.

"Most of the men are out working. The women too. These women care for the compound, watch the children, and do the cooking for the others."

Jessie nodded, looking around, pleased with what she saw. Jason might be proud enough to set a bondslave in his place and disdain the company of one "beneath" him, but his slaves fared well. He did not stint them adequate necessities, and they did not cower in fear of him or glare in hatred. To her, that said more than the elegance of his house, his grand manners, and his fine horses.

She smiled at him. "I think I've seen all I need to."

The interior of Jason's home was as elegant and tasteful as the exterior. Wood floors gleamed, brasswork sparkled, and there were fine carpets and curtains. In spite of its polished, well-kept air, it was warm and welcoming, cozy. A perfect reflection of Jason's effusive warmth. It was, she thought, what she had hoped to find when she had arrived at her own plantation.

"It's beautiful, Jason. I never expected a bachelor's home to be so comfortable," she said.

"I must admit," Jason said, guiding her to a chair, "that I am not entirely responsible for the decor." He sat opposite her and poured her a cup of tea that a discreet servant had brought. "My mother lived with me until she remarried last year."

"Does she live in Charles Town?"

"Yes. On Church Street, very near the Walkers. I shall have to introduce you soon," he said, his voice heavy with meaning.

"I should like that very much," Jessie answered, wondering whether he had meant the remark as a prelude to a proposal. She set her cup down, rattling it nervously in the saucer. "I really must go. I have enjoyed seeing your place, Jason, but I fear I am neglecting my own."

"You must come again, my dear," he said, and led her outside where his efficient servants were already bringing their horses.

She patted her horse's nose. He seemed much happier with a belly full of oats. "Now that I know the way, you may get tired of seeing me," she said, laughing.

He took her hand, pressing it eagerly to his lips. "Never!"

Shyly, she pulled her hand away, but he did not take offense nor press her, for which she was glad. He helped her to mount, and she waited for him to mount, then set her horse into an easy canter.

When they reached her overgrown drive, she stopped, not allowing him to accompany her to the house.

"Will you ride with me again tomorrow?" he asked.

"I shall be going to Charles Town again for just a few days," she told him to ensure he did not come again until her parents were gone.

He looked crestfallen. "I think I will move into my house in town. Then I would see more of you."

"I shall ride over to see you to let you know when I return." She put out her hand to bid him good-bye.

He took her hand gladly, seeming to cherish it for the few moments he possessed it, then reluctantly let it go. "It will be a thousand years till then." Turning his horse, he galloped away.

Coming into the gloom of the house from the bright daylight, Jessie did not see Sean in front of her until she had hurtled headlong into him. His arms came around her, and his head bent near her neck.

"I missed you," he murmured, nibbling one ear lobe.

"I was gone but an hour," she replied.

Her breath seemed to flee before the onrush of chills his nibbling sent through her. It left her completely when his hands cupped her face, bringing her mouth up to meet his in a hungry encounter. The kiss seemed all too short, yet a lifetime of longing seemed stored within its brief length. Then his arms enfolded her again and hers wound around his neck.

"Two hours," he growled, holding her tight. "I was ready to come after you."

She laughed lightly. "Jason is perfectly trustworthy, my dear jealous 'husband.' He's a—"

"I know," he said, cutting her off with a derisive snort, "a gentleman. But I've known some so-called gentlemen who are not so trustworthy."

"Jason is not one of them."

"Let's not talk of Jason," he said fiercely. "Come upstairs with me."

She leaned her forehead against his chest, hiding the smile his invitation brought. "My parents will be up soon. I must see to breakfast."

"They are already breakfasting on the veranda."

She pushed away from him in alarm. "They could come in any minute!"

He held her tighter, grinning mischievously. "They would but find you in the arms of your loving husband."

"A rutting bondslave, you mean!" She tossed her head proudly, but there was a teasing sparkle in her eyes. "Were you truly my husband you would be seeing to our guests."

"Were I truly your husband I would take exception to my wife riding off alone with a lecherous neighbor."

"Would you rather I ride completely alone and unprotected?" she asked with an innocent air.

"I would rather that we rode together abovestairs," he answered, giving her a leer that made his suggestion hard to resist.

"As I said, naught but a rutting bondslave!" She leaned against him in impish response to his suggestion. "I must see to our guests since I have no real husband to do it for me."

Sighing, she pushed against the bonds of his arms.

"They are well cared for," he said, reluctant to let her escape. "Letty is stuffing them with dozens of delightful dishes."

"Then unhand me, oaf! I am famished and would not miss one of her meals. There will be too few ere she is gone!"

Laughing, she turned out of his embrace to go out to the veranda and was propelled on her way by a playful slap to her rump.

After breakfast Jessie and her mother walked toward the slave quarters. Jessie carried a handful of comfrey leaves cut from the kitchen herb garden which she had promised to one of the women to help sooth a cough. She only hoped that this trip amidst the slaves would go as well as their first time, with no one mentioning Sean's true identity.

As they neared the quarters, the bustling sounds of hammering and sawing met them. Hammer in hand, Sean waved to her from the roof of one of the cabins. Holding a wooden shingle in place, he hammered it down, instructing a young black man in the roofing process. Jessie looked about in amazement at the transformed area. She had managed to get it cleaned up, to improve the diet of the slaves, to provide better clothing. But she had not known how to go about the actual repair of the buildings, and Jackson had been no help at all. He thought the quarters were fine the way they were. But in the few days Sean had been "master" here, he had accomplished more in this respect than she had in nearly two weeks.

Jessie had already decided that when Jackson returned, she would fire him. Not only was he a poor manager, his cruelty to the slaves was intolerable and she was sure she could manage better on her own. But Sean's presence and help had shown her that she couldn't manage as well as she wanted to. She had a lot to learn. Would she be able to handle everything and get the harvest in before it was ruined?

Turning the roofing job over to his assistant, Sean slid to the edge of the roof and dropped to the ground. He was once again dressed in his work clothes. Though a smile seldom left his face, even working side by side with the slaves and indentured servants, it was clear at a glance that he was in charge.

She watched as a bondslave approached Sean with a problem. Sean bent his head, listening intently, nodding occasionally. In a few brief words Sean gave the man his answer, bringing a satisfied smile to the man's face. Clapping the bondslave familiarly on the shoulder, Sean sent him off as if the man were doing Sean a favor rather than merely obeying orders.

Sean came toward them, his ever present smile adding a sparkle to his eye, a lilt to his step. His shirt sleeves were rolled to the elbow and the collar open at the throat, and he was dirt begrimed. But watching him, Jessie thought it would be hard to decide how he appealed more to her. Did she prefer him as he was last night, in his fine clothes, playing the role of a gentleman, polite and formal, or as he was now, casually dressed, happily at work? She blushed as she thought of one more way she had seen him. Naked and aroused, his lips warm with passion, his eyes alive with desire.

Happily, she did not have to make a choice. They were all the same man and for a short space of time, they were all hers. She did not want to think of the time, too soon, when he would be gone.

While he was yet across the compound from her, his gaze locked with hers, and even at that distance, she could feel the desire his merest glance ignited within her. As he came toward her, it was as if all the rest of the world ceased to exist. There was only Sean and his eyes saw only her.

She felt her mother plucking at her fingers. "I'll take these to Sally," Mrs. Pierce said.

Jessie loosened her grip on the comfrey leaves, absently felt them leave her hand, saw her mother walk down the compound with them.

Amid the bustle of the compound, she was alone with Sean.

He stood before her, his gaze warm upon her, his smile, one of contentment. "Have you come to check on your hired bondslave? I assure you my time is well spent." His fingers toyed with the tie at the front of her dress.

So near my heart, she thought, mesmerized by the play of his slim fingers. "You have wrought wonders in the place in so short a time, Bondslave Winthrop. My coin is well invested."

"You are paying off a year of my indenture. I must work hard to see that you do not go unsatisfied." The back of his fingers brushed against her breast, making it stiffen at that brief attention.

"I was well satisfied until now," she said, her voice husky. "Now I think I need more proof of your competence."

"I shall be glad to provide it, my lady." He leaned toward her but a slave passing by reminded them where they were and he drew back.

Clearing his throat, Sean said, "I have set a crew to replant the slope that was logged."

She nodded her approval. Jackson would never have considered the idea, and it was something she should have thought of herself. How long would it be before she found her footing and was able to handle a plantation this size on her own? She would sorely miss Sean when her parents left. *In more ways than one*, she thought, blushing.

"I gave the leaves to Sally and told her how to brew them," Jessie's mother said, returning.

Hastily, Jessie stepped away from Sean, her cheeks burning anew for having forgotten herself so completely in such a public place. Her mother might think she and Sean were wed and smile indulgently, but Jessie knew it was all deception and felt a double edge of guilt.

"You are an angel of mercy," Sean said, smiling down at Mrs. Pierce. "Several of the women told me how you and Jessie helped them sew new clothes for the children yesterday."

Mrs. Pierce sighed happily. "It was fun to do for little ones again. My own chicks are all grown now."

A slave woman plucked at Sean's sleeve, and he turned to give her his attention. "How big you want dem rice sacks, Massa Sean?"

Jessie shot Sean a horrified look. Had her mother heard what the slave called him? Sean merely grinned and shrugged, then excused himself to go with the woman, leaving Jessie to handle the situation alone.

When she looked at her mother's face wrinkled in puzzlement, Jessie knew her mother had heard the remark.

"Why did that woman call your husband Sean ?"

"Sean? I'm sure she said Jon, Mother. It's just that the accent here can be so slurred, sometimes."

"I suppose it's the heat," Mrs. Pierce laughed. "It can sap anyone's strength and make them sloppy."

"Are you hot, Mother? Perhaps we should go back to the house for a cool drink." *And to safer ground,* she thought to herself. She took her mother's arm and they headed back up the path.

Rice sacks, Jessie mused, again chiding herself that that was something she had not thought of at all. With the coming harvest, they would need them. What would she do without Sean?

Jessie was setting out food on the table on the veranda for lunch when Sean came up behind her, surprising her with a kiss on her nape. She turned and would have gladly accepted his embrace, but he stepped away from her, holding out his sweaty and dirty arms.

"As much as I'd like to hold you, Jessie, I think you'll appreciate me more after a bath."

She nodded her agreement, her nose wrinkling. "For once you look like the bondslave you are."

"I feel like one. And hungry as a field hand. If you'll just make me a sandwich, I'll finish those repairs before I call it a day."

Jessie sliced bread and buttered it, adding ham and cheese. "I appreciate all you're doing, Sean, but this wasn't part of our bargain. There's no need for you to work so much."

She handed him the sandwich, stepping close to caress his cheek in spite of his grime.

"There certainly would not be the need to work so hard if your overseer were here to do his job."

Jessie jumped away from Sean at the sound of her stepfather's voice. He was just coming onto the veranda, but Jessie wondered how much of their conversation he had heard.

"I don't understand how you could send your overseer off on errands at such a busy time, Jessie," he continued, seating himself. "When did you say he would return?"

"I didn't say, sir. But I'm sure it will not be until after you have gone."

Jessie thought she heard a muttered "Damn!" from her stepfather and wondered again why Jackson's absence should concern him at all.

"Was there some reason you needed to see our overseer, Mr. Pierce?" Sean asked.

Though the question seemed casual enough, Jessie saw Sean's narrowed eyes as he studied her stepfather.

"No. No, of course not. I was merely wondering," he answered, turning his attention to the table full of food.

"Perhaps there is something I can help you with?"

Jessie was surprised by the hard glare her stepfather gave Sean.

"I think you've done enough already!" he snapped.

"Then if you'll excuse me, I'll get back to work and see you this evening." He bent to brush Jessie's cheek with a kiss, but she turned and the kiss landed full on her mouth. Sean gasped at the unexpected contact and desire kindled in his eyes. "Later," he mouthed in promise to her and was gone.

When she turned back to the table, her mother was just coming out, following Letty. The cook carried a steaming pot and placed it on the table.

"It smells delicious, Letty," Jessie said.

"It's a pepper pot," Letty said proudly. "I learned to make it in Barbados. If you like it, Mrs. Pierce, I'll give you the recipe."

"Along with about a dozen others, Letty. Unless I can convince you to come to Boston with us."

"No, ma'am. I had enough of cold winters in Ireland. This is as far north as I go!" She ladled out three bowls of the spicy West Indian stew and left.

The three ate in satisfied silence for a few minutes. A willet sang from the river and except for bird calls and the distant hammering from the slave quarters, all was still.

"I do hope you won't be lonely out here, Jessie," Mrs. Pierce worried.

"I've been far too busy to be lonely, Mother. It isn't Boston, but there are plenty of people around."

"I'd like to meet some of your friends, Jessie. So that when you write to me I'll know who you're talking about."

Jessie gave a little laugh and thought of the close call with Jason. Her mother would love Jason. They had the same kind of gossipy warmth. "I haven't been here long enough to make many friends, I'm afraid."

"But surely Jonathan has friends?"

Jessie leaned over and gave her mother's hand a squeeze. She was genuinely sorry that she could not introduce her mother to Jason, sorry that her visit would be short, but relieved that it gave her the excuse to keep her mother isolated. "Your visit this time is just too brief, and I want to keep you all to myself. Next time you come I promise you you'll be caught up in a social whirl that will leave you dizzy."

"Samuel insists that this is purely a business trip and he has to get back to Boston," her mother said, darting a glare at her husband. "Next time I come, I'll stay longer—if I have to come by myself!"

Jessie laughed at what, for her mother, was a daring declaration.

Jessie and her mother spent the afternoon erecting a loom they found in the attic. It was old, but serviceable, and between them they set up most of the warp to make blankets for the slaves. It was late when they finished, and Jessie had to hurry to her bath.

She had laid out her blue dress, but because she was already late, Jessie did not protest when Maybelle slipped her green silk over her head. A few hurried touches to her hair and Jessie slipped downstairs to join her guests.

When she came into the parlor, she knew why Maybelle had changed her dress to the green one. Sean was dressed in a deep bottle-green coat with lighter green breeches and a waistcoat embroidered with dark green silk. As always, his presence seemed to make her come alive. Her heart seemed to beat joyfully within her and she smiled, not at all loath to be decked out in similar colors. She only wondered whose idea it was.

Sean bent over her hand in a courtly gesture. No one but Jessie saw the promise in his eyes or the way he eyed the low cut of her gown as if remembering well the part of her it concealed. His gaze brought a rush of color to her cheeks, and drew a thrill of anticipation through her.

The talk at dinner was about the next day's departure. They would go back to Charles Town in the wagons and spend the evening with the Walkers before the Pierces boarded the *Harper* to sail on the next morning's tide.

After dinner they played whist, Sean and Mrs. Pierce winning against Jessie and her stepfather. The seating arrangement at the card table offered many opportunities for Sean to touch her. Each time he did, she was tormented, for she knew where such touches led, and she anxiously awaited the end of the evening for their culmination. Each brush of his fingers on hers, each time his leg pressed against hers beneath the table, each time his glance told her he desired her, her senses were quickened, her desire heightened. His gaze often rested on the lush fullness of her bosom, and she leaned toward him to offer him further enticement, and his rising desire fueled hers.

By the time the cards were at last put away and her parents headed for bed, Jessie was anxious for a repetition of the previous night with Sean. When they entered their room, she turned into his ready embrace, giving him little time to put down the candle.

His mouth caught hers, and she clung to him with a moan of anguished hunger. Their clothing was quickly discarded and dropped in a trail from the doorway to the pallet.

He bent to trail kisses across her shoulder, but she pulled away coyly.

"The bed would be more comfortable," she invited, remembering last night's bruises on the hard floor.

Sean sighed heavily, a teasing twinkle lighting his eyes. "Ah, but I promised to keep to my pallet and not even to think of sleeping in the bed with you," he reminded her with feigned regret.

The twinkle in her eyes matched his as she turned away from him to twitch enticingly across the room. "So who said anything about sleep?"

With a laugh, he caught her up in his arms, and they fell onto the bed together to do very little sleeping.

"I suppose I should sign that deed over to you now," Mr. Pierce said, pushing away from the Walkers' dinner table.

They had arrived in Charles Town that afternoon, and, at her stepfather's insistence, he and Mr. Walker had spent a couple of hours at the shipping office. Until they had returned and Mr. Walker had given Jessie a reassuring nod, she had hardly dared breathe for fear that someone at the office had learned of Jonathan Twill's death and mentioned it. Now there were but two hours before her mother and stepfather would board the *Harper*. They would sleep aboard since the ship would sail on an early tide, a good hour before dawn.

Suddenly very nervous at the culmination of all her deception, Jessie rose to make a place to write at the table. The dishes rattled in her hands as she collected them and helped a servant girl carry them to the kitchen.

Mr. Walker brought ink, pens, and extra paper while Mr. Pierce got his copy of the deed. Seating himself at the table, Jessie's stepfather smoothed out the deed and began making the transfer copy in his tight, neat hand.

"The deed is to be made out to me alone, sir," Jessie said.

Mr. Pierce stopped writing so suddenly he almost made a splotch on the paper. He looked up at Sean incredulously as if expecting him to refute his wife's statement.

Sean put an arm around Jessie, a comforting touch she welcomed, and, nodding his assent, said, "That's the way we want it, Mr. Pierce."

Her stepfather's eyes widened a bit in amazement, then with a disgusted shake of his head went back to his writing, muttering, "You're a fool, Jonathan Twill."

Jessie watched as her name, her full name, Jessica Kathryn Ashbrook Twill, appeared from the tip of the pen and spread across the paper as the new owner of the upriver plantation. A complete description of the property followed. When the deed was completed and properly dated, Mr. Pierce looked up at Sean once again before adding his name. Sean nodded his assent and Jessie's stepfather signed the deed. Mrs. Walker signed as a witness and Mr. Walker signed as the notary. Samuel Pierce handed both copies to Jessie.

At last holding the deed in her hands, Jessie was not sure whether she wanted to laugh or cry in relief. Sean gave her a reassuring squeeze and bent to kiss her cheek. Her mother came over to hug Jessie, adding her congratulations. The Walkers hugged her in turn, each giving her looks that promised their continued support.

Mr. Pierce stood up, clearing his throat. "It's not officially yours until you record it. Take care of that detail as soon as possible," he cautioned.

"I will," Jessie said. Always ill at ease with her stepfather, she at last held out hand to him, which he took almost grudgingly. "Thank you, sir."

He merely harumphed. Turning to his wife, he said, "I suggest we get our things together. We should be going aboard shortly."

At the mention of their departure, Mrs. Pierce again took Jessie into her arms, bravely trying to hold back her tears. Jessie patted her mother on her back, trying hard to cheer her with a smile. At last Mrs. Pierce wrenched herself away and went upstairs to ready herself for her forthcoming ordeal on the high seas.

It was already dark when Sean and Jessie walked down to the docks with her mother and Mr. Pierce and stood at the gangplank watching the last of the Pierces' trunks disappear down a hatch. Captain Adams met them at the foot of the gangplank, greeting Mr. Pierce with the deference due the owner of the line.

Mrs. Pierce looked nervously toward the *Harper*, obviously reluctant to go aboard any sooner than she had to. "Is it true what they say? Are there pirates preying on Charles Town shipping?" she asked shakily.

"You'll be out of the harbor before dawn, Mrs. Pierce," Captain Adams assured her. "Even if there are pirates out there, I doubt if they'll see our ship."

"I've heard that hardly a ship goes in or out without being challenged," Mrs. Pierce worried.

"We weren't stopped on our way in, Amanda," Mr. Pierce said. "There's no need to borrow trouble and worry about our departure."

Sean bent to kiss Mrs. Pierce's cheek. "You have less to fear than others, Mrs. Pierce," he said. "Ashbrook ships are attacked less often than any. I look forward to seeing you again."

Mr. Pierce shot Sean a glare, and Jessie thought it best if she got her mother safely aboard and away from talk of pirates. "I'll help you get settled, Mother," she said, taking her arm. The two of them went up the gangplank and down to the cabin.

"Stand out to the open sea as quickly as you can, Captain Adams," Sean advised. "The danger from pirates is very real, but most of them seem to prefer clinging close to Charles Town. And they do seem not to attack Ashbrook ships quite so much as they do others." His glance quickly darted from one man to the other to see if his shot found a sore point. Pierce merely continued to glare at him.

"Yes," Captain Adams agreed, smoothly. "The *Harper* is too fast for them." Bowing, he went aboard, leaving Sean alone with Mr. Pierce.

"Don't get the idea you'll get anything more from me by your loose talk of the piracy in this area," Pierce almost growled. "You've been paid and paid well for your silence. If you're so besotted with my 'daughter' that you let her have the whole plantation for herself, that's your problem." He grinned maliciously. "You might find that the little twit is not so easily managed as you thought. Good-bye, Mr. Twill." With a curt bow, he went aboard.

Sean looked after him in surprise. So, Jonathan Twill had not been the ringleader but somehow had stumbled onto some incriminating information. Information which involved Ashbrook Shipping, perhaps Pierce himself. And Twill had been paid for his silence with the offer of the plantation he was managing. Was Jessie also part of that payoff? Or had she been sent as added insurance to keep Twill quiet with hope of more gain?

But if Twill had not been the ringleader, then who was? Was it the woman Mr. Campbell had seen and shot at? He couldn't believe it was Jackson. Nor Captain Adams. The captain was not in Charles Town often enough nor at the times when all the attacks occurred.

Jessie appeared at the head of the gangplank, giving her mother one last hug. Then she turned and smiled down at Sean, giving his heart a wrenching tug. He looked up at her, so beautiful in the soft summer darkness, lit only by the glow of the ship's lanterns. *Please,* he prayed silently, *don't let it be Jessie.*

Chapter Twelve

Jessie gave her mother one last hug then turned toward the gangplank. Looking down at the dock, her heart leaped to see Sean, tall and handsome, leaning casually against a barrel, waiting for her. Suddenly she realized that it was all over. Sean would go back to his master, and she would return alone to her plantation. He was looking up at her, his face hidden in shadow, unreadable. But she knew how she felt. Her heart was wrenching so badly it was hard even to breathe. How could she face the loneliness now that she had experienced the warmth of Sean's embrace? Though she longed to fly into his arms and never leave them, she forced herself to walk sedately down the gangplank and turn back to wave.

"I'll send those dishes as soon as I get back to Boston," Mrs. Pierce called. "I love you!"

"I love you, too, Mama," Jessie answered.

Waving once more, she turned away. She felt Sean's comforting touch at her waist as they walked down the dock and into Church Street. A touch she would now have to do without. She had known from the beginning that it could not continue. Their lovemaking, heady as it was, was wrong. Now she would have to face that. Lifting her chin, she moved away from his touch and felt his hand drop.

"I suppose this means I am reduced to being a mere bondslave again," Sean teased, his voice softened with a chuckle.

"Yes," she said, forcing a light smile. "But a very special one. Thank you, Sean." They had reached the Walkers' and Jessie put out her hand to say good-bye.

He took her hand and held it as if that was where it belonged. "As soon as you file your deed in the morning, I'll take you back upriver and collect my things."

There was no question about it. Sean would be moving out, and Jackson would return. She shuddered at the thought of the overseer. She had promised herself that she would fire the man as soon as the plantation was hers. But the harvest had to be brought in. Now she knew that she could never bring in the crop alone. If she just had some experienced help this year to teach her, she could handle it in following years. She looked up at Sean. Did it have to be Jackson who helped her? Could Sean stay? Just long enough to help with the harvest?

"Sean, do you have to go?"

He glanced toward the Walkers' door, his brow cocked in amusement. "I hardly think Mrs. Walker would approve."

Jessie jerked her hand away, frowning at his purposeful misunderstanding. "I meant could you stay on at the plantation?"

He moved closer, sliding an arm around her, a suggestive smile on his face. "It would be a pleasure."

Jessie pushed his arm away, and spoke as firmly and businesslike as she could standing this close to him. "As overseer. You would have to move out of the house, of course."

"Ah." He stepped away from her, clasping his hands behind his back as if disappointed but considering her proposition.

She hurried to add, "But we could fix up one of the cabins for you. I know you belong to Mr. Fortune, but you only need stay until the harvest is over and until I have learned a little more about running a plantation. Two or three weeks."

Sean seemed to be thinking it over. "What about Jackson?"

Jessie spoke through clenched teeth. "Mr. Jackson may be useful for some things. Running a plantation is not one of them. I plan to fire him as overseer soon as I see him."

Sean seemed disturbed by that statement, and his brow creased in thought. "Perhaps," he suggested thoughtfully, "he should stay on for a while." He held up a hand to halt her protest. "Just through the harvest."

Jessie's shoulders slumped. "Does that mean you can't stay on?"

He grinned down at her, his eyes raking her warmly. "It so happens that Mr. Fortune is out of town and I'm at liberty for a while. I shall be glad to help out."

She smiled happily, her heart soaring. "Thank you again, Sean."

He took up her hand and bending to kiss it said, "The pleasure is all mine, my lady. Or it would be if I didn't have to move out of the house!"

Jessie gasped. But before she could think of a retort to his boldness, he was gone, swinging down the street, whistling.

* * *

The *Fortune* docked early the next morning, having successfully slipped by the infestation of pirates. After recording her deed, Jessie went on board with Sean for the trip upriver. Josie and Jackson were aboard and made their report to her as Sean helped with the trimming of the sails.

"We got ever'ting you tell us," Josie said, hitching a thumb in the direction of a stack of boxes.

At Jessie's thank you, Josie merely shrugged and sauntered across the deck where she found a coil of rope to sit on near Sean. Jessie gritted her teeth as she watched the shapely quadroon flash a pretty grin at Sean and display a length of leg to gain his eye.

"Mr. Winthrop will be staying on for a while, Mr. Jackson," Jessie said. "He seems to have some expertise in the running of a plantation and you will work with him in directing the harvest."

"You're putting a slave in charge?" Jackson seemed barely in control of his anger, towering over her threateningly.

Jessie clenched her teeth and refused to back down. "A bondsman, Mr. Jackson," she corrected.

"Don't make no difference what you call him. You put a slave in charge of slaves, you got trouble." He leaned close to her, leering down at her. "I can take care of you as good as him."

Jessie glared at him but refused to dignify his crudeness by acknowledging it. "Mr. Winthrop has had no trouble this past week, Mr. Jackson. I expect there will be none in the next two. Unless you give it!"

He seemed to mull that over. His eyes narrowed and his gaze swept over her, leaving her feeling slightly soiled. It was all Jessie could do not to shudder as she saw his tongue slide lecherously over his lips. Abruptly, he turned away to go sit

233

beside Josie, and the two of them soon began to talk.

As she checked the goods Jackson and Jessie had bought in Williamsburg, she watched Sean as he hoisted a sail under Captain Reading's orders. Dressed once again in his simple work clothes, his muscles straining against the white cloth, he worked alongside a seaman. He seemed perfectly content working the little ship. And perfectly at home, Jessie thought.

Having finished checking the supplies, she leaned back against the railing, feeling very at home herself. Wouldn't it be wonderful, she thought, if things could go on as they were? If they were truly man and wife they could. She could picture sleeping in Sean's arms at night and working with him on the plantation by day. Eventually, they could buy a share in a ship, build their own shipping line.

She shook her head clear of such a dream. Sean might happily pitch into any work at hand, but it was questionable whether he could stay the distance. Was there not proof of his spendthrift ways sitting in the clothes chests at home? And there were his past crimes. She still did not even know what they were. Besides, when had Sean ever mentioned anything about marriage? Certainly, he wanted her physically as much as she wanted him. He gave her proof of that every time he came near her. But never once had he said anything about marriage.

No, she told herself sadly, she could not consider Sean in her future. She wanted . . . needed . . . a husband she could count on. Someone steady. Someone who respected her for more than just a night's tumble. Someone she could build a future with. Someone like . . . Someone like Jason Soames.

She smiled thinking of the flamboyant Soames. He was dashing in quite a different way from Sean. But he was certainly steady. A rock. And she was sure he cared for her. It was only a matter of time before he asked her to marry him. If he did ask, would she accept? There was no fire with Jason as there was at Sean's merest glance, but was a good marriage built on fire or on solid, steady rock?

"A fine day for sailing," Sean said, leaning beside her. Crossing his arms across his chest, he looked up at the rigging, his eye roving critically over the set of the sails and finding all as it should be.

Jessie lifted her face into the wind. "Especially on such a trim little craft as this," she agreed.

Sean's eyes sparkled proudly as they moved over the ship. "I've always had a fondness for the *Fortune*," he said. "Clean-lined and quick with enough kick to her heels to outrun anything her size afloat."

Jessie laughed. "She does have a bit of spirit to her," she said, noting the wide-spread sails. "I thought at first she had too much sail for a ship this size, but she handles it well."

"You have a good eye," he said, looking down at her appreciatively. "Not many people would have noticed that."

"I grew up with ships," she reminded him.

"So did I."

She grinned up at him, a mischievous twinkle in her eyes. "Ah, yes. Your pirate father. The family roots run deep, I see. Is that why you were sentenced? For piracy or something else?"

"Pirates are not enslaved. They're hung."

"Was your father hung?" she asked, the twinkle in her eyes softening to concern.

Sean smiled wickedly. "Not yet. But my grandfather was."

"For piracy?"

"For treason."

"A family history to be proud of," she said dryly.

"Yes," he answered, nodding, "it is."

She looked up at him expecting to see a hint of teasing in his eyes and was surprised to see that he was serious.

Catching her look of surprise, Sean smiled and reached over to chuck her under the chin. "Someday I'll tell you the whole of it."

She started to ask him more questions, but he leaped into the rigging in answer to Captain Reading's orders to change the sails for the starboard tack. She watched him work, realizing that again he had avoided telling her why he had been sentenced to slavery.

Maybelle had not approved of her mistress's activities of late. Not that she would mind seeing the handsome bondslave really become Miss Jessie's husband, she thought, bobbing her head over her embroidery. She just didn't like them sharing a room when they weren't truly wed. She pushed a brown curly lock off her forehead. Now they had gone off to Charles Town and would spend yet another night as man and wife. She sighed. Well, it would soon be over. If all went well, they should be back this afternoon, he would clear his things out of the room that should belong to Miss Jessie alone, and he and that insufferable manservant of his would be gone.

Not that Matt Webb was so awful to look at, she thought, jabbing a new thread into her needle. And not near so uppity as she had thought at first. He had been downright entertaining at the supper table in the kitchen every night. She just might miss having him at meals. And his recipe for starch really was an improvement over her own, she had to admit.

Miss Jessie had even said Matt and Sean might be returning to Barbados. At that thought, she was surprised to feel a pang of disappointment. She might actually miss that big lummox! Not that he was all that big. He was just a bit taller than she was. But he was wonderful well set up with them brawny arms and all, with just enough heft to him to have a good solid feel about him. Solid and secure. Dependable. Now wouldn't he be just the one to grow old with?

"Humpf!" she said, wondering where *that* thought had come from.

Suddenly a shadow fell on her work, and she colored when she looked up to see the object of her thoughts standing over her. He was also turning a bit red and shifting uncomfortably from foot to foot. It was the first time she had ever seen him ill at ease and somehow it made her heart go out to him—a heart that now beat more quickly than before.

"Miss Maybelle?" Matt said.

"Yes?" she answered, surprised at how little breath she seemed to have to get out that one simple word.

"Walk with me?"

He looked so much like a man resigned to refusal she gave him an encouraging smile as she put down her work. "I would enjoy that," she said, sliding her arm though his, feeling how right they seemed to fit together as they walked off the veranda and headed down the path beside the hedge.

They walked in silence for a few moments, and she gave a great sigh of contentment. It was so easy walking with Matt, she thought, comfortable. She leaned closer to him and that seemed to give him the confidence to speak.

"I'll be going back to Charles Town today."

"I'll miss you," she answered, knowing now it was true.

"I would like to come back and see you if you would permit it."

She stopped and turned to face him, surprised that he would want to court her. "I think I would like that very much."

"I made something for you." From his pocket, he pulled a little wooden horse and handed it to her. It was excellently made, prancing and graceful.

Maybelle was so touched by the gift made just for her she was speechless. She had had gifts from men before, but they had been typical things, ribbons, flowers, trinkets. No one had ever given her something so special, something they had made themselves. Quickly, before she thought, she reached up and gave him a kiss on the cheek, and she was not sure who was more surprised. Then she, who had always been such an outrageous flirt with every other man but this one, turned and ran into the house, embarrassed as a schoolgirl.

As soon as Jessie and Sean arrived at the plantation, Matt began clearing Sean's things from the house. Jessie stood in the doorway, watching as Matt helped Sean pack the last of his things into his trunk. She was amazed at the deference Matt showed Sean, as if Sean were his master instead of a fellow bondslave.

Sean helped Matt lift a small trunk to his shoulder, and Jessie moved out of Matt's way as he left the room with his burden. It was then that Sean looked up to see her standing there.

"Jessie!" he said, striding to her and reaching out to pull her close.

She should have fended off his embrace, but she leaned into his arms instead. "Your cabin is nearly ready," she said, trying desperately to breathe steadily, to keep her senses from reeling at the onslaught of his nearness.

He nuzzled her hair. "I am not adverse to remaining here."

She closed her eyes for a moment, savoring his presence, the touch of his lips on her hair, the strength of his arms around her. She wanted nothing more than to have him remain here with her. But she knew it was not right. She had already transgressed far beyond the bounds of propriety, of moral rightness, because she could not resist him. Her only hope of retaining some decency was to keep him at a distance. It was not much of a distance from the house to the little slave cabin she had had cleaned and readied for him. But perhaps it would be enough for the next two weeks. Then there would be the miles from the plantation to Charles Town between them. Then from there to Barbados. At that painful thought, she wrenched away from him.

"I know," she said, "but you can't."

Matt returned at that moment to help carry down the big trunk, and as Sean bent to take one end, he looked up at her. "You know where I'll be if—"

"I'll check on you later to make sure you have everything you need, Mr. Winthrop," she said primly, interrupting Sean, wanting him settled in his cabin far away from her.

Sean smiled lecherously at her as he went past her. Not until the two men had left the room did she realize that Sean seemed to think that "everything you need" meant her as well!

Sean was arranging his belongings in his new quarters when the door to his cabin burst open, banging against the wall, and Sean looked up in surprise to see Jackson looming in the doorway.

"Do come in," Sean invited sardonically.

"I heard what you been up to while I was gone," Jackson accused.

Sean merely lifted a questioning brow and waited for the man to have his say.

"She must not've liked it too good, though, since she throwed you out." He laughed, nodding at the simple straw-stuffed ticking in one corner.

"Is there something I can help you with?" Sean asked, ignoring Jackson's brazen innuendos.

Grimacing at his adversary's lack of response, Jackson shrugged and moved on to his reason for coming. "Information," he said. "*J* wants to know if you got any information."

"*J?*" Sean's brows came together in a puzzled frown.

"The boss," Jackson said. "That's what we call her."

Sean's guts twisted. *J*. And a woman. *J* for Jessie? "A woman?"

"Nobody but me knows who she is and that's the way she wants it." Jackson hooked his thumbs into his belt. "You got anythin' for us or not?"

"Maybe," Sean said, crossing his arms. He needed to be more than a mere informer to catch the elusive *J*. He needed to be a member of the gang.

Jackson drew out some coins and tossed them onto the pallet.

Sean scoffed at the money. "I'll need more than that."

Jackson fingered another coin, holding it up for Sean's inspection. "Let's hear what you got first."

Waving negligently at the money the overseer held, Sean sat on the one stool the sparse room contained, stretched out his long legs, and crossed his arms. "A mere pittance," he said. "I have needs—and expenses—far greater than that."

"I heard about all them fancy clothes," Jackson sneered as if dressing well was beneath him.

"It seems there is little you haven't heard about," Sean said as if admiring the man's astuteness.

Jackson preened under the scant praise, swelling importantly, then brought himself back to the subject at hand. "So you need money, eh? There's greater rewards to be earned for sure. But you got to be willin' to take more risk."

Sean shrugged. "That seems only fair. What can I do?"

Jackson leaned forward conspiratorily. "We can use another man. That is, if you've got the stomach to go raidin'."

Sean let a slow smile light his face. "I have the stomach, Mr. Jackson. And the willingness to fight if need be. When and where is the raid?"

A crafty look glinted in Jackson's eyes. "I'll tell you that when the time comes."

"And when will that be?" Sean asked, still trying to nail down the next raid. If he could have Colonel Rhett waiting with some men, the raiders could be followed. This band of raiders had to be rendezvousing with the pirates plaguing Charles Town to dispose of their loot and to give them any information they could about future shipping. And that's who they wanted to catch. This band could lead them to the pirates.

"I'll let you know. Just be ready any time. Get yourself a mask of some kind and some dark clothes and weapons." He turned to leave then turned back. "And any information you got from now on helps us all." With that, he scooped up the coins he had thrown onto the bed and left.

Sean had just finished washing when a light tap sounded at the door. Jackson had just left but moments before. Could it be the overseer returning with news of a raid already? Lacking a towel, he grabbed up his discarded shirt to dry himself with and wrenched open the door.

It was Jessie, holding two large fluffy towels.

"I couldn't ask for better service," he said, laughing. Tossing his shirt back with his other laundry, he took a towel and began rubbing it briskly through his hair, motioning Jessie inside.

She entered the cabin and sat on the stool, looking around. There was little enough to see. There was the straw-stuffed pallet in one corner, a small table in another with Sean's comb, soap, razor, and a small mirror neatly arranged beside a washbasin. Two of Sean's clean work outfits of cotton shirts and nut-brown trousers hung on pegs. His small trunk was tucked under the table, but there was no sign of his large trunk.

"Where is your trunk?" Jessie asked.

Sean ran his comb through his still-wet hair and turned to her, grinning. "Matt took it back to Charles Town on the *Fortune*. Now that I'm a bondslave again, I didn't think I would be invited to any formal balls."

She started to ask why he had the clothes in the first place but held her tongue on a point that could only lead to a disagreement. "Letty stayed here." It was as much as question as a statement.

Sean shrugged into a clean shirt. "She likes to cook for an appreciative audience. Since Mr. Fortune is out of town, she thought she might as well give us a few decent meals."

Jessie smiled. "It will certainly be appreciated. Maybe she can give Josie a few lessons while she's here."

Sean leaned back against the cabin's sturdy center pole and looked down at her, his eyes growing warm as they surveyed her. Her straight hair had been pulled severely back into a knot at her nape, and he wanted nothing more at that moment than to loosen it and let it flow through his fingers.

He stretched out his hand to touch her, and she jumped up as if burned.

"I'm sorry it isn't much," she chattered nervously, indicating the simplicity of his surroundings.

He caught her by the arms and pulled her close. "It's all I need now that you are here."

She stared up at him, stock-still, her lips softly parted. He bent to kiss her, but before his lips touched hers, she wrenched out of his grasp and fled from the cabin, not even bothering to close the door behind her.

Jessie fled down the path from Sean's cabin. She had been a fool to go there. She should have known what would happen. What *almost* happened, she corrected herself.

She went to her room and undressed, her hands shaking so badly she could hardly unfasten her stomacher. Her glance fell on the soft, wide bed. She had shared it once with Sean. Now it seemed too wide for one. How could she miss someone so much, she wondered, when she had known him so short a time?

After hours of restlessly tossing in bed, she got up to pace. Her steps led to the window, and she paused when she realized that this was where Sean had slept on his pallet. Where she and Sean had . . . She moved away, back to the bed, only to toss and turn again. At last she sat up and pushing the hair back from her eyes, wrapped her arms around her knees and decided to face her sleeplessness head on.

She missed Sean and wanted him. Whether it was right or wrong, she wanted him here with her. She knew he wanted her. So why shouldn't she have him? *Because society says it is wrong,* the answer came back. *You are not wed.*

"Then society doesn't have to know," she muttered, kicking off the covers. "I can't let him move back in here, though," she continued her mutterings to herself as she searched along the floor with her feet for her slippers. "But I can go to him and who will be the wiser?"

Finding her shoes at last, she slipped her feet into them and grabbed a warm robe from the wardrobe, flinging it around her as she went softly down the hall.

Sean's cabin was dark and quiet as she approached it. Thankfully, she had chosen one for him that was set a bit apart from the others and screened somewhat by a clump of pines. Tapping softly on the door, she waited in vain for an answer. Growing bolder, she pushed the door open. There was no one there.

The pallet in the corner had been used, the covers flung aside. *Perhaps he has gone to answer nature's call,* she thought, smiling to think of his surprise when he returned, sleep rumpled, to find her there waiting for him.

She wandered about the one room of the cabin, fingering Sean's things on the table, touching his clothing on the pegs. She sat for a few minutes on the stool, then got up to pace again. He should have been back by now, she thought. She waited a few more minutes then grew restless. Where could he be?

If there had been a problem in the slave quarters, she would have heard the commotion on her way here. All had been quiet. Then a disturbing thought struck her. When she had moved him out of the house, then let him know she was no longer available, had he sought solace elsewhere?

That he was a virile, lusty man she knew well. Had he found another so quickly? Maybelle had been attracted to him until she met Matt Webb. But Maybelle, for all her man-watching and flirting, was the most straight-laced of Bostonians when it came to actually . . . No, it was not Maybelle.

Josie! The quadroon slave had left no doubt that she would welcome Sean's attention. Could he have gone to her? Was he even now clasped in the dusky woman's embrace?

Her cheeks burning, Jessie fled the cabin even more rapidly than she had earlier that evening. He must not find her there if he returned. Her flight led her through the kitchen, and she paused for one slight moment, the thought of flinging open the door to Josie's cozy room behind the fireplace crossing her mind. Then she fled up the stairs to her room. As she well knew, she and Sean were not wed. It was no business of hers if he were pillowed in a lusty brown embrace.

It was hardly a lusty embrace that pillowed Sean. A sharp rock jabbed into his side as he lay outside Jason Soames's palatial home in the darkness, a sturdy saber in hand. He could hear Jackson's anxious breathing a few paces away as they watched a furtive figure dart to the house to peer through the windows.

The figure, though dressed in trousers and wearing a close-fitting hat pulled low over a masked face, was clearly that of a woman. The darkness and her attire hid the other indications of her femininity, and Sean had not been allowed to get near enough to her to tell who she was. To tell, he thought, whether it was Jessie.

The woman motioned them forward. He and Jackson took up positions at the front and back of the house. They watched while two other men, masked as Sean was, quietly and expertly pried the lock of the door and entered the house, led by J.

Sean heard small shuffling noises from within, the sliding of drawers, the rattle of silver, all of which sounded to him like alarms in the dark stillness. He heard the woman's husky whispers directing the ransackers as if she knew well where the valuables were. Had she been to this house before? Sean wondered. A welcome guest at the end of an early-morning's ride?

He pushed such thoughts away, concentrating on watching. If someone did raise an alarm, he wanted to be sure no one was hurt.

The raiders began to emerge with bulging sacks slung over their shoulders, when a shouted, "Who's there?" came from abovestairs in Jason Soames's clear ringing tones.

The woman paused in the doorway, pistol in hand, half turning back toward that challenge. Sean jerked her out of the house and gave her a shove down the walk, then hurried behind her, shielding her with his body.

A shot rang out, and Sean felt a sharp pain crease along his upper arm before he was hidden by the trees. They ran down the path to the dock and clambered aboard the skiff they had come in. One man had been left in charge of the boat and had the sail up and oars out. In moments they were well away before chase could be given.

Sean took the place he had been given in the bow and held a hand to his bleeding arm, studying the woman. She took a place at the stern, her hand on the tiller, directing a closer trimming of the sail. Clearly, she was a woman well versed in sailing. His heart twisted.

Sean examined his wound. It was barely a scratch and the bleeding soon stopped.

The raiders sailed in silence until they reached the dock at the Twill plantation where Sean was ordered ashore. The woman whispered something to Jackson.

"*J* says you did all right. You'll get your share later." With that, the little craft changed the set of her sail and went off upriver.

There was no more to be learned tonight so Sean made his way to his cabin, thinking of the woman who led the raiders. If *J* really was Jessie, there was one piece that just didn't fit. Jessie seemed to loathe Mr. Jackson, yet he seemed to fit in well with *J*'s plans. But hadn't Jessie said that though she no longer wanted the man as overseer, he had his uses? Was piracy and theft what she meant? Sean shrugged tiredly. A person could dislike someone and still use them.

*　　*　　*

Jessie dozed fitfully, unable to sleep much that night. It was nearly dawn when she rose and paced again to gaze out the window toward Sean's cabin. A white blur at the dock caught her attention, and she peered through a thin screen of trees in that direction. She moved to the other window in the room for a better view and saw, to her surprise, what looked like a skiff docking. One person got out and headed up the walk. The sky was just beginning to lighten, but it was still dark out and from this distance she could not be sure, but she thought it was Sean. When the man came closer, then turned down the path toward the slave cabins, she was nearly certain it was Sean.

At first her heart soared. He hadn't been with another woman! Then a worried frown creased her brow. Just where had he gone and with whom? Relieved but still wondering, a while later, she dressed and yawned as she made her way down the stairs by dawn. A furious knocking fully awakened her, and she hurried to the door, wondering who would be calling at such an early hour.

She opened the door to a nearly frantic and totally disheveled Jason who took one look at her and gathered her to him, nearly smothering her in a crushing embrace. Taken by surprise, she endured his hug while he hung on to her as if she were a long-lost treasure.

Finally, she pushed away. "Jason, whatever is wrong?"

Suddenly aware of the great liberty he had taken, Jason stood back but kept his hands on her shoulders as if afraid she might disappear.

"Forgive me, my dear Jessie. But I was so worried about you."

"Worried?" She laughed to dispel his fear and, taking his arm, pulled him into the parlor and pushed him into a seat.

Without hesitation, she went to the liquor cabinet and poured a shot of brandy and gave it to him.

He looked at it distractedly a moment as if he didn't quite know what it was, then set it aside. "You're sure you're all right?" he asked, taking her hands and pulling her down beside him.

"Of course, Jason. Why wouldn't I be?

"My house was robbed less than an hour ago."

"Robbed! Jason, are *you* all right?"

He waved away the question as if it were unimportant. "They were pirates. They came from the river. I got off one shot before they got away in a skiff, and I think I hit one of them. But I was afraid they might have come here."

"I doubt that they would come here," she said, indicating the shabby room. "There's nothing here of value."

Jason leaned forward earnestly. "There's you."

Surprised and touched by his tender regard, Jessie smiled and squeezed his hands.

"Come with me to Charles Town," he urged. "You can stay in my townhouse where you'll be safe from any danger."

"Thank you, Jason, but I couldn't."

"You would be well chaperoned, I promise you. I'll stay at an inn. You would have no fear for your reputation."

Jessie shook her head, smiling to reassure him. "I appreciate your concern, but I'll be fine. We start the harvest today and I need to be here."

Jason sighed as he stood. "I'm going into Charles Town this morning to report the robbery, but I'll be home this afternoon. If you need me—for any reason—you have but to send word."

"I will," Jessie said, holding his arm as they walked to the door.

"It might be best to post guards until these brigands are caught, Jessie."

"I will. Thank you for the warning."

He turned to her, lifting his hands, and she thought he would take her in his arms again. But he merely nodded and, turning on his heel, went out to leap onto his lathered steed and to pound away down the drive.

By the time Jessie reached the compound, the sun was up and the slaves were gathering their tools to head out into the fields. They had spent the previous day sharpening the sickles and finishing the bags to hold the harvested rice. Sean was there, dividing the men into gangs of workers. The first group marched out of the compound with Mr. Jackson, others under the direction of indentured servants.

"Good morning, Mrs. Twill," Sean said, tipping his wide-brimmed straw hat.

"Good morning, Mr. Winthrop," she answered. "Did you sleep well?"

"Well enough," he said, studying her closely. "But it doesn't look as if you did."

She shrugged and looked away. She couldn't tell him that it was because of him. She couldn't say she had come looking for him last night, only to find him gone. And she had no right to ask him where he had been. "Excited about the harvest, I suppose," she answered at last.

The last gang marched out of the compound, and Sean turned toward a water wagon. It was hot work in the paddies and it saved time to take the water to the workers. "Want to come?"

She nodded, and he lifted her up to the seat, his hands warm and exciting at her waist.

He leaped up beside her and slapped the reins over the mules' backs. The wagon started with a lurch, and Sean guided it in a tight turn, then out toward the fields.

"We're starting with the field farthest from the river. They have the best drainage and are the driest, and we'll work down to the lowest fields."

"Will you have to help with Mr. Fortune's harvest?" she asked.

"Yes, but his field won't be ready for two or three weeks yet, since it was planted later."

When they arrived at the field, the slaves had just begun cutting, bending to chop the stalks close to the ground. They cut for a while then gathered the stalks into sheaves. Others carried the sheaves to the levees and placed them right side up to dry in the sun.

Sean stood beside Jessie, watching the work for a few minutes; then, unable to stand still when there was work to be done, he stripped off his shirt, took up a sickle, and joined a line of slaves. The slaves grinned and worked faster as if challenging this white man to keep up. Sean was well up to the challenge and worked with a will. It was not until he tied his first sheaf and turned to hand it to a slave woman that Jessie saw the long, narrow wound on his upper arm.

She started to call out to him, then stopped, her mind suddenly putting pieces from last night together. Sean had been out on the river last night in a skiff. Jason's house was robbed. He had shot at the retreating pirates and thought he had hit one of them. And Sean had a fresh wound that looked suspiciously like the crease of a bullet. Was it all coincidence, or were Sean's piratical roots sending up fresh sprouts?

Her knees suddenly felt weak, and she leaned back against the wagon. Could Sean really be involved with the pirate raids in the area? She didn't want to believe it, but it would explain how he came by enough money to buy his elegant clothes.

No, she wouldn't believe it. She didn't want even to think it. Without saying good-bye, she turned and headed back to the house. There was a lot to do to help prepare the noon meal for the workers. It would keep her busy enough not to have to think at all.

Chapter Thirteen

It was a long, busy day. From sunup to sundown, the workers labored in the fields. Somehow Sean had managed to make a game of it, offering prizes to the ones who cut the most sheaves and to the gangs who cleared their field first. Sean worked for one group for a while, then helped another gang, challenging the slaves with his own efforts instead of threats.

The midday meal was brought to the field in wagons, and the work continued. At the end of the day, Sean passed out prizes, a new shirt, new hats, new pots. Jessie promised a dance for the end of the harvest, and then the evening meal was served.

Jessie went to the house to clean up for her own supper. She didn't feel like facing the loneliness of dining alone at the big table, so after preparing for bed, she took a tray Letty made for her and went into her office to work and eat.

The supplies Josie and Jackson had purchased in Williamsburg and the prizes for the harvest had seriously depleted her meager supply of money. The additional purchases of food for the slaves had eaten into the money she had set aside for Sean's indenture and now only a few assorted coins remained in her cash box.

It might be weeks before she saw any money from the harvest. The sheaves of rice had to be dried, threshed, milled, winnowed, and dried further before they could be put into the readied sacks for transport down the river and eventual sale. She needed money now for clothing material for the slaves, nails, and tools.

She pushed her half-empty tray aside to go over the accounts once again. There was no pleasant surprise. She only found another bill that would take more cash than she had to pay it.

"Money problems?"

Jessie lifted tired eyes to see Sean standing in the doorway, his hair neatly combed but still glistening wet, a clean shirt hanging loosely to mid-thigh. His eyes seemed to warm at the sight of her attired in her nightgown and thin cotton robe, and her body answered with a growing warmth of its own that even pulling her robe tighter about her failed to subdue.

Nodding despondently, Jessie leaned her folded arms on the ledger, not realizing how enticingly that simple act displayed the rounded swell of her bosom to eyes eager to feast on that sight. "I won't have the money to give you, and there are things I need but there won't be any money until I sell the harvest or . . ." She trailed off reluctant to mention her minuscule investment in a ship's cargo.

"Or?" Sean prodded.

Jessie shook her head. "Nothing that can be counted on."

A disconcerted look crossed Sean's face as he looked at her closely. "Jessie, if you are in need of money, I'm sure Mr. Fortune would give you a loan against your harvest. You needn't worry about paying my indenture for now nor do anything desperate," he finished lamely.

"That's good of you, Sean, and Mr. Fortune's been so generous already, I would hate to ask him now for a loan." She sighed. "But I may have no choice."

"I'll take you into Charles Town whenever you need to go."

"Thank you again, Sean," she said, standing up and coming around the desk to place a hand on his arm. "And thank you for being willing to wait until I can pay your year's indenture and for helping out with the harvest. It seemed to go well today." Sean's sharply indrawn breath elicited a similar shortening of her own.

"There is still a long way to go," he said, his voice husky and low.

"Yes."

His arms came around her slowly, caressingly, as if she were the most fragile thing in the world. "I've missed you, Jessie."

As ever when she was this near to him, all else faded in importance. She let herself be drawn nearer, laying her head on his chest, her hand smoothing the coarse fabric of his shirt and feeling the firm flesh beneath. "As I have missed you."

"Come to me tonight," he rasped into the softness of her hair.

She almost told him that she had come to him the night before to find him gone. Disconcerted about the possible reason for it, she held her tongue. But almost of its own will, her head was nodding its assent to come to him. Kissing the top of her head, he left her as silently as he had come.

Jessie was hurrying down the path to Sean's cabin, her long, dark cloak wrapped about her, when an arm shot out from the shadows and caught her, pulling her beneath the trees. She gasped and was about to scream when a mouth came down on hers, strong arms embraced her, and she was held close to a lean, rock-hard body that she knew even in the darkness. Letting out a sigh, she relaxed into Sean's arms.

"I was waiting for you," he said huskily.

"You nearly scared me to death," she accused, snuggling closer.

Chuckling, he swept her up into his arms to carry her the few feet to his cabin. Kicking the door shut, he bent to claim her mouth once again, then lay her down on his pallet, pushing aside her cloak. He ran his hands over her entire body as if they were as hungry to touch her as his mouth was to kiss her.

Just as eager for him, she lifted his shirt to caress his lean ribs, the solid flatness of his belly, the smooth muscles of his back.

Kneeling beside her, he pulled her nightgown up and over her head, casting it aside to waft down in a cloud of cambric and lace, his own clothing landing a moment later.

"You're beautiful," he breathed.

She laughed softly into the darkness. "You can't see me."

His hands touched her body where they had caressed her through her clothes but moments before. "Not with my eyes."

She lifted her hands to play softly over his face. "And you are most handsome."

She felt his lips land on her shoulder, search downward until they found their goal at the tip of her breast. "You taste good, too."

Hungrily, her mouth nibbled at him, first his ear then the strong corded muscles along his neck. She delighted in the deep curve of his collar bone so unlike her own, savored the rich abundance of muscle on his chest, and nuzzled in the crisp curls of hair there, nipping his skin while her nails raked gently across his back.

Growling, he captured her wrists and held them captive above her head. "Would you eat me alive, minx?"

Holding her gently imprisoned with one hand, he freely explored her with the other. He smiled, feeling her body respond to his caresses.

At last, unable to withstand this loving torment, she pulled free of him and twisted to push him down, imprisoning his wrists as he had done hers. "Now, bondslave, it is time you learned your place."

Smiling, Sean submitted to her. "What will my lady do to me?"

She leaned on his chest, her face close to his. "Perhaps I shall exact a kiss," she said, moving closer until she felt his breath mingling with hers. When he lifted his head, she let his lips catch a bare, tantalizing taste of hers before she moved her head away, laughing softly. "Or perhaps not," she said.

Keeping one hand firmly on his wrists above his head, she let her other hand trail down the center of his chest, across the flat plain of his belly and to the edge of the thicker tangle of hair between his thighs, teasingly reversing her course time and again.

"Perhaps, temptress," Sean muttered between clenched teeth, "you will drive me mad."

Time and again her breasts brushed across his chest, and she tempted him with lips that barely touched his body before darting away. Time and again he tried desperately to capture the sweetness of her mouth before she took it away, chuckling, while he groaned with the torment of the unattainable temptation.

Melting against him as if at last giving in to his needs, she let her mouth linger on his for a moment. He had time only to let out a sigh of relief before her mouth was gone again. It was too much. Moaning, he brought his arms around her, but her strength was nothing compared to his, and, twisting, he brought her beneath him, at last bringing his mouth down upon his elusive goal, obtaining its complete and total surrender.

Greedily, they sought each other—she, open and inviting; he, eager to fill her and make her his. Replete at last, they lay entwined. Her head rested on his shoulder, and her fingers played across his chest, twining the crisp hair around them. His hand trailed along the curve of her back.

"It seems the bondslave has conquered after all," she said, sighing contentedly.

He laughed and squeezed her. "How so? I find I am more your slave than ever."

She scoffed at that. "You are no one's slave. I don't think you are capable of being a slave."

"Mr. Fortune might dispute that."

"It would probably do him little good. I sometimes wonder just who is master there, Mr. Fortune or you." She sat up, groping for her gown.

" 'Tis true he gives me much latitude," Sean agreed, crossing his arms behind his head. "And I am thankful else I would not have the time to dally with young widows."

Finding their clothes, she took her gown and dropped his shirt on his face. "Widows?" she asked. "How many other widows do you know?"

"At least a dozen," Sean said, pushing the shirt away.

"Do you dally with them all?" she asked as she pulled on her gown.

"Only you." His hand reached out to pull her down to him again.

"Why am I so honored?" she asked, ruffling his hair.

"Now, let's see," Sean said, running a finger absently along her jaw as if trying to recall his reasons. "Was it your wealth or your beauty that attracted me?"

"Since I have neither," she chuckled, sitting up to put on her robe, "it must have been convenience. I was near to hand and you but took advantage of that fact."

He pulled her to him, his voice changing from its easy bantering tone. " 'Tis true you are near, but having once seen you, I would have sought you out if a thousand miles had separated us."

"If your master takes you back to Barbados, would you then come back to me once you are a free man?"

"It will not be so long as that, Jessie. I'd not wait that long to claim you."

What did he have in mind? she wondered. Had he joined the pirates to gain the money to purchase his freedom? She had no certain proof that he was engaged in that trade, yet she felt a sudden fear for him. Clinging to him, she whispered, "Be careful, Sean!" Then, wrenching free of him, she fled, running down the path back to the cold comfort of her own bed.

Jackson had come for him in the early hours before dawn, not long after Jessie had left him, and now Sean motioned the two men and the woman following him to silence as they crept toward Mr. Fortune's upriver warehouse. He had known that, sooner or later, he would have to prove his usefulness to this gang of pirates to gain their confidence. He had planned this raid with Mr. Meachum, making sure that the goods stored here were worth the effort but not so much that their loss would be seriously felt. He had hoped to use this raid as a chance for Colonel Rhett to trail the gang back to their leaders. Unfortunately, *J* had insisted that the raid take place tonight and Sean had not had the chance to warn Colonel Rhett. He had also not had a chance to warn Bill Flinders, the shy watchman, to stay out of harm's way and was worried that the man would get hurt.

Mr. Meachum had complained that too much was being sacrificed to the cutthroats. But Sean felt that these goods would be a small price to pay if he could eventually lead Colonel Rhett to the pirates this small gang worked with. The same pirates who were devastating Charles Town's shipping seemed to have a particular fondness for Fortune Company's ships. After tonight there would have to be another trap set, one the wily *J* would have more trouble evading.

Now as he crept along the dock at the Fortune holdings, he could not help wonder if the woman following so stealthily behind him was really Jessie. Mr. Jackson had said that *J* had not liked having Sean as part of the gang, but had had to accept him after Jackson had let him in on that other raid. *J* was always careful to stay well away from Sean as if fearful of being recognized. She whispered her commands to him, and her voice was further muffled by the mask she wore. Even her figure was often, as tonight, hidden in the folds of a long, dark cape.

They had just come up to the shed containing the furs when Bill Flinders stepped out from behind the building, aiming a musket at them. "Hold!" he cried.

From the corner of his eye, Sean saw *J* raise a pistol. The movement distracted Bill, and Sean took the chance of diving at the watchman, grappling with him for possession of the musket. The watchman was burly and strong but no match for the steellike strength in Sean's arms. Pinning the watchman down, Sean leaned close to his ear. "Bill Flinders! It's Sean Winthrop!" he whispered.

The watchman stopped his useless struggles, looking up at Sean with amazement.

"Go limp, Bill, and stay still until we are through here. Then go to Colonel Rhett."

Flinders opened his mouth to protest, but Sean clamped a hand over it. "Trust me!"

Bill's eyes shifted uncertainly a moment; then he gave as much of a nod as he could within Sean's hold. Then he went limp so suddenly Sean wondered for a moment if he had really hurt the man. But the watchman's steady breathing assured him that Bill was fine.

Sean stood up to nods of approval from his fellow thieves and *J* put away her pistol. Would she have really used it? Sean wondered.

Jackson and the other man were pounding on the door, but the sturdy structure was holding firm. They were about to take a hatchet to the lock when Sean pushed them aside. "Here," he said, holding out a key. "There's no need for that."

The door was soon opened, and Jackson turned to *J*. "Told you he'd come in handy!"

J shrugged noncommittally and pushed her way into the warehouse. Lighting a lantern, she looked through the furs quickly, choosing only the best ones. Then each of them took up a load to carry to the skiff. When the skiff held all it would carry, they clambered aboard and set off downstream.

A few minutes later they were stopping again, this time at the edge of the Twill plantation. The skiff fit neatly into a small inlet well-screened with undergrowth. A narrow path led to the shed Sean had investigated before—the shed Jackson had claimed to be dilapidated and vermin-ridden.

This time *J* had the key. She unlocked the stout door, and they began carrying furs inside. When the furs were stored, Sean surveyed the contents of the shed. He noted the gathered loot from other raids, including several silver pieces with an engraved *C*, probably from the Campbells.

"When do I get my share?" he asked.

"When we sell the goods," Jackson answered as if Sean were a dolt.

"When will that be?" Sean prodded.

"When we meet with the others," the other man chortled. "We got to take this stuff to another colony to sell it. Can't rightly sell it in Charles Town, now can we?"

Sean opened his mouth again to ask when, but Jackson cut him off, snarling impatiently, "It'll be soon, Winthrop. We'll let you know."

Now that they had revealed the location of their hidden cache, Sean hoped they trusted him enough to reveal themselves to him, for he still had not seen the faces of anyone but Jackson. He also needed to know the time and place of their rendezvous with the other pirates. But again he was disappointed.

"You know the way back from here," Jackson said, pointing down the path.

"What about you?" Sean asked. "And *J?*"

"We'll take the skiff."

"Why can't I go in the skiff?" Sean complained, hoping to be allowed to come along this time to find out just where *J* was let off. Would it be at the plantation house?

" 'Cause you ask too many questions," Jackson sneered.

Sean thought of pleading further, but *J* had taken out her pistol again. Whether she was Jessie or someone else, he wanted to give her no excuse to use it. Shrugging, he set off down the path at a leisurely walk.

As soon as he was out of sight, he quickened his pace to a near run. The way by the river to the house was shorter and, with the current, much quicker. But if he hurried, and they dallied long enough, he just might be able to get there about the same time—if that was their destination.

As he jogged along the path, Sean thought of Jackson's words. If Jessie were *J*, she wouldn't like him to take part in the raids. Hadn't Jessie left him just hours before with a hasty plea of "Be careful" as if she knew he would be raiding before dawn? He knew she had money problems. Was raiding her answer to them? She had said that she was waiting for some investment to pay off. Or was it the sale of her loot she was waiting for?

Jessie woke in the early predawn. She had left Sean with an injunction to be careful, and as she lay in bed alone, she wondered if Sean could really have been part of anything so terrible as theft. Unable to go back to sleep, she decided that she might as well get dressed and go down to the quarters for the start of the day. Since the path went past Sean's cabin, she would wake him with a kiss. Surely he would be there. Surely her worries were groundless.

She finished dressing and headed out of her room, then stopped to put a cloak around her. It would still be a bit chilly this early.

As she passed through the kitchen, Jessie was surprised to see Josie, already awake and stirring up the fire. She nodded to the woman and left the house, heading down the path that branched just ahead to go either to the river or to the quarters.

She stopped at the branch, listening to the sound of running feet. Then Sean burst into view, coming from the direction of the fields.

"Sean!"

Sean stopped a few feet from her, his shoulders slumping as if in disappointment. "Jessie," he said somberly.

Then he held out his arms to her, and she came into them, trembling with fear that he had been out raiding again.

"Oh, Jessie," he repeated, and buried his face in her hair.

The harvest continued the next day. The slaves worked even more diligently now that they knew that the offered prizes were real and not just airy promises. When Jessie arrived with the food wagons for the noon meal, she saw Sean working alongside a huge black man, both grinning at the other, as if there were a personal challenge between them to finish their row first. They were both naked to the waist, glistening with sweat in the hot sun, their movements rhythmic and sure. The black finished well ahead of Sean and straightened, his hands on his hips, to wait for the white master to catch up. Sean finished his row and tossed down his sickle, shaking his head, acknowledging defeat.

The clatter in the wagon reminded Jessie of her purpose there, and she jumped down to help feed the slaves who were already queuing up. Josie had already filled one bowl, however, and was carrying it to Sean, her hips swaying provocatively, her smile enticing. In one hand she held a gourd of water, and he took the drink gratefully, grinning down at the slave woman. Josie took the opportunity to preen before him, holding the wooden bowl of stew up to her breasts as if to draw attention to her shapely bosom.

Gritting her teeth, Jessie watched them. It seemed to Jessie that Sean was not at all reluctant to give Josie's bosom all the attention the quadroon wanted. Turning away, she grabbed up a ladle and began filling bowls, handing them to the workers as they passed. But she continued to watch Josie's flirtations with vexation. Her attention was only diverted when she noticed that Maybelle had stopped handing out her bowls and was gazing out across the field.

The workers had all been served, and Jessie looked to see what Maybelle was staring at.

"It's Matt!" Maybelle said, lifting her skirts and heading toward the still-distant figure.

Jessie shook her head, wondering how Maybelle had made out the identity of the man from so far away and was even more surprised to see her maid nearly throw herself into the arms of the man she had claimed to despise so short a time ago.

Absently chewing a chunk of Letty's homemade bread, Jessie watched the couple come closer, purposely avoiding looking in Sean's direction. Just hearing his laughter as he joked with Josie was enough to bear.

When Maybelle and Matt reached the wagon, Matt handed Jessie a letter. "Mr. Soames sent this to you from Charles Town," he said.

Jessie could have guessed who it was from by the looping script that was every bit as flamboyant as Jason.

"My Dear Jessie," she read. "So many of our neighbors are in town this week, I thought I'd give an impromptu ball. Do say you'll come so I can introduce you to everyone. It's this Saturday night at my townhouse. The Walkers send their invitation to stay with them. Fondly, Jason."

Goodness, she thought, *that's tomorrow night.* There was no problem about something to wear, but did she dare go off and leave the harvest in progress? Her eyes sparkling at the thought of a ball, she looked out across the fields. It seemed an eternity since she had danced!

Sean had come up to them to see if Matt had some message for him, and Matt handed him a letter as well.

Sean broke the seal and glanced at the note in his hand. "Mr. Fortune has need of me in Charles Town," he told Jessie, refolding the note and tucking it into his pocket. He looked at

Matt. "You can stay the night, can't you?"

Maybelle squeezed his arm happily and Matt nodded. "Certainly, S . . . Sean."

Jessie glanced sharply at Matt. She was sure he had almost said "sir," but had changed it to Sean.

"Would you like to go into town, Jessie?" Sean asked. "We could leave tomorrow afternoon and return Sunday morning. We wouldn't miss much of the harvest that way."

"I'd love to go!" she said so enthusiastically that Sean cocked a questioning brow at her. Suddenly embarrassed by the exuberance she had shown, she hastened to explain, "It's just that I have an invitation from Jason to attend a ball tomorrow night."

She saw a scowl start to form on Sean's face but turned away. What right did he have to scowl at her relationship with Jason when he had just been flirting so outrageously with Josie?

Not wanting to make too much of her relationship with Jason in front of the others, she continued, "I wanted to go into town anyway, to talk to Mr. Fortune about that matter we discussed, Sean."

She noticed a look of surprise, almost of alarm on Matt's face as he looked quickly toward Sean, but an almost imperceptible shake of Sean's head suppressed it. Before Jessie could wonder about this surreptitious communication, Jackson was bellowing for the hands to return to work.

Sean handed her his bowl with a smile and a wink and turned back to the field, directing the women to gather up the sheaves and stack them along the dike.

Jessie stood by her window, washed in starlight and shadow. But not even the cooling night breeze that continually brushed the sheer curtains against her could cool the heat that flowed through her. Sean had started it when he had left the kitchen after supper. His lips had brushed her cheek and he had whispered a single word to her. "Come," he had said. Simply, "Come."

It was enough. He wanted her. She wanted him, wanted his arms about her, wanted his body next to hers, wanted to lean on his strength. She ached for the touch of his hand and her loins cried out with desire. But there was more to her longing than physical passion. She wanted the comfort, the belonging, she felt in Sean's arms. She had never felt so cherished, as if she were the most precious thing in the world to him.

Yet she stood here, uncertain. There were so many logical reasons not to go. Not the least of which was that what she had done was against all the moral teachings she had been raised to respect. And Sean had never once offered to rectify the situation, to marry her. Perhaps because he had little future to offer her. There were still nearly seven years of his indenture to serve. His bondage no longer bothered her, but the thought that he might not have forsaken a criminal path, that he might yet be involved in theft and piracy, gave her pause. If he were involved, was there any way she could stop him?

She stood there uncertain for one moment longer, her heart crying out. Then reason gave way to emotion and she ran from the room, down the stairs, out into the night, and into Sean's arms once more.

The moment she threw open his door and flung herself at him, his arms went around her as if he were desperate for her. She clung to him fiercely, wanting, needing some assurance from him that all was well.

But it was an assurance he could not give her. He held on to her just as tightly, just as fiercely as she clung to him. He took her with a furious urgency that she matched with an almost insatiable craving of her own. Like wildfire through dry kindling, their passion raged, consuming them until they lay spent in each other's arms.

The next afternoon Jessie went downriver in the skiff with Sean, Matt, and Maybelle. Matt and Maybelle sat in the bow, lost in their own world, while Jessie settled in the stern near the tiller watching them. They seemed as happy as two puppies. She had watched Maybelle moon after men many times, but never had she seen her this giggly, schoolgirlishly happy. Matt would be good for Maybelle, she thought. Maybelle needed his solid competence. She hoped things worked out well for them.

She turned to watch Sean sail the little boat, wondering anew if his pirate father had passed on more than skill in seamanship. Was this the skiff she had seen at her dock that early-morning hour right after the raid on Jason's? Then Sean turned to her, his eyes two dots of blue sky in a sun-browned face, and her fears fled in the light of his smile.

When they reached Charles Town, the two servants took Jessie's trunk to the Walkers', her ball gown packed carefully inside between layers of sheeting to prevent wrinkles. Sean took her hand to help her from the skiff, then, like a good bondslave, walked sedately beside her to Mr. Fortune's house.

The house was a new, comfortable-looking brick set back from the street and screened by a high lattice fence. Sean held the gate open for her, and she hurried up the walk, anxious finally to meet and to thank Mr. Fortune who had been so helpful to her. She hated that at their first meeting, however, she would have to ask for the further kindness of a loan. But at least she would be repaying that kindness.

Sean opened the door and ushered her inside, and it was

clear even from the entry that this house belonged to a gentleman of good taste who could well afford to indulge himself with riches of every sort. From the rich Turkish carpet to the polished brass wall sconces to the lace-trimmed curtains, all was in harmony and gleamed with evidence of good care.

"Mr. Fortune's office is at the back, Mrs. Twill," Sean said, indicating the passage through the house.

Jessie wondered if Sean's sudden formality was due to his presence in his master's house. But a quick glance at the bondsman's face showed that his words were uttered with a touch of amusement which assured her that there were no limits to the man's audacity.

Jessie preceded Sean down the hall where Sean again surprised her by opening the door to Mr. Fortune's office without so much as knocking. Mr. Meachum was seated behind the large desk that dominated the room, going through some papers. He looked up at their entrance, looked in surprise from one to the other of them, then hurriedly rose to his feet to sketch her an awkward bow.

"Mr. Meachum," said Sean, "I'd like you to meet Jessie Twill."

Mr. Meachum's eyes grew wide as if not sure how to react. Then he bustled from around the desk to bow again over her proffered hand. "Pleased," he mumbled bruskly. "Charmed."

"Mrs. Twill is here to see Mr. Fortune," Sean said and smiled when his statement sent poor Mr. Meachum into a state of nervous anxiety.

The secretary's eyes flitted back and forth from Sean to Jessie, and he seemed to have trouble finding a resting place for his hands which seemed to fly about frantically.

"Mr. Fortune?" Meachum gulped. "Uh, Mr. Fortune is . . ." He cleared his throat and seemed to be appealing to Sean for help. "Uh, Mr. Fortune is . . ."

"Indisposed?" Sean offered.

Mr. Meachum let out a long sigh of relief, and his hands at last found a comfortable spot folded across his paunch. "Yes, yes. Indisposed."

Jessie tried not to let her disappointment show. "I'm sorry. Perhaps I could come back tomorrow?"

"Tomorrow?" Her question seemed to set off the jitters in Mr. Meachum again. "No, I don't think so. That is, I'm not sure. I mean . . ."

"It must be the migraine again, eh, Mr. Meachum?" Sean asked.

Mr. Meachum flustered until he found a yes in answer to Sean's encouraging nodding.

"Which is why you sent for me, isn't it?" Again Meachum nodded in the affirmative, seemingly soothed not to have to offer explanations of his own but merely to agree with Sean.

Sean shrugged deprecatingly to Jessie. "I seem to be the only one who can ease Mr. Fortune's discomfort when he has a migraine. I'm sure I'll be able to go back upriver with you tomorrow, but I'm afraid Mr. Fortune won't be able to see you."

"Oh," Jessie said, trying not to show her disappointment. She really needed that loan to tide her over, especially if she gave the slaves the party they so well deserved at the end of the harvest.

"But I'm sure Mr. Meachum can help you in the matter of the loan. Can't you, Mr. Meachum?" Sean said brightly.

"Loan? I, well, that is . . ."

"Just a small loan to Mrs. Twill until the harvest is sold," Sean said smoothly, taking Mr. Meachum's arm and guiding him back to his seat behind the desk. "I can assure Mr. Fortune that it is a good harvest and Mrs. Twill should have no difficulty repaying the modest sum she needs."

"Well, now, if you say so, Sean." Mr. Meachum seemed much assured by Sean's pat on the shoulder.

"Here's the amount she'll need," Sean continued, pulling out a piece of paper, then writing down a figure.

"Ah, yes, my boy," Meachum said, recovering himself now that there was solid business at hand. "I'll take care of it." He took the paper and finished writing out the loan, then pushed it toward Jessie to sign.

Mr. Meachum had just finished counting out the money from a cash box and given it to Jessie when a knock sounded at the office door.

Sean cocked one brow questioningly as if to ask Meachum if he were expecting someone, and Meachum rose, becoming more agitated than ever. Sean opened the door to a tall elegantly dressed man wearing a wig even more elaborately curled than Jason's. The man entered the room and stopped to lean on a silver-headed ebony cane.

"Colonel Rhett! How good to see you again," Sean said, holding out a hand in welcome.

Jessie had been amazed before at Sean's audacity but for a bondslave to offer his hand to one of Charles Town's leading citizens might well be considered an affront by some. She was more amazed when Colonel William Rhett took Sean's hand and shook it warmly.

"Sean," the colonel said, "I'm glad to find you here."

"I suppose it is Mr. Fortune you have come to see," Sean said pointedly. "May I introduce you to Mrs. Jessie Twill?"

Jessie curtsied. "I am honored to meet you, Colonel Rhett. I have heard a lot about your exploits."

"As I have heard much of you, dear lady." Colonel Rhett took her hand and bowed low over it.

"You've heard of me?" Jessie asked in amazement.

Colonel Rhett's eyes twinkled. "Quite a bit. But for once I

find that Jason Soames has not exaggerated. if anything, his descriptions of your beauty are understated."

Jessie was now the one to grow flustered in the light of such compliments. "You flatter me, sir," she said at last.

"Not at all," the colonel insisted. "I never flatter. I am merely honest."

"Thank you, Colonel," Jessie accepted graciously.

"May I hope to see you tonight at Mr. Soames's?"

"Yes, I'm looking forward to it." Jessie could not help smiling at the thought of the coming ball.

"Mr. Soames has told everyone you are invited. All of Charles Town looks forward to meeting you."

"Then you must have the most gracious and hospitable citizens in the colonies."

"We pride ourselves on our charm. If you will excuse me, dear Mrs. Twill." He bowed apologetically and turned to Meachum. "Would it be possible for me to see Mr. Fortune?"

The rotund secretary was nearly apoplectic and wiped his brow with a kerchief hastily pulled from his sleeve. "Mr. Fortune is . . . ah . . ."

"Mr. Fortune is indisposed today, Colonel Rhett," Sean furnished smoothly. "Perhaps if Mr. Meachum will see the lady safely to the Walkers', I might be able to help you."

"Yes, that would be acceptable," Colonel Rhett answered, a trace of amusement glinting in his eyes.

"Meachum?" Sean asked, turning to the secretary.

"Oh, yes. Glad to see the lady safe. Be good to get out. Take a walk." Meachum straightened his vest and took up a tricorn.

"Jessie," Sean said, facing her, "if you don't mind, Meachum can see you to the Walkers'. I'll pick you up there in the morning. Perhaps," he added with a mischievous gleam in his eye, "you can induce Mr. Meachum to help you make the purchases you need. He's very good at bargaining."

"Madam," Meachum said, offering his arm.

Jessie curtsied briefly to Colonel Rhett. "I'm glad to have met you, sir," she said.

"Until tonight, dear lady," Colonel Rhett said, bowing. "I would be honored if you would save a dance for me."

"Assuredly, Colonel." Smiling, Jessie took Meachum's arm and, nodding to Sean, left.

Mr. Meachum took her to several shops where, as Sean had promised, he proved to be an avid bargainer. Her purchases made, Jessie arranged for their transport upriver, since they would not fit into the skiff, and then Mr. Meachum took her to the Walkers'.

Chapter Fourteen

Although it was not far from the Walkers' to Jason Soames's townhouse, Jessie and Mrs. Walker took a carriage. With Mrs. Walker's bad leg, it was too difficult for her to walk even such a short distance in the hooped skirts and heeled shoes fashion dictated. The fact that she would be unable to dance did not dampen Mrs. Walker's enthusiasm one bit for the social occasion. Her eyes glistened in anticipation of an evening full of cozy chatting with the friends she had made since coming to Charles Town.

Though he wouldn't admit it, Mr. Walker was also looking forward to the evening. So much so that he had gone earlier on foot to Jason's to talk business and to size up his competition.

For Jessie, it was not just a chance to meet her neighbors for the first time, but she also looked forward to getting to know Jason better, to see him interact with others, to dance with him. She smoothed her fingers over the dark purple silk of her dress, her hand trembling slightly in her excitement. Mrs.

Michele Stegman

Walker's hand closed over her, squeezing reassuringly.

"You look lovely, Jessie," she said.

"You're sure I need not wear deep mourning and stay away from parties?" Jessie asked.

Mrs. Walker shook her head. "Jason Soames assured me that he has talked with all the important people who are coming and explained your situation, a lovely young woman married by proxy who never really knew her husband. Everyone agrees that there is really no necessity for deep mourning. This dress is cut conservatively enough and is a somber enough color." She gave Jessie's hand another squeeze and smiled. "Just don't dance every dance or appear too carefree."

"I'll have to thank Jason for smoothing my way into Charles Town society and for inviting me to this ball," Jessie said.

"The man is obviously smitten with you, Jessie," Mrs. Walker told her.

Jessie shook her head. "He's been very kind to me."

"Listening to him sing your praises, I think it's just a matter of time before he asks you to marry him."

That was something Jessie already knew. She just wasn't sure what her answer would be. Was Jason Soames the man who would fit her dream? Was he the man she could share a life with? Build a plantation and a shipping line with? Could it be a marriage full of passion and fire?

"Jason isn't your only conquest in Charles Town, though," Mrs. Walker continued.

Jessie looked sharply at the older woman.

"Don't think I haven't seen how Sean Winthrop looks at you." Mrs. Walker studied her cane. "It's quite a choice you'll have to make, Jessie. A rich plantation owner or a bond-slave."

"You make it sound like a very simple and obvious choice."

Mrs. Walker chuckled. "Do I? Perhaps I've left out a few details."

"The major one being that neither of them has asked me to marry him. Perhaps I will have no choice to make at all, Mrs. Walker."

"I doubt that, Jessie. I doubt that very much."

There were a few other carriages clustered near Jason's townhouse, but most people had chosen to walk on this balmy evening. When Jessie alighted from the carriage with Mrs. Walker, several other arrivals turned to look at her, some nodding politely and smiling as if they already knew who she was.

Jason's house was brightly lit, and happy sounds of music and chatter floated out to the street to greet them. There was no need for Jessie to knock. The door stood open, and Jason was there to welcome her, taking her hands and pulling her inside with a delighted sparkle in his eyes.

"Jessie! Dear Mrs. Walker! How glad I am to see you at last. Come in, come in!"

Jessie smiled at the customary warmth in Jason's greeting. "Thank you for inviting me, Jason. It's been an age since I've danced."

"Invited you?" Jason seemed aghast. "How could I not? You are the entire reason for the ball."

"I am?" Jessie looked at Mrs. Walker in confusion.

"But, of course," Jason went on, tucking one of Jessie's arms through his to lead her inside. "It was the only way I could think of to get you to safety in Charles Town." He shrugged and waved a negligent hand in the air. "Well, perhaps not the only way. But certainly the most fun."

Jessie wasn't sure whether to believe such an outrageous

story. "Jason! Surely you didn't give this whole ball simply to get me to come to Charles Town!"

He leaned close to her, squeezing her arm. "You're here, aren't you?"

Speechless, Jessie looked at Jason in amazement, overwhelmed that the man would go so far to try to get her to come to the relative safety of town in the face of the pirate attacks.

"Mrs. Townsend!" Jason pulled a short blond woman away from her circle. "How lovely you look in that shade of yellow!"

"Why, thank you, Jason." The woman looked up at her host as if she were quite shortsighted.

"Jessie, I'd like you to meet Monica Townsend, Charles Town's foremost woman with a needle." He pulled out an elaborately embroidered handkerchief. "Can you believe she made this for me? Isn't it the most exquisite work you've ever seen?"

"It is lovely," Jessie said, examining the handkerchief. "I don't think I've seen lovelier work."

The woman colored. "Jason is such a flatterer."

"Not at all, Mrs. Townsend," Jessie insisted. "I could never do anything this delicate."

Smiling, Mrs. Townsend said, "I'll make one for you, Jessie. What colors would you like?"

"Oh, I couldn't ask it of you!"

"Red, Mrs. Townsend," whispered Jason. "Red roses."

"You must be Jessie!" A tall, slender woman with large, sparkling brown eyes took Jessie's hands in hers and beamed down at her. Her black hair was thick and wavy and caught back in a simple chignon.

Jason smiled proudly at the woman's intrusion. "Jessie, may I present Mrs. Barbara St. Germain. My mother."

Jessie looked from one to the other in surprise. She should have guessed right away, she thought. The two had the same eyes, the same smile radiating warmth and welcome, the same exciting energy about them.

"How nice to meet you, Mrs. St. Germain," Jessie said, dropping a quick curtsey. "Jason has told me so much about you. I have seen for myself how beautifully you decorated Jason's plantation house. Did you also do this one?"

Jason's mother smiled at her compliment. "Jason collected most of the pieces for his townhouse. I just added a few touches here and there."

"You have a rare gift, Mrs. St. Germain."

"Call me Barbara," she said. "Everyone does. Come, let me introduce you around." She took Jessie's arm from her son. "Go greet your guests," she told him. "I want to get to know this lovely lady I've heard so much about."

Shrugging and shaking his head but smiling, Jason went back to the door to greet more newcomers.

"Now, tell me all about yourself," Barbara insisted.

Jessie smiled thinking how alike mother and son were. She did not feel the least bit intimidated. She only felt a comfortable warmth. Barbara led her about the large room, introducing her to everyone, asking questions about her in between introductions. Colonel Rhett greeted her warmly, surprising Barbara that they had already met. Governor Johnson and his wife, Margaret, were there. Mrs. Johnson stood by her husband's side while the governor stood by the punch bowl, surrounded by Mr. Walker and several other prominent citizens.

When Barbara introduced her, Governor Johnson bowed low over her hand. "So this is Charles Town's newest belle. Jason has not praised you enough, Mrs. Twill."

"Everyone has been so kind," Jessie responded.

"It is not hard to be kind to so lovely a lady!" Governor Johnson said.

"I'll just leave you here with Margaret," Barbara said, patting her hand. "If you'll excuse me, I must see to more refreshments."

Mrs. Johnson seemed glad to have a lady join her in the group of men around her husband and pulled Jessie closer to ask about her plantation. But it was not long before the angry male voices around them silenced them. As usual, in a gathering, the topic had turned to pirates. There was not a man there who hadn't lost something to the brigands, including Mr. Campbell whose house had recently been raided.

"Gentlemen, gentlemen, please," Governor Johnson was saying. "I assure you that we are doing everything we can to track down and arrest these thieves."

"I hear the Fortune Company lost another ship yesterday," Mr. Campbell was saying.

"They seem to have lost more than anyone lately," Colonel Rhett commented.

"Most elusive, this Mr. Fortune," Mr. Campbell said. "He came to Charles Town two months ago, and I don't know a soul who's actually met him."

"I have," Colonel Rhett said.

"As have I," Governor Johnson added.

There was a pause as the onlookers waited for further embellishment. "Well, what's he like?" Mrs. Johnson prodded.

Colonel Rhett and Governor Johnson exchanged glances. "Oh, fine man!" Colonel Rhett exclaimed. "Fine man!"

"Ah, yes," Governor Johnson harumphed in agreement. "Fine man!"

Mrs. Johnson rolled her eyes in disgust and shrugged at Jessie as if to say, "Men! Don't they know how to tell a woman what she wants to know?"

"I lost a large shipment on that ship from London that was taken three days ago," a merchant complained.

"So did I," another joined in angrily.

"Gentlemen, we've all had losses, including myself," Governor Johnson placated. "Colonel Rhett is outfitting ships now and I assure you, the pirates' next attack will be their last. You'll see pirates hang in Charles Town by the end of the season!"

An angry murmur of agreement ran around the circle.

Jessie took a long drink of punch worriedly. If Sean was helping the pirates, he was in danger. These men were rightfully angry over their losses, and they were determined to catch and hang the outlaws. Somehow she had to stop Sean.

"Gentlemen!" Jason poked his beaming face into the group beside Jessie. "This is a social occasion. Let's have a bit more levity!"

"You've had losses yourself, Soames," a large, florid man said. "Aren't you anxious to have these brigands brought to justice?"

"I am even more anxious to dance with the lovely Mrs. Twill," Jason replied, his eyes twinkling. Holding out his arm to her, he asked, "Will you honor us all by opening the ball with me, Jessie?"

"The honor is mine, Jason."

Curtseying to the group, she allowed Jason to lead her to the center of the room.

Jason held her hand and nodded for the musicians in one corner to begin. He guided her expertly through the slow graceful steps of a minuet, holding the handkerchief from Mrs. Townsend delicately in one hand. Soon they were joined by other dancers until the floor was crowded.

Jason seemed to have eyes only for her, and Jessie could

279

not help feeling a sense of pride that this man, so well liked by so many people in Charles Town, should single her out for his attention. She watched as Jason bowed and moved through the steps of the dance. He was in his element in the midst of the elegant dance. It was a world she could easily be part of, she thought, a world of genteel people, easy laughter, elegant clothing, and high finance.

Coming close to her in the dance, Jason smiled down at her, and she felt the warmth of his eyes on her, filling her heart with an answering warmth. He squeezed her hand, and she could not help responding with a slight gasp and a smile.

The dance seemed to end all too soon. Reluctantly, Jason surrendered her to another man for the next dance. Feeling bereft, Jessie labored through the steps of a country dance with an ox of a man whose creased brow gave evidence that it was only by extreme concentration that he managed to remember the order of the steps.

She was not at a loss for partners. Every swain in the room seemed determined to have at least one dance with the lovely widow whose virtues Jason had extolled. But after several dances Jessie remembered Mrs. Walker's advice not to dance every dance or appear too gay. Excusing herself, she slipped out the back into the coolness of the garden.

Several other people had escaped the stuffiness of the room and stood on the back veranda or walked sedately along the garden paths. Jessie headed down one darkened path where she thought she might be able to be alone, her shoes crunching on the crushed shell walk. Rounding a curve, she was surprised to see a man leaning casually against a small stone fountain. He was obviously not dressed for a ball. He wore no coat nor even a vest. Only a simple white cotton shirt with the sleeves rolled up. She was about to turn around and leave when the man called her name.

She inhaled sharply, instantly recognizing that voice. "Sean! What are you doing here?"

Unfolding his arms, his lean form pushing away from the fountain, Sean came forward to bow mockingly to her.

"A bondslave may not be invited to join the dancing, Mrs. Twill," he said, "but I can enjoy the music as much as any man."

She cocked her head in surprise. "And how is it that a bondslave son of a pirate enjoys good music enough to risk sneaking into a private garden?"

The familiar smile of his, half suppressed, twitched about his lips. "The same way he would also enjoy a dance with the fairest lady present if access to the lofty circles she enjoys were not denied him."

Taking up her hand, he brought it to his lips, then brazenly turned it over to nuzzle her palm, seeming to draw her breath from her. The strains of the music floated to them on the soft warm air, the beginning of another minuet. Expertly, Sean moved into position to begin the dance, bowing low over her hand.

Without quite realizing how, the subtle flood of music and Sean's guiding hand moved her into the dance. She felt the rhythm of the beat mingle the rhythm of her heart's beating with his. Sean was perhaps not quite the elegant dancer that Jason was, but he moved with a grace of his own. The grace of a swordsman, the grace of a sailor used to keeping his feet on a bounding deck, the grace of a wild animal barely tamed to this gentle movement. He moved beside her closer than would have been acceptable in the house. She could feel the warmth of his body next to hers, not quite touching yet close enough to stir her blood.

He moved closer to her until their bodies, still not quite touching, swayed as one. It was mesmerizing, this slow sinuous movement of one body rhythmically responding to another. Separated now by a mere hairsbreadth, caught by the look in their eyes, breath touching breath through lips parted in quivering anticipation, they moved. Only their hands touched, and through that touch all their passion flowed, skimming over nerves and urging further contact with a body that danced only a breath away.

Jessie's breathing became more rapid and labored, yet it was not from any exertion. The dance was too ponderously slow, the rhythm steady.

Suddenly, laughter intruded upon them, and Jessie stopped, realizing that the music had ended and that the dancers were moving into the garden for air. She was frozen for a moment with Sean's lips hovering above hers. Her mouth longed for his, her body longed to press along the hard length of him, to feel the crushing embrace of his strong arms. How long she stood there she could not have said, but it must have been but scant moments before Sean straightened, moved away, and she heard the shuddering intake of his breath. People were moving closer down the walks, and with a nod and the slightest of smiles, he faded into the shadows and was gone.

Jessie felt limp and drained yet curiously alive. To return to that other life inside, prancing properly with Jason, now seemed a travesty. Her life, her breath, her heart, had just melted into the darkness, and she would not see them again until morning.

After Jessie's return from Charles Town and in the days that followed, the harvest continued. In the evenings there was never any need for words between Jessie and Sean. His eyes merely sought her out. Hers shone in answer. When she made her way to his cabin, he was always waiting. Wordlessly, he would sweep her to him, giving her the ecstasy that clouded her thoughts all day.

One day, she saw Sean's early-morning return in the skiff. The next day Jason brought word of yet another pirate raid, and she desperately told herself that it was merely coincidence.

The last day of the harvest arrived amid much joyous banter among the slaves. It would be a short day since they were nearly done, and the women were already at work, fixing the extra food that would be consumed. There were still long days of threshing and winnowing ahead. The straw would be used for thatched roofs, woven into mats and hats and even shoe soles. But the crop would be in, the heavy, bending, backbreaking work in the hot sun over. Tonight they would celebrate.

That evening, the compound came alive as it never had before Jessie had arrived. Slaves, newly bathed, their hair trimmed, sported the new clothes they had won in the harvest contests and ate their fill. Even the cabins preened under their new coats of whitewash. A group of slave musicians tuned their instruments, and one couple who had decided that tonight was the night they would "jump the broomstick" stood shyly eyeing one another.

When they were all assembled, Jessie stood in the center of the compound looking around her. Jackson, unpopular at best, had wisely absented himself from the party. Sean stood with a group of the men, his arms folded across his chest, watching her with a quiet smile of approval on his face. A hush fell over the group, and the slaves turned to her, their eyes bright and expectant, their teeth gleaming in happy smiles. What a change from the day she had first seen this compound. Here, at least, was one accomplishment she could be proud of.

" 'Lisha!" Jessie called out. "Sally!"

The engaged couple came forward with two friends holding a broom. Sally was radiant in a gown Jessie had given her. Flowers were twined in her hair.

Although there were no legal marriages among slaves, Jessie went through the words of the ceremony with the couple anyway, asking if they would love, honor, and cherish each other. At the end, the two friends held the broom out, and the couple jumped over it together, signifying that they were now wed. A huge cheer went up from the crowd, and the musicians began playing as men and women chose partners to dance with.

Sean took Jessie by the hand, and they led the reel, skipping and twirling in happy abandon. The dancing was joyous and grand and a little disorganized, a far cry from the sedate dancing she had done at Jason's. But far more fun. She danced and laughed until she was near to collapse. There were no matrons to arch their brows disapprovingly that she danced so freely or that she danced every dance with the same handsome partner.

At last the party began to wind down, and Jessie went to her bed alone. There would be too many eyes for her to go to Sean's cabin tonight. She lay alone in the great, soft bed and longed for the simple straw mat on the floor—and Sean's company beside her.

Three days after the party Jessie knew Sean would have to leave soon. The threshing was well underway. Threshed, winnowed rice was drying, and she was again visiting Sean by night. But tonight she was late. There had been a sick child and she had helped the mother gather healing herbs from the kitchen garden to boil into a poultice. After several hours, the child finally slept peacefully. Now Jessie hurried along the walk to Sean's cabin, her long, dark cloak wrapped about her and hiding her in the soft summer darkness.

She paused outside Sean's door, her hand poised above the latch when she heard the voices inside. It was Jackson, his low, evil chuckle sending shivers of revulsion through her. She didn't intend to eavesdrop, not until she heard what they were talking about.

"How many men will we need to sail the *Fortune*?" Jackson was asking.

"You, me, two others," Sean said.

Jackson chuckled again, "We'll wait until they've finished loading Fortune's goods; then we'll take her. No need doing all that work ourselves."

"I don't want Captain Reading or any of his men hurt," Sean said sternly.

"What for? So they can stay behind and be witnesses?" Jackson sneered. "Maybe you do not want to come back here and be a slave again, Winthrop, but there's some of us who might want to come back."

"What reasons?"

"That doxie up there in that big house, fer one." Jessie could hear the man licking his lips. "She won't even look at the likes of me, but one of these days I'm goin' to take her an'—"

"Let's get back to the matter at hand, shall we?" Sean said, cutting him off. "The men from the *Fortune* are not to be hurt."

"You're not givin' the orders, Winthrop. I say we slit their throats and take no chances."

"There are better ways of dealing with them," Sean suggested.

"Such as?"

"Sugar planters in Barbados are crying for slaves. I know some who'd be glad to buy three healthy men and never ask

285

where they came from. Why kill them when we can turn a handy profit on them in a few days?"

Jessie's stomach turned. Maybe selling Captain Reading and the crew from the *Fortune* into slavery was better than killing them outright, but maybe not. She had heard too many horror stories about the cane plantations. Could Sean really contemplate doing that to men he had known? Yet he had suggested it.

"Yeah, Winthrop, maybe you're right. And after we take the *Fortune,* we'll sail her down to our shed, load our pickin's, and sail right past Colonel Rhett's nose in Charles Town. Like you said, he'll never suspect pirates usin' Mr. Fortune's own ship to slip past him to our rendezvous."

"Which is?" The question from Sean sounded casual.

"You'll find out when we get there!" Jackson snapped.

"Still don't trust me, Jackson? After all the help I've given you?"

"More like *J* don't trust you. She still don't like the idea of you comin' along."

Sean laughed. "As if I'd stay behind and miss my chance for wealth and freedom."

Jessie heard shoulders being clapped, feet shuffling toward the door. Quickly, she threw herself behind some bushes as the door to Sean's cabin opened.

"In the mornin' then, Winthrop," Jackson said, and strode off up the path.

Sean went back inside and shut the door. Jessie didn't move. She didn't think she could. She leaned her head back against the wall of the cabin, closing her eyes. It was true. All her suspicions of Sean, suspicions she had tried to ignore, things she had tried to pretend were only coincidences, were true. He had thrown in with the thieves who had plundered the area. Now he was leaving with them.

What had she been to him but a fleeting pleasure? He had used her knowing that he would leave and never see her again. She opened her eyes, anger and shame at his betrayal welling within her. Yet she wasn't the only one he had betrayed. Mr. Fortune's trusted bondslave had obviously given information to the pirates more than once about his master's goods. Now he had told them exactly when and where the *Fortune* would be so it could be taken. And he planned to run from his bondage.

She had had few illusions about her relationship with Sean. But she had thought he cared for her. Maybe he had in his own way. But it was over. She tried not to let the pain of that press too sharply. But that pain told her one thing. Whether he had cared for her or not, she had cared for him. She still did. She always would and because she cared, she knew she had to stop him. Hadn't Governor Johnson hinted at some trap being laid for the pirates? She couldn't let Sean be taken and hanged. She couldn't.

Jessie stood away from the cabin. It was not too late. No one yet knew that Sean was involved with the pirates. If she could stop him until they were gone, he would be left behind and could go on with his life. Even if that life did not include her, at least Sean would not hang.

Jessie came out from the bushes and hurried down the path toward the quarters. There was only one way to stop Sean.

After Jackson left, Sean lay back on his pallet, expecting Jessie any moment. When the door to his cabin crashed open, Sean sat up with a jerk, but was no match for the two burly blacks who set upon him. Under Jackson's tutelage, they had dealt expertly with more than one recalcitrant slave. Though he thrashed and kicked, they had the advantage of surprise and position. In a matter of moments they had him held down and subdued. One held his arms securely behind him. The other weighed down his legs. He looked up. Jessie stood over him, a length of chain in her hand.

"What the—"

Bending, she snapped one end of the shackle about his ankle. The other end, she fastened to a ring set stoutly in the wall of the slave cabin for the purpose of detaining slaves. She nodded to the blacks, and they released their hold on him. Grinning apologetically and shrugging, they left, shutting the door behind them. Jessie stood by that door, the key to the shackles in her hand.

"Jessie," Sean said shaking the length of chain, "what's the idea? Get this thing off me."

She laid the key on the small table by the door, enticingly out of reach. "You're not going on the raid, Sean." She spoke calmly, frighteningly calmly, her voice almost tonelessly dead.

He looked up at her and something seemed to die within him. She *was J.* Until now he had tried to rationalize the coincidences, to tell himself that even if she were involved, it didn't matter. Now he knew she was involved and, strangely, it still didn't matter. He still wanted her, cared for her. But how could he protect her if he was chained while she went off to rendezvous with the pirates? Did she really know what she was getting into? Know what cutthroats pirates could be?

He got to his feet, the chain rattling loudly in the stillness of the night. "Jessie, you've got to let me go." He eyed the distance to the key on the table. He couldn't reach it, but he could reach Jessie. He snatched her arm, pulling her to him.

She struggled briefly to get away, but he held her close. "Oh, Jessie," he said, burying his face in her hair. Her nearness, her fragrance, the feel of her in his arms made him forget all else.

For a moment she stood stiffly, resisting him, but she had never been able to resist him for long. Now she only wanted to be held by him one last time. She melted against him, her face against his chest. Her arms went around him, savoring the strength she felt in the muscles of the arms that held her, the feel of those on his back, his shoulders. She felt his mouth nuzzling its way through her hair, down her neck to the curve of her shoulder. His hand pushed aside her cloak. It dropped to the floor. Her gown was low-cut and slid easily from her shoulders crumpling at her feet. His hands moved over her as if hungry to touch her.

He drew her down to lie beside him, and she heard the scrape and clatter of the chain that bound him to the wall, felt the cold length of it across her leg as he lifted himself above her. Her arms held him, urging him on, shuddering at the consummation of their need for each other.

For long moments he held her, cherishing the feel of her. Then he heard the rustling and twittering of birds beginning to stir in the predawn and knew he had tarried too long already. He rolled off her. "Jessie, you have to let me go."

She sat up, grabbing her gown and yanking it over her head. "Is that why you made love to me? To bend me to your will?"

"I'm the one who's chained," he said, jerking angrily at the end fastened to the wall.

"And that's the way you'll stay," she retorted, throwing her cloak about her and striding to the door. She took up the key and turned to face him.

"Jessie, you've got to let me go. There's too much at stake."

She turned, her hand on the latch. *Yes*, she thought, *your escape, your freedom, your chance for wealth, my everlasting loneliness.*

She heard his angry jerking on the chain. "Jessie, I can't spend the rest of my life like this!"

She leaned her head against the door, fighting the tears. No, she couldn't keep him chained forever. And when she let him go, what would keep him here? If he chose to leave her, he would go. If not now, then later. If he went with the pirates, at least he would have a chance at the things he seemed to want. But he couldn't want her.

She whirled again to face him, her jaws clenched to keep back the tears, the angry words of farewell she longed to throw at him. But what, after all, had he ever promised her? Never once had he ever told her he loved her, never once asked her to love him. Even if she kept him here tonight, he would leave her. If he wanted to go so badly, then let him go.

"Then go!" she snarled, flinging the key at him. "Go to hell in your own way!"

Before she could change her mind, she ran from the cabin, promising herself that if they caught him, she would be glad when he was hanged.

Chapter Fifteen

From the concealment of the underbrush, shadowed from the early-morning sun, Sean, Jackson, two other men, and *J* watched Captain Reading direct the loading of the *Fortune* from the goods stored in Mr. Fortune's upriver warehouse. Rich furs and deer hides went into the hold. When the last bale had been put in place, *J* gave a signal. The skiff with the last two members of their gang moved into position to block the *Fortune*, the two men aboard her training their muskets on the *Fortune's* crew. Sean, Jackson, and the third member of the gang whose name, Sean had learned this morning, was Twitch, ran forward, guns at the ready, to take the sloop. The fourth man, whom Sean had heard referred to this morning as Fleming, held back with *J*, his pistol ready in case they needed backup.

They raced down the dock and jumped aboard. Sean grabbed Captain Reading from behind and jammed his pistol into the man's back, ordering him to surrender.

Instinctively, Captain Reading fought back but quickly stopped his struggles when he heard Sean's voice. He knew Sean and had been forewarned to expect this attack. He had, in fact, been waiting for it and had brought only two crewmen with him to endanger fewer men. Seeing their captain surrender, the two crewmen also gave up and were being bound tightly by their captors. Captain Reading allowed his own hands to be bound behind him. With his men already helpless and several pistols aimed in his direction, there was little else he could do.

When he and his men were shoved toward the hold, however, he turned questioning eyes on Sean. "What are you going to do with us?" he asked. The plan had been to leave them ashore at the warehouse.

Sean jabbed him with the pistol barrel and nodded in the direction of the hold. "Which do you prefer, Captain? To be sold as a slave in the sugar islands or to have your throat cut here and now?"

Captain Reading's eyes widened, but Sean's almost imperceptible nod gave him assurance. Tight-lipped, Captain Reading and his two crewmen did as they were told.

The *Fortune* was cast loose from her moorings, and *J* took her place at the tiller. No sails were set. It was but a short distance to the shed on the Twill property where they would load the last of their plundered goods. The river's current would take them that far soon enough.

Sean watched *J*, wondering how long she would keep her identity hidden from him now that they were on their way to the rendezvous. Expertly, she steered the sloop, nosing it toward the little inlet in the bank until it slowed to a stop in the shallow water. Twitch jumped out to secure the craft to a tree, and they went ashore to begin loading their stolen treasures.

Dawn was just lighting the sky and they worked quickly and in silence while *J* stood watch, a pistol in one steady gloved hand. The sound of approaching hoofbeats startled them, and the men stopped their work, putting down their burdens to surprise this early-morning rider who interrupted their escape with their goods.

After leaving Sean to unchain himself, Jessie went dispiritedly to her room. It was early still. Now that the harvest was done, the workday started a little later. No one would be up for an hour yet. She tossed her cloak aside and sat on the edge of her bed. Sean was well away by now, and she would never see him again.

She wondered what his life would be like on the high seas, as part of a cutthroat pirate crew. Was it a life he was well acquainted with? His father had been a pirate. Had Sean been raised in that life? Had he missed it so much he had to return to it?

She shook her head. There was too much about Sean that could not be explained if he had led only the rough life of a pirate. His speech, his manners, his dress, all attested to a better upbringing. So what had he hoped to gain by joining the pirates? Freedom? There was less freedom for him as a hunted man than as the pampered bondslave of Mr. Fortune. There was also the trap hinted at by Governor Johnson and Colonel Rhett.

She stood up, pulling at her hair and pacing in frustration. What if he were caught? Would Colonel Rhett have any mercy because he knew Sean, had greeted him warmly? Or would he be even more merciless because he had been betrayed by a friend? No, she thought, if Sean came in voluntarily and surrendered, then he had some chance at a pardon. But if he was caught in the act of piracy, in a well-laid trap, he would be shown no mercy. Only the end of a rope would await Sean.

She nearly gagged thinking of him dangling on the gallows. Not Sean! She whirled, throwing off her nightgown and snatching up her riding clothes. She had to find him, bring him to his senses. The harvest had been good, better than expected. She could now well afford to pay off her loan and purchase his freedom for him if that was what had motivated his thievery. Even if he didn't care for her, surely he would return if she promised him his freedom and some further funds besides to start a new life with, she thought. She would offer him whatever it was he wanted. If only he could be convinced not to go off with the pirates! If he were hanged, she would never be able to face Charles Town again. Even if he left her, he would have his freedom and her funds, and she could go on knowing he was alive somewhere in the world.

She yanked open a drawer and rummaged until she found the old pistol she had there. It was not loaded and she had no ammunition, but the pirates wouldn't know that. She tucked it in at her waist, tossed her cloak about her, and flew down the stairs and out to the stable.

She had to hurry. Too much time had gone by already. What had she heard Jackson and Sean saying? Something about loading the goods from the shed. Of course! That shed Jackson had claimed was dilapidated and vermin-ridden. The one she had explored and found sound and sturdy with a stout lock on the door.

Slipping a bridle on her horse, she urged the animal out of the stable to a block where she could mount. She didn't bother with a saddle. There was no time. She threw her leg across the animal's back. It would be faster and easier to ride astride. Kicking her mount, she leaned forward, grasping a handful of mane, and headed down the lane toward the shed.

Jessie slowed her horse to pick her way along the narrow path. She was almost to the shed when a man appeared in the path, grabbing her horse's bridle. Rough hands pulled her down, and she wrestled with her assailant, trying desperately to get her hands on her pistol. At last her fingers touched the stock, but strong hands pinned her arms behind her back, and other fingers snatched the gun away.

"Jessie!" Sean stood in the path, a dark mask hanging loose about his neck, a pistol she was sure was loaded held threateningly in one hand. The look on his face was one of astonishment at seeing her, and Jessie thought she saw a flash of joy in his eyes before he quelled it.

"Well, if it ain't the high-and-mighty Miz Twill," Jackson sneered, tightening his hold on her and running one hand over her body.

"Leave her alone," Sean growled, leveling his pistol in Jackson's direction.

J's pistol moved to center on Sean with deadly calm. Her mask had become twisted in her brief struggle to take Jessie's gun, and she pulled it down to dangle about her neck like Sean's. Sean's eyes widened when he at last saw the face behind that mask. Hers was the last face he would have expected.

"Josie!" Jessie cried in surprise.

"Yassum, Miz Twill," she said in singsong mockery of a slave's dialect. "It's bumbling, incompetent Josie."

"But you're . . ."

"A slave?" Josie laughed, drawing herself up proudly. "When you walked into your house and saw a nigger gal standin' there, you just had to assume I was a slave. Well, I've never been a slave. I just happened to be there bringin' instructions from my boss. I was supposed to stay and lead the raids until it was time to rendezvous since our last man had been killed. When you came and started handin' out orders, I figured pretendin' to be a slave was a good way to have a place to stay and to avoid suspicion at the same time."

Josie threw back her head and laughed. "I guess I was right. You just thought I was another one of your slaves. But I was born free. I may not know how to cook and clean, but I can do other things quite well. For instance," she said, checking Jessie's pistol, "I know better than to chase after pirates with an unloaded gun. And I know that this one is worthless." She tossed it into the bushes. "I can shoot straighter than most men and I know how to trim a sail and hold a ship on course. And"—she swayed her hips provocatively and looked enticingly at Sean—"no man has ever left my bed with any complaints."

Jessie scowled at Josie's implication that she and Sean were lovers. Seeing the scowl, Josie tossed her head and turned, laughing, to Jessie. Jangling the new gold bangles she had sported shortly after her return from Williamsburg.

"You thought he gave these to me, didn't you?" Josie tossed her head proudly. "How I laughed at you! I could see you burnin' for him. But it was me he smiled at. But I'm a free woman. I don't take up with no slave. Not even a bondslave!" She smiled and lifted her head proudly. "I got me a man better than any man here! And we are going to him now. Stede Bonnet!"

"Stede Bonnet!" Jessie echoed in wonder.

"You've heard of him, I presume?" Josie asked mockingly.

"Who hasn't heard of the most notorious pirate in the area?"

"Well, that's *my* man!" Josie said proudly.

Jessie looked to Sean with real fear in her eyes.

"You've done real well for us, Winthrop," Josie said. "You want her we'll take her along."

Jessie looked to Sean, her eyes pleading. "Sean, don't go with them."

"Why should he stay here and be a slave," Josie sneered in Jessie's face, "when he can be free like me?"

"Let her go," Sean said through clenched teeth.

Josie shook her head. "We can't let her go for the same reasons we didn't let the good captain and his crew go. Witnesses. You got first choice on her is all, Winthrop. You don't want her, I'm sure Stede's crew will."

"If you don't want her, bondslave," Jackson said, running his hand over Jessie again, "I do. Fact, I'll even be willin' to take this one after you're done with her."

Jessie's eyes widened, and she cringed from Jackson's touch.

Sean snatched Jessie's arm and yanked her away from Jackson. "I'll take her," he said, glaring a warning at Jackson. "And as long as I want her, nobody else touches her." Sean held her firmly in front of him, daring any of them to challenge him.

Jessie shuddered. As long as he wanted her? She had thought he had some feelings for her. Enough that he would not just use her and then throw her to a pack of piratical wolves. She could barely find her voice, but she managed to inject pride into it when she asked, "And how long will that be, Mr. Winthrop?"

Sean leered at her as he pulled her hard against him. "I'll let you know, Mrs. Twill."

"Tie her up," Josie snapped. "And get back to work. I'll stand guard."

Twitch brought a length of rope and tied Jessie's hands in front of her, and Josie shoved her down to sit on the ground while the men continued loading the *Fortune*.

Jessie watched bales and bags disappear into the hold of the *Fortune*. Sean helped with the work, glancing her way whenever he passed, but she refused to look at him.

She heard Josie's chuckle and looked up into the barrel of the pistol the woman had trained on her.

"He don't look so good now, does he?" Josie asked.

Jessie turned away, refusing to be baited. But Josie continued, "You'd've had him as a bondslave, wouldn't you? But a pirate's not good enough for you, is he? Well, he's a free man now, Miss High-and-Mighty Twill. And you got no choice in the matter. Come night we all gonna hear you and that buck makin' music together."

Josie poked the pistol in Jessie's face. "I ain't sorry you showed up here. I bet you are. But I ain't. It's gonna be fun givin' you orders for a change. I got so damn sick of hearin' you all the time tellin' me what to do. 'Josie, stir up that fire! Josie, scrub that floor! Josie, fry up that bacon!'" The quadroon straightened up. "Yassir, It's gonna be fun havin' you along just to watch you squirm. I hope you make the biggest fuss any woman ever made when Sean takes you. I want to hear your pleas for mercy changin' to moans of pleasure then to pleas for more! Let's see you hold your head up so proud when he gets tired of you and passes you on down the line!"

"All done, *J*," Jackson said.

Josie prodded Jessie with her toe. "Get up now, Miz Twill. Time to go."

Jessie scrambled to her feet before Jackson could "help" her and, holding her head up proudly, marched onto the ship. Sean was just stowing his last load and turned to help her, but she pulled away from him and went to stand by the rail, clutching it with her bound hands.

Josie took her place at the tiller, shouting directions to the others on setting the sails and casting off. Soon they were skimming down the river toward Charles Town with a following breeze.

They passed a few other ships on the river, but the pirates were careful to give them a wide berth so Jessie had no chance to call out for help. They passed Charles Town, staying on the far side of the river. Jessie noticed that the attention of all the pirates, including Sean, was locked onto the town. But no fire burst from the one hundred cannons that lined the fortifications of Charles Town, and the *Fortune* crossed the bar into the open sea completely unopposed.

The pirates slapped each other on the back in congratulations. Now it was only a matter of sailing up the coast to the rendezvous point and rejoining their brethren. They soon relaxed, one pirate taking out a Jew's harp, twanging a discordant tune on it. Sean, however, seemed to be ever on the alert, constantly skimming the horizon through a spyglass. He had not spoken to her since she had been brought aboard, and she wondered if he had already grown tired of her. He seemed to have had no qualms about leaving her to join the pirates in the first place. What would happen once they joined up with Stede Bonnet? Would Sean stand by while she was passed from one man to another?

She, too, scanned the horizon, hoping that Colonel Rhett would appear or some British warship. She shook her head. There was no reason they would stop them, even if a warship did come along. The *Fortune* flew the Fortune Company flag and was well known in these waters. The pirates had been right in making their escape in her. No one would suspect that she was now in pirate hands.

"Hey, Winthrop!" Twitch called. "What ye lookin' fer? If 'n it's a woman, ye got one right here! Or did ye fergit about her? I'll be glad to break her in good fer ye if ye've no mind to do the job yerself!" The man laughed at his own cleverness.

Jessie clutched the rail, white-knuckled at the man's jibe. How soon would his suggestion become reality?

Sean turned, and his gaze locked with Jessie's for a brief moment. Then he slapped the spyglass shut and walked over to her, but his attention was on Twitch. She half turned to him, wondering what he was going to do.

He plucked casually at the fastening of her cloak and gave her a leering grin. "You're right, Twitch. I have a far more pleasant sight here than an empty sea."

Twitch, Jackson, and Fleming now focused their attention on Jessie and Sean, their feral eyes gleaming, hoping for a show.

"Are ye goin' ta take her here and now, Winthrop?" Twitch asked, licking his lips in anticipation of at least enjoying her vicariously.

The color drained from Jessie's face. What kind of animals were they?

Sean ran a finger along Jessie's jaw, seemingly considering the matter. She stiffened, glaring at him, but he didn't seem either to notice or to care about her feelings in the matter. Could she have known so little about Sean after all? Even now she found it hard to believe that he had actually fallen in with pirates. Yet he seemed as naturally one with them as if born to it. Well, maybe he was. There was that pirate father of his.

"I'll take her when I'm good and ready."

Jessie closed her eyes for just a moment to gather her courage. She could not believe he would force her. He had been too considerate in his lovemaking, too gentle, to rape her now. No, this was not the Sean she knew. But did she know the real Sean? She opened her eyes to his, full on her, saw a brief flicker of concern before he wiped it away, and she knew, knew for certain that the Sean she was seeing now was not the real

300

one. Her eyes widened at that brief revelation from him. She almost started to speak, but a quick negative shake of Sean's head, coupled with a momentary creased frown between his brows, assured her that she was right. Sean was acting a part, at least when it came to his treatment of her.

Jackson sauntered across the deck and leaned on the rail next to Jessie. He looked across at Twitch. "A fine gentleman like Mr. Winthrop don't like no audience to his pleasures." He turned to Sean. "Take her down below to the captain's cabin, Winthrop, if you've a mind. But take her. The sooner you spend yourself on her, the sooner you'll be ready to let the rest of us have a go at her."

Great guffaws of agreement greeted this statement, and Twitch nearly undid himself laughing.

"Aye," Sean said, ogling her and letting his eyes rake over her appreciatively.

Gathering the front of her cloak in one hand, Sean pulled her to him, cocking one brow. Then, shoving her before him, he took her below and into the cabin recently occupied by Captain Reading.

As soon as the door closed behind them, Sean's whole demeanor changed. His arms went gently around her. At this proof that she had been right about him, Jessie leaned against him, letting his strength and his gentle caresses soothe her. He held her close to ease her trembling and spoke soothing words between the kisses he placed in her hair.

When her trembling eased and she relaxed against him with a great shuddering sigh, he took her by the shoulders and held her away from him and began working at the knots that bound her hands.

"Oh, Sean!" she said. "I was so afraid. I didn't know what to think when you said . . . when you . . ."

"I know," he said, giving her a half-smile. "I was worried that you seemed to be taking every word I said at face value." The rope came loose and he tossed it aside, gathering her again into his arms. "What made you realize I was only playing along with them to protect you?"

She snuggled deeper into his embrace. "I suppose I've come to know you a little. To trust you. That first night we made love was when it began, I think. You were more than ready to complete what we had begun, yet you would have stopped if I had asked you to. I don't think you could ever treat any woman with less than complete respect."

She felt the chuckle rumble from deep within him. "I would like to think that is true."

Jessie threw back her head to gaze up at him. "Yet you joined these pirates. Why? Your life was not so onerous, was it? You seem to be fond of Mr. Fortune. How could you betray him?"

He cupped her chin in his hand, ignoring her questions. "Why did you follow me?"

"I wanted to try again to stop you. I was going to offer to purchase your freedom, to give you funds to start a new life, with me or without me, as long as I could stop you from joining them."

He thrust one hand into her hair and held her close to him, bending to kiss the top of her head. He was moved more than he could say by what she had tried to do for him, the risk she had taken. She was here now and in danger because of him. If he had questioned how he felt about her before, those questions were now answered. He had hoped to make her his, even if she had been *J*. Now, more than ever, he wanted to make her a part of his life.

"With you," he said huskily into her ear. "With you."

"Yet you left me."

It was a statement, but it demanded an answer as much as any question. But he was not sure he could or should give her an answer now. There were still too many uncertainties ahead of them. They were on their way to meet with Stede Bonnet, a most ruthless cutthroat. For her own sake, it was better if she remained ignorant of his real purpose among the pirates, or Brethren of the Coast as they called themselves.

He pushed her away from him. "It was something I had to do," he said gruffly.

She shook her head. "That's not a very good explanation coming from the Sean I know."

"It's the explanation you'll have to settle for, for now," he said.

She lifted her chin. "Very well," she answered stiffly.

He couldn't bear seeing a barrier go up between them. Taking her by the shoulders, he looked into her eyes. "You've given me a great deal of trust already, Jessie. Give me just a little more. Please."

It was almost more than he could stand, waiting for her to make her decision. He didn't think he could bear losing her now. But finally, he saw the barrier fall again, saw her resign herself to trust him further without any assurances, and his heart sang with love for this woman who could give so much, trust him so much, and ask for nothing in return.

When he spoke, his voice was soft with awe and gratitude. "Thank you, Jessie. I promise I'll do everything I can to get you out of this. In one piece," he added grimly, and she glanced upward to where the other men were waiting, knowing just what he meant by that promise. Gently, he again gathered her into his embrace.

"And what about you?" she asked worriedly, leaning contentedly against him.

He grinned down at her rakishly. "That's where the trust comes in."

"Even when they hang you for piracy?" she countered with a small, wan smile.

He chucked her under the chin. "Hopefully, it won't come to that."

She did not look too hopeful but nestled closer to him. "So what do we do now?"

He cocked a brow and let his gaze rove over her. "Sea voyages can be long and dull unless you have something interesting to occupy your time. We could do exactly what they think we're doing."

"I think, Mr. Winthrop, that you are a complete, unmitigated rogue and have fallen in with the exact company that suits you," she told him. But she spoke the words with a smile and she lifted her face to him in invitation.

It was nearly evening when Sean began putting on his boots, tying his sash. Seeing him, Jessie began putting on her cloak, but his hand stayed her.

"Stay here, Jessie. You'll be safer."

"I can't cower here the whole voyage, Sean," she answered. "Besides, what's to keep one of them from coming down here while you're gone?" She shook her head. "I'd rather stay close to you."

He hesitated a moment, then reluctantly agreed, knowing that keeping her out of sight for now would only buy him a limited amount of time. He was going to have to face the others eventually and fight for the privilege of keeping her to himself. They went back on deck together in search of food and drink.

The ship was still making good headway to the north. Josie had relinquished the tiller to one of the pirates and sat by the railing, chewing on biscuits and jerky. A bottle of ale sat by her side to wash down the dry stuff.

Twitch spied them first and started to chuckle. "Was she worth bringin' along, Winthrop?"

Sean's grip on Jessie's arm tightened, warning her to silence. "You'll never know, Twitch," Sean answered, grinning good-naturedly for the benefit of the crew.

"Sure I will," Twitch grinned back, leering openly at Jessie. "We drew lots whilst ye was down there makin' the beast with two backs. Jackson's after ye, all right. But I'm after him." He poked his thumb toward his bony chest for emphasis.

"Think you can handle her, Twitch?" Fleming jeered from the tiller. "She looks pretty strong to me."

Twitch never lost his grin, but turned to eye Jessie more speculatively. "Maybe, maybe not," he answered. "But I doubt ye'll have trouble with her, Fleming, seein' as how ye're last. Won't be no fight left to her at all by then."

Jackson had sauntered up and stood eyeing her, running the back of his hand over the stubble on his greasy, pockmarked face. "Why did you bother bringin' her up, Winthrop? You could've left her down there on the bed all naked and waitin' for me."

A high giggle sounded from Twitch. "What's the matter, Jackson? Need a little help? What else ye want him to do for ye?" He giggled again. "Maybe ye'd like it if he plugged her for ye an' all ye had to do was watch?"

The others joined Twitch's joking and Jackson scowled. "Maybe I'm just a little anxious to get started, is all," he said.

He reached for Jessie, and she cringed from his filthy hand. But that hand never touched her. Sean's fingers closed over Jackson's wrist with crushing force, making the man wince.

"I said you could have her when I'm done with her," he said, flinging Jackson's hand away. He smiled pleasantly at Jackson, but there was deadly steel in his eyes as he continued quietly, "I'm not done with her."

Irritated calls of "Ye had her all afternoon!" and "Pass her around, Winthrop. Ye can have her again when we've had our turns!" came from the others.

Josie watched the threats and baiting with a satisfied smirk on her face as she continued chewing the dry jerky.

His courage bolstered by the catcalls of his comrades, Jackson again reached for Jessie. "You're done with her for now, Winthrop. If there's anythin' left when we've had our turns, you can have her back."

Sean shoved Jessie behind him. "I'll let you know when I'm done with her, Jackson."

Growling, Jackson stepped back, giving himself room to jerk out the saber that hung by his side. He waved the tip threateningly at Sean. Sean was unarmed but did not flinch.

"Now move out of the way, Winthrop," Jackson sneered, "or I'll have to run you through before I take my pleasure on Miss High-and-Mighty Twill." His eyes shifted to Jessie's and he continued, "You looked down your nose at me long enough. Thought you was too good for me, didn't you? Well, I'll have you beggin' for mercy afore I'm done with you!"

He made a lazy jab at Sean. "Now move out of the way, Winthrop!"

"Winthrop!" It was Josie. She was on her feet now, her eyes bright with anticipation as she tossed a saber to Sean.

Sean plucked the saber deftly from the air, his hand fitting comfortably to the grip. He fell immediately into a defensive stance, motioning Jessie to keep back.

"Bitch!" Jackson spat at Josie, but the quadroon only laughed.

Jessie backed away at Sean's command, but she shook with fear and was glad to have the support of the railing behind her. She looked around wildly for some way to help Sean. Grabbing a marlinspike, she stepped forward only to be confronted by the end of Josie's pistol. There would be no interference with the fight. The others had gathered around to watch, eager for blood. Jackson would offer Sean no mercy, she was sure. She could only hope that Sean's pirate father had taught him as much about fighting as he had about sailing. Otherwise, he would soon be sprawled on the deck in his own blood and she would be left in the hands of the rapacious crew. She gripped the marlinspike. If worse came to worse, she was determined to give a good account of herself before they took her.

The two combatants circled each other warily, saber touching saber in light beating attacks, one saber circling the other to disengage and gain a clear line of attack, testing, testing. Suddenly, Jackson lunged but Sean moved to the side, deftly beating the overseer's saber away with a graceful economy of motion, letting the point of Jackson's saber slide harmlessly by, a mere inch from his body.

Jackson recovered quickly for a man his size. He was taller than Sean and carried more bulk, but his weight hung about his middle. He did not have the breadth of shoulder, the slender quickness of Sean.

Jackson feinted to his right, disengaged Sean's parry, and again lunged low and to the left. Sean's blade swept down and around, pushing the overseer's saber harmlessly away. Jackson attacked again and again while Sean gave ground, his own weapon always seeming to be just ahead of his opponent's, parrying, disengaging, challenging.

The pirates moved along with the running battle, shouting encouragement to Jackson. He, after all, represented their interest. If he won, Jessie would be shared by all.

307

Jessie watched wide-eyed, her heart seeming to stop with each attack Jackson made. Yet Sean seemed to have little trouble fending off any attack. His blade worked smoothly, efficiently, coolly. While Jackson worked himself into a sweat, laboring and lunging, Sean's hand moved almost imperceptibly to flick away each ungainly thrust while Sean seemed hardly to move. To Jessie's amazement, he actually seemed to be enjoying himself.

Jackson was becoming winded. His attacks grew wider, wilder, were repelled more easily. Sean seemed to be as fresh as when the fight began, and now he began a counterattack. With very little more effort than he had expended on his defense, his flying blade forced Jackson to back away. Jackson was propelled back across the deck little by little. He was fighting in desperation now, and the smirk was gone from his face as he literally fought for his life.

Sean's grin seemed to infuriate Jackson, but his fury served only to defeat him. He attacked mindlessly, lunging so far he could not recover before Sean's blade forced his further downward to the deck itself. Sean's foot came down on the saber just in front of the bell guard, pinning the saber to the deck with Jackson's hand beneath it. Sean's saber lay across Jackson's throat, and the man froze in his awkward pose, his eyes nearly popping out of his skull, staring at the cold steel that threatened to end his life.

"You don't really want to die, now do you, Mr. Jackson?" Sean asked pleasantly, the grim smile never leaving his face.

Jackson was too frozen with fear to speak and too afraid of the sharp blade at his throat to shake his head more than a trifle.

"I thought not." Sean moved his foot just enough to kick Jackson's sword away, sending it skidding across the deck.

With the edge of his saber, Sean forced Jackson upright until the man was nearly on tiptoe to avoid having his throat cut.

"Jessie is mine, Mr. Jackson. She will remain mine. You will keep away from her. Understood?"

Jackson swallowed, nodding his reluctant agreement while his eyes glared hatred. Sean moved away, allowing Jackson his first free breath in minutes, then walked away from him as if he were no longer of any importance.

Twitch's laughter rang out, and the little man doubled over in his merriment at seeing the giant Jackson so humiliated. Jackson was further angered when the others, including Josie, joined in.

"What are you laughin' at?" Jackson growled, kicking Twitch in the rear. "You don't get her 'til I do!"

That realization that Jackson's loss was his as well sobered the man, and he scratched his head puzzling the truth of it.

Jessie wanted to rush into Sean's arms, to touch him, to reassure herself that he was all right, but she held herself in check in front of the others, touching Sean only with her gaze. He came to her then, prying the marlinspike from her fingers and returning it to its place.

"I'm sorry, Sean. You could have been killed."

He smiled tenderly at her, his expression hidden from the others since his back was turned to them. "It's all right, Jessie. That fight was inevitable."

"Thank you for protecting me, Sean," she said, lowering her eyes. Then she grinned mischievously at him. "For once I'm glad your father was a pirate if he's the one who taught you to fight like that."

He eyed the saber he still held. "He taught me a few tricks," he admitted. "I'll get us something to eat."

He brought some of the biscuits and jerky and a bottle of ale for each of them.

"I don't think I can eat," she said, refusing the unappetizing food.

With a smile, Sean eyed the hard biscuit and tough, dry jerky. "I must admit, Josie's cooking hasn't improved, but you do need to eat and keep up your strength. We don't yet know what else we may face."

Squelching a smile, Jessie glanced at the quadroon. Josie was again at the tiller. The others were finding blankets to sleep in for the night or going below to sling hammocks. Sighing, she took the food and began to gnaw on it. "It's too bad Letty didn't turn out to be part of your gang of thieves, too," she mumbled.

Chapter Sixteen

In the days that followed they continued to sail northward. Sean took food to Captain Reading and the two other prisoners, assuring them as much as he could. Jessie kept to the cabin as much as possible, coming on deck only on brief occasions and always with Sean. The pirates made tentative approaches twice, but a glare from Sean made them move away. They had seen and appreciated his skills in swordsmanship. They did not want to experience it.

Even Josie had been somewhat subdued by Sean's duel with Jackson. She still tended to swagger about with her pistols stuck into her waistband and to taunt Jessie with threats of what would happen when Sean turned her over to Bonnet's crew. But, getting no reaction from Jessie, she soon tired of that sport.

It was late afternoon when the pirates sighted their goal, the great headland of Cape Fear. There the Cape Fear River emptied into the sea, and there they were to rendezvous with

Captain Stede Bonnet. Josie sat at the tiller, a map spread out beside her.

"A good place to hide," Sean muttered to Jessie as they made their approach. He pointed ahead. "The mouth of the river is filled with shifting sand bars. Without a pilot familiar with these waters or a map like Josie has, there's a good likelihood of running aground. Even with those aids, it's not unlikely. Especially at low tide."

Paying careful attention to the map, Josie guided the sloop through the maze of sand bars.

Once they rounded the cape, Jessie nudged Sean. "There!" she said. Sticking up from around a point of land were the masts of two ships.

"I think I would have anchored a little further upriver," Sean said quietly. "We spotted those masts as soon as we entered the mouth of the river. Anyone looking for Bonnet will find him just as easily." With his spyglass, Sean peered out from the stern as he had done often in their brief voyage. When he turned back, he had a satisfied smile on his face.

As they rounded the point and neared the two pirate ships, Sean turned his spyglass toward them. "One is an Ashbrook ship," he said.

When they drew closer, Jessie's eyes grew wide and she tugged at Sean's sleeve. "It's the *Francis*!" A worried crease formed between Jessie's brows. "I hope Captain Manwaring and his crew are all right."

They were now close enough that calls of welcome were being exchanged ship to ship and with the pirates ashore. The *Fortune* dropped anchor next to the *Royal James*, Bonnet's ten-gun sloop. She was a fast-looking ship with a bowsprit almost as long as her hull for piling on more canvas. Most of the pirates were ashore, including a tall, well-dressed man who stood with arms akimbo, grinning a welcome at Josie. With his powdered wig and clean-shaven face, the portly man looked oddly out of place amongst the unkempt buccaneers.

"Who is that gentleman?" Jessie wondered, aloud.

Sean smiled as if relishing his answer. "That, my dear Mrs. Twill, is the pirate Stede Bonnet."

She shook her head in wonder. "He certainly doesn't look like my idea of a pirate."

"Too gentlemanly looking for you?"

Jessie colored and shrugged. "I suppose if a bondslave can play the part of a gentleman, a pirate can."

"Ah, but you're wrong there, Jessie." Sean was chuckling outright now. "Mr. Bonnet is truly a gentleman. Or was."

She looked at Sean in puzzlement.

"Bonnet was a businessman in Bridgetown, Barbados. He was a major in the Barbadian Army, honorably retired, and an owner of a very profitable sugar plantation. In short, he had everything a man could desire—wealth, property, respect."

"And?" Jessie encouraged.

"And one day, he sold it all, outfitted a sloop, and turned pirate." He cocked one brow at her and smiled in grim vindication. "So much for the honor of gentlemen!"

Jessie tossed her head. "One exception does not ruin the whole."

"I could name others," he said, bending close enough to brush her ear with a brief kiss. "But this one's bad enough. It will be best if you stay aboard and keep out of sight."

Jessie nodded her understanding.

"Launch the longboat!" Josie called.

Sean went to help, and soon the crew was scrambling over the side and into the boat.

"You, too," Josie said, beckoning imperiously to Jessie.

Sean frowned. "There's no need for her to go ashore."

"I say she comes, so she comes," Josie snapped, her hand going to her pistol.

Nodding reassuringly to Jessie, Sean went over the side and reached up to help her into the boat. Josie was the last, and she took up a position in the bow.

As soon as the boat scraped bottom, Josie was over the side, splashing through the surf, her arms outstretched to Bonnet. Laughing, she flung herself at him, and he scooped her up, twirling her around and bussing her soundly to the cheers of those crewmen who had come to welcome the newcomers.

"Josie, my girl, you're a welcome sight! It seems you've done well," he said, nodding toward the *Fortune*.

Josie preened in the attentions given her by this infamous pirate captain, tossing her head proudly at Jessie while she clung possessively to her man. "It used to belong to the Fortune Company," she said, expecting further praise.

She was not wrong in her expectations. "Well done!" Bonnet exclaimed, walking closer to the edge of the water to examine the prize. "A fine-looking sloop. 'Twill set the Fortunes back a bit. We'll burn her here and now."

Sean stepped forward. "She carries a fine cargo, sir. Why not use her to carry it and sell the whole of her? Your crew will appreciate the gold it puts in their pockets."

"Who is this?" he asked, looking Sean up and down.

"A newcomer to our crew," Josie explained. "A fine swordsman, as Mr. Jackson can attest." She caught Jackson's eye at this last statement and laughed.

"Sean Winthrop, at your service, sir," Sean said, inclining his head politely. But, Jessie noted, he did not offer his hand.

"Haven't I seen you before?" Bonnet eyed Sean speculatively, his brow knotting with thought. Then he shook himself free of Josie, reaching for his saber. "Now I remember!

314

It was in Barbados. You were with that scoundrel Fortune! No friend of his is a friend of mine!"

Sean held out his empty hands placatingly. "You remember correctly, Major Bonnet. I was with Mr. Fortune. But does a bondslave have a choice of masters?"

Bonnet stopped with his saber half out of its scabbard. "Bondslave?"

Josie stepped in to smooth things over. "It's true, Stede. He was Fortune's bondslave. But he's run away from Fortune to join you."

Bonnet slammed his saber back home and held out his hand to Sean. "Run away from Fortune, eh? Then his loss will be our gain. Welcome."

"Thank you, Major," Sean said, shaking hands.

"But it isn't Major anymore, my boy," he said, clapping Sean on the back. He leaned conspiratorily close. "It's Captain now. I'm no longer in the Barbadian Army, but a pirate captain and now calling myself Captain Thomas just to throw my detractors off the scent."

"I see. Captain Thomas, it is, sir."

"So, what cargo does the *Fortune* carry?"

"Furs, hides, the silver, and valuables we've taken from some of Charles Town's finer homes," Josie enumerated proudly. "Three healthy male prisoners to sell in the sugar islands, and"—she pointed smugly to Jessie—"this little bundle for your crew."

Bonnet's gaze shifted to Jessie.

She tried not to cringe before the glittering eyes that scrutinized her. Her courage was held together only by the hope that, somehow, Sean would be able to protect her.

"For my crew?" Bonnet bellowed. He glared at the motley collection who had surrounded them and who now looked at Jessie like a pack of rats ready to devour some tempting tidbit.

315

"For this lot?" Bonnet jerked out his saber, brandished it wildly, then began laying about him with the flat of the blade, driving his men back. "Back, you vermin-ridden cowards! Not one of you is decent enough to touch a lady of quality like this one! Off with you now!"

Grumbling and snarling, the pirates backed away, returning to their games of chance and other pursuits that had occupied them before the arrival of the *Fortune*.

Returning his saber to its scabbard, Captain Bonnet took Jessie's hands in his own and smiled down at her like a kind father. "My dear, pardon my men. They have not the upbringing to appreciate the delicacy of a lady like yourself. In the absence of a mutual acquaintance of good quality, may I introduce myself? Captain Thomas, at your service."

Jessie was not sure just what to make of the notorious Stede Bonnet. She had expected a pirate of the lowest sort, but here he was bowing over her hand and introducing himself like any gentleman invited to her mother's Bostonian drawing room. She had half expected to be thrown unceremoniously, as Josie had threatened, to that feral pack he called a crew to be fought over and torn apart. Her amazement and relief threatened to overwhelm her. Whether he really meant to treat her well she did not know, but she thought it prudent to treat him like the gentleman he claimed to be.

She managed to give the captain a shaky curtsey and a tremulous smile. "I am honored, Captain Thomas. I am Mrs. Jessie Twill."

Bonnet glared at Josie, Jackson, and the rest of that gang. "They haven't harmed you, have they?"

Josie's face was contorted with hatred. This was not what she had planned for her captive. Bonnet had further insulted her with his statement that there was no person of quality there but Jessie and himself. She had dragged Jessie along to see her humiliated. Now Jessie was being treated with a courtesy Bonnet had never shown her. She might even fall into disfavor if the Twill woman complained of her treatment.

Not willing to indict anyone and incur further enmity, Jessie shook her head. "I have been treated with every courtesy, Captain."

" 'Tis lucky for them that you have," Bonnet said, again glaring at his quadroon lover. Holding out his arm to Jessie, he said, "Will you have tea with me, my dear?"

At that, Josie spun on her heel and stomped away. Jessie forced a smile to her lips, and, glancing at Sean in a silent plea to stay close, she took the pirate's arm and headed up the beach with him.

He led her to a tent where a small table had been set up for tea and a man was just bringing a hot pot to the table. He seated Jessie on a stool, apologizing for the poor accommodations.

Jessie sat down, her back half to the opening, but she could still see out and was relieved to see that Sean had indeed stayed nearby. He was leaning against a tree, casually cleaning his saber, but she noticed that his attention was on the tent more than on his work.

"Sugar?" Bonnet asked in his best drawing-room manner.

Jessie nodded and he added sugar to her cup.

"I'm sorry there's no cream," he apologized.

Jessie smiled and hastened to reassure him that her tea was just the way she liked it. If she had not still felt in imminent danger and worried about how she would make an escape, she would have laughed at the incongruity of her situation, calmly having tea with one of the most notorious pirates of the time.

"You must excuse Josie," he said. "Most of the time I enjoy her raucous exuberance but occasionally I miss the quiet gentility of a lady of quality like yourself. It is seldom I have the chance to entertain a lady, barred as I now am from the finer homes."

"Surely, sir," Jessie dared to suggest, "a fine gentleman like yourself could obtain a pardon?"

Captain Bonnet sighed. "Alas, fair lady! I have already done so. But I fell again into wicked ways and now there is naught left for me but the buccaneer's life or the hangman's rope. But," he continued brightly, "let us not be morose."

Bonnet chatted easily of his travels up and down the coast, his meeting with Governor Eden of North Carolina to receive the King's pardon, his return to piracy.

"I see you've had a prize dropped into your lap, Captain Thomas."

A man stood outside the tent, just out of Jessie's sight, but she froze at the sound of that voice, for it was quite familiar to her.

"You'll be glad to note that we've more than earned the money you paid us," Bonnet replied, sipping his tea. "She was a Fortune ship and her hold is full of Fortune goods. Your rival cannot continue to take such losses and still compete successfully with Ashbrook Shipping. Not even the very wealthy Mr. Fortune."

"We should drink to the downfall of our mutual enemy. But I would like to be on my way. With the *Fortune* at your disposal, you can let the *Francis* go."

"The *Francis* is mine," Bonnet said, inclining his head politely as if he were, indeed, in polite drawing-room company. "I took her and the prize must be shared with my crew according to our articles."

"Your articles be damned! She belongs to Ashbrook Shipping! We have an arrangement! You've been well paid to take Fortune ships and to leave mine alone."

"The payments have been welcome," Bonnet agreed.

"Rest assured that more payments will follow as you take more of Fortune's ships," the man continued, his voice more strained, "but I need my freedom and the use of my ship to return to Boston! Only then will the payments continue."

"The *Francis* is quite a handsome payment. I don't think we'll need anything more from Ashbrook Shipping," Bonnet said, effectively ending the partnership and his need for the man.

The man stepped forward menacingly. A pistol appeared in Bonnet's hand. "You have been given the freedom of the camp, Mr. Pierce. Would you prefer hell?"

Mr. Pierce had stepped far enough into the tent that he now saw Jessie. His mouth dropped open in surprise. "Jessie! What are you doing here?"

Jessie had been astounded to hear her stepfather's voice and had been speechless during his exchange with Bonnet. But her fury had also mounted. She had never liked Pierce and would not have been surprised by his engaging in underhanded business dealings. Even a bit of smuggling. That was a common enough practice. But she had never thought that he would stoop to piracy to achieve his ends.

Steadily, she set her cup down and coldly glared with unwavering calm at him. "I could ask you the same question, sir."

Pierce laughed nervously. "I was on board the *Francis* and have been captured," he said. "As I am sure you were captured."

"I have heard enough of your conversation to believe that that is not quite the truth, sir."

319

Bonnet stood up, looking from one to the other. "I assume you know this man, Mrs. Twill?"

"I regret to say that he is my stepfather."

Pierce turned to Bonnet. "What are you going to do with her?"

Bonnet sat down again and picked up his tea, a wide smile on his face. He seemed to be relishing the situation. "What would you like me to do with her?"

Jessie stiffened, her hands clutched in her lap. Surely her stepfather would plead for her safety and her release. Or would he? She had witnessed enough to implicate him in a hanging offense. If Captain Bonnet let her go, she could accuse her stepfather of piracy. Bonnet knew that and was enjoying watching Pierce squirm. But would the pirate captain release her knowing that she could implicate not only his erstwhile partner but could testify that Bonnet himself had returned to piracy after receiving a pardon?

Pierce eyed her coldly as if she were a roach, an annoyance to be stepped on and gotten out of the way. "Do what you will with her," he said. "She is no concern of mine."

"Tsk, tsk," Bonnet chided. "Such unfeeling coldness from the lady's own kin."

"He's no kin to me," Jessie said, lifting her head proudly.

"So he's not, so he's not," Bonnet agreed. "Which is to your credit, dear lady."

"What will you do with me, Captain?" Jessie asked, unable to keep a slight waver from her voice.

"I suppose it is up to me to decide, isn't it? For the time being, I am enjoying your company quite thoroughly."

It was not much of an answer and gave her little assurance of her future. She could only be thankful that she was being well treated. For now, her only hope was that Sean could help her escape when the opportunity arose She looked up to see him approaching.

"You!" Pierce growled when he saw Sean. "If I had known you were involved with the pirates yourself," he sneered, "I wouldn't have had to give you a plantation and a stepdaughter to keep quiet!"

Jessie gasped. So that was why her greedy stepfather had agreed to give her the plantation once she was wed to Jonathan Twill. Somehow, Twill had found out about the raids Pierce had paid the pirates to launch, using the plantation as their base. She was part of a bribe to keep Twill from talking.

Bonnet chuckled, enjoying Pierce's discomfiture immensely. "It seems you have been paying everyone and not always getting what you bargained for."

"Much less," Sean said. "It makes you wonder how profitable dishonesty really is. Perhaps introductions are in order." He bowed to Pierce mockingly, but as elegantly as any gentleman. "Sean Winthrop, at your service, sir."

"Winthrop?" Pierce was thrown into confusion. "You're Jonathan Twill!"

"My husband is dead, Mr. Pierce," Jessie said.

Pierce looked from one to the other, trying unsuccessfully to puzzle out what had happened.

"A part," Sean began to explain. "I merely played the part of Jonathan Twill. It seems Jessie was right in thinking that you would refuse to give her the plantation if you knew Jonathan Twill was dead."

"You little cheat!" Pierce snarled at Jessie.

Jessie was not affected. "You accuse me of being a cheat? That plantation was but a tithe of what my father was supposed to have left me. I would have been content with only

321

that, but I had to be sure that I was not defrauded out of it as well. Can you really blame me for my deception?"

"Aagh!" Pierce growled as he lunged for Jessie's throat.

Jessie shrank back from her stepfather. A shot rang out. Pierce halted, his fingers clutching convulsively mere inches from her neck, a look of surprised anguish on his face. Slowly, he crumpled, his twitching fingers grasping the hem of her gown. Then he lay still, her gown, as well as all else he had sought, slipping from his dead fingers.

"Amusing for a bit, but he was beginning to bore me," Bonnet said grimly, blowing the smoke away from the end of his pistol. Her charming, elegant tea companion had reverted to being what he really was—a cold-blooded pirate.

Jessie stood frozen, her eyes wide with shock.

"Ships coming!" Josie shouted as she ran up the beach to the tent.

As if her stepfather were merely a log, Captain Bonnet stepped over him and out of the tent, peering intently toward the sea.

Carefully, Jessie edged around the dead man, and went outside, taking in deep breaths of the fresh air. Sean gave her a long, questioning look and, grateful for his concern, she nodded that she would be all right. She looked toward the sea. What ships had blundered into this nest of pirates? she wondered. But with that point of land in the way, nothing of the other ships could be seen.

"Who's on lookout?" Bonnet demanded.

"Parkins," a burly pirate answered. "But it's gettin' too dark to see. Can't tell what ships they are, nor nothin' about 'em."

"You! Jackson, Stark, Slash!" Bonnet called. "Each of you take an armed crew in longboats around the bend. See who's come to call."

The three men ran down the beach, gathering their crews as they went. Three longboats full of armed pirates pushed into the river and set off downstream.

"Damn!" Bonnet said, beginning to pace.

Jessie wanted to pray but was unsure just what to pray for. If the ships were merchantmen, they would be at the mercy of the pirates. If they were warships, she might be rescued, but Sean would hang. She could only wait as Captain Bonnet was doing.

The rest of the pirates had left their various activities and had joined their captain to gaze down the river. Some of them laughed at what a joke it was going to be when some fat merchant realized he had sailed right into the arms of pirates. Others were silent, concern on their faces.

Josie edged closer to Bonnet, and the pirate captain unconsciously put an arm around her. The quadroon sneered at Jessie as if she had won some victory, then turned to wait for the return of the longboats.

Jessie could almost feel Josie's hatred of her, and she clasped her arms to keep from shaking. She would not let the woman see her fear. It helped that Sean stood close by, one hand on the butt of a pistol tucked rakishly in his belt.

It was not long before the longboats reappeared, their crews straining on the oars against the current. Jackson's boat was the first to reach shore, and he jumped over the side and hurried up the beach to report.

"It's Rhett!" he blurted out.

Bonnet stiffened. "You're sure?"

Jackson nodded. "It's the *Sea Nymph* and the *Henry*," he said, naming Colonel Rhett's two ships.

Jessie looked at Sean with alarm. To her surprise, there was the hint of a smile on the bondsman's lips.

The man Bonnet had called Slash had arrived. A great, ugly scar ran slantwise across his face, growing red as he stood glaring at Josie. He pointed a hairy finger at the quadroon. "She led them to us!" he accused. "She come straight from Charles Town and he followed!"

As if suddenly aware that he had his arm around her, Bonnet pushed the woman away as if she were a viper.

"Fool!" Bonnet gritted, giving Josie a backhanded swipe that knocked her to the sand.

Rubbing her jaw, Josie glared at the gathered pirates then jumped up, standing defensively with her feet wide apart. "Why would they have followed us?" she argued. "Nobody knew the *Fortune* had been taken. Why would Rhett follow a ship he thought belonged to Mr. Fortune?"

"How else could they have found us?" shouted Slash. He started toward Josie threateningly, but Bonnet held the man at bay with his saber.

"However they found us, they are here," Bonnet said, calmly in command again. "What armament do they carry?" he asked, directing his question to the one called Stark.

"Both are sloops, eight guns each," the man stated succinctly.

"Twice our strength,"Bonnet muttered.

"But right now"—Stark smiled—"they're both aground on sand bars."

"The tide has turned," Bonnet mused. "They'll be free by midnight."

"Let's make a run for it now," Jackson urged.

"They could still use their guns" Bonnet said, shaking his head. "And in the dark, at low tide, we could go aground to be picked off at their leisure." He fingered his chin, then straightened, coming to a decision. "Our only chance is to wait until morning. The tide will be in our favor, the wind at our backs.

We'll make a fighting run for the sea right through them. It's risky, but the best chance we have."

His men nodded their agreement with the plan, and the camp came alive with activity as Bonnet gave orders. The men hastened to strike the camp, ferrying everything out to the *Royal James*.

In answer to an order, Sean began helping strike tents, folding them, and carrying them to the longboats.

"You will come with me aboard the *Royal James*, my dear," Bonnet said to Jessie. He took her by the arm, his grip firm and unyielding.

"Shouldn't I go back aboard the *Fortune*?" she asked. She tried to catch Sean's eye without Bonnet seeing the direction of her gaze. If she were separated from Sean aboard the *Fortune* and Bonnet escaped, there was no telling when and where the two ships might rendezvous again.

"The *Fortune* stays here with the *Francis*," Bonnet said. "With no guns, they'll be no help to us. It would only take men to sail them who could otherwise be used for fighting."

Relieved that Sean would be aboard Bonnet's ship, she exhaled a deep breath.

Bonnet pulled her along toward a longboat. She did not want to offer too much resistance and earn his ire, but she wanted to assure herself of the safety of Captain Reading and his two men. "What of the prisoners aboard the *Fortune*? Will you just leave them?"

Bonnet shrugged and gave her an irritated jerk. "I will leave them for Rhett to deal with." He paused to look over the two ships he had taken. "It won't be the first time I've had to abandon a rich prize," he muttered more to himself than in answer to her.

He pushed her toward a longboat, helped her in, and clambered in himself. Suddenly a hand closed over hers, and something cold and hard was being given her. Startled, she looked up into Sean's eyes. She had looked for him so frantically further up the beach she had not seen him until he was beside her. Under the pretense of helping push the longboat into the water, he had pressed a small dagger into her hand.

As the boat pulled away from shore, she kept her eyes on Sean until he turned away to work.

On board the *Royal James*, the activity was no less frantic. The disordered clutter on the deck gave evidence of the dissipation and the inactivity of the crew. But now the supplies from shore were being hauled aboard and stored below, while the decks were being cleared for the action they knew would greet them on the morrow.

Josie was already aboard and came to stand before Bonnet as soon as he came aboard with Jessie, an angry challenge in her stance. "Why don't you leave her behind with the other prisoners?" she demanded, tossing her head at Jessie. "She'll only cause trouble here."

"Leave her behind?" Bonnet asked as if surprised. "It was you who brought her here for the crew."

"You givin' her to the crew?" Josie's attitude changed immediately. Her eyes lighting with triumph, she leaned against Bonnet seductively, her hands running possessively over him.

Jessie's eyes widened, but otherwise she managed not to show the sudden fear that clutched at her. When Captain Bonnet had greeted her so civilly this afternoon, she had been ready to give the lie to Sean. The captain certainly didn't seem to be the blackguard Sean had made him out to be. But she had changed her mind when she had seen her stepfather lying dead at her feet and Bonnet coolly blowing smoke from the end of his pistol. His treatment of Josie had also been less than chivalrous. Earlier, she might have doubted that he would turn a captive woman over to that wolf pack of a crew. Now, she thought that what he did with her depended entirely on his mood and his whim. If he could commit murder so calmly, she did not doubt for a moment that he was fully capable of giving her to the crew for their enjoyment without a single guilty thought.

Josie laughed, throwing back her head in delight. "I didn't think you'd tire of your milk-and-water 'lady' this soon. But you always did prefer *café-au-lait*, didn't you?" she asked in a husky voice, caressing the pirate captain's hand with one that was just the color of coffee liberally laced with cream.

"It's satisfying enough when it's all I can get," Bonnet said, plucking Josie's fingers off him as one might rid oneself of a leech.

Josie straightened, fire in her eyes, her hand reaching for the pistol in her belt. Bonnet's fingers closed over hers, tightening until the quadroon winced.

"Leave be, Josie," Bonnet warned, "or you'll find it's yourself I give to the crew."

Josie's nostrils flared with her sharply indrawn breath, but she did not flinch from that threat. With a grin that was more of a sneer, she said, "There's not a man among them brave enough to dare touch Josie!"

"Not," Bonnet agreed, "as long as you have my protection."

Tiring of the game, Bonnet turned away to direct the more important matters at hand. It was a battle to the death he faced come morning and he wanted all in readiness.

Josie turned on Jessie, and her fingers curled into claws as she glared at her erstwhile mistress. "You!" she snarled. "You think you can take Stede from me? You might be a fine lady, but you are only a momentary diversion." The quadroon preened, tossing her head proudly. "My Stede knows no woman has the fire of Josie in bed! And I will see that you never know his touch!"

Jessie stood silent, her head held proudly. She knew it would do no good to tell Josie that she did not want Stede Bonnet, in or out of bed, nor to remind Josie that she would not even be here if Josie hadn't brought her.

Giving Jessie a final glare of hatred, Josie flounced away.

As the last of the things from shore were brought aboard, the pirates hauled up the longboats. Sean was one of the last aboard and not until Jessie saw his feet firmly on the same deck with hers did she breathe a sigh of relief.

Chapter Seventeen

Through most of the night the pirate crew worked to ready the *Royal James* for action. The decks were cleared, and the guns uncovered and cleaned. Powder and shot were placed close to each gun. Each crewman looked to the cleaning and loading of his own pistols and the sharpening of his saber and knives. The sails were set in order, ready to be run up at the first hint of the morning breeze.

Sean labored like the rest, but Jessie noticed that he never seemed far away and his eye was on her constantly. Josie spent her time sauntering around the deck, stopping to talk to one crewman then another. Occasionally, her glance would turn toward Jessie and the crewman's would follow, and Jessie knew that the quadroon was trying to brew some trouble for her. If only Jessie could tell her and convince her that she did not want Stede Bonnet's attention. But Josie seemed to crave the power that being Stede Bonnet's lover gave her. Naturally, Josie thought that Jessie, that any woman, would take her place if she could.

The crew was naturally keyed up by the impending battle, and once the work of preparation was done, the hardest part began—the waiting. One or two brief squabbles broke out over who should do what or over the possession of a particularly fine pistol. Captain Bonnet was not loath to bang heads together or to lay about him with a belaying pin or the flat of his saber to halt a quarrel or to force the men to greater effort.

Jessie had managed to find a quiet corner near the stern where she tried to make herself as inconspicuous as possible, sitting with her back to the railing. Once or twice she managed to doze briefly, the small dagger Sean had slipped her held out of sight but ready for use. It would do little more than delay the crew should they set upon her, but it gave her comfort to know that she had the means of putting up some show of resistance.

She was wakened from a doze by a rough hand across her mouth and another hand groping for her breast. Alarmed, she opened her eyes to Slash's grinning face, the ugly scar that gave him his name seeming to stand out red and livid as he pressed her down to the deck. She struggled with the pirate, bringing up her hand with the dagger to strike wherever she could. With a shock, she felt it find flesh, cutting a gash down the length of Slash's arm.

He growled in anger and drew back his other arm to strike her, but the blow never landed. He was lifted off her and hurled away, skittering across the deck to land crumpled against the mast. Sean stood over her, his worried gaze checking her from head to toe. Shaken, she managed to give him a wan smile and to nod her head to reassure him that she was all right. He turned then to take up a defensive stance before her, his feet planted wide, his saber in one hand, a pistol in the other, ready to challenge any who dared molest her.

Several crewmen had gathered around, some of whom had hoped to take their turns when Slash was done. They snarled now as they edged closer, a pack of ravening wolves whose prey had been snatched from them. Jessie saw Josie across the deck, lit by the ship's lanterns, a smug smile on her face at the turmoil she had caused.

"Out of the way, Winthrop," one of the pirates snarled. "You'll have your turn when we're done!"

"Aye, bondslave," another agreed, and Jessie was not surprised to see that Jackson was one of the eager participants in her planned rape. "These men have been without a woman long enough. You can't keep the bitch to yourself forever."

"Perhaps not," Sean agreed lightly, "but I can send to hell the first two or three who come near her."

Jessie had slowly gotten to her feet, and she now looked at Sean with amazement. He was smiling grimly at the menacing men, but stood relaxed, seemingly undaunted by their anger and overwhelming number.

"Here! What is this?" Bonnet's voice boomed in anger as he charged into the snarling group, shoving them back.

"We want a bit of tail, Cap'n," one pirate argued belligerently.

"Aye!" shouted Slash who stood holding his wounded arm but still eager for his turn at a woman. "We've been here careening and refitting for weeks now. It's a woman we all need to ease ourselves a bit afore we fight!"

"There's a good chance we'll die fighting our way out of this trap tomorrow," another challenged, "we deserve a bit of pleasure tonight."

"Agh! You disgust me!" Bonnet snapped. "Fighting over a pair of tits and not a man of you on watch. You'll have plenty of time for wenching after we fight our way clear tomorrow. Now get back to your posts!"

Complaining but somewhat mollified by the captain's promise, the crew turned back to their posts, eyeing Jessie hungrily.

Bonnet's gaze raked over Sean standing defensively before Jessie, and he nodded with approval. "Guard her!" he ordered curtly, and turned away.

Her knees weak, Jessie slid to the deck. She looked at the knife in her hand, thinking how ineffective it would be if the crew seriously attacked her. Not even Sean could defend her for long against so many. Her only hope was that Colonel Rhett would be victorious tomorrow. Yet that could mean Sean's death.

Sean sat down beside her, and she leaned against him, feeling his strength and drawing comfort from it. Someone put out the lanterns, and Sean put his arm around her in comfort. Gratefully, she sank into the curve of his embrace, trembling.

He held her silently, gently caressing her arm and kissing her hair. After a while she was able to stop trembling and to relax against him.

"Here," he said, pulling a large gold watch from his pocket, "I have something for you."

He put the watch into her hand, and she looked up at him in amazement. "Where did you get this?" she asked.

"We buried your stepfather ashore. It was in his pocket. I thought you should have it."

She looked down at the timepiece, opening the cover and running her hands lovingly over it. "It was Papa's," she whispered, her eyes bright with unshed tears.

"I thought as much," he said softly.

She looked up at him in surprise.

"From the inscription," he explained. "'To Papa From Jessie, July 8, 1708.'"

"I gave it to him when I was ten years old. Thank you for saving it for me, Sean." She hugged the treasure to her for a moment, wondering how her stepfather had come to have her father's watch, then put it carefully into the pocket of her riding skirt.

"Colonel Rhett will win tomorrow, won't he?" she whispered fearfully. "I've heard the men talking. They say he has twice the guns and twice the men and two ships. The tide will free his ships from the sand bar tonight, and he commands the mouth of the river."

"Yes," he said. "I think Rhett will win tomorrow. He's a capable commander. Bonnet has never been much of a seaman. What he knows, he learned in the last year under the tutelage of Blackbeard."

"Oh, Sean," she cried, throwing her arms around him, "what will happen to you?"

He would have told her the truth then if there hadn't been so many ears nearby. "I'll be all right," was all he could promise her.

"I'm so afraid for you, Sean."

He looked down at her in surprise. "For me?" he asked incredulously. Here she was surrounded by pirates who would like nothing better than to ravish her, about to face a dangerous battle, and her fears were for him. Could any declaration of love be sweeter than that?

Her eyes were shining up at him, her softly parted lips more tempting than he had ever seen them. He bent and kissed her gently, but quite thoroughly. He felt the softness of her breasts pressed against him, the slimness of her waist. He could never quite get enough of her. The more often they made love, the more he desired her. If he hadn't been involved in helping Rhett settle this piracy business, he would have long ago asked her to marry him, even if she had been *J*. But she had proved to be as innocent as his heart had hoped, and his own charade would hopefully be over on the morrow. But there was no reason to wait until then to tell her of his love for her, to ask her to be his wife.

She looked up at him, and even in the near darkness he could see the tears glistening in her eyes. "If you're taken tomorrow, I'll plead your case with Colonel Rhett. You have protected me. And maybe Mr. Fortune will help. He is fond of you, isn't he?"

He could not hide his smile. "He's very fond of me."

"Then maybe all is not lost. I'll do whatever I can for you, Sean. I promise." She spoke quickly, hopefully.

"You can promise me one thing right now," he said, brushing her hair back from her face.

"Anything!" she said, looking up at him with anxious eyes.

His mouth twitched in that familiar way that told her he was trying to suppress a grin as he thought of what her reaction to his proposal might be. "Promise to marry me," he said.

Disbelief widened her eyes, and her mouth dropped open.

Seeing the disbelief on her face, all hint of a smile deserted his face. He clenched his teeth, making the muscle in his jaw jump. What other reaction could he have expected? he thought. To her, he was a runaway bondslave fallen in with pirates who might be hanged for his crimes within the month. If there were not so many pirates within hearing, he would have told her the truth about himself. But he had to know she really cared for him. Could she give up her fascination with the idea of marrying a "gentleman" to marry only for love? If she could accept him now, for what she thought he was, there would never be any doubt that it was he she really cared for. Not his social status, not his money, not his shipping business. His jaw clenched tighter, as he waited anxiously for her answer.

She nodded in the direction of Colonel Rhett's blockading ships, and her voice was strained when she spoke. "A pirate on his way to the gallows can offer little to any woman," she said. "I do not relish being twice widowed in the same year."

"I am not dead yet, my love."

At those words, she clung harder to him. She could hear the strong thudding of his heart. Her hands touched his vibrant flesh. She could see the life dancing in his eyes. She could not imagine him cold and lifeless. Yet his hanging was not improbable.

He took her hands and looked solemnly down into her eyes. He could very well understand her hesitation. How he wanted to crush her to him, to explain everything, and to watch her hesitation vanish. But he had to know beyond doubt that he was more important to her than wealth and social position.

"Jessie, I love you and care for you. You must accept me and love me as I am. Whether my hands are full or empty, they are ready to love you, serve you, and protect you. Can you ask more of any man?"

Jessie leaned her head on Sean's shoulder, her mind in utter turmoil, the declaration of his love for her warming her as much as the kisses they had shared. How many times had she dreamed of being truly wed to Sean, banishing that dream because he was a bondsman, not a gentleman? But what was a gentleman? Stede Bonnet could have claimed that title once. So could her stepfather. Yet Sean was more of a gentleman than either of them.

How many times had she suppressed her feelings for Sean by telling herself she wanted someone with whom to build a future and that Sean might be a spendthrift? Certainly, his wardrobe was elegant and costly, but tasteful. In what other way had he spent money?

She had wanted someone with whom to build a future. She had envisioned a great plantation, a far-flung shipping line. Could she ask for anyone more competent than Sean? Or a more willing worker? She thought of the things he had done unasked, from repairing the outhouse to nailing a roof on a slave cabin.

How many times had she told herself that he had never declared his love for her, that he made love to her merely to satisfy his physical cravings, not because he truly cared for her or would ever want to marry her. Now he had declared his love for her and asked her to marry him. What else, as he had said, could she ask of any man?

He was waiting for her answer. She could feel the tension in the arms that held her, the arms in which she had so often found not only comfort but a fire and passion no other man had ever stirred in her. She knew now that she wanted to be a part of Sean's life, to share in it as much as she could for as long as she could. If their life together was short, so be it. What guarantee did anyone have of long life?

"Yes," she whispered. "Yes."

His arms tightened around her and she found her face smothered in happy kisses until she could not help but laugh, delighting in their commitment to one another.

The ship stirring to life around her woke Jessie. Her arms were still around Sean's waist, and her head was pillowed on his shoulder. She opened her eyes to see him smiling down at her, his saber still held defensively across her lap.

"Good morning, my love," he whispered. "My wife-to-be. Unless you have changed your mind?"

A slight smile played about her lips, and she could feel the tension in his arms as if he were afraid that she would change her mind after sleeping on his proposal.

"You'll not get out of marrying me that easily, Sean Winthrop."

She felt the tension drain from him, and he planted a hasty kiss on her nose.

Smiling at him, she sat up, brushing back her hair and pinning up the loose ends.

"Do you know how to use this?" he asked, holding out his pistol to her.

She shrugged. "Point it in the right direction and pull the trigger."

Sean gave her a grim smile. "Good enough," he said, handing it to her.

She pushed it back at him. "You can make better use of it than I."

"I can find another. There's no lack of weapons aboard. I want you to take this and use it if you must."

His eyes were serious as he looked down at her, and she understood that he meant it for her defense in case something happened to him in the coming battle. Or was the bullet in that gun for her? She gasped and looked up at him with wide, frightened eyes. His mouth hardened into a tight line. She wanted to hold him close, to keep him safe with her, but she only nodded and accepted the gun with a hand that was less than steady. There was no use adding to his worries at the beginning of a battle.

"Awake, you whoresons!" came Bonnet's bellow as he came down the deck, alternately kicking backsides or swatting them with the flat of his saber. "Awake! 'Tis almost dawn! We want to show Rhett a clean pair of heels afore he knows 'tis morning!" Bonnet was elegantly attired, his wig carefully curled and powdered as if he had not spent most of the night on his feet preparing for the coming life or death battle.

There was some grumbling as the men who had not been on watch came to their feet, coughing, spitting, calling for a bit of biscuit with which to break their fast.

Sean brought Jessie food and some well-watered wine. She choked down as much of it as she could as the sky lightened in the east.

"I want you to go below until we are out of danger," Sean said.

She nodded, but she had no intention of cowering below decks, unable to at least see what was happening. But she knew it would be no use to argue with Sean. When he escorted her to the hatch, she obediently went down the steps. When he turned away, she came back to take up a position just inside the doors where she would be somewhat protected and unseen, but have a clear view of the deck.

Bonnet began calling out orders, and the men scrambled to set the sails. The gaff and the jib were let out, and the ship swung round in the breeze. The vessel hove short, standing over the anchor chains. The capstan was manned, and with a great deal of rattling, the anchors were hoisted to the deck. The rest of the sails were then run up to catch the freshening morning breeze which was blowing straight off the land and out to sea. Captain Bonnet's own black flag was run defiantly up the mast. Emblazoned with a skull, with a heart to one side, a dagger on the other, and a single long bone beneath, it declared to all the nature of the ship beneath it. With her hull newly careened and her sails newly patched and refitted, the *Royal James* went skimming down the river.

Bonnet paced the quarterdeck above Jessie. She could hear his orders and his encouragement to his crew. "We'll catch 'em asleep, lads, and sweep through them afore they're awake! They'll wake up and find the fox escaped from the trap!"

But above the sound of the wind and the crying of the morning gulls, Jessie thought she could hear the rattle of other anchor chains. Colonel Rhett would not be caught sleeping this morning. He would be waiting for them to try to make an escape.

As they rounded the point, Rhett's ships moved to intercept, taking a position on either quarter of the pirate ship.

"They're going to try to board, Captain!"

"Steer closer to shore!" Bonnet ordered. "We'll run around them!"

Jessie could feel the list of the ship as it changed course slightly.

"The *Sea Nymph* is trying to cut us off, Captain," Slash called, pointing toward the bow.

Jessie had left the door ajar and she could see Rhett's second ship pulling ahead of them, desperately trying to cut in front of them, to halt their run for the sea.

Suddenly, she felt the ship lurch, heard the scrape of sand against the hull, as the *Royal James* plowed into a sand bar. Slowly, the vessel halted, and Jessie clutched the door as the ship tilted to the side, fast aground. Pandemonium seemed to break loose on deck. Sails were reset but to no avail. They were stuck fast and the tide was going out. Until the tide turned and the water level rose, they were helpless, at the mercy of Colonel Rhett's two ships.

Jessie could see the *Sea Nymph* ahead of them. In her hurry to cut them off, she, too, was headed for the shoals. The men on board were working frantically to change the set of the sails to come about, but it was too late. The *Sea Nymph* ground into the sand and stuck fast, as helpless as Bonnet's *Royal James*. One or two pirates fired shots in her direction, but she was too far out of range either to receive or to answer their fire. A cheer went up from the pirates, but it was short-lived. The *Henry* was still bearing down on them.

"Prepare to repel boarders!" Jessie heard Bonnet order just before a second cheer went up. Colonel Rhett's flagship had also run aground.

Jessie could see the Carolinian ship just off the bow and easily within range even of the pirates' small arms. Her heart sank as she realized that Colonel Rhett's ship had careened in the same direction as Bonnet's with the result that while only the hull of the *Royal James* was exposed to fire, the colonel's entire deck was vulnerable.

The tilt of his deck was not so great, however, that he could not use his guns. She could clearly see the Carolinians aiming their cannons, saw the flash from the guns' mouths, and felt the impact of those shots on the hull of the sloop. Other men kept up an exchange of small arms fire with the pirates. Even though they were treacherously exposed, and the pirates' hull their only target, Colonel Rhett's men stayed with their guns, launching one broadside after another.

Bonnet was not slow to take advantage of his superior position. His guns were also firing at a steady rate, and with much more disastrous results as he freely raked the entire deck of Colonel Rhett's ship.

Jessie looked about the deck for Sean. Was he safe? She spotted him near the stern, hunched down behind the railing, firing his pistols toward Colonel Rhett's ship.

No! she thought, beginning to run toward him without further thought. She couldn't let him kill anyone! How could she plead his case with Colonel Rhett if his shots found their mark in the flesh of the Carolinians so exposed to that murderous fire?

Keeping low, Jessie made her way up the slanting deck to Sean's side. At the first touch of her fingers on his arm, he whirled. Then, seeing who it was, he scowled at her and shoved her head even lower. He fired once more over the side then took her arm and, making sure she kept her head down, hauled her back to the companionway, shoving her inside.

"Stay here!" he ordered sternly. But when he turned to go, she clung to his arm.

He looked down at her, and his expression softened, and he tucked one of his pistols away to free his hand to caress her cheek. "Do you think I could bear it if anything happened to you?" he asked softly.

His words were barely audible over the raging battle, but her heart understood.

"Sean, you can't fight! Do you think you will get a pardon if you kill those men? Our neighbors are over there. People I have met and talked to. How can I make a case for your freedom if you hurt them? Do you think Colonel Rhett will offer his hand to a pirate who has murdered his friends?" Her fingers dug into his arm as her eyes pleaded with him more eloquently than her words.

"Hey, Winthrop!" one of the pirates called. "Get your ass out here and help!"

"You can dally with the doxie later, Winthrop!" another called.

"Hell, we all get a turn later!" Slash bellowed, bringing guffaws from a number of pirates.

"What choice do you think I have?" he asked, nodding toward the pirates.

Again he caressed her face and leaned close. She thought he meant to kiss her. Instead, he took the chance to whisper in her ear. "Be assured, my love. My shots are all going wide."

She gasped and was about to reply, but he was already hurrying back to his place. She leaned her head back against the wall, a sigh of relief shuddering through her. How could she have doubted him?

"He'll have to share you when we're out of this."

Jessie opened her eyes. Josie was leaning indolently in the doorway, chewing a piece of jerky. Her dark sloe eyes glittered with hatred as her gaze raked over Jessie.

Jessie held her chin higher, determined not to be intimidated. "How do you know Bonnet will win?" She gave the quadroon a slow smile, showing a lot more confidence than she felt. "I may yet watch all of you hang in Charles Town," she challenged, hoping Josie would flounce away and leave her alone.

Josie threw back her head and laughed. "We have him at our mercy while he can only batter away helplessly at our hull and you think Rhett will win?"

"Are you really so certain of the outcome?" Jessie questioned.

Josie pointed her thumb proudly at her own chest. "I have been in battles before. I have seen many times the reaction of the crew. Do you think they would be in such a mood if they did not see victory ahead?"

Jessie scanned the deck. There were jubilant smiles on the faces of the men. Crude jokes were exchanged and laughed at. One of the men had found an old flag, its black faded to gray, and was waving it mockingly at the helplessly mired Carolinian ship. Jeers and taunts were hurled at the *Henry* as often as bullets.

"Come on over!" shouted one pirate. "We'll see you get a proper welcome!"

Others took up the cry, waving their hats to beckon a derisive invitation to Colonel Rhett's trapped crew to come and get them if they could.

Pinned down as they were, exposed to the deadly fire, the

Carolinians' own humor did not desert them. They answered the insults with cheerful yells.

"It will be your turn soon enough!" one Carolinian called, undaunted by the barrage of bullets that struck around him.

More shaken by the pirates happy bravado than she cared to reveal to Josie, Jessie retorted, "It doesn't sound as if Colonel Rhett and his men have quite given up yet."

Throwing down the last bit of her jerky, Josie jerked her pistols from her waist. "Nor have I." She started out onto the deck but turned to sneer down at Jessie. "Josie does not cower in doorways while her man fights for her!" She smiled viciously at Jessie. "I will help win this battle. Then I will look forward to seein' you lyin' on your back on deck with your legs spread while the men ease their lust on you!"

Jessie watched Josie duck and dodge her way across the deck to the rail where she immediately fired both pistols at the Carolinians, then crouched down to reload. Jessie could not help but shudder at the future Josie had planned for her. Tightly gripping the pistol Sean had given her, she vowed that, if necessary, she would use it on herself before she allowed herself to be submitted to that indignity.

Chapter Eighteen

The battle seemed to go on forever, the broadsides coming as steadily as ever, the musket and pistol fire never letting up. Jessie could see the carnage Bonnet's guns were wreaking on the *Henry*. Because of the its position, the rigging of Colonel Rhett's ship had sustained a lot of damage. As the hours dragged by, Jessie noticed that the pirates became less boisterous. They continued to pour a relentless barrage onto the deck of the Colonel's ship, but they had lost some of their cockiness.

The Carolinians were far from beaten and had managed to find some targets among the pirates. Five pirates lay dead on the deck. Seemingly without remorse, their comrades simply moved them out of the way and continued with the grisly battle. Three others lay wounded. One man was giving them what poor aid was available aboard ship.

Jessie continued to watch Sean. Two pirates, who seemed a little cleaner, a little less loutish than the others, had taken up positions next to him, and she noticed that between rounds the three talked together quite seriously.

Indeed, there seemed to be a swell of mutterings among the crew and she craned her neck to try to see what was causing the consternation.

"The tide's comin' in!" Slash announced. He pointed over the side to the waterline of the *Henry*.

Jessie caught Sean's eye, and he gave her a small smile of satisfaction. She nodded her understanding of the situation. For hours the two ships had been locked in combat with neither side seeming to gain an edge. Now the outcome would depend on the tide. Whichever ship was freed from the sand bar first would no doubt be the victor. And the *Royal James* was closer to shore, less likely to be first. No wonder the pirates' jubilation had fled. The hangman's rope was looming closer.

Jessie offered a brief prayer. This time she knew what to pray for. She prayed for a quickly rising tide that would free Colonel Rhett's ship and she prayed that the Colonel would listen when she asked for a pardon for Sean.

Crouching low, Sean came over to her, darting through the companionway door and leaning against the opposite wall. He began reloading his pistols while he talked.

"Rhett's ship will be free first," he said, pouring a measure of powder down the muzzle of one pistol. "There might be some heavy fighting unless we can talk Bonnet into surrender."

"Surrender? Do you think he would?"

"He might have little choice," Sean told her grimly, ramming a ball home. "The odds are against him. If he surrenders before it's too late, there's a chance for a pardon."

"Do you really think there's a chance of a pardon for Bonnet?" Jessie scoffed. "He's already been given one pardon and returned to piracy."

Sean stopped his work to look over at her, his mouth a hard, tight line. "No. Not for Bonnet," he said, shaking his head. "But his men have a chance, some a very good chance. A few, like Pence and Craft over there, were honest seamen who signed aboard just after Bonnet's pardon. They thought they were going privateering. Bonnet surprised them with his announcement to turn pirate, and they were forced to go along with him. They know they have a good chance of acquittal and a pardon. They'll push hard for surrender."

Jessie glanced at the two men who had been fighting beside Sean. They had called another pirate over and the three of them were deep in conversation. She looked back to Sean. He had finished loading the first pistol and was working on the second.

"Hungry?" she asked, holding out some jerky and biscuit she had found below.

He nodded and took a piece of the jerky from her, pausing a moment to smile at her when their fingers touched. Chewing on the jerky, he continued loading. When he tucked the second pistol into his belt, Jessie handed him a jug of water and he drank long and deep. Glancing out the door, he set the jug down and pulled her into his arms.

She came into his embrace gladly. Uncertain of the future, the present became crushingly important. With her arms about him, she ran her hands over his smoothly muscled back, hugging him to her as if trying to store up as much of him, his feel, his scent, his taste, as possible before he left her again.

He seemed no less eager for her. His kisses rained down on her face, her hair, her neck. It was as if he wanted to eat her up and carry her with him, and she could not help but laugh knowing he wanted her as much as she wanted him.

A cry of dismay from the crew on deck brought them back

to their senses, and, giving her a last kiss, Sean wrenched himself away from her and went back to his place.

Jessie looked out to see the sway of the *Henry's* rigging as the ship moved with the incoming tide. Water surged around her bows, lifting the Colonel's ship slowly upright. Already her crew worked to repair the rigging, determined to be able to sail to board the *Royal James* the moment the ship was free.

"Captain, we've got to surrender now!" Craft said, coming across the deck to stand belligerently before Bonnet.

"Surrender?" Bonnet boomed. "Better to die fighting than to die at the end of a rope!"

"They outnumber us two to one!" Slash growled. "We can die here and now, but if we surrender, at least we'll live a few weeks yet. Who knows what can happen? I hear Charles Town don't even have a jail. How're they gonna hold us?"

Jessie felt her arm gripped in a desperate hand, and she turned to see Josie holding her, the quadroon's eyes glaring fanatically. The pistol Sean had given her was in the hand Josie held behind Jessie. She struggled against Josie, but the quadroon's pistol came up under her chin and Josie hauled Jessie out onto the deck.

"Why surrender when we got a hostage?" Josie prodded Jessie's chin up with the muzzle of her pistol. "We bargain with them. They let us go, we give them the woman."

Jessie struggled but Josie held her fast. She saw Sean move forward but pause when Josie cocked the pistol.

With a snarl of rage, Bonnet plunged between the two women, shoving Josie away. Josie's pistol discharged into the air, the ball whistling close to Jessie's head. Furious, Bonnet towered over his ex-lover. "Captain Bonnet doesn't bargain. And he doesn't surrender, either!"

"If we surrender now, there's a chance for a pardon!"

Pence shouted, turning to appeal to the crew and pleased to find them nodding in agreement.

"Pardon!" Bonnet spat. "What chance do I have of a pardon?"

"Maybe you don't have a chance," Jackson said, coming forward, "but some of us do. I say we surrender now."

In a sudden change of mood, Bonnet pulled Josie to him, and he looked down at her for a long moment. For a brief moment Jessie thought she saw between them a spark of what she had felt with Sean, an urge to savor a last touch before an uncertain future. Then Bonnet turned disdainfully to the crew.

"Surrender! What does a pirate have to do with surrender? We fight! This little one here," he said, squeezing Josie briefly, "has more courage than the lot of you! Do you hear her mewling for surrender?"

Her eyes gleaming with pride at Bonnet's words of praise, Josie grabbed a saber from the lifeless hand of a pirate sprawled on the deck and leaped onto the railing. Holding onto the rigging with one hand, she brandished the saber with the other. "I say we fight!" she shouted. "Fight, and a pardon be damned!"

Josie had expected a rousing acclamation. Instead, a shot rang out and a look of surprise covered her face before she slowly let go of the rigging and fell heavily, face down, onto the deck. Some Carolinian's ball had found its mark.

Bonnet stood silent and stunned for a moment, then bent to touch Josie. His fingers came away stained with her blood. Almost as if the blood were a contagious disease, he pulled a lace-edged handkerchief from his sleeve and, wiping the blood away, tossed the handkerchief down.

Bonnet turned then, whipping out his saber, his eyes lit

with a feral gleam. "Captain Bonnet does not surrender!" he snarled.

But there was a different opinion among the crew. A mutter of disagreement ran around the circle of pirates.

"We say surrender!" Craft shouted.

His shout was answered by a spattering of ayes.

"I'll fire the magazine myself and send the *Royal James* and all of you to hell with her before I surrender!" Bonnet snarled.

A cheer from the other ship caused them to look in the direction of the Carolinians. The *Henry* had righted herself and was floating free while Bonnet's ship still listed to the side caught on the sand bar. The *Henry's* crew was hurrying to clear away the damaged rigging and set the sails that would carry her closer to the pirates for boarding.

"Captain, we've got to surrender now before they come aboard," Pence pleaded for all of them. Having seen their imminent danger, a chorus of agreement rang out from the crew, calling for surrender.

Bonnet pulled out a pistol, turning it in the direction of the crew. "I'll scatter the deck with the brains of any man who refuses to fight to the end!"

Strong fingers reached out to grip the hand that held that pistol so threateningly, forcing the muzzle downward. Frightened, Jessie watched as Sean pried the pistol from Bonnet's hand. Bonnet started to bluster, to bring his saber into play, but Sean brought his own saber up to rest against Bonnet's throat.

"It's all over, Captain," he said.

Bonnet's shoulders slumped, and the fight drained out of him. Beaten, he looked for a moment at the saber in his hand, then handed it to Jessie, as if placing it in her keeping until he needed it again.

She nodded to him in understanding. He had been kind to her once. She would keep his saber for him.

Seeing their captain disarmed, the pirates wasted no time in running up a flag of truce.

Jessie recognized Colonel Rhett's voice calling from the *Henry*. "Do you surrender?"

The pirates appointed Slash as their spokesman, and he stepped to the rail. Cupping his mouth with his hands, he answered, "We ask for pardons!"

The *Henry* had edged closer, her guns trained on the helplessly caught pirate ship.

"Surrender unconditionally!" came Colonel Rhett's voice.

There was a hasty conference among the pirates.

Without surrender, death seemed sure and soon. "We agree!"

The pirates' weapons clattered to the deck, and they lined the rail, waving their arms over their heads and calling out to the Carolinian ship that they surrendered.

Grappling hooks were thrown from the *Henry*, and the two vessels bumped together. Colonel Rhett was the first to clamber over the rail onto the deck of the *Royal James*. Other Carolinians followed, their weapons warily in hand. The men from Charles Town began rounding up the pirates on deck and checking below for others.

Still holding the saber Bonnet had given her, Jessie started forward to plead for Sean, pushing her way through men surprised to see a woman on board. Colonel Rhett's jaw dropped when he saw Jessie. "Mrs. Twill! How the devil did you get aboard?"

"I was captured at my plantation, Colonel Rhett," Jessie said, holding out her hand to him.

Recovering himself somewhat, Colonel Rhett remembered his manners and bowed over her hand. He could see that she was unhurt as he looked her over. But he noticed the saber she held. "You make a lovely pirate, Mrs. Twill. Do you plan to use that against my men?"

She looked down at the saber in her hand and gripped it tightly. "Captain Bonnet gave it to me, Colonel, when he surrendered."

"Stede Bonnet?" Rhett spluttered with surprise. "I had no idea it was that notorious renegade we were pursuing." The Colonel motioned for his men to bring the captured pirate captain to him. "You are Stede Bonnet?"

Captain Bonnet gave Rhett a courtly bow. "At your service, sirrah. Surrendering myself to you in good faith in hope of obtaining a pardon for my misdeeds."

Colonel Rhett's eyes hardened. "You may plead your case before a judge, Captain, but I think, sir, you have received one already. I doubt you'll get a second."

Bonnet paled and Jessie could see him actually shake. He would have protested, but the Colonel motioned to one of his men who came and led Bonnet away.

Jessie started again to plead Sean's case, but Colonel Rhett was called away by one of his men, and she was suddenly caught by the arms and turned to face Jason Soames.

"Jessie! My God! What are you doing here? Are you all right?" Jason ran his hands down her arms as if checking for wounds, and scanned her quickly to assure himself that she was unhurt, then hugged her to him briefly.

Jessie laughed. "I am quite all right," she said, pushing away from him. "As I was telling Colonel Rhett, I was captured at my plantation, but was ably protected from harm by Mr. Winthrop."

Sean had come to stand beside her and Jessie was surprised to see that he was still armed.

Jason's hands dropped from her, and he turned to study

Sean. "You're Mr. Fortune's bondslave, aren't you?"

"Yes," he answered. "Sean Winthrop."

As if coming to a momentous decision, Jason slowly held out his hand to Sean. "I want to thank you. Jessie says you protected her from the pirates."

"I could do no less." Sean shook Jason's hand.

Perhaps, Jessie thought, it was Jason's naturally effusive nature or Sean's ability to meet any man as an equal, but the handshake that began as a simple gesture of thanks from a gentleman to a bondsman changed into an expression of warmth and sincerity.

"I'll do my best to see that you are acquitted of any charges against you, and I will personally pay the bond for your freedom," Jason said.

"I doubt that any of that will be necessary, Soames." Colonel Rhett came up between the two men, a wide smile on his face.

"Colonel! Your arrival was most welcome." Sean held out his hand to the Colonel, and Jessie was amazed when Colonel Rhett took it gladly, clapping Sean on the shoulder.

"Thank God, you're safe, Sean!" Colonel Rhett said, gripping Sean's hand and patting him on the back at the same time. "Did you not see us trailing you?"

"I hoped it was you, but at that distance, I could not be sure. I didn't see your ships in the harbor as we went past Charles Town."

"Your plan to catch the pirates almost went awry, Sean," Colonel Rhett said a bit red-faced. "I heard that the pirate, Captain Vane, was making repairs to the south of Charles Town and went after him. To no avail, I might add. I had returned to Charles Town but was just outside the bar when the *Fortune* sailed out. Since you were using her as bait and had said the *Fortune* would not cross the bar unless taken by pirates, I assumed the thieves were aboard and on their way to their rendezvous with their captain. As we planned, I followed. I never thought we would net such a big fish."

"You planned all this with Colonel Rhett?" Jessie turned wide, questioning eyes on Sean.

"I was never in league with the pirates, Jessie. Except to gain information to help Colonel Rhett bring them to justice."

"Oh, Sean!" Heedless of the many eyes watching, Jessie threw herself into Sean's arms, holding him close, relief flooding her, knowing he was safe from prosecution, knowing that her faith in him was not misplaced. "You should have told me."

He smiled down at her wryly. "There were reasons why I couldn't. Reasons I've already promised to explain to you later."

Jason watched the two of them together, saw the love shining from their eyes, and he knew there could be no place for him in Jessie's life. His jaw clenched. He could almost hate the bondsman, but he saw the happiness on Jessie's face, the glow of love in her eyes, and knew that Sean was who she wanted, who she loved.

It was difficult for him, but Jason forced a smile to his lips. "My offer still stands, Mr. Winthrop. I will pay your bond for you. It is the least I can do to thank you for protecting Mrs. Twill."

"As I said, I don't think that will be necessary, Jason," Colonel Rhett said with a twinkle in his eye. He turned to Sean. "May I?"

Sean gave a brief nod of consent, and Jessie noticed the familiar twitching of his lips as he tried to subdue a smile.

Colonel Rhett drew himself up proudly. "I'd like to introduce to you Mr. Sean Winthrop Fortune, son of Mr. Jeffery Fortune of Barbados."

"You're Mr. Fortune?" Jason's mouth was agape. "No wonder he was never home when I called."

Jessie's head was whirling. Things were moving too fast for her. Scarcely moments ago she had been ready to plead for the case of a runaway bondslave involved in piracy who had protected her. Now Colonel Rhett was telling her Sean was not only free, but had helped catch the pirates, and was one of the richest men in the colonies.

"We thought it would be easier for me to infiltrate the pirates' gang as a bondslave in need of funds," Sean was explaining to Jason. "Only Colonel Rhett, Governor Johnson, and some of my people knew who I really was."

As the story, with Jason's help, spread among the colonel's men, they came to shake Sean's hand, congratulating him, welcoming the wealthy Mr. Fortune to Charles Town.

Jessie stood still, watching Sean and the men with stunned eyes, not quite able to take it all in. She felt like the eye of a storm as the men milled around her. Why hadn't Sean told her before? Why had he kept his secret from her? He had asked her to marry him, yet had not trusted her enough to share his true identity with her. Did the Sean she was in love with exist at all?

"Colonel Rhett," Sean was saying, "I'd like to take a long-boat upriver to the *Fortune*. Captain Reading and two of his crew have been locked below decks all day without food or water."

"Of course!" Rhett ordered some of the crew to man and lower the longboat from the *Royal James*. "I'll have cabins prepared for you and Mrs. Twill on board my flagship for the return trip to Charles Town."

"If you don't mind, Colonel Rhett," Sean said, giving the colonel a small but elegant bow of thanks, "I'll sail aboard the *Fortune*."

"Certainly, Sean. She's yours. Thank you again for risking her in our cause," Colonel Rhett said.

"It was a cause as much mine as yours," Sean said.

The Colonel held out his arm to Jessie. "Mrs. Twill, may I escort you aboard my flagship?"

"I was hoping Jessie would return with me aboard the *Fortune*, sir. She has agreed to become my wife." Sean slid his arm around Jessie's waist and looked at her with concern when he felt her stiffen.

Colonel Rhett beamed happily. "May I be the first to offer my felicitations?"

"Thank you, Colonel Rhett," Jessie replied numbly. Why hadn't he told her kept thrumming through her head.

Rhett shook Sean's hand again in congratulation; then Sean held his hand out to Jessie, looking down at her with pleading in his eyes. "Will you come aboard the *Fortune* with me, Jessie? We have a lot of talking to do."

She almost refused to go with him, but she saw the pleading in his eyes and heard the promise in his voice. "Yes, we do, don't we?"

She allowed herself to be helped into the longboat. Sean seated her in the stern then took up an oar and sat facing her, pulling with the rest of the men. Like a bondslave would, she thought. Was he so fond of that role that he was not yet ready to give it up? Even now it was hard for her to believe that Sean was Jeffery Fortune's son, that he was himself Mr. Sean Fortune. Fool that she was, she had been taken in by his charade like the rest of them.

No wonder he had been able to play the role of gentleman so well during her mother and Mr. Pierce's visit. No wonder he had never quite seemed to know his place as a bondslave. No wonder the manners, the clothes, the air of a gentleman had fit him as if born to them! Yet he had scoffed at the very

355

idea that a gentleman was better than a bondslave. Was that part of his masquerade as well?

She watched Sean pull on his oar, his muscles bunching, straining. He didn't get those muscles sitting in a parlor in elegant clothes, ordering servants to do his bidding. She thought of the work he had done on her plantation. He had not learned how to shingle a roof sitting in a parlor, either. Nor how to plant rice or to handle a wagon and team or to sail a skiff. Yet she couldn't deny that Sean was every inch a gentleman, from the artless way he wore the tasteful clothes he chose to his flawless manners and constant courtesy. Whether he spoke to slave, bondsman, or freeman, he treated all with equal respect. Even now, Sean bantered with the men rowing with him, sharing their work.

Yes, he had scoffed at the idea that a gentleman was better than any other man. Many gentlemen may admit they were no better than those who served them, but only a true gentleman would dare to live it. Sean had no need to look down his nose at someone less fortunate to make himself appear more the gentleman. Only a true gentleman could work beside a slave in the field without losing an ounce of dignity or a shred of respect from that slave. She had seen Sean do just that.

Watching him row, Jessie realized that when Sean had worked beside her slaves, when he had hauled boxes on the docks, he might have been pretending to be a bondslave, but he was the same person he was now. He hadn't changed. Here was the same Sean she had fallen in love with. Everyone knew him now for the wealthy shipowner he was. He didn't have to pull that oar. He could have sat in the stern with her at his ease, yet he still pitched in to help when there was work to be done. He still laughed and joked with those around him, treating them as equals. She had respected that quality in him when she thought he was a bondsman. Now that she knew what he really was, she had to admire it all the more.

She admired him. She loved him. But, she thought, feeling the hurt and anger build, he still had a lot of explaining to do. It was all she could do to keep that anger and hurt from spilling over. She clenched her teeth, glaring at Sean each time he smiled at her, biding her time until they were alone.

The longboat was soon bumping the side of the *Fortune*, and the men scrambled on board, Sean helping Jessie. Standing on deck, Jessie looked around with new eyes. No wonder Sean's eyes had always shone so when he looked at this ship. It was the pride of ownership. She could see it in him now as he hurried down the companionway to free Captain Reading and the men.

Thanks to Sean's care, the men were no worse for their experience but thankful to be free and out of danger. Captain Reading was soon in charge again, working to restore the *Fortune* to its former trim neatness, leaving Sean free to seek Jessie out.

Wordlessly, he led her to the captain's cabin, the same one they had shared on the voyage.

Closing the door behind him, he reached for her. She held him at bay with a hand firmly planted in the center of his chest. She knew that once he took her in his arms her will to resist him would be gone along with her anger and her need for explanations.

"Not until you answer a few questions," Jessie told him firmly.

He nodded seriously at her, one hand briefly caressing the line of her jaw before he moved away. He sat down in a chair, stretching out his legs and laying his arms along the arms of the chair as if leaving himself completely open to her scrutiny—and her questions. "You deserve answers and explanations," he said.

"I need more than that from you!"

He cocked his head questioningly.

"Where is the trust?" she demanded. "You have asked me time and again to trust you, believe in you, and I have. But when did you ever trust me? You lied to me, Sean."

"Did I?"

"You told me you were a bondslave."

"I let everyone believe that. I had to. Do you think I could have infiltrated *J*'s gang as the wealthy son of Jeffery Fortune?"

"You let me believe you were involved in theft, piracy. Why didn't you tell me what you were doing? Why did you have to lie to me? Why didn't you trust me?" The hurt in her voice was almost painful.

"You were the one person I thought I could trust least of all."

Her eyes rounded and filled with pain as she took in a deep breath.

He gave her a rueful smile. "I thought you were *J*."

Her eyes grew even wider, incredulous. "Me?"

He smiled softly. "I didn't want to believe it. At first, I spent time with you to get information on the thefts." He shrugged. "You had married Twill, and I already knew that the thefts were centered in that area. The more time I spent with you, the more evidence I seemed to find that you were *J*. But I also found more and more reason for loving you. From the first moment our eyes met on the docks, I felt irresistibly drawn to you. That night when you made a gift to me of your innocence, I knew you would somehow always be a part of me."

He sat forward in the chair, his elbows resting on the arms, his chin resting on his folded hands. "I felt torn apart. Everything I found out about the thieves pointed to you. Everything

I found out about you pointed to your innocence. I wanted to believe in your innocence, but I didn't dare trust you because of the evidence."

"What evidence?"

"I found out that *J* was a woman newly arrived in the colony."

Realizing that that fact did fit her, she nodded for him to continue.

"After I infiltrated the gang, I saw *J*'s competence for myself, her strength, her ability to sail."

"And I knew how to sail."

"You're strong and competent, too. You may have been afraid of Jackson, but you never backed down from him. Neither did *J*," he said. "Then that one morning, just as I expected *J* to be returning home, I ran into you, wearing a long cloak just like hers. The clues kept leading back to a woman living at the Twill plantation."

"But it was Josie all along," she concluded.

He nodded. "Then, too, the pirates seemed bent on destroying the Fortune company. Ashbrook ships seemed to have some kind of immunity from attack. You were an Ashbrook."

Still unsatisfied, she crossed her arms angrily. "Why didn't you tell me after you knew Josie was *J*? We sailed up the coast for five days. Don't tell me you didn't have a chance during all that time. We certainly had time for . . . other things."

He frowned, shaking his head. "I could have told you then. But I didn't know what we were heading into. At first, I thought that the less you knew, the better it would be for your safety. I was worried that Bonnet might remember me and take out his hatred of the Fortunes on you. I had met Bonnet once or twice with my father in Barbados. The man seemed obsessed with hating my father, not only because of my father's success in business, but because people were fascinated when they found out that he had once been a pirate. Quite a famous one."

"You did tell me your father was a pirate," she admitted. "But I find that hard to believe now."

Sean grinned. "That part, at least, was true. My father was forced to ply that trade for a number of years after the Monmouth Rebellion. But he was eventually pardoned and his holdings restored to him. After that, running a shipping business came quite easily to him. I think Bonnet always felt overshadowed by my father. Maybe that was part of the reason Bonnet turned pirate, to prove he was as interesting as Jeffery Fortune." Sean spread his hands.

Even from across the room, she could see the anguish building in Sean's eyes. "Why didn't you tell me who you were last night? Before you asked me to marry you?" she probed softly.

He looked up at her over his folded hands. "I loved you. By then I didn't care whether you were *J* or not. I loved you and wanted you, but I didn't know how you felt about me. Would you really marry me for richer, for poorer, for better, for worse, knowing I was a bondslave? Your head was so set on having a real gentleman, on having wealth, I couldn't be sure. Perhaps I was selfish, perhaps I have felt a little overshadowed by my father, too, but I had to know it was me you would be marrying, not the Fortune name and money."

"My head was set on wealth and security, yes, but my heart found something else." She crossed to where he sat and knelt between his legs, looking up at him. "In a runaway bondslave turned pirate, I found all the wealth of love, the gentleness of touch, the passion, and the security of competence I was looking for."

He put his hands on her shoulders, drawing her closer,

smiling down at her. "Do you still want to marry me, even though you know I'm not really a pirate or a bondslave? That I was given a fine education, am quite wealthy in my own right, and come from a good family? That I am, in short, considered a gentleman?"

She gave him an impish smile of her own. "I suppose I can make an exception in your case since your father was pirate."

He bent to kiss her, but she turned away. "Are you sure you still want to marry me? When I accepted your proposal, I thought of how much I could give you, how much I could help you. Now I find out you need none of it. Can you still want me when I can give you so little?"

He drew back to stare down at her in disbelief. "So little? You are an incredible woman, Jessie Ashbrook Twill. You have strength, compassion, intelligence, and a heart full of love."

The corners of his mouth twitched briefly; then a wide smile spread over his face as he stood, pulling her up with him. Sweeping her into his arms, he held her tight as he carried her to the bed. "So little? Let me spend the next hundred years showing you just how much we have to offer each other!"

AUTHOR'S NOTE

Stede Bonnet was captured by Colonel William Rhett on September 27, 1718, in the Cape Fear River. Bonnet's ship, the *Royal James*, along with two of Bonnet's prizes, the *Francis* and the *Fortune*, were also taken. Stede Bonnet was hanged in Charles Town in November, pleading for a second pardon, even telling the court they could keep him from returning to piracy by "separating all my Limbs from my Body, only reserving the Use of my Tongue, to call continually on, and pray to the Lord." There were some who pleaded that his life be spared, and as he was hanged, friends placed flowers in his hands. Some of his men were acquitted because they had joined him after his pardon and had been forced into piracy.

TERMS OF LOVE

SHIRL HENKE

Winner of 6 *Romantic Times* Awards!

Cassandra Clayton could run her father's freighting empire without the help of any man, but without one she could never produce a male child who would inherit it all. When Cass saved Steve Loring from a hangman's noose, he seemed to be just what she needed—a stud who would perform on command. But from the first, Steve made it clear that he wanted Cass's heart and soul in the bargain. Although his sarcastic taunts made her dread the nights she must give him her body, his exquisite lovemaking made her long to give him all that he asked—and more!

_3345-3 $4.99 US/$5.99 CAN

SAVAGE Promise

CASSIE EDWARDS

"Cassie Edwards is a shining talent!"
—*Romantic Times*

From out of the driving snow the silver-eyed warrior appeared to rescue the young maiden from a vicious polar bear. And deep in Kanuga's embrace, Letitia discovered ecstasy in the frozen north. But when Kanuga vowed to rid Alaska of all white trappers, Letitia's fervid ardor changed to icy reserve. For how could a woman unaccustomed to the primitive ways of the Tlingit Indians forsake family and friends for a life she might not survive? Only Kanuga's fiery passion could overwhelm her fear, subdue her doubts, and convince her that life without him would be a vast and empty wasteland.

_3226-0 $4.99 US/$5.99 CAN